# THE SPIRIT BARES ITS TEETH

Published by Peachtree Teen
An imprint of PEACHTREE PUBLISHING COMPANY INC.
1700 Chattahoochee Avenue
Atlanta, Georgia 30318-2112
*PeachtreeBooks.com*

Text © 2023 by Andrew Joseph White
Jacket illustration © 2023 by Evangeline Gallagher

Edited by Ashley Hearn
Design and composition by Lily Steele
Jacket design by Melia Parsloe

Printed and bound in July 2023 at Lake Book Manufacturing, Melrose Park, IL, USA
10 9 8 7 6 5 4 3 2 1
First Edition
ISBN: 978-1-68263-611-4

Library of Congress Cataloging-in-Publication Data

Names: White, Andrew Joseph, author.
Title: The spirit bares its teeth / Andrew Joseph White.
Description: Atlanta, Georgia : Peachtree Teen, [2023] | Audience: Ages 14 and Up. | Audience: Grades 10-12. | Summary: Set in an alternate Victorian England where mediums control the dead, sixteen-year-old autistic transgender boy Silas must expose a power-hungry secret society while confined to a cruel finishing school designed to turn him into the perfect wife.
Identifiers: LCCN 2023020823 | ISBN 9781682636114 (hardcover) | ISBN 9781682636183 (ebook)
Subjects: CYAC: Transgender people--Fiction. | Autism spectrum disorders--Fiction. | Boarding schools--Fiction. | Schools--Fiction. | Ghosts--Fiction. | Secret societies--Fiction. | Great Britain--History--Victoria, 1837-1901--Fiction. | Horror stories. | LCGFT: Gothic fiction. | Horror fiction. | Novels.
Classification: LCC PZ7.1.W4418 Sp 2023 | DDC [Fic]--dc23
LC record available at https://lccn.loc.gov/2023020823

# THE SPIRIT BARES ITS TEETH

ANDREW JOSEPH WHITE

PEACHTREE
Teen

*For the kids with open wounds*
*they're still learning to stitch closed*

—A. J. W.

# LETTER FROM THE AUTHOR

One of the cruel injustices of the world is that survival hurts sometimes. Open-heart surgery, for example, looks a lot like murder. Amputation before the advent of proper anesthesia was just a bone saw and a rag to bite. On that note, I will make this clear: *The Spirit Bares Its Teeth* contains transphobia, ableism, graphic violence, sexual assault, discussions of forced pregnancy and miscarriage, mentions of suicidal ideation, and extensive medical gore.

But I will also make it clear that this book is not a necessary procedure. You don't have to endure it. You can get off the operating table and walk away at any time. I won't blame you.

For those still reading—do you have a rag to bite?—I want to make note of some context. Ghosts and mediums and alternate histories aside, *The Spirit Bares Its Teeth* was inspired by Victorian England's sordid history of labeling certain people "ill" or "other" to justify cruelty against them. Threats of violence enforced strict social norms, often targeting women, queer and disabled people, and other marginalized folks. I have included another note about these realities at the end of the book, including some that this book does not cover. True history is often much more heartbreaking than any horror novel can depict.

So, if nothing else, I hope this story means something to you. I hope the scalpel is kind to you. I hope your sutures heal clean. You deserve that much; we all do.

Yours,

*Andrew*

*Mors vincit omnia*

Death conquers all

At least the doctors had the decency to kill me before they opened me up. At least they killed me quick. Its funny when you die from bleeding out because it doesnt feel like dying. You just get tired and tired and tired and then youre gone.

After i was dead i watched them cut me apart. They took out my eyes and sliced them thin like paper. They shaved my head and opened my skull to the brain. They wore masks to conceal their faces and trapped me in this dark room so i could not bring the world down with my anger. Because they know how angry dead girls can be.

When the doctors were done with my eyes and my brain they moved on to the rest of me. My hair teeth skin tongue. Not to study but out of rage. To punish me for failing them. They took a saw to my ribs when i did not crack under their hands. They said my name FRANCES FRANCES FRANCES i am a haunting i am a poltergeist i am stuck here screaming.

What were they looking for? did they find it?

Are you listening?

I

The last time I spoke to my brother was six months ago. I remember the date exactly: the twenty-second of April, 1883. How could I not? It's burned into me like a cauterized wound, an artery seared shut to keep from bleeding out.

It was his wedding, and I was on the edge of hysterics.

I wasn't being difficult on purpose. I wasn't, I swear. I never mean to be, no matter what Mother and Father say. I'd even promised it would be a good day. I wouldn't let the too-tight corset send me into a fit, I wouldn't tap, I wouldn't fidget, and I certainly wouldn't wince at the church organ's high notes. I would be so perfect that my parents wouldn't have a reason to so much as look at me.

And why shouldn't it have been a good day? It was my brother's *wedding*. He'd just returned to London after a few months teaching surgery in Bristol, and all I wanted was to hang off his arm and chatter about articles in the latest *Edinburgh Medical Journal.* He would tell me about his new research and the grossest thing he'd seen after cutting someone open. He'd quiz me as he fixed his hair before the ceremony. "Name all the bones of the hand," he'd say. "You *have* been studying your anatomy, haven't you?"

It would be a good day. I'd promised.

But that was easy to promise in the safety of my room when the day had not yet started. It was another to walk into St. John's after Mother and Father had spent the carriage ride informing me I'd be married by the new year.

"It's time," Mother said, taking my hand and squeezing— putting too much pressure on the metacarpals, the proximal phalanges. "Sixteen is the perfect age for a girl as pretty as you."

What she *meant* was, "For a girl with eyes like yours." Also, it wasn't. The legal marriageable age was, and still is, twenty-one, but the laws of England and the Church have never stopped the Speakers from taking what they want. And it was clear what they wanted was me.

It was like the ceremony became a fatal allergen. While Father talked with a colleague between the pews and Mother cooed over her friends' dresses, I dug my fingers into my neck to ensure my trachea hadn't swollen. The organist hunched over the keys and played a single note that hit my eardrums like a needle. Too many people talked at once. Too loud, too crowded, too warm. The heel of my shoe clicked against the floor in a nervous skitter. *Tap tap tap tap.*

Father grabbed my arm, lowered his voice. "Stop that. The thing you're doing with your foot, stop it."

I stopped. "Sorry."

On a good day, I could stomach big events like this. Parties, festivals, fancy dinners. Sometimes I even convinced myself I liked them, when George was there to protect me. But that's only because a legion of expensive tutors had trained me to. They'd molded me from a strange, feral child into an obedient daughter who sat with her feet tucked daintily and never spoke out of turn. So, yes. Maybe, if it had been a good day, I could have done it. But good days had suddenly become impossible.

In the crowd, I slipped away.

Sometimes I pretend my fear is a little rabbit in my chest. It's the sort of rabbit my brother's school tests their techniques on, with grey fur and dark eyes, and it hides underneath my sternum beside the heart.

*Mother and Father are going to do this to you*, it reminded me. I pressed a hand against my chest as I searched the pews to no avail. The church was long, with stained glass stretching up like translucent membranes. *And when they do, you'll cut yourself open. You'll pull out your insides. You promised.*

I stepped out into the vestibule, and after all this time, there he was. My brother with his groomsmen, friends from university I'd never met. Stealing a drink from a flask. Swinging his arms, trying to get blood to his fingers. Bristol had changed him. Or maybe he'd just matured while I wasn't there to see it, and it'd be better if I turned him inside out and sewed him up in reverse so I no longer had to watch him age. At least, now that he was back, he'd be serving the local hospitals and nearby villages, and he wouldn't be so far away from me. Nothing all the way out at the coast, not anymore.

I said, barely loud enough to hear, "George?"

My brother met my eyes, and his first words to me in months were, "*That's* the dress you picked?"

Right. I'd tried awfully hard to forget what I was wearing. The corset was specifically made to accentuate curves and the dress was gaudy, with a big rump of a bustle as was the fashion. Or Mother's idea of the fashion. I'd studied diagrams from George's notes of how tightlacing corsets could deform bones and internal organs, memorized them until I could draw them on the church floor with charcoal. Flesh and bone make more sense to me than the people they add up to.

"It was Mother's idea," I said plainly, resisting the urge to chew a hangnail. "May I speak to you? For just a second?"

George flashed a grin at his groomsmen. "Sorry, lads. The sister's more important than you lot."

So he broke away from the flock, even as his friends groused and jabbed their elbows into his ribs—and then he led me to a quiet corner in the back of the sanctuary. Away from the people and the noise.

Without Father to snap at me, I couldn't stop fidgeting. My hands wrung awkwardly at my stomach, and I bit my cheek until I tasted blood.

*It's pathetic you ever thought you'd avoid this*, the rabbit said.

George got my attention by putting a hand in front of my face. "In," he said. I scrambled to follow his instructions, breathed in. "Out." I breathed out. "There we go. It's okay. I'm here."

*As soon as you were born with a womb, you were fucked.*

I couldn't take it anymore. The mask I'd built to be the perfect daughter cracked. The stitches popped. I began to cry.

George said, "Oh, Silas." My name. My *real* name. It'd been so long since someone called me my real name. I clamped a hand to my lips to stifle an embarrassing gasp. "Use your words," George said. "Tell me what's wrong."

I didn't mean to do this at his wedding. I didn't do it on purpose. I didn't, I swear.

I said, "I need to get out of that house. It's happening. Soon." I started to rock back and forth. George put a hand on my shoulder to hold me still, but I pushed him away. I had to move. I'd scream if I couldn't move. "*No.* Don't. Please don't. I just—I don't know, I don't know what to do."

"Silas," George said.

"If I get away from them, I could buy a little more time." Could I, though? Or was I just desperate? "Don't leave me alone with them, *please*—"

"*Silas.*"

I forced myself to look at him. My chest hitched. "What?"

Then, one of the groomsmen, leaning out to the pews, bellowed: "The bride has arrived!"

"Shit," George said. "Already?"

"Wait." I grabbed for his sleeve. No, he couldn't walk away now, he couldn't. "George, please."

But he was backing up, peeling me from his arm. When I remember this moment months later, I recall his pained expression, the worry wrinkling his face, but I don't know if it was actually there. I cannot convince myself I hadn't created it in the weeks that followed.

"We can talk about this later," George said. "Okay? Sit, before someone comes looking for you." Nausea climbed up my throat and threatened to spill onto my tongue. "Afterwards. I swear."

He walked away.

I stared after him. Still shivering. Still struggling for air.

What else was I to do except what I was told? I never learned how to do anything else.

I scrubbed my eyes dry and found my place with our parents. Mother smiled, holding me by the shoulder the way surgeons used to hold down patients before anesthesia. "How is George doing?" she asked me, and I said, "He's well." The organist ambled into a slow, lovely song, and the sun shone through stained glass in a beam of rainbows. George stood at the end of the aisle. He met my gaze and smiled. I smiled back. It wavered.

The bride herself, when she walked in on her father's arm, was tall, with honey-colored hair. She was not the most beautiful woman in the empire, but she didn't have to be. She radiated such kindness that it was as if she were made of gold.

But.

She had violet eyes.

And a silver Speaker ring on her little finger.

The rabbit said, *Soon, that will be you.*

When I was younger—ten, I think, or maybe eleven—I dreamed of amputating my eyes. It seemed easy. Stick your thumb in the socket, work it behind the eyeball, and take it out, *pop*, like the cork in a bottle of wine. If they were gone, I reasoned, the Royal Speaker Society would leave me be. They came over every Sunday to savor cups of Mother's tea, talk with Father about ghosts and spirit-work and economic ventures in India, and calculate the likelihood of their children having violet eyes if they had those children with me. "You've never played with a ghost, have you?" a Speaker said once, teasing my sleeve. "Because you know what happens to little girls who play with ghosts."

And it has never stopped. It has only gotten worse, louder and louder as I grew into my chest and hips. Now they kiss my knuckles and run their hands through my hair. They wonder about boys I've been with and offer ungodly sums of money for my hand in marriage.

"*Is she lilac, heather, or mauve?*" they would ask my mother, holding my jaw to keep my head still. Sometimes they gave me their silver Speaker ring to wear, just to see how I'd look with it one day. "*Oh, Mrs. Bell, when will you let her marry?*"

Mother would just smile. "*Soon.*"

I'd grown out of the juvenile fantasy quickly enough. The eyes were a symptom, not the disease. If I wanted to resort to surgery, I'd have to go to the root: a hysterectomy, a total removal of the womb. Until my ability to continue a bloodline is destroyed, these men don't care how many pieces of myself I hack off—but that doesn't mean I haven't popped the eyes out of a slaughtered pig just to feel it.

George's wife had violet eyes like mine.

He was doing to a girl everything that would be done to me.

I got up from the pew. Mother hissed and reached for me, but I stumbled into the aisle, clamping a hand over my mouth. I slammed out the front doors and collapsed onto the stairs.

I spat stomach acid once, twice, before I vomited.

Father came out behind me, dragging me onto my feet. "What are you doing?" he snarled. "What is wrong with you?"

*It will hurt,* the rabbit said. *It will hurt it will hurt it will hurt.*

✦

George has not been able to face me since.

He knows what he did.

2

November descends upon England, dark and uncaring
like consumption, and I'm almost grateful; after all, it
is easier to be a boy in the winter.

I fret in front of the vanity mirror as embers gleam in my
bedroom fireplace. Darker tones are blessedly more fash-
ionable in the later months; heavier fabrics and long coats
break up the silhouette, obscuring more feminine features.
There's nothing to be done about soft cheeks and pink lips,
but with my hair tucked into a cap and a scarf wrapped
round to conceal the pins, I just about pass for a boy. A
feminine, baby-faced boy from the poor side of the city—
funny, then, that my bedroom is full of fine dresses and
imported rugs—but a boy nonetheless. Very *Oliver Twist*, I
think. I've never been one for stories.

Still, my chest aches as I fill out my brows with powder
stolen from Mother's vanity. How cruel is it, that I only get

to be myself as a costume? I do not get to savor the masculine cut of my clothes, or the illusion of short hair, or the
fleeting joy of my skin feeling like mine. Instead, I have to
worry if my boyhood is convincing enough to keep me safe.

There is no joy in that. Only fear.

*You think you'll fool them?* the rabbit chides as I work. *So
many men would do terrible things for you. So many of them
have begged for the chance. They'd know your body anywhere.*
Look at the trousers bunching at my full hips and the linens
tied around my breasts that never feel tight enough. *See?
You're nothing more than a little girl playing dress-up.*

*And you're going to walk right into their lair.*

The rabbit is right. If I have any time left, it's not much.
Mother and Father have nearly decided on my husband.
That's what they're doing at this very moment: perusing
the Viscount Luckenbill's annual Speaker gala with a
list of names. This year's costume theme is literature, so
they're busy in whatever inane outfits Mother has devised,
cross-examining the men who have fawned over me all my
life. I can nearly hear them weighing the advantages of
each potential marriage contract. How many connections
do they have? How much money? How much power?

So, yes, it would be safer to stay home. But tonight is my
best, and maybe my only, chance to escape.

Because a young medium is set to receive his spirit-work
seal at the gala tonight—and with any luck, it will be me.
The plan is simple enough. Go to the gala, get the seal, and
*run.*

I close the tin of powder and remind myself to breathe.

I do not give a shit about being a medium. I want nothing to do with the Speakers, or spirits, or hauntings, or any of it. But if a silver Speaker ring marks you as a member of the brotherhood, a medium's seal grants you the freedom of a king. Violet eyes make spirit-work possible, and a seal makes it legal. Speaker money will fund your travels and businesses. Opportunities rise up to meet your feet. Of course, England regulates its mediums brutally, but to be officially recognized as one with that mark on your hand—it might as well be *magic*, the way the empire will bend for you.

So I'll take the seal, proof of my manhood branded on the back of my hand, and go where no one knows my face. I'll enroll in medical school and begin my life in earnest. Nobody will know I had been a daughter once. I won't need Mother and Father. I won't need George; I won't need any of them.

I'll be . . .

My heel clicks again, *tap tap tap*, but it's not enough to get rid of the tension creeping up my trapezius muscles. In a burst, my hands flutter, and I shake myself out until I'm calm enough to breathe again.

After this, I'll be free.

I've forged my invitation to the gala. According to Mother's friends, the young man who is supposed to get his medium's seal tonight, who has eyes like wisteria and traveled all the way here from York for the chance, has fallen ill. Nobody has met him in person, so I've borrowed his name for the evening. I will take his place, and his seal, and I will be gone before a soul learns the truth.

It's just that if I'm caught, if they figure out who I am, that I was born a girl—

*They'll fucking hang you.*

✦

The gala is not far. I slip down the front steps of my family's townhome—not nearly as impressive as some of the other houses of London, but still grand enough to reflect well on the family—and huddle into my coat. Despite the cold, I refuse to hail a cab. I need to walk. It's the only way I can reliably clear my head these days. Especially since I don't let my hands flap in public. *"You look like an imbecile,"* Father said once, which was far more effective than any of my tutors' attempts to get me to stop. *"You look* stupid, *girl."*

I tried telling my family the truth exactly once. When I was younger, back when I thought they still cared, I told them I did not ever want to be married. Stories that took the shape of fairy tales sounded like Hell to me. My eyes would give me a good marriage and a life of privilege, a life of plenty, if I'd only let them. But wedding dresses, big bellies, the miracle of childbirth? I'd rather cut myself open. I told them I didn't want any of it. I told them I was scared.

Mother called me silly, and Father told me to get over it. I knew what they really meant, though. The rabbit translated for me. *Entitled. Selfish.* How dare I ask to be treated differently than anyone else? Every man and woman in England has a duty, and I couldn't expect to escape mine just because I was *scared*.

I don't think *scared* was the word I should have used.

It doesn't take long to find the South Kensington Museum. It's a grand cathedral of art and finery, lit up so brightly against the dark night sky it looks like it's been set on fire. The Speakers have swallowed it whole. Violet banners hang from the marble façade, framed by thousands of lavenders and lilacs woven into wreaths and ivy arches, all of which will shrivel and die in the cold as soon as the event is done. Carriages wait obediently in the street, horses huffing and puffing while the drivers try to catch a nap. It's almost as if the Royal Speaker Society will dissolve into violent chaos if they don't spend half their taxpayer funding on decorations and overworked servants.

At the entrance, a violet-eyed doorman blows into his hands to warm them. He has a seal, but only a small place-holder design, a circle freeze-burned onto the back of his hand. This is an indentured medium: a man who couldn't afford his full medium's seal and so signed himself away to the Speakers in exchange for the funds. It's a nasty deal, but there will never be a shortage of people willing to take nasty deals in exchange for a better life. This indentured medium will get the rest of the seal, an intricate eye, once his debt is paid off—as long as the hand doesn't succumb to gangrene first. At least he gets to wear a fancy ring while he waits.

Through the twin sets of double doors, I hear laughter. It's muffled, as if underwater. I'm late.

"This is a private event, boy," the doorman drawls as I approach. There's a thrill at being accepted as male, but I refuse to let myself linger on it. It doesn't matter nearly as much if they're seeing the wrong boy.

"I'm aware," I say, and produce the invitation.

The doorman frowns, skimming the forged document up and down. His eyes are droopy and his hands seem to be permanently stiff. "Roswell? My, uh, sincere apologies. Glad those rumors about you being ill were just rumors." He doesn't sound particularly glad. "Well, they haven't started the ceremony yet, so you're in luck. *Mors vincit omnia* and all that. Come in."

He opens the door.

I hate that anything having to do with the Speakers could be beautiful. Inside, a towering ceiling looms toward marble balconies; gas lights flicker, turning everything gold. Irreplaceable works of art have been brought out for the occasion, placed behind tables overflowing with purple bouquets. The air smells of liquor and pollen and ozone. And the costumes—a woman with cheeks painted pink in homage to Heidi. An Edgar Allan Poe carries a model heart. Some bored-looking man has opted out of the theme by carrying around a portrait of a horse, claiming to be one character or another from *Black Beauty*. So many glimmering silver rings, a smattering of seals, too much drinking and laughing and noise. It is so overwhelmingly *jovial* in comparison to the sick feeling in my stomach. The mismatch makes me want to dig my nails into my arms. It's just like the wedding all over again. I hate it, *I hate it*.

*Just walk away*, the rabbit says. *You don't belong here and you know it. Leave. Go.*

But I don't leave. I can't. As I step into the museum, I imagine the branding iron so cold it smokes in the air. It will crackle and hiss as it touches my skin. The pain will be worth it in exchange for the freedom it will grant.

I have to do this.

The doorman steps in behind me, ushered by a gust of air so frigid that I turn to make sure a spirit hasn't followed him.

"George Bell?" he says. "The Roswell boy showed up after all. He's yours."

The sickness in my gut blossoms into nausea.

My brother, holding a flute of champagne just inside the door, stares as if he's uncovered a medical cadaver only to find my face looking back at him.

He has a Speaker ring on his little finger.

✦

Did you know that someone like me had once been a surgeon?

It sounds like a myth, but it's true. His name was James Barry. George told me about him when I was young, offhandedly, as if he knew something about me that I didn't. Barry was a right prick with no sense of decorum or tact, but brilliant doctors have no use for either. He was a high-ranking military surgeon, George said, who improved conditions for the poor and sick all his life—and when he died, it was discovered by a nurse that he'd been a woman all along.

"Though," George continued, "you'd think someone like Barry would've wanted to make a fuss about that on his deathbed. Fuck you all, you've been bested by a woman, rot in Hell, all that mess. But he didn't." He didn't look up from his studies. "You think, perhaps, he was happier as a man? And that nurse should have left his damned body alone?"

I'd said nothing in return, but I hadn't had to. He snuck a chest of clothes under my bed that night. Formalwear, patched linen trousers fit only for poor street boys, and everything in between. The accompanying note read: *Some of this is mine, some of it not, but hopefully all will suit you one day.* I'm wearing those clothes now.

I wish I could feel anger. I wish that, when I was upset, I could scream and yell and rage, do *anything* other than cry. I would feel so much more like a man than a little girl playing pretend. But there I am, shaking, my eyes burning with tears.

He left me.

He joined the Speakers and left me with *them*.

The doorman says, "You all right, Bell?"

"I—yes." George bobs his head in a jerky nod. He has a moustache now. That's what I focus on. He has a moustache now, and it looks very strange on his face. "Yes. I'm fine, just relieved I don't have to rework the schedule is all. And, yes, it's a pleasure to finally meet you, Mr. Roswell." He plays the part well. I struggle to do the same. If I'd known George would be chaperoning the boy, I never would have come. I would have found another way; maybe I would have faked the seal, I could have carved it into the skin myself. "Why don't I show you around? Come with me."

He gestures for me to follow him as the doorman leaves to deliver the news of my arrival. I tuck close to his side despite the lead weight in my stomach. No matter what he did, I don't think I'll ever outgrow the instinct to use him as shelter.

George, after a second of hesitation, puts a hand on my shoulder.

There are so, so many people at this gala. A man with blue eyes boasts of the number of indentured medium contracts he holds, though I heard from Father that he feels as if he was cheated out of violet eyes—and, therefore, spirit-work itself—thanks to his mother's infidelity. An older, lavender-eyed gentleman with an ivory cane rubs his seal as he discusses his time as a medium in Prince Albert's private service decades ago, traveling to hauntings across the world. I recognize nearly all of them. *That one*, the rabbit says as we pass a brown-eyed bachelor set to inherit his father's shipping company, *didn't care how old you were when he tried to kiss you in the parlor.* Men will do a lot of things to weave spirit-work into their bloodline. If they cannot have violet eyes themselves, they will find ways to control those who do. Marrying them, fathering them, hosting their contracts—whatever's most convenient.

But there are more dangerous people at this party than men with God complexes. I skim the crowd for Mother and Father. I'm not sure what they've dressed up as. Mother loves any opportunity to make a scene, so maybe I should be looking for the most ostentatious outfit in the room, but it's all just a blur of bright light and shades of purple and servants, marble statues and oil paintings and alcohol. I hate alcohol. The smell makes me ill.

George drains his champagne, places the flute on the tray of a passing butler without slowing down, and ducks his head to hiss, "What the hell do you think you're doing here?"

"I could ask the same of you." I ball my hands together so they don't do something they shouldn't. "You said you were working in the countryside today."

"I *was,* but now I'm *not,*" George says. "Now, let me ask again: What are you doing here?"

"I'm getting my seal."

George makes a noise like I've put a knife in his gut.

"No," he says. "No. Have you gone mad? Mother and Father are here, you know that."

"They can't stop me."

"They can if they recognize you," George says, as if I am not fully aware of that. The rabbit reminds me: *They'll hurt you they'll hurt you.* "You've done none of the reading, taken none of the oaths, attended none of the chapter meetings— Oh, don't look at me like that. When would you have had time, between sneaking into operating theaters and cutting up slaughterhouse rejects?" I breathe carefully to steady myself. Like he taught me. "And then you have no money to pay the dues—"

I say, "Roswell already paid, and I took the deed to my dowry. It's the country house. I'll pay him back with it."

"The *country house?*" George splutters. "Christ, Father really is desperate. So, you're going to run away? Trade the deed to some ne'er-do-well for a few thousand pounds to pay back a man you've never met, then what? Take a train or ship to wherever will have you? If James Barry was found out, you will be too, and you know what will happen if you are."

We stop by one of the pillars holding up the balcony, my back to the cool stone. We always end up like this. Because of me. I wrap my arms around my stomach and stare past him, over his shoulder. Looking anyone in the eye is gut-churningly difficult.

It wasn't supposed to happen like this. He wasn't supposed to be here.

"If the Speakers catch you—" George chokes on his words. "I have had lots of bad days, but seeing you at the gallows would be worst of all."

What stings the most—out of everything, out of all of this—is that George had been on my side once. When I was little, he was the only one who understood me. He ate the food I couldn't stomach so Mother and Father wouldn't snap at me for leaving my plate half full; he let me hide in his room when we had company over, and tapped three times on the doorway when it was safe to emerge. He indulged my curiosity and defended my stubbornness until I learned to hide it. I thought it was the two of us against the world.

Now, we are this. Whatever this is.

My lip wobbles. I'm crying. Again. Like I always do. And here I am, still trying, still begging him to see reason. Because it's still *him*, isn't it?

"Fine." I try to force my voice level but it doesn't work.

"If you truly don't want me to do this, then help me." He pinches the bridge of his nose as if I am a child pitching a fit for attention. His glasses go crooked. "It'll be more difficult without the seal, but I can still do it. All I need is to get to Edinburgh. Even to York, or Leeds—I can make it from Leeds."

He says, "No. I can't. Elsie . . ."

That name makes a spark of rage flash behind my eyes. Of course. Elsie. Over and over, Elsie. It's his wife, always his wife, never me. Ever since she came into his life, he has been distant, and he never answers my letters, and he's never home when I visit, and every attempt to ask for help ends with him hemming and hawing about how it will affect *her*.

And maybe I'm jealous of her too. I am jealous that she got to pick her husband. I am jealous that she did not have to marry someone before her body had even finished growing. I am upset that I will never get the chance for a marriage based on love like everyone else. Why does *Elsie* get to be happy when I don't?

I regret it before I even finish the sentence, but I can't stop myself. "Can you leave her out of this for *once*?"

Something snaps in George's expression. His nostrils flare. He slams a hand into the pillar by my head.

*"She just lost a child!"*

The noise of the gala disappears into a low, droning hum. A child.

His statement, corrected for a medical context: a miscarriage. Or an early stillbirth, maybe, the dead fetus expelled from the womb like the body rejecting a splinter. This sort of thing is hardly talked about. It is described as a cold, an unwellness, something to be brushed away and hidden from polite company.

And if I were Elsie, I would be relieved. So terribly relieved, sobbing, thanking God that the awful thing was gone.

Is that cruel of me? Am I monstrous for being unable to understand why someone would want to subject themselves to a parasite? For being disgusted that my brother would dare to put her in that position at all?

My tutors would say so.

"Is that what you want to hear? Is it?" George's hazel eyes flash with a horrible thing I do not recognize. I think he might be crying too, or maybe it's just the flickering of the gas lamps. "I didn't want to tell you, I didn't want to tell *anyone*, but here we are. And maybe you don't care at all—I know you hate her—but do you want to be the person to put her through this now? When she's *ill*?"

I don't hate her. I don't. I hate what she means. Like she is a metaphor, not a living person.

"No," I say. "I didn't know. I'm sorry."

George's lips draw into a thin line.

"Nothing is as black and white as you think it is," he says.

It's been a while since someone has called me slow to my face. The rabbit tells me I deserve it.

Behind us, in the grand atrium of the museum, someone taps their fork against a glass. George tears his eyes from me. I peer around the column, arms wrapped around my chest. It always feels like there's an anvil on my sternum whenever someone is upset with me. The chatter of voices slows, then stops.

At the front of the room, the Viscount William Luckenbill—host of this party, president of the Royal Speaker Society, and the most forgettable man I've ever seen—stands at a podium in silly safari attire, flanked by ancient statues that were once carefully excised from their proper resting places, wrapped in linen, and brought to London. His face is devoid of any distinguishing features, and his eyes are a muddy every-color. He fiddles with his ring. I can smell the champagne and imported cologne from here.

His green-eyed son, about my age or perhaps a little older, stands beside him, inspecting his nails with a pouty lower lip.

His son is as sharp and striking as a scalpel.

"Your attention, please!" Lord Luckenbill calls. This man is not a scalpel at all. He is dull forceps, or a tongue depressor. "Ladies and gentlemen, thank you for spending your Sunday evening with me. I will, of course, spare you a lengthy second welcome—we have better things to be doing." A ripple of polite laughter. "Tonight, we have the honor of performing one of the Royal Speaker Society's most sacred of traditions: welcoming a new brother into our fold."

As if on cue, two butlers carve through the party. One carries a bouquet of lavenders and lilacs; the other, a branding iron in the shape of an eye.

"Sixty years ago," the Viscount Luckenbill says, "when the Lord gave us our first children with violet eyes, we were a baffled people, but a grateful one. How blessed were we, to be graced with this new beauty?" He sweeps his hand grandly. "But when the Veil began to thin, we realized the deeper truth of this blessing. These violet-eyed sons had been sent here to keep us safe. To help us navigate the strange new reality we'd found ourselves in, where the dead are now just a breath away from the living."

That is why I am doing this. If I cannot escape their system, I will use it. And why shouldn't I? I have reached into the Veil before. I have put my hand to a haunting without realizing what I'd done, before I grasped the punishment that would befall me if I was ever caught. I was only curious as to why the world warped and shone. I was a child then, and it was nearly effortless, even if I hated how it felt. Whatever the test is, it can't be that hard. Can it?

Lord Luckenbill steps away from the podium. His footsteps echo off the tile, going up, up, up to the ceiling. This story must be recounted at every meeting the same as prayers at church, or the Hippocratic oath at the end of a doctor's training: *I will abstain from all intentional wrong-doing and harm. . . .*

"And so the Royal Speaker Society was created," he says. "To support those who guide us through God's new world, to provide brotherhood for our guardians, and to punish those who would do them harm."

He pauses for dramatic effect. It feels as if the entire world is leaning in.

"We further that purpose here tonight," Lord Luckenbill says. "Mr. David Roswell?"

It's now.

It's happening.

I raise my trembling hand—before the rabbit can scream, before I can stop myself, before my mind can work through all the possible, terrible consequences of failure—and say, "I'm here."

3

I said it.

*I'm here.*

Every head in the room turns to pin me with their eyes, but all I can think of is freedom. I'll take the seal and disappear, leaving my parents with nothing to remember me by except the dresses hanging in my wardrobe. I'll cut my hair, take a new last name—maybe Barry—and make my way north. I'd like to visit the Edinburgh Medical School before I apply.

The Royal Speaker Society will never get to have me.

But the rabbit *howls.* It says, *Your parents are here.* It says, *They made you, they raised you, they'll recognize you no matter what you PRETEND to be.*

At the center of the atrium, standing with the butlers, Lord Luckenbill narrows his eyes, lifting his chin as if that will help him see across the crowd.

"Mr. Roswell?" he calls. "You must be quite short, my boy, where are you?"

George nudges me forward. *You wanted this*, the rabbit translates, rabid with fear. *So go.*

I do. The pale crowd parts like a wound as I step toward him, opening a path between us. The rabbit tries to convince me everyone is picking me to pieces, looking for parts of my body that will identify me as a liar. If my hands are too small, if I walk too daintily, if I breathe from the chest like a woman instead of from the belly like a man. Do those distinctions actually exist? Or am I creating them to fuel my own anxiety, a closed loop feeding on itself?

"Roswell!" Lord Luckenbill claps his hands as I approach. His demeanor puts my teeth on edge. "Oh, I'm so glad you were able to make it; what a blessing that you're feeling better. I would have hated to have to reschedule all this, you know. And, Lord, you're such a little thing! Take after your mother, I presume. No matter, you look wonderful, come up, come up. Mr. Bell, is that you there with him?"

George clears his throat. Yet another reminder that I don't know my brother anymore; since when would a viscount know him by name? "Yes, my lord," he says.

But.

At the edge of the crowd, near the front, there they are.

Mother and Father.

My vision blurs when I see them. Their faces are screwed up in mutual confusion, as if trying to remember if they've seen me before, and if so, where. Father seems incredibly uncomfortable, having refused to don any costume for the occasion, while Mother has found a horrific green dress: taxidermy birds sewn between flowers and feathers like a fairy or some kind of goddess. Her corset is cinched so tight I could span her stomach with my hands.

*They'll hurt you they'll hurt you they'll hurt you.*

When I get close enough—I'm so nervous I could vomit—Lord Luckenbill takes my hand in his and holds it up high. I never considered myself a particularly small person, but his fingers make mine look frail in comparison.

"May the ceremony be swift and may the branding iron treat you well," Lord Luckenbill says. *"Mors vincit omnia!"*

And the crowd echoes, *Mors vincit omnia*, one voice, one cadence. Death conquers all. Everyone will die and there is not a soul who can escape it. The phrase is inscribed on the inside of every Speaker ring, written at the bottom of all official correspondence, carved above their doorways so it can never be forgotten. One day, when I am a surgeon myself, when I open my own practice—where I will accept every body as it is, with kindness, without question—I will do the same. "Not because I am one of them," I will explain, "but because it is true. Not even a surgeon can defy the will of God. Isn't that a comfort to know?"

Lord Luckenbill says, "Bring out the traitor!"

. . . the traitor?

One of the inconspicuous doors along the side of the museum atrium swings open with a tremendous bang, and two mediums—big men, violet-eyed men, with a seal etched into each of their large right hands—drag a tattered woman onto the cold tile floor. She is dressed in rags, eyes swollen and whirling. The bruises on her bare arms and throat are dark wine stains against her white skin. Her lacerations border on septic.

A gasp rises from the audience, as if this is some sort of performance. Mother covers her mouth with her hand, scandalized.

The woman's irises are violet too. They remind me of orchids.

A million possibilities stretch out in front of me, and all of them are monstrous. I glance back to George, but with the barest twitch he shakes his head. He doesn't know what's happening either.

"This woman," Lord Luckenbill bellows, "has been found guilty of violating the 1841 Speaker Act, for the crime of practicing unlicensed spirit-work and falsifying Speaker documents." The woman picks up her unwashed head, staring at the twisted expressions around her. I take a half step back, but George catches me. *You wanted this.* "Miss Neuling, stand up straight, please. Give yourself some dignity. You had so much gall before; where is it now?"

All I can think of is that man who said, "*You know what happens to little girls who play with ghosts.*" Miss Neuling digs her feet into the floor, but they just scuff and slide against the tile. Her body is made of sharp angles, edges pressing against her prisoner's dress.

It's written there, in the 1841 Speaker Act, section 3, paragraph A, that women are prohibited from practicing spirit-work: reaching into the Veil, using speaking tiles, or even being allowed near hauntings at all without the presence of a chaperone. I am not a woman, but as long as I am seen as one, I will be forced under the jurisdiction of the law all the same. It is, of course, for our protection. If violet-eyed men are a gift from God, violet-eyed women are an unfortunate side effect. We are prized for giving our husbands violet-eyed sons and hated for our weakness of mind. For us to tamper with the dead will make us unstable, unfit, dangers to ourselves and others. In the interest of preserving the peace and stability of the empire, those who violate this law are to be either locked away for the rest of their lives or—depending on the severity of the crime—summarily executed.

(It's no wonder, then, that the Indian accountant Father once employed sent his newborn daughter away in a panic when she was born violet-eyed; he saw England stacked against her and made the only choice he could. It's no wonder the rage that erupted in the colonies when the law was passed. It's no wonder that English soil was the only place the law was accepted with applause.)

Miss Neuling rasps, "You are a rancid, disgusting piece of shit." Her voice is misshapen, like something in her throat has been broken. "All of you."

Her eyes slide right over me, as if I am the same as all the rest of the men staring down at her, the same as the Speakers who have doomed her. She does not recognize what I am.

No. No, I'm not—

*How would she know?* the rabbit says. *If you want so badly to be a man, you don't get to object when you're mistaken for one.*

"Right," Lord Luckenbill says. "Let's not delay this any longer. We have a test to finish."

I need the seal.

The lights are dimmed, gas lamps tightened to only a trickle of flame. Everyone hurries to sit, crowding the tables dotting the room, some bachelors standing in the back. George stays close, refusing to meet Mother's eyes. The doors are locked. I turn my gaze to the roof of the museum to look somewhere, anywhere else.

The delicate joints of the architecture move as I watch. A haunting. A place where the Veil is so thin you can see the edges of spirits distending the fabric of the world. Where a medium can tear it, if they want, to reach through to the other side.

"It's a simple way to go," Lord Luckenbill explains as he brings me forward. He gives me a single item: a piece of a statue, about the size of my palm. It warps and changes in my hand. This chunk of stone is, like the ceiling, a haunting. Holding this feels like plunging my arms into ice. "And it is a peaceful way to go too. We're a merciful brotherhood, Mr. Roswell—I detest hangings with a passion. They're barbaric and prone to miscalculation. All you have to do is open the Veil, and the gentlemen here will place her head through. Simple suffocation. It won't even be long enough for her to catch frostbite. Are you ready?"

If I don't speak now, I won't be able to say anything at all.

I need the seal.

I say, "Yes, sir."

But I'm not ready. This is the test? *This?* Not just opening the world and reaching through to the other side, something every damn person with purple eyes can do, but to see if you're willing to kill for the brotherhood? Committing a public execution?

I bite the inside of my cheek until the mucus membrane pops between my teeth.

"Godspeed," Lord Luckenbill says, and backs away.

I stand at Miss Neuling's head now. Readjust my grip on the stone. She's only a few meters away, close enough that I can smell the mustiness of her prison cell, the vague smell of decay. She's in her thirties, maybe. She has no wedding ring.

"You're a child," she says when her attention lands on me. The weight of her gaze is horrible. "They make children perform executions now?"

It's just suffocation. Suffocation isn't painful, right? So long as you can breathe out? She won't feel it. She can't.

I peel at the edge of the world around the piece of statue. It comes too easily. With just a gesture, the world ripples the way a puddle would when you step into it, thrums like the bobbing of a swallowing throat.

The air shifts. It changes.

I hate how intangible the Veil is. How ethereal it is against my hands. What's behind the Veil begins to show through: emptiness, sheer emptiness, and the vague shape of a person-thing. Like most spirits, it has no face, only a caul-like membrane and a jagged slash-mouth. And another one. Another. Most are strange, elongated, recognizable. One, though, is dark around the edges, as if charred, proof that it pressed too hard against the edge of its world and burnt itself in the process. What was it trying to reach? How many souls are bound to the works of art in this museum? How many mediums wander the halls beside the patrons, keeping them quiet, keeping them hidden so London never knows the suffering this place enacts on the dead? I've never bothered to count them. I should have.

Then the Veil opens entirely. Ripping apart with a sound like bones breaking. It strains at the corners, and a gust of cold air screams through the room. Something hisses, loud and low.

This is what all these men reach for. The dead no longer have reason to lie, so they never do. They carry the knowledge of their life, of their times—warped by perspective and time and rage, sure, but it is always truth. That medium in the service of Prince Albert called upon the dead for accounts of what the world had once been and what it may be one day. Capitalists shell out pound after pound for mediums to keep dead workers from rattling factory windows until they shatter. Rich men travel thousands of miles to hauntings guarded jealously by British rule, to locations irreversibly warped by death or suffering, hoping that a ghost will whisper some secret and change the world. A haunting can never be destroyed, only hidden or quieted. A haunting can never be owned, either, but that has not stopped the empire from trying.

I don't want this. I want meat and bone, vessels and blood, things I can *touch* and *know*. I want to stitch together a person's body, not dissect their soul. Not this.

The mediums pull Miss Neuling closer, grab her by the hair, shove her across the floor. She struggles, throwing her head back with a snarl. One of them clocks her on the temple. Her eyelids flutter.

Once they get the head through, they'll hold her there until she chokes to death. Asphyxiation can take minutes. I have to keep this open for minutes. Painless minutes, but they'll still be dying minutes, and she'll know what's happening when her vision begins to blur and her head starts to feel a bit too light.

Spirit-work. Falsifying Speaker documents. She did what I'm doing *right now*.

*You came all this way, into the mouth of the beast, to object on moral grounds? You can't always feel things so strongly. Sometimes you need to do the dirty work.*

I can't.

*Everyone else can do it, why not you?*

I don't know why people do the things they do. All I know is that I *can't*.

I drop the piece of statue and close the Veil.

It's a thunderclap, the world stitching itself back together with a crack of air. Or maybe it's the stone hitting the tile floor. *Snap.* Just like that. It startles one of the mediums so badly that his hand slips from Miss Neuling's arm.

She yanks herself from him, and from the apron of her prison dress, she pulls a sharpened piece of metal. Roughly filed with a strip of cloth wrapped around one end.

She jams in into his stomach.

It's quick. In through all the layers of cloth right under

the ribs, and then a *rip*, cloth and flesh all at once. She throws her whole weight into it to tear through the vest and undershirt. Through the epidermis. Through the subcutaneous tissue. Through the muscle, into the belly, where the blood is so thick it turns black. Snap. Lunge.

There is a moment of uncomprehending silence from the crowd.

The first person to move is the other medium. He grabs Miss Neuling by the throat, takes her head, beats the side of her skull. *Thud thud thud.* The makeshift knife clatters to the tile.

But the medium with the ripped stomach puts his hand to the wound. Stares at his hand when it comes away red. Whispers, "Oh, hell."

He falls.

The party starts to scream.

My vision narrows to the smallest point: the wound. I've snuck into hospitals and watched doctors from the balcony of the operating theater. I've straddled dead hogs behind the abattoir with a surgeon's kit at my knee. This is what I was made for. Not the Veil. Not the Speakers or the children they expect me to bear. This.

George and I start for him at the same time.

I get to the medium first. I start yanking the buttons of his vest, pulling up his shirt, getting to the skin as quickly as possible. George stumbles down beside me but the medium grabs him. George hisses through his teeth.

"Sir, I'm going to need you to stay still," George says. "I know it hurts." Then, to me: "What's going on down there?"

I can't tell. The wound ebbs and flows with his breath, opening and closing as his lungs expand and contract. It reeks too. Just from the smell—rancid, half-digested food—I can guess what's been hit, but I yank off my jacket and sponge up the blood to get a better look anyway. The medium thrashes. George grunts and grabs his wrists.

*You did this*, the rabbit says.

Shut up. Let me focus.

"It's open to the abdominal cavity," I say. "Perforated large intestine." Inside, the guts writhe like worms. Everything is alive, struggling and squirming. Then it all fills with blood again, and it's gone. "Nearest hospital?"

"St. Mary's," someone offers in a shaky voice. "Ten minutes to the north, by carriage."

"Does he have ten minutes?" I ask.

"Not when he's bleeding that much, Christ, organs like to *bleed*," George says. "Does anyone have a sewing kit! Are there any other doctors!"

I don't know who it comes from, but a sewing kit ends up in my hands. How lucky that we're at a costume party. I open it up and go for the thread.

"Give it to me," George says.

"No."

*"Give it—"*

I show my teeth. I got here first. This patient is mine. *"No."*

George stares at me, eyes blown wide, before he must realize there's no use fighting. He says, "Fine." He puts more of his weight on the medium, adjusts his grip. "Fine.

Okay. Close the bowel, then stop the bleeding. Look at me. You know how to do that, right?" I nod. Of course I do. "Good. I'm right here. Are there *any other doctors!*"

The rabbit says, *This is your fault.*

Shut up shut UP.

I take a spool of thread—it's bad thread, cotton thread, not silk like a surgeon would use—and get it through the needle. Can't disinfect it, no time to find and strike a match.

George pins the medium's arm with his knee. "Sir, I need you to stay still." I have to be quick. George can't hold him for long.

I straddle the medium, reach into his cut belly, and pull the intestine through the wound. Find the injury. There: it's an inch or two long, carved into the slippery thin organ. I pinch the sides together and begin to stitch the jagged gash closed. This loop of small intestine sticks out of the hole like an umbilical cord. My fingers smear with blood and chyme, pulpy chunks of digested food mixed with bile. The smell is rancid, but that's because it's one step away from shit.

"What stitch are you using?" George asks.

"Running," I answer. The world blurs until it's just the thread, just the wound. "Don't have the time to cut each knot individually."

"Good."

Breathe in. Stitch. Breathe out. Stitch. I don't know what's happening around me. I don't care. It's not a clean wound, no straight lines or careful placement like I'm used to, and my needlework is shoddy. But it doesn't matter what it looks like as long as I get it closed. The edges pucker tightly together.

Once I get to the end, I hunker down and bite the thread close to the medium's stinking insides to sever it.

"I got it," I gasp, packing the organ back into the abdominal cavity. "George, I got it."

"The *bleeding*," he says.

Right. The bleeding. I can fix that too.

But another pair of hands comes down over mine.

"I'm a doctor," a man says. "It's all right. I'll take it from here, son."

*No.* I jerk away from him, lurch protectively over the wound. "Don't *touch* me."

But across the torso, George gives me a desperate look.

"Please," he says.

My fingers loosen around the needle, and the strange man takes it. He takes the thread, takes the patient.

Without the needle, I don't know what to do. My body and mind grind to a halt. I don't back away. I don't run. Should I? Maybe.

Eventually, the man is taken too. He leaves a red smear on the floor.

✦

The first time I really, truly saw blood, it was George who showed me. "If you want to be a surgeon, you can't be squeamish," he told me. It was his first year of medical school when he discovered me reading his notes. He took me to an abattoir. The air smelled of innards and rot. The animals screamed. "Dr. Abney brought us here on our first day of class. Had us kill a pig with our hands. Told us that if we killed something first, before we took our oath, it'd be easier when we open someone up to save them."

I'd cried and begged him to take me home, but then snuck out to visit on my own and watched the slaughterer cut throats until my vision blurred.

This is my fault.

✦

Someone is yelling at George now. The rabbit is yelling too. I can feel the hysterics coming on, building in my head like an aneurysm or encephalitis.

Move. Think. Do something.

"It was your job to keep an eye on him!" There's another man in George's face and spittle on George's little round glasses. "You shouldn't have let him do it if he felt ill! This is gross negligence, and you're not fit to be a Speaker, let alone a doctor!"

The rabbit was right. I should have stayed home. This wouldn't have happened if I hadn't showed up and made a mess of things. Why is everything so loud, why are so many people looking at us, go away, stop, *stop*.

"I'll get your license revoked for this, Bell!"

No.

No, not that. It's the only thing George wanted his whole life. To be a surgeon, to help people, to reclaim the profession from its ugly roots. The Speakers can't take it from him. Not because of me.

"Wait!" I cry. My hands flutter and slam against my chest because the alternative is digging my nails into my face until I draw blood. "It's my fault. My name isn't David. I'm not Mr. Roswell."

George's face goes white. Whiter than it already is.

"Son," a stranger says, stepping closer to me, "what are you talking about?"

I tear off the hat. My long blond hair falls out in a knotted mess. Some of the pins fall out and clink on the tile floor.

"I'm not David Roswell," I say. "I'm sorry. George tried to stop me."

And then Mother.

Screaming a name that isn't mine and never was.

*"GLORIA."*

4

The South Kensington Museum is a digestive tract of rooms and corridors, all filled with beautiful things that aren't ours to display. Haunted relics are held behind glass. The partygoers who didn't leave have scattered, little polyps dotting the maze, desperate to avoid the bloodstain in the atrium. And me. Avoiding me.

I can still feel the intestine slipping through my fingers, pulsing like a snake, spilling bile and hot, stinking mess. I felt grounded. *Real.* For the first time in a long time.

Not that it will ever matter again.

Now, my family and I are in some secluded wing with high ceilings and crowded displays: paintings, porcelain plates, carvings taken from some foreign dig site or another. George stands in front of a still life, a statue himself. Father says nothing. Mother paces back and forth. I wish I could do that. I want to so badly, but she is allowed to pace, I've

learned, and I am not. Instead, I rock on my feet, away from
them.

If Mother and Father are talking, I can't hear it. I'm
too busy asking the rabbit if it knows how to tie a hang-
man's knot. It's not really a *cruel* way to go, not like Lord
Luckenbill said. It's only when the rope is too short or too
long that it becomes barbaric. Too short, and you dangle
there and choke; too long, and the force of the drop will
break the head clean off. I'd rather be hung than whatever
they were going to do to Miss Neuling.

Whatever *I* was going to do.

Mother stops pacing and reaches for Father pathetically.
"I feel faint," she says. I don't know how much of this she's
putting on, as she tends to do, and how much is because she
hasn't eaten for a day to get that corset so tight. I imagine
all the organs shifted out of place, the same way pregnancy
rearranges the innards. "Please. I fear I'll be sick."

"You're fine," Father says.

*"Fine?"* Mother squeals. Her voice is high enough that
it hurts my ears, but I know better than to cover them.
"They're going to *kill her!*" She walks away from him again,
waving tears from her face. "I thought—oh, I thought we'd
done everything right. We did everything we could. Didn't
we? What did we do to deserve this?"

"When the police arrive," George cuts in, "I'm sure we
can explain. She's still practically a child, she meant no
harm, she has a history of mental frailty, she even helped—"

Father turns on him. "Shut the fuck up, boy."

George recoils.

"In fact," Father continues, "it'd be best if you turned and left right now. *Now.* Because if you keep talking, maybe I'll stop paying for that house. Even your fancy surgeon's salary can't support a wife there alone, not now. You're too busy paying the loan you took out for that bride price. Isn't that right?"

I know, I *know*, that violet-eyed brides fetch a high price. It's an antiquated system, bride prices, but everything about the Speakers is antiquated—arranged marriages, young brides, executions. None of it would be accepted outside of their fold. It's just that their fathers see the demand and take advantage of husbands willing to pay, willing to bend the rules of the land to get what they want. And I know that George paid that price, because there's a price for my hand too, and it's impossible to forget about something like that. It disgusts me so much I want to tear off my skin.

But he's still my brother. I still need him.

"George," I whisper. Didn't he see what we did together? We saved that man. Doesn't that mean anything to him? "Please don't leave."

He chokes. "I—"

I can see him working through the possibilities, the logical conclusions, the likelihood that Father is telling the truth. What he's willing to lose if he dares disobey.

The answer, it seems, is not in my favor.

George grabs the back of my neck and pulls me into a half-hug. I don't hug him back. "Be strong," he says.

Then he's gone, the click of his shoes fading as he leaves.

*Maybe you'll get to meet Miss Neuling. Maybe they'll execute you together.*

Executions in line with the 1841 Speaker Act are the only executions still performed publicly in England. They're exceedingly rare, on British soil at least—I think there's only been ten since the law was enacted forty-two years ago—but three of those were in the last two years. It's a pattern I don't like.

"I fixed it," I say.

"What?" Mother whimpers.

"I sewed him up." Even if that man took the patient from me, I did it, *I* did it, not him. "He won't bleed out, and he probably won't go septic. I fixed it. I fixed him. He'll be okay."

Mother only says, "My God," and covers her face as if I am too awful to bear.

The blood has begun to go tacky. I still smell of human insides. My fingers stick together when I move, and the dried bodily fluids crack as my skin folds.

*You know what happens to little girls who play with ghosts.*

"We're going to stay right here until the police come," Father says. I think, in the distance, I hear Miss Neuling screaming, or spirits pressing their faces to the Veil, opening their slash-mouths to howl. I can't tell the difference. "Don't you *dare* move."

✦

When someone finally comes for us, it is not the police.

"Oh dear," Lord Luckenbill says with a genteel dishevelment, dabbing politely at his forehead with a handkerchief.

He's changed out of his awful safari getup. Good. If he'd come in dressed for an African expedition, my mind may have broken in half.

His son follows closely behind, rumpled and a bit green in the face.

When the son sees me, he stops in the middle of the aisle.

"There you are," Lord Luckenbill says, hurrying up to my parents. "I've been searching everywhere for you and, well, George was in a bit of a rush. I'm glad I've caught you before the police."

I'll be lucky if the police don't beat me to pieces before they drag me off. Like what that medium did to Miss Neuling. I'm not sure I'd even make it to the gallows. Going by the sketches in the cheapest newspapers, I'm shocked any of us do.

"The police are *here?*" Father says.

"Not yet," Lord Luckenbill says, causing Mother to press her hand to her chest with a desperate gasp, "but soon. We don't have much time." He looks toward his son, then toward me. "Lord, I'd really hoped the two of you would have met under better circumstances. This is an awful way to begin an engagement, isn't it?"

I'm—

They—

The boy says through gritted teeth, "A bit of an understatement."

The Honorable Edward Luckenbill, the only son of the Viscount William Luckenbill, wants to marry me.

*Wanted*, the rabbit counters. *Past tense. After this, he wouldn't dare touch you. Isn't that what you wanted? Aren't you, by all accounts, getting what you wished for?*

The scalpel of a boy watches us. I can make out the details of him now. Striking, pink-lipped, long-legged, improper. A bit too feminine for today's fashion, with smooth skin and long hair that curls behind the ears.

He catches me looking. I taste metal on the back of my tongue.

"It *is* awful," Mother agrees, "and I am so, so sorry."

"I don't know what's left to discuss," Father says, "unless you're here to give your side of the story to the police. I apologize that this has been a waste of your time, and I hope you find a more suitable wife for your son."

But Lord Luckenbill ignores them both in favor of me. He approaches, leans a bit to make himself smaller, holds out a hand. I back away. Please don't touch me. My clothes—*your costume*, the rabbit reminds me, because these clothes are not allowed to be mine—feel like coarse sand where they meet my skin.

"Miss Bell," he says, "do you have a habit of dressing up like this?"

"What kind of question is that?" Father snaps.

Lord Luckenbill turns with a huff. "I was asking *her*, not *you*, Mr. Bell! Please, let her answer." And then, to me: "It's okay, dear. You can speak freely here."

I don't see the point in lying. It's not like this can get any worse. "Sometimes."

"Sometimes," Lord Luckenbill says.

Behind him, the boy won't stop *staring*. His eyes, jeweled like emeralds, are blown so wide I can see the red at the corners. He's clearly sick to his stomach. It's almost funny how this worked out. In another life, I'm not sure I could have respected a husband with a weak stomach.

"Sometimes," Lord Luckenbill says again. "I see. How interesting. And the way you saved that man's life—how did you know what to do? One would think you've been practicing."

Again, there's no point in lying. "I have."

"I'm so sorry," Mother whispers. "You don't have to humor this any longer, my lord."

Lord Luckenbill pays Mother no mind. "Well," he says. "Well, well. What a fascinating specimen we have here."

I can't follow his train of thought. That's nothing new; I usually can't. People have a nasty habit of speaking in non sequiturs and confusing questions that leave me scrambling to follow. Still, most of the time, I can dig up the meaning after a moment too long, find the right angle to pick at the knot. Not this. Because why would he say these things to me now? As if I haven't committed a capital crime? Opening the Veil is bad enough, but trying to defraud the Royal Speaker Society . . .

Lord Luckenbill straightens up, tugging at his suit jacket as he goes. "Mr. and Mrs. Bell," he says, "have either of you heard of Veil sickness?"

Veil sickness? In all my studying, I've never come across an ailment with such a name. I almost turn to ask George, but he's not here anymore.

Father says, "No. We haven't."

"It's not a disease, per se," Lord Luckenbill says. "At least, not one of the body. It's a sickness of the mind. It's the name given to the set of symptoms that arise in females after exposure to spirit-work. In advanced stages, it looks something like Miss Neuling. In fact, there's been a rash of advanced Veil sickness afflicting violet-eyed women these past few years. It's what brought the situation to our attention."

Lord Luckenbill glances to me. His expression is soft. Pitying. Something isn't right.

"But in early, treatable stages," he says, "it looks like your daughter here."

"Oh God," Mother whispers. "Oh God, no. Not again."

This is not news. I have always been sick to them. Because I am a boy, because I want to be a surgeon, because of the way my mind works. Because they gave birth to something they do not understand, because they tried so many times to fix me and they *failed*.

Like George told me: Breathe in. Breathe out.

"What is the point of telling us?" Father snaps, taking a threatening step forward. Lord Luckenbill does not budge. "Once the police arrive, we are handing her over. We are so very sorry for wasting your time, and I apologize profusely, but—"

"I tell you," Lord Luckenbill says, "because it is, as I said, treatable."

The gallery room falls into an uneasy silence. Mother and Father glance to each other. Lord Luckenbill's son won't stop looking at me. Don't look at me. I don't want anyone to look at me.

"I never said I wanted to call off the engagement," Lord Luckenbill says. "In fact, I do not one bit. I think Miss Bell—yes, even acknowledging the struggles she faced in childhood, even acknowledging today—is a strong, intelligent, good-natured girl who will offer much to the Luckenbill bloodline. Just because she has made a few mistakes doesn't mean I am not willing to do a lot of things to help make her a proper wife."

He pauses to look at Father, and then Mother, in turn.

"If only you'll let me."

A heartbeat.

Another.

Father reaches into his pocket to produce a pack of imported French cigars. He offers one to Lord Luckenbill, who does not accept, the look on his face bordering on offended; one to the viscount's son, who also does not; then takes one for himself. *Click, click.* The lighter. The crackle of paper burning. He might as well be drinking in broad daylight.

"What do you have in mind?" Father says.

"*Father,*" the viscount's son says. His voice is soft, like the intestines slipping through my fingers. "This is unnecessary. We can smooth it over without this mess, can't we? Let me talk to her."

"Hush." Lord Luckenbill flicks a hand at him. "Mr. Bell, have you heard of Braxton's Finishing School and Sanitorium? Just outside of London. It's still an experimental facility, attempting to treat early stages of Veil sickness, but they have produced astounding results. In fact, they've created some of the most wonderful wives a man could ever ask for."

Smoke rises from Father's lips. It obscures his face like a haunting.

All the implications click into place, a dislocated joint slipping back into the socket.

They wouldn't just make me a wife. They'd break me into a perfect one. The name *Silas* will disappear, never to be said again. One day, someone will put a hand on my stomach and look to the viscount's son as if to ask when he'll finally make a woman of me, and at least if I died in the middle of a hysterectomy I could convince Heaven that I didn't *mean* to kill myself, it was an accident, I didn't mean it, promise.

Lord Luckenbill continues, "If you give Miss Bell over to the school's care, I can make all of this disappear—and if you sign your consent for the marriage, I will even cover tuition."

The rabbit *screams*.

I bolt.

Mother squeals, jumping back. The boy plasters himself against the wall and Lord Luckenbill goes, *"Whuff"* as I break for the door.

I don't know what I'm doing. I can't run from this. I can't hide. *Don't do this don't do this don't don't don't.* The Speakers will tear London apart and they will make me hurt for it. They'll have every policeman and every dog on my trail until they find me, and they will make me hurt *make it hurt make it hurt.*

I catch myself on the doorframe and lunge for the hall—
Father grabs me.

He wraps an arm around my stomach and wrenches
me back. My head hits something hard enough to split the
skin. *Crack.* I wonder if that's what a fracture sounds like
from the inside. If my brain rattles around my skull like
weak gelatin. I fall. Something warm trickles down the side
of my neck.

Then Father is on top of me. "Stop it," he's saying. "Stop
it, you ungrateful bitch." His words slur in my ears. I try to
push him away and he grabs my hands and pins me down.
Like when I was a child, when Father grabbed me and shook
me to stop my crying fits. I'm crying now. "You should be
grateful. You should be so grateful that we're doing this for
you after everything you've put us through. Do you hear
me?" I want to cut myself open. I want to peel out my eyes.
For the first time I believe, wholeheartedly, that execution
may be the better option. "So shut the fuck up and go with
him."

For those who have never seen one before, a hysterectomy works like this.

A small incision is made below the navel, only a few
inches but longer than you'd think. There are layers to the
skin, to the membranes beneath, and each of those are
opened in turn. Be sure to push the intestines and bladder
away to get a better view without perforating either; doing
so will lead to sepsis. Clamp any arteries so you don't bleed
out on the table, or the bathroom floor. Metal implements will protrude from the incision like saplings. Grip

the uterus like a sack of meat and cut the first ligament, then the second. The fallopian tubes look like dead worms. Clamp. Cut. Sew it shut. Clamp. Cut. Sew it shut.

"I'm sorry," I sob, "I'm sorry." It's the only thing I can say. "I'm sorry."

Lord Luckenbill seizes Father by the collar of his jacket and drags him off me. The viscount's face is red and warped with rage. Beside me, the dropped cigar burns on the tile floor. Lord Luckenbill shoves Father once in the chest, and they're yelling. It hurts. The viscount's son leans against the wall as if it is the only thing keeping him upright. Mother says, "Oh God, oh God."

"If you put a hand on her again—" Lord Luckenbill snarls. I roll over, prop myself up on one elbow, cough through the tears. I try to wipe my eyes but I only smear half-dried blood across my face. If Father tries to defend what he's done, it doesn't register in my mind. Mother begs them not to fight. My ears ring. The viscount's son takes a step towards me but my lips curl back and my teeth snap.

*Imbecile,* the rabbit says. *Wild animal. Maybe they'd be better off killing you anyway.*

But then Lord Luckenbill is by my side. He presses his handkerchief to the wet spot behind my ear and mops up the hot blood on my neck. Even George never held me so kindly. "Poor thing," he says. "I won't let him touch you again. Let's go."

5

Lord Luckenbill wraps his heavy winter coat around my shoulders, sends one butler ahead to call for a carriage, and beckons for another, instructing them on what to say to the police and how much money to pass along in exchange for their silence. The number he gives is nauseating.

"Would you like a maid to go with you?" the servant asks, peering at me. "Or a chaperone?"

Lord Luckenbill clears his throat, as if this is a horribly embarrassing question to be asked. "No time. An emergency, you know."

"Of course," the servant says. He rubs the half-brand on the back of his hand. "An emergency."

Then Lord Luckenbill leads me outside. I do not look back.

"Watch your step," the viscount says as he guides me down the front stairs. His son hurries beside us, swearing as freezing rain spits from the sky. The moon shines white in puddles on the street. The viscount's voice is soft and so close to my ear. "Hold the handkerchief for me, love. Keep pressure on it. There we go." I know how to staunch bleeding. "Easy now."

"Is she all right?" the boy asks. "Miss Bell? Are you all right?"

If he really cared, he wouldn't be here in the first place.

"I'm fine," I rasp, and then I spit bile at my feet. Lord Luckenbill sighs and pulls me against his side, rubbing my arm to warm me. Poor thing, he keeps calling me, little dear.

*A girl who will offer much to the Luckenbill bloodline*, the rabbit says. *You know what that means, don't you?*

I know. I know, I *know*. It's been my lot as long as I can remember, and it always will be. I don't get to be surprised anymore.

Lord Luckenbill's carriage clatters up to the pavement, a pair of matching chestnut mares snorting steam, and the viscount bundles us all in. I am alone with two strange men I have never met, and nobody is doing anything to stop it. I shouldn't be surprised—Mother and Father left me in the parlor with those Speakers before I was ten years old. The rain picks up. It drums in an incessant rumble on the roof. The viscount shouts directions to the driver and we lurch forward with a snap and a clatter.

*At least you don't have to deal with Mother and Father anymore.*

In stories of girls being taken away for whatever reason— of brides stolen for kings, classic tales of barbarians and monsters—the young mistress desperately presses her face to the carriage window, or flings herself away from her captors, screaming and fighting, straining to see the last remnants of home as it fades away. She says if they don't return her to her mother and father, she'll kill them, or herself.

I do none of those things. If I tried to speak, nothing would come out, not really. Just acid and *I'm sorry, I'm sorry* stuck in my throat until it becomes meaningless.

Then the boy says, "Your father shouldn't have done that to you."

I laugh. It comes out strangled with tears, almost frantic. The hysterectomy scar aches even though it doesn't exist yet. He shouldn't have done that to me? *It's a little late for that*, the rabbit says, and I agree, yes, it's a little fucking late for that.

There are lots of things my family shouldn't have done to me.

"Edward," the viscount chides, "let her rest. She's had a long night."

◆

I don't know how far into the ride it takes for the bleeding to stop. The red spot on the handkerchief has gone tacky by the time I check. I fold the cloth and scrub my hands until the smell of chyme lessens. I'd dunk my hands in chlorine if I could, rinse these clothes in salt and lye until the stains burn away.

Beyond the carriage window, London passes in a stream of gold. Streetlights and bright windows blur together. Hauntings glimmer. I can spot them if I try, watching where the world warps under the pressure of the Veil. What was it like when the Veil began to thin all those years ago, back when my grandparents were young? Did they think it was all ending? Did the churches preach of the Second Coming?

For a moment, I entertain the urge to yank open the carriage door and fling myself onto the wet cobblestones. To get out, to run. But I'd twist my ankle when I hit the ground, or break my arm, and Lord Luckenbill would simply stop the carriage and pick me up, and it'd be so, so much worse.

*Be a good girl and do as you're told.* The rabbit likes to take words and regurgitate them; this time it mimics the tutor who used to pet my hair when I forced myself not to cry. He called me a good girl. I wrap the viscount's coat tighter around myself and curl into the corner of the seat.

Lord Luckenbill talks to fill the air. Taxes. New laws. Explaining the letter he will write to the bank about my father's appalling behavior. Anything to keep the carriage from silence.

It's been a long time since I've had an outburst like this. So much of my life has been spent suppressing my hysterics: being quiet, being still, doing exactly as I was told. See, when Mother and Father hired my first tutor, he set about adjusting me the same way one would alter a piece of clothing. My strangeness was not a hereditary defect, as George would later theorize to the rage of our parents, but instead a failure to thrive, my own weakness of will. Therefore, I could be fixed, if only the right pressure was applied. There was to be no more chewing on my hair. No more flapping my hands or rocking. I would eat my dinner, no matter how awful I found it, and I would sit through parties politely with my legs crossed at the ankles. I was to be just like everyone else, no matter how much distress it caused me. *It is the only way anyone will ever tolerate you*, the tutor said.

And it worked. He, and the others Mother and Father brought in as I grew, changed something in me. As if they'd opened me up and rearranged my organs into a more pleasing configuration. I am not perfect, but I am no longer an embarrassment, and any flaws are now small enough to be outweighed in favor of my potential motherhood. Not a single thing I do is truly my own. Not even when I'm by myself. The bastards dug themselves so deeply into my psyche that I feel them on the back of my neck at all times, pulling my strings.

And then—on top of everything—I've managed to convince myself that I am a boy. Despite all the evidence to the contrary, I believe wholeheartedly, in my soul, that I am a boy. How arrogant of me, to think I could change something so God-given as my sex.

What is sickness, if not that?

The rabbit says, *The only reason you survived committing a capital crime is because some rich man wants his son to fuck you.* Maybe if I am still enough, quiet enough, Lord Luckenbill and his son will forget that I'm here, and I can disappear for good. *The only reason you survived is because of that womb you want to cut out and discard.*

*You pretty little sick girl.*

✦

The carriage slows and stops. My eyes hurt and my body is heavy with exhaustion, but I stay awake by compulsively chewing the inside of my cheek into a wound.

It's only now that Lord Luckenbill decides to explain what, exactly, Braxton's Finishing School and Sanitorium is. We all know its purpose, so that is not what he focuses on. He says Braxton's is a two-acre campus encompassing a large school with a private library, a greenhouse, and all sorts of nice and calming things. A winter garden party is held every year, and in fact it's coming up soon, how wonderful is that? There are games of croquet in the spring and summer, and so few students that every single one of us receives the individual attention we deserve. It's run by a man who is the foremost expert in helping girls like me.

*Girls like you.*

Looking out the window, I can tell that it is, at most, a pleasant lie. The world is empty here. I can almost see the pale, twinkling lights of a village in the distance, the closest vestige of civilization that is not farmland or forest. In front of us, the gate is so high and long that it feels like a prison wall. Is this meant to be better than Bedlam? I can't tell the difference.

A moment, and then, a long, low squeal: the gates opening.

The carriage trundles forward once more. The boy picks up his head from where he had fallen into an uneasy, fitful sleep. His hair has dried oddly, making his head lopsided.

We come around a curved path, putting a building in view: three stories, wider than it is tall, imposing columns standing at attention. Though illuminated only by the moon and two dull lanterns, it feels more like the idea of a building, or half-remembered sketches of an ancient asylum, than an actual structure.

In front of the front doors, the coach stops for good. The viscount's son slips out into the misty dark and offers a hand to help me down. I take it unwillingly. His palm is soft, untouched by hard labor. A cutting wind blows and the lanterns sway; the horses steam. Around us, the walls go on forever, swallowing a garden of dead, leafless shrubs and a marble fountain with no water. For some reason, I was expecting to see a haunting. There aren't any.

Lord Luckenbill walks the front steps, lifts the giant metal knocker, and lets it drop.

*BANG.*

"Isn't there a quieter way?" the boy demands, blearily rubbing his eyes. "You'll wake the whole bloody school."

Lord Luckenbill flicks a hand at him again. The viscount seems fond of dismissing him. "It's fine. Get acquainted, the two of you."

We look to each other. I've done my best to avoid doing so the entire ride, and revulsion roils in my stomach. The boy's expression is unbearably haughty. Eyes half-lidded, mouth stuck in a perpetual pout. The only concession he makes is one foot warily braced behind him, as if I am something to back away from. Yes, reaching into a man's split stomach to pull out a rope of intestine might warrant that reaction. Or the lingering smell of insides on my hands. I can't imagine what I look like now, hair ragged and clothes stained brown. *Clothes that aren't yours and never will be.*

Did this not change his mind? What if I showed him the fetal pigs I've taken apart at the back of the abattoir?

*Fuck him*, the rabbit says. *Or, rather, don't.*

The boy says, "Did you actually think it would work?"

"What?"

"Getting your seal. Did you think you could?"

I don't like the way he says it. Like the failure to do so didn't ruin my life. Like my own inability to swallow one, single cruel act didn't bring me here and dash all my dreams like broken bones.

"Yes," I say. "I did."

"Right." He looks away, frets with his collar. "I'll, ah, take the handkerchief if you want. So you don't have to carry it around."

I shove it in my pocket. "I'll keep it."

The front door of the school swings open. A young woman peers out, squinting against the dim light of the candle she carries in one hand. She has the stereo-typical look of a harried governess, which all board-ing-school teachers are in a way: in her nightgown with a shawl wrapped around her shoulders, hair a mess and eyes squinted with sleep. Her feet have been jammed into lumpy, misshapen socks.

"Lord Luckenbill," she grouses, "do you have any idea what hour it is?"

He dips his head in remorse. "Indeed, and my apologies—but, if I may, you have a new student."

The woman looks past him to me, and her brows knit together in confusion, betrayed by the shadows playing across her face. With the men's clothes and the long, loose hair, I must hardly be recognizable as one sex or the other.

The two of them talk in whispers for a bit—the woman's harsh, the viscount's growing more and more stern. I look away from it all and stare at the dark, wet grass.

"Fine," she eventually says. "I'll wake the headmaster." Then, raising her voice: "Come in, dear. You'll catch cold."

The viscount's son takes a step, then waits for me, pausing until I follow.

I almost don't. I almost resist, try to explain, beg them to let me go. But George would tell me to reduce the spread of damage; to find what will do the most good, or barring that, the least harm. Resisting now will only make it worse. I have no information about the situation, no upper hand. It'd be like starting a surgery without so much as asking where I should be cutting.

So we walk across the cobbled path, heads down against the wind, and step into Braxton's—and when the heavy doors slam behind us, I know, in an instant, that this is Bedlam dressed in silk and flowers.

The woman holds up her candle, illuminating the vague impressions of polished wood floors, lilac tapestries, botanical wallpaper creeping around us the same way parasitic vines choke their host trees. Dark hallways stretch out to either side of us, disappearing into voids as the light runs out, and a grand stairway juts out from the center of the foyer. There is one window, at the landing above us, showing nothing but empty black sky. It is utterly silent.

At the top of the stairs, carved into the wood above the window: an eye.

Underneath, it reads *MORS VINCIT OMNIA*.

The woman gestures down the hall. "The two of you, to the office. Headmaster will be with you shortly. And you?" She seems utterly unfazed by the blood on my hands and knees. "My name is Mrs. Forrester and you shall address me as such. Give Lord Luckenbill back his coat, and we'll get you cleaned up from whatever this is."

I hand over the coat, and as the men disappear, I hurry to follow Mrs. Forrester down the opposite hall.

Even with her limping walk, she is beautiful. She has the lips and soft cheeks of a classical painting, her hair piled into a fraying bun, hauntingly alluring despite (or perhaps because of) the plain gown and dismal lighting.

But when she turns back to glance at me—

Her eyes. Violet with a rotting tinge. Utterly lifeless.

A school for sick girls indeed.

6

In the dressing room at the end of the hall, lit only with a single unsteady gas lamp, Mrs. Forrester pushes me in front of a massive silver mirror and drops a basin of water at my feet.

"Strip," she says. She pushes a ring of keys back into the pocket of her nightgown; this room had been locked. I don't like that. "Wash yourself."

A rag hangs limply over the side of the basin. Soap has been provided in a little porcelain dish. I'm desperate to get the blood off my hands, the innards and the reek, but—

Strip?

"Did you hear me?" Mrs. Forrester snaps. "I won't do it for you. Take off your clothes and clean up all that mess."

My reflection is a haggard thing. When I meet its eyes, my first instinct is to recoil from the thought of it as human, let alone as me. My eyes are bloodshot, my puffy face framed with pale, limp hair. And the clothes; they sit bunched on my hips, straining around the chest, rolled at every hem. My hand thumps against my chest, as if jamming my wrist into my ribcage will stop the disgust burning in my thoracic cavity. I don't know why I thought any of this ever looked right on me. I don't know how I fooled a soul. When I see my body through Mrs. Forrester's eyes, it's misshapen. It's *ugly*.

*How did you ever think you could convince anyone you were a boy?*

But I am. I *am*. I know it; I know I am.

*If you were meant to be a boy, you wouldn't have to fight so hard to prove it.*

I wash my hands. I roll up my sleeves, scrape under my nails, soak my forearms to get out the blood that's dried to the fine hairs. Mrs. Forrester glares at the back of my neck.

At Bedlam, there would be no privacy either.

Once my hands are clean, after I check for splatters on my neck and face, I take off the waistcoat. My fingers fumble over the buttons. Then the suspenders. The trousers. I do what I'm told because I can't do anything else. Mrs. Forrester pushes the bloody clothes into a corner with her toe. She tries to get the handkerchief from me, but I pull it away from her, and it seems like she isn't willing to fight that particular battle. I wash it too, and lay it out to dry.

I'm just in my linen underclothes now. I stop. Gooseflesh rises on the back of my neck, on my bare calves. My shirt is unbuttoned and hangs around my arms, revealing the cloth I use to bind my breasts.

It's okay. I can do this. It's just my body, and there's nothing wrong with that. There's nothing to be ashamed of.

It's just—

I hiccup, pressing a hand to my mouth.

It's a violation. No matter that she's not the one wrestling the clothes off my body. Just because it's my hands does not make it better.

"Well?" Mrs. Forrester says. "Go on."

I take off the rest.

I cross my arms over my bare chest, clumps of hair clinging to my shoulders. I want to curl up into a ball and stitch myself together so I can never be unraveled. I want to peel off all my skin, if only so I could be anything other than a naked body, something horrifying instead of vulnerable. Nobody looks at a pig corpse and thinks it could be made beautiful.

Mrs. Forrester puts out a hand and takes a tentative step forward. Another, and then another, until she's circling me, tilting her head, humming softly.

"How long were you alone with the viscount and his son?" Mrs. Forrester asks.

"I don't know," I rasp. "An hour. Or two." I swallow hard to keep tears from choking me. "They didn't do anything."

"I see."

There is nothing wrong with my body. When I am alone, I am in awe of it. I've studied myself in the mirror, comparing myself to the copy of *Gray's Anatomy* George bought for my fourteenth birthday. The systems, the patterns, the interconnecting weaves of veins and arteries and sinew—it is all a grand work of genius, and I could never begrudge the one that was given to me. I hold no hatred for the shape it takes. Not for the breasts that overflow my cupped hands, nor for thighs and hips drawn with red lines where they have grown faster than the skin could handle.

It is only when I step back to see it all through another's eyes that I want to unravel it and carve the meat into a new, different, more acceptable shape. *The only thing that will ever matter is how others see you.* I want to take myself apart into something else, and if I cannot do that, I want to destroy every part of it that could ever be used against me. And if that is my eyes, or my womb, or *all of it—*

"You're beautiful," Mrs. Forrester says. She stops behind me, hands on my shoulders. I do not wipe away the tears. I am too afraid to move. "I don't know what the Veil sickness tells you, but I need you to remember that. You are beautiful, well-bred, and so, so lucky. Women across the world would kill to have everything you do. To have a chance like the one you have now with that boy. Do you understand?"

I dig my nails into the soft parts of my arms because it is the only thing keeping me from jamming them into my eye sockets. I should just do it. Just push them into my skull until my vision bends and my fingers slip into the waiting hollows.

Just a few seconds of pain. Just like the brand. That would be all.

"Yes, ma'am," I say. "I understand."

"Good." Mrs. Forrester squeezes my shoulders, then hands me a white gown and cotton stockings. "I'll wake one of the girls to show you around. I'll see you in the morning."

She takes the bloodstained clothes and leaves.

The nightgown is beautiful, with lace cuffs and ribbons. I don't know how long I stare at it. This isn't *me*.

But I have to put it on. I justify it to myself: I have to keep my boyhood safe. I have to keep it hidden, deep in my chest where nobody else can have it. It will stay next to dreams of my own operating theater, my name, the rabbit. I just need to find a way out, because there has to be one, because there is always one, right? And until then, I will keep myself safe.

That is not self-betrayal. That is self-preservation.

The door opens. I stumble back, blundering for the gown to cover as much of me as possible. The girl in the doorway covers her eyes with a yelp.

"Sorry!" she says. "Sorry, sorry. I didn't think you'd still be— Oh, I'm so sorry."

"It's all right," I say on reflex.

The girl peeks out from between her fingers before looking away again. She must be the student Mrs. Forrester said she'd send—another sick girl. Her hair is long and dark, tied in braids for sleeping. She has a year or two on me. She is lovely. I focus on that. She wears her womanhood like fine jewelry, not like an ill-fitting skin forced upon her.

Still, as a surgeon, I know better than to assume sickness or health by a person's appearance. It is a fallacy to assume health when faced with beauty; the two have nothing to do with each other. So I make no assumptions. I can't allow myself to.

"You might want to," she says, "um . . ."

Right.

Holding my breath the way I would if I were stepping into a mortuary, I slip into the gown. The lace cuffs make me want to scratch until my wrists are raw. To distract myself, I yank the stockings up, tying them maybe a bit too tight to keep them up over my thighs. The seam presses horribly into my toes. I used to cry about these seams when I was younger. I don't anymore, as much as I want to.

While I'm down there, I cram the soggy handkerchief into the nightgown pocket.

"Okay." Deep breaths. "You can look."

The girl drops her hand. Her face is soft, round, Italian in complexion—and her eyes are so violet they're almost blue, like the sky just before nightfall. Her smile is sad.

"Much better," she says. She begins collecting things from the room in her arms: a comb, a ribbon. "You can call me Isabella if you'd like; we're not particularly formal about names here. What's yours?"

It's Silas. Nothing but and only Silas. "Gloria."

"Gloria. That's a beautiful name." It's tolerable; I'd rather be called *Gloria* than *Miss Bell*. Isabella takes a stool from a back corner and drags it over to me, one of the legs catching over a bump in the wooden floor. "Here, sit. How long before they took you did they tell you that you were coming?"

*Took you.* I don't like to sit, but I do as I'm told. "A minute, if that."

"Mm. A bit less time than most of us, a little more than me."

Isabella stands behind me, runs her fingers through my damp hair, gently untangles a knot. Her hands are strong but not cruel or demanding, not the way Mrs. Forrester's were. Her gaze holds no malice. When she begins to comb my hair, it is calming. Mother used to do this back when she still loved me, or at least when she acted as if she did.

"So," Isabella says, "Mrs. Forrester says you came here in boy's clothes."

I freeze.

"She's a bit prone to exaggeration," Isabella muses as she holds the back of my head to keep it steady while she works. My heart beats in my throat like I'll choke on it. "For all I know, your jacket was cut too close to a man's style for her liking. So I suppose the best course of action is to ask you directly—were you?"

For once, the rabbit has nothing to say. Neither do I.

Unhurriedly, Isabella picks out a stubborn tangle near the wound behind my ear.

"I'm going to give you some advice," she says softly. "Never, ever, admit that." Her voice has a dangerous edge. "Listen to me when I say that they brought you here to fix you, and they are willing to do a lot of things to that end."

She clutches the comb tight, leans over me, forces me to meet her eyes in the mirror. There is so much there, so much emotion and feeling, that I have to jerk away.

She says, "Don't make it any worse for yourself than it already is."

I think her hands are shaking.

I think I see bruises on her wrists.

I think I should have thrown myself from the carriage when I had the chance.

✦

When Isabella is finished, it's as if I'm a different person entirely. My hair is tied back with a white ribbon, a bit of warmth bringing pink back to my cheeks. I am trying my best to make it look like this skin belongs to me. *See? You make a beautiful girl. It's so exhausting to fight it.* I know the rabbit isn't actually me—it says the worst possible thing, contradicts itself, claims it is only trying to help—but it hurts anyway. Isabella hands me two folded uniform dresses, the kind a nurse would wear under her apron: plain, dark, and high-collared, with no room for a bustle or a crin-oline cage. Nothing like the intricate gowns I'm used to. A small mercy.

Isabella says, "Let's get you to bed."

She explains as we leave the room: the first floor is for visitors, the second for classes, the third for girls. As strict and clear as a hospital. The eye carved into the wood watches us as she points out a sitting parlor, Headmaster's office, a library, a dining hall. With a school as large and beautiful as this, it feels as if the place should be bustling with staff, but there's none. Isabella makes a tired-sounding noise when I ask and explains that, with the exception of the groundskeeper, there are only ever maids and servants on special occasions.

Headmaster believes our "treatment" requires debasing ourselves to the point of doing menial chores, such as laundry and dusting. "Can't kick up a fuss if you're too busy or too tired to do anything about it," Isabella says.

On the second floor, we are swallowed by more polished wood, more violet tapestries. Tiny ice crystals form in the corners of the window at the top of the stairs. I peer through the glass only to see leafless trees, a dark greenhouse, the groundskeeper's shed. The classrooms are up here, along with Headmaster and Mrs. Forrester's room on one end of the hall. The fact that they're married feels weird at the base of my throat. There are more rules too: if a girl expresses any interest in a possible husband, do not even deign to look at him unless you're willing to risk a fight with her; after all, a girl will do lots of things for a husband she doesn't hate. Do not talk back. Do not leave yourself alone with Headmaster if you can help it. And do not, under any circumstances, even *mention* the Veil.

"Wait," I say. "Why shouldn't we be alone with Headmaster?"

Isabella shoots a resigned look over her shoulder. "Private lessons are bad enough as they are. You don't want him to start thinking you like them."

On the third floor, there is the dormitory and only the dormitory. Isabella ushers me inside.

It is one big, long room with beds lined up against opposite walls, facing each other like rows of teeth. Lace curtains cradle bay windows that look out over dead grass and, beyond the walls, miles of nothing. A reading nook huddles by the fireplace, strewn with books opened to pages of pressed flowers. Each of the beds has a quilt and a chest for our clothes. It is quiet here. I try to tell myself that the quiet is serene.

But right now, in the middle of the night, it is hard to convince myself that the girls in their beds are breathing. Curled under their blankets, faces soft with sleep, one even with her pillow cradled to her chest the way one would hold a baby, they all look too much like cadavers.

Isabella brings me to an open bed near the middle of the room. "This can be yours," she whispers, sitting me down on the mattress. "I'm there, by the fire. The washroom is through that door if you need it, and wake-up is at seven sharp."

The moonlight coming through the window turns her skin silver, her hair ebony. If it weren't for the dresses in my hands, I might have reached for her, tried to clutch her sleeve so she couldn't walk away. I don't want to be alone. Not here.

She notices my hesitation. Her eyes soften.

She leans down to kiss my temple.

It should be noted that I do not define my manhood through my love of women. There are lots of men who do so: their hunger to dominate feminine things, their power over their wives and daughters, are the building blocks of their maleness. That is not me. Yes, I could love a man if I ever found one who accepts me as I am, and I've dreamed of being so lucky—but I love women too. I love women as men are expected to, but the way only one who has ever experienced womanhood can.

"Stay quiet," Isabella says, "do as you're told, and you'll be okay."

I nod. "Okay."

Then, another voice: "That was Frances' bed."

The girl in the bed across from me has awoken and is sitting up, gold hair tumbling over her shoulders. Her eyes are violet, not like flowers, or night, but like morning. She has a face that would suit a wolf.

"Now isn't the time, Mary," Isabella says.

"Change beds," Mary tells me.

"Don't listen to her," Isabella says. "You don't have to do what she says."

Mary shows all her teeth. "If you don't get out of that bed, I'll tell Headmaster you put a hand up my dress."

She'll do *what?*

Isabella storms over. "Quit it. Frances is *gone.*"

But I'm already on my feet, gathering up the uniforms and skittering away from the bed like it's burning me. Around us, I hear the shuffling of blankets, the flutter of sudden waking breaths. "No, it's fine. It's fine, I swear. I can take whatever bed. I just—I won't be here long. I don't mind."

I'm not sure why I say that. I don't even know if it's true. It reminds me of how much work my tutors put into teaching me how to lie: how sometimes it's better to say nice things that are false than cause a whole fuss by saying what you actually mean. People would rather be told things they like to hear, and then eventually be disappointed, instead of being told the truth.

Mary tilts her head. Curls spill down her chest. Isabella clasps her hands tight in front of her stomach, the muscles in her throat bobbing.

"What was that?" Mary says.

That didn't work. I backtrack and apologize. People like apologies. "I said," I manage slowly, "I'm sorry."

Mary smiles. It doesn't look right. "Yes. Of course."

I hurry to the empty bed closest to the door, pack the uniforms in the chest, and crawl under the covers. Mary's stare disappears.

I've already made a mistake. I always do.

So I take the handkerchief from where I'd tucked it in my nightgown and hold it to my mouth to smell the copper. At least it doesn't reek of bodily fluids anymore. I press the stiff, dried stain against my lips. Then my tongue. It's cold and damp and bitter, almost rancid. My head aches where Father hit me.

Between my ribs, the rabbit settles down to sleep, nestling next to my lungs so I cannot take a full breath, and its eyes flick open with curiosity when I gasp for air and it hurts.

They left my body in the dark room for i dont know how long. Could have been hours could have been days. But they came back because they cannot leave a dead girl alone. They came back with their medium. No no no let me warp the air let me haunt this place let me haunt *them*. Let me do something other than watch my body rot. Bury me burn me i dont care just please please please—

They asked one another if they found anything. They said no. They said my body is no different than anyone elses. Even the sickest of Veil-sick girls bear no mark of it in our brains in our cells in our eyes.

They said that is a problem.

They said they will keep opening us until they find what they want.

7

The first time I dreamed of taking out my eyes, I didn't actually do it. I wanted to, but I believed that when they were finally removed from my skull, you'd be able to reach into the socket and touch the brain with a finger; that without the eye, you could poke the gelatinous mess and stir it up like a soup. How terrible. How disgusting. How badly Mother and Father and my tutors would have wanted to do so if they thought it would change me.

This, of course, ignores the existence of all the meat separating the brain from the soft membranes of the eye socket, but you can convince yourself of just about anything at a young age. It was George who explained this to me when I raised the point as a hypothetical.

It was also George who knew what I *really* wanted to ask.

"You know," he said, "violet eyes only came on the record in 1820." He gestured at a map he pulled from his notes.

"First here, in the Russian Empire. Then all at once: Britain, Peru, Ethiopia, everywhere. Less a biological mutation than a sudden miracle. So if I can't convince you to keep them in your head through, oh, normal means, can't I ask you to preserve your own piece of history?" Then, as if realizing who he was speaking to, he added: "Or at least promise me you'll disinfect your hands?"

Anyway, I dream of it again that night. It's so easy when it isn't actually happening; when it's a pig, or a cow's head, or a sheep with its face hanging off the back of a slaughter cart, when you don't have to feel the pain yourself. Maybe one day I'll want it so badly that it'll be like a dream, and the want will overshadow the pain enough that it'll be like the pain doesn't exist at all.

✦

I wake to the screaming ring of a little bell, so loud and high-pitched it hurts. I sit up with a strangled gasp. The handkerchief is still clutched in my hand. Around me, the sound of blankets being taken off all at once, like a flock of birds.

"Good morning, ladies! Up! Up!"

The gas lamps along the wall are lit, one by one, as Mrs. Forrester goes down the aisle. All of the girls cringe from the sudden light, blinking and scrubbing sleep from their eyes. The sky is still inky black, turning the windows into giant mirrors, reflecting each of us back at ourselves. There's Isabella and Mary, of course, but then there's a tall girl with a nose that looks as if it was once broken and did not heal quite right; a redheaded girl with a small mouth and doeish eyes; another who fumbles for large, round glasses and perches them on her face with an owlish blink. In the bed across from me is, I think, the youngest of us all— mousy, tiny, plain in a way that makes her charming, like the subject of a pastoral watercolor.

All of us have violet eyes. As is to be expected.

Therefore, it stands to reason, all of us are Veil-sick.

As she paces restlessly back to the door, Mrs. Forrester silences her bell by pressing the mouth of it against her dress, the way one would suffocate a small animal.

"Up!" she says again, as if repeating it will make us go any faster. But it does, it seems. We get up and pull our hair out of their sleeping braids. I don't know what to do, so I watch the girl next to me—the one with red hair—and copy her exactly. Make the bed. Lay out the uniform. I stuff the handkerchief in the little pocket of the skirt. "Up! Why are we all so sluggish today? A wife should be out of bed and made up before her husband even thinks of waking. He will never see her unmade." She rings the bell again, just once but harder. It stings. "Miss Warwick! Hurry, please. Dr. Bernthal will be here to pick you up today."

The youngest girl falters and suddenly, instantly looks sick.

The rabbit notices.

The girl whispers, "Yes, ma'am."

"Good," Mrs. Forrester says. "And you—new girl."

Me. That's me. I fumble a bit, duck my head in

acknowledgement because that seems like the proper thing to do.

Mrs. Forrester says, "Headmaster will do your intake assessment this morning. After breakfast, go to him."

Isabella's warning sits heavy in my stomach like a calcified tumor. I nod.

Mrs. Forrester continues as we dress—critiquing bed-making, straightening Mary's uniform skirt, calling one of us lazy for not having our underclothes laid out the night before. But once she has sufficiently chewed all of us into shape, she whisks Miss Warwick away and leaves us all alone.

A moment of silence. Another. And then:

"Dr. Bernthal can rot in hell," Isabella says as she laces her corset, pulling the strings tighter behind her back.

"She's lucky," Mary says. "She's getting out."

The girl with glasses says, "Exactly. You're simply jealous Agnes has made such good progress. If you're still sick, it's nobody's fault but your own." She sniffs listlessly. "Would you rather go to Bedlam? That's where you'll end up, acting like this."

Isabella whirls on her. "I'm not *jealous*; she's *fourteen*."

Fourteen. She hasn't even made her debut on the social scene yet—she should still be playing with dolls and cats, not dressing up for a soon-to-be husband. Her father would have had to sign off on the marriage, like all of our fathers or guardians will, which means they know, which means they're okay with it.

The Royal Speaker Society rots the morals of everything it touches.

The tall girl cuts in, without looking up from her hair, "Is the little bitch pregnant already?"

"Ellen," the redheaded girl whimpers, "please don't."

We finish getting ready in silence.

In the meager dining hall on the first floor, the tall girl—Ellen—and Mary are on breakfast duty. They prepare leftover ham and fresh eggs, porridge and rolls spread with preserves. The meal is wasted on me. I scrape the preserves off my bread with the back of my knife and fold it in half to eat so the remains don't touch my tongue. I cannot stomach anything else. There are no empty chairs, as if the number of them has been adjusted so there is no hole where Miss Warwick—Agnes—should presumably be. By the time I'm getting ready to leave, the redheaded girl is already collecting the dishes to wash them.

Ellen begins to twitch.

"Easy now," Mary croons. "Don't want to do something you'll regret."

"She doesn't get to leave," Ellen says. "Not like that."

Mary regards her. Hums. Fiddles with a little ring hanging around her neck. It's too small to fit on any of her fingers, as if it was made for a young child, and it is the only personal item I've seen of any girl here.

"I think she'll have to come up to get her things," Mary says, tucking the ring away under the neck of her dress before Headmaster wanders close enough to notice it. "I'm sure the two of you can have a chat before she goes."

Ellen grits her teeth, and I swear I hear the enamel crack under the pressure of muscle and bone.

✦

Headmaster answers my knock on his office door with a soldier's voice. "Come in!"

Inside, a man with a dignified beard sits at a long, shining desk. He doesn't seem old enough to have gone as grey as he is, but there's a distance in his eyes—such a light violet they are almost see-through—that tells me he's witnessed too much. His right hand bears a medium's seal that has almost faded. *Captain Ernest Forrester*, the placard on his desk reads. What little decoration he has are all military medals, and there is a shelf of artifacts from theaters of war. Trophies, more like it.

The artifacts are hauntings.

All of them. The Veil shimmers around them like the piece of statue I was given at the gala. If I reached out, I could pluck one from its shelf and tear the world like spider silk. I am reminded, coldly, of something I read once, while looking through the newspapers Father brought home. It said that when the Veil first started to thin all those years ago, spirit-work had been the purview of women. It was emotional work, especially suited to the strengths of women and women alone. It was only when Englishmen, the Speakers, realized what spirit-work could be used for— war, power, control—that the 1841 Speaker Act was passed. Headmaster, Captain Ernest Forrester, is proof of that.

"Ah," Headmaster says. "Miss Bell. Please, sit."

Again, I don't like sitting. It makes me nervous when I can't move around. I have to pace, to shift my weight, to do anything in place of flapping my hands or chewing on my hair or all the other little things my tutors scrubbed from me.

But the rabbit says, *You know better than to provoke a man, don't you?* So I sit.

"Hello, sir," I say, balling my hands in my lap.

Headmaster doesn't look at me. He flicks through his papers and leans back calmly in his chair. His demeanor is too easy. Too affable. It'd be better if he were cruel from the start, so at least I know what to expect.

"Oh, don't look so nervous," he says. "We're just here to discuss the notes from my conversation with the viscount last night. I have to understand you to discover the best path forward for your treatment, after all." He slides another bit of paper toward himself, regards it curiously. "Let's see here. You arrived late last night with Viscount Luckenbill and his son, Edward. A rough evening, it seems." He does not have to elaborate. "You were hurt as well?"

"Only a little." I refuse to touch the scab crusted behind my ear.

"I see." Back to the papers. "You were admitted to our care after disguising yourself as a man to receive a medium's seal, including binding your breasts." My stomach curdles. "You have a history of needing specialized tutors and, it says here, mutilating animals?"

It wasn't mutilation. It was practice. "They were already dead."

Headmaster and I look at each other for a silent moment. When he says it aloud, I sound like a monster. Some kind of wretched devil. As sick as Miss Neuling, ripping open a man's stomach with a makeshift blade for half the world to see. Granted, all surgery looks like that to the untrained eye.

Headmaster says, "You are very, very lucky to be here. Do you recognize that? Lord Luckenbill is a generous man."

"Yes, sir." Is that what we're calling it? "He is."

"I expect to see that gratitude reflected in your behavior during your time here." *That is a threat*, the rabbit points out. But Headmaster just folds up the paper and sets it aside. "We here at Braxton's have a unique outlook on situations such as yours. Violet-eyed women find themselves in a sad predicament, don't they? Day in and day out, battling the realities of their minds and bodies, a burden that the fairer sex simply is not meant to bear."

I want to lay out my dissected body next to his and show him the pieces of us that are the same. Could he tell his arteries from mine, the folds of my brain from his own? If I excised both our eyes and laid them out on a microscope, would there be a difference?

"Because of that," Headmaster continues, "our approach toward the treatment of Veil sickness is not punishment, but healing. Our program takes into account both the body and the mind, and seeks to help them align with your true nature as women. It's much kinder than what happens in those hospitals in the city." He sounds so proud of himself. So assured. "But that means we must know where to start. Does that make sense?"

I have heard this before, in so many different forms. I know how sick girls are treated. I know how it works, I know, I know. "Yes, sir."

"Good. A few questions, then." He smiles as if rewarding me for my subservience. "Is there anything you can tell me about yourself that may have led to your adoption of men's clothing and mannerisms? When did it start?"

I could tell him about George. About James Barry. I could tell him about my name, recognizing myself in the mirror for the first time when I put on trousers and pressed my chest flat, realizing that I could survive as a woman but only truly *live* as a man. How a medium's seal was merely a means to an end. But I don't.

"Has this been a pattern in your life?" Headmaster says after my silence. "I'd appreciate your cooperation, Miss Bell. Uncooperative girls end up in hospitals, you know."

*Like Bedlam.* And after what I did, I'd be lucky to get a hospital at all.

"Somewhat," I say. "I don't make a habit of it." That much is true. As much as I love it, as much as it means to me, it's not worth the risk of being caught. For the sake of safety, being seen as myself for more than a few hours at a time is an impossibility.

"Mm," Headmaster says. "And are you prone to self-pollution?"

I don't know what that means. "Excuse me?"

"Self-abuse. Onanism. The disease of self-abasement." Headmaster gestures broadly. "It's a terrible mental condition. Affects young men far more than women, but it isn't unheard of in those such as you."

It takes me a moment to sort through the words he's using; euphemisms, all for the same thing. But what . . . ?

Oh.

The floor tilts under my chair. Why would he ask that? I jam my hands into the skirt of my uniform to keep from twisting my fingers to the point of dislocation. Sure, I have inspected myself against my notes and looked at myself unclothed in the mirror. I have considered doing those things, because who hasn't? But I have not yet *touched*. It just seemed to be an undertaking I was not ready for. All the discussion of it as a moral evil seemed silly to me, but I still found myself hesitating.

I'd just—I'd wanted to wait.

*Answer him.*

"No," I whisper. "No, I haven't."

After a beat, he says, "I see," as if unconvinced, and makes a note. "I've heard rumors—perhaps unsubstantiated, but nevertheless, I must ask—of young women manually manipulating each other. Given your history of men's clothing, there is a possibility . . ."

I can guess what that means. I feel ill. I have thought of this too, but I have never. I've never even had a real friend I could talk to, let alone one I could touch. He doesn't need to be asking these questions. I can't decide if it's better or worse than Mrs. Forrester stripping me bare in front of the mirror, forcing me to look. My teeth chatter.

"No," I say.

He seems shocked by this. "Really."

"Yes."

He asks a few more questions, and I answer them the best I can: about my parents, my tutors, my history, I think;

I don't remember. He pokes and prods at my past, as if looking for cracks. I resist the urge to cry. I won't let myself.

*You saw Isabella's hand shaking. You saw the bruises.*

"This is all very, very interesting," Headmaster finally says, looking over his notes. "I will spend the day looking over this, perhaps have another discussion with Lord Luckenbill, and determine what the best treatment plan for you will be. Once I do that, we can begin private lessons—lessons tailored specifically to you. I truly do think your condition is something we can learn to soothe in time. It's only a matter of finding a way to help you do so. Welcome to Braxton's, Miss Bell."

I do not feel very welcome at all.

He finishes the intake assessment. He says there is a winter garden party for me to look forward to. He sends me from the room. I nod politely and ease the door shut so that the click of the latch does not bother him the way it bothers me.

As soon as it clicks, my lip wobbles. No, I can't cry, I can't. I press the heels of my hands into my eyes, but it's not enough. *"It's like you're trying to bully us whenever you don't get your way!"* Mother always said. Her voice sounds like the rabbit's voice, sounds like Father's, sounds like mine. *"All these tears!"* I dig my nails into my cheeks, then press my knuckles into my neck when that doesn't work. *"Not everything works out for you, Gloria. Nobody likes a spoiled brat."* My skin wants to crawl off, and I can't stop it, I can't get enough air in my lungs. Don't cry. Don't cry. I'm not trying to bully anyone, I swear. Didn't they hear me apologizing?

I never wanted to be upset, it's not as if I *liked* it, like I was doing it to *get* something. I was never trying to be difficult on purpose, I promise.

It's just—

Hasn't it been enough? All the years haven't been *enough*? First the tutors, and then this, the Veil sickness, whatever it is. They can't keep scraping away layers of me thinking they can find the girl they want underneath. I'm not the dead flesh on top of a healing injury, devoured by maggots making way for the tender meat underneath to bloom. I am not the septic organ or the infected tooth. *All* of this is me. They can't just remove whatever they want.

*Do you touch yourself? Have you lain with a woman? How far have you debased yourself, so we know how much is wrong in that fragile, breakable skull of yours, so we know how to cut it out of you?*

What is wrong with him? Why would he ask those things?

The rabbit says, *Do you really think you're getting out of here in anything other than a wedding dress or a casket?*

I don't know. I hurry away from the door, toward the stairs.

Then, at the top of the steps, at the second-floor landing above me—Isabella hissing, "No. No, don't you fucking dare, get your hands *off her.*"

8

The words are so quiet I can hardly hear them past my own breathing; for a moment, I convince myself it's the hauntings on Headmaster's walls, spirits on the other side gnashing their teeth. It's not my problem. I should just stay here. I can't handle anything else right now, I can't.

Muffled whimpering. The thump of a shoe on the carpeted floor, a rasp of annoyance. Above me.

"Well?" Mary's voice. "Are you going to do it or not?"

"Ellen. Put her down."

I take one step up the stairs—wiping tears from my face, breathing deep as if wringing all the oxygen from my lungs—and then another. Just to look. Just to see.

Ellen stands at the second-floor landing, eyes blown wide like a cornered animal. She has Agnes bent backwards over the banister. One hand fisted in her dress to hold her, a beautiful winter gown for her future husband, the other hand clamping her mouth shut. Agnes' feet scrabble in the air like a hanged man. Only a few centimeters more, a slipped hand, and she'll fall. Maybe to the stairs, maybe all the way to the first floor. She'd hit the ground right beside me.

Halfway up the stairs, the two other girls—the redhead, the one with the glasses, neither of whose names I know— look up, mouths open.

"Just put her down," Isabella says, hand out, placating, "and walk away. We won't tell Headmaster. Right?"

The redhead grabs the girl beside her. "Right. We won't tell."

But Ellen gasps for air, nearly senseless with rage. "Why does she get to leave? Headmaster barely *touched* her. She's not healed, she can't be. It's because she's pregnant. Isn't it? He wouldn't pick you if you weren't— Are you pregnant, Agnes?" Agnes tries to shake her head, voice muffled against Ellen's palm. "You lying whore. You are."

"Ellen, listen to me," says the girl with glasses. "This is the sickness. You can fight it, I promise."

Ellen keens. "Fuck. Fuck."

"Might want to make it quick," Mary says. She nods over the railing. "New girl's here."

Me.

I straighten up, opening my mouth to say something, but I hesitate. One of Ellen's eyes, wild, peers out from the mess of her hair that's fallen from its bun. Agnes must have ripped it out in a fight. Her chest heaves. Agnes tries to scream again. The two girls on the steps stare at me like twin ghosts, or at least the way ghosts would stare if they had eyes.

"Shit," Isabella says. "Gloria." She motions for me to stay, then to come to her. I don't know what to do, so I back away instead, grabbing the railing to steady myself. I'm already breathing so hard I can barely hear. It's so loud. I want to clamp my hands over my ears. I shouldn't be here. "Just—"

Agnes digs her nails into Ellen's arm, tries to tear the sleeve, kicks and squirms and pushes away. Her feet slide further from the ground. She tips a little farther over the banister.

Isabella stops moving. Even Mary hesitates, eyeing all of us as if Ellen will drop Agnes if anyone does a damn thing wrong.

Is this what Veil sickness is? This, Miss Neuling, Mary's sneer, me, all of us?

"It's not fair," Ellen whimpers. "I've been here so long, I'm *better* I *swear,* but you had go to and let him fuck you—"

Isabella says, "Ellen, you don't have to do this." Beside me, the girl with glasses repeats, "*Put her down, put her down, you have to put her down.*" Ellen squeezes her eyes shut. "Charlotte's right. Just put her down. It's okay."

"This is taking too long," Mary says. "Honestly, Ellen, what are you talking about? You really think any man would pick you?"

Ellen lets out a gut-wrenching scream.

And tips Agnes over the edge.

It takes forever for her to hit the ground, and no time at all. She collides with the wood at a bad angle right in front of me. *Thump.* The sound is like a sack of flour falling off the back of a cart. There's no wet snap, not like I expected, and if she makes any noise, it's covered by the shriek of the redheaded girl, begging, "No, *no.*"

A fall like that is unpredictable. I've seen case studies on either side: Agnes could be totally fine, or she could be dead. We could be looking at a nasty bruise, or a brain injury so brutal she never gets up again. The most likely outcome is somewhere in the middle. Cracked bones, a concussion, lots of awful things that add up to a mess.

I should do something. Like I did at the gala. Lunge forward, check the damage, triage and fix what I can.

I just stand there.

Isabella stumbles down the stairs, saying, "Agnes, Agnes, get up, it's okay, you're okay, you're okay." The girls with me on the stairs gather her up, pat her cheeks, shake her—one of them, Charlotte I think, pries her eyelids apart. Is she moving?

Headmaster slams out of his office. Mrs. Forrester limps toward us from the dining hall, a hand over her mouth.

Ellen and Mary and I look at each other in silence.

Agnes moans pathetically. Her hands instinctively wrap around her stomach. Good. Movement is always good—and it seems Ellen was right after all, as protecting the belly means protecting the baby. Blood soaks her mousy brown hair, staining her scalp and big forehead. Her arm looks broken. Down near the wrist. It needs to be maneuvered back into place before the bone begins to stitch.

I should do that. I should have someone hold her down while I grip the hand, the elbow, straighten the bone and line the pieces up. It's an excruciating procedure if you don't have nitrous oxide or ether-chloroform to ease the pain (and even then, it doesn't always smooth it over entirely; anesthesia is notoriously difficult). Get it over with now, while she's still in shock from the fall, make one moment worse instead of extending the suffering across time.

But I don't.

*Good*, the rabbit says. *Don't draw attention.*

"Who did this?" Headmaster demands. "Which of you—"

"Nobody," Mary says.

"She fell," says the redhead. "I promise. It was an accident."

I can't open my mouth. There's blood on the stairs, a broken bone repeating itself in my head, snapping and stitching and snapping again, and I point to Ellen because it's the truth.

Isabella looks as if she'll be sick. Mary turns on her heel and walks to class.

Headmaster storms past us, up the stairs, and snatches Ellen by the arm. "Thank you, Miss Bell," he says. Ellen turns like she means to run, but Headmaster pulls her close. "Oh, don't make this difficult. Why don't we go to my office to talk?"

*Uncooperative girls*, the rabbit reminds me.

Ellen is taken away. Mrs. Forrester snaps at us to go to class. I don't move. Agnes is between me and the upstairs.

Isabella eventually slips around her, takes my hand, and pulls me.

Agnes reaches for the hem of my dress as I go.

✦

Mrs. Forrester's classroom is at the end of the east wing on the second floor, with a large bay window letting in trickles of weak sun. It would offer a beautiful view of the garden if it weren't rapidly approaching winter. When the lot of us arrive, Mary is already in her seat, reading a little booklet. Mrs. Forrester herds us in.

"Quickly, quickly," Mrs. Forrester snaps when we don't move fast enough for her liking. She pushes two desks from the middle of the classroom to the side, removing them from the group. "I have to call for a doctor. Read quietly today." She shoves a booklet at me: *The Angel in the House* by Coventry Patmore. Isabella has to nudge me to take it and sits me in a chair because I can't do it myself. "Cross out the name and add your own. We're on canto eleven, so be sure to catch up."

I open the front cover. This one is—was—Ellen's.

The rabbit makes an awful noise somewhere in the back of my head.

"The rest of you," Mrs. Forrester says, "discuss how the narrator feels about his wife. I expect a full report by the end of class. Miss Carter, keep an eye on them, will you?"

Mary smiles placatingly. "Of course, ma'am."

And then Mrs. Forrester leaves. She calls, "Agnes, dear,

it's all right. Dr. Bernthal will be here soon— Yes, he has a telephone, yes. Can you sit up for me?"

I should be down there. I should be helping. I should make sure she doesn't go into shock, soothe the pain, anything.

But I'm not, and I don't. I stare at the poetry booklet on my desk because it's the only thing I can bring myself to do.

From what little I know of it, *The Angel in the House* is an instruction manual on how to be a perfect wife. An aspiration for all young girls. This is what Mother and Father dreamed of when they looked at me as a baby, what they hoped I'd be when the tutors were done.

A strange thing about being a boy like me is how difficult it is to untangle the truth of yourself from the world's perception of you. Because, yes, I am a boy. I am just as much a man as my father and brother, just a different kind. Acknowledging this has made my life almost bearable; it's taken a terrible weight off my shoulders, given me an answer for why I feel the way I do. But I still connect with women. I find companionship with them, closeness that cannot be denied, because the world will always do its damnedest to see me as one of them. As long as we are seen the same, we will experience the same. Our lives will be linked. I will be held to the same unfair standards, punished under the same unjust rules. To separate how you are *seen* from who you *are* sometimes feels nigh impossible.

On the other side of the room, pulling me out of my thoughts, a girl says: "Why would you tell Headmaster that?"

It takes me a moment to understand what's going on. The redhead is looking at me like she might cry. That anvil on my chest from the gala returns.

"What?" I say.

"Why would you—" Her voice cracks. "I know what she did was awful, but now she'll never—"

"Leave Gloria out of it," Isabella says, snapping her booklet shut. Charlotte, the girl with the glasses, watches each of us curiously, as if we're animals in a zoological garden. "If you're going to blame anyone, blame Mary."

"Blame Ellen," Mary says. "I didn't throw a pregnant girl down the stairs."

"You told her to do it," Isabella says, "didn't you? And you knew she'd never come back if she did." When the redhead opens her mouth, Isabella continues, "Even if Gloria said *nothing*, Headmaster still would have figured it out."

"I didn't know she'd be taken away," Mary hums innocently. "You don't know she's not coming back."

Isabella says, "Frances didn't come back."

All the air goes out of the room. That name again. *Frances.*

Mary glares. Her canines are oddly sharp, as if she attempted to file them to points as a child.

"Dear me," she drawls. "Don't act like you're *sad* Ellen's gone. And certainly don't act as if you're innocent! You were supposed to explain the rules, and I think you missed one." Mary stands with a rush of skirts. "New girl. Miss Bell, is it?"

Everyone falls silent. Not even Isabella says a word.

Mary walks through the desks to stand inquisitively in front of me, and then taps my book to force my attention to her. Her face is open in an almost childish way—sweet lips, raised brows—and it takes me a second too long to realize it's not an honest face. She's putting it on. To make fun of me. The cord of the necklace, the ring, puts weight on the side of her neck, and now that I know it's there, I can't unsee it.

"I'm so sorry," she says. "It seems Isabella didn't do a very good job of explaining how things work around here. She probably didn't even introduce anyone! Why don't we do that now?" She gestures at herself. "I'm Miss Carter; my father is the first Carter of Carter & Carter, so I'm sure you've heard of him. That crow over there is Isabella Rossi. She's a bit of a slut. Then, of course, we have Charlotte Hudson, another tattle; you'll love her, and—" She gestures to the redhead. "Louise Hare, the coward of the group. But they're not particularly interesting. Not when we have a shiny, pretty, *new girl*. Who just so happened to make sure Ellen got whisked away for good."

*Frances didn't come back*, the rabbit repeats. *And Ellen won't.*

"So," Mary says, "I have a question for you, since you clearly think you're better than all of us." I don't think I'm better than anybody. How could I? "When you said you weren't going to be here long, what exactly did you mean? You think you're not as sick as the rest of us?"

I look anywhere but her eyes. *It means you were lying to get her to leave you alone.* I just want to her stop. If I answer, maybe she'll stop.

"No," I say. "It's just that I'm engaged."

That seems like the safest thing to say, and it is technically true. Edward and I aren't betrothed—there's been no ceremony, no official acknowledgement in the eyes of the Church or anything of the sort—but it's the most correct way to describe our situation. We're meant for each other, whether or not I have a choice in the matter.

Mary laughs. "Oh, really? I can't believe it." I can't blame her. It's not correct, like opening up a patient to find that all of the organs grew in mirrored. "And just who is this mysterious future husband?"

Leave me alone please, please, please. "Edward Luckenbill."

There is no breath. No shuffling of fabric. No scuff of shoes on the floor.

"Luckenbill?" Mary says finally. "As in the son of the Viscount Luckenbill?"

And all of a sudden she is showing her teeth in something that I think might be a smile but probably isn't. She breathes in, long and sharp, her chest rising and nostrils flaring.

"*You?*" she says. *"And the fucking Luckenbills?"*

The door lock clicks.

Mary straightens up, her face instantly pleasant again. Mrs. Forrester limps into the room, eyes flicking between each of us in turn.

"Hello, Mrs. Forrester," Mary says. "We've had a wonderful discussion. The author makes a stunning comparison to the story of Eve we'd love to explore in class today."

I sink further into my chair, wrap my arms around myself, and try not to cry. Again.

✦

An hour or so into class, Louise points out the window, interrupting Mrs. Forrester's discussion on wifely duties. "Look," she says. "There she goes."

Mrs. Forrester goes quiet. Charlotte rushes across the room. Even Mary leans back a little to watch. Out the window: a carriage with wheezing horses, a doctor in a black coat, a girl curled up in his arms. She looks up, violet eyes watery.

Moving. Alive.

"She's beautiful," Charlotte breathes.

For the first time, Mrs. Forrester smiles. It looks odd, like her face isn't quite meant to move that way. "She's *cured*. Everyone, please, take heed. Remember Miss Warwick and her progress. You should all aspire to be just like her. And you should be nothing, nothing at all, like Miss Ellen Wright."

✦

The rest of the day is quiet. After tea, Mrs. Forrester reads from an instruction manual on how to best oversee servants in our future husbands' households, and Headmaster urges us to sing along with the piano in the library. At dinner, I watch the other girls. Louise has a sweet voice, but almost everyone ignores her when she speaks. Mary moves like a predator has been taught the most feminine of manners and is showing off to the other predators how well she has memorized them. Isabella is the quietest and oldest of us all, always pulling the cuff of her sleeve over bruises. Charlotte unsettles me the most. I understand anger, or sadness, but her obsession with finding the perfect husband feels almost parasitic. Like this school has burrowed into her like a Guinea worm.

After dinner is chores. When I am put on laundry with Louise, Isabella objects to me being given one of the most difficult jobs, but I don't mind. It's mindless, repetitive work—the second best thing to surgery. I used to beg Mother to let me peel the potatoes or clean the floors, to let me work with the servants for just a little while. For a while, as I boil and bleach cloth after cloth, my mind is blissfully quiet.

I'll take any quiet I can get. Anything to keep from tearing off my skin.

When we return to the dormitory for the night, Isabella is stripping Ellen's and Agnes's beds. Nobody claims one of them, even though Ellen's bed is a good spot closer to the fire.

"Do you think Agnes will be okay?" Louise asks nobody in particular.

"Dr. Bernthal will take great care of her," Charlotte says. "I swear, the lot of you are so paranoid. It's unfair. Has anything actually terrible happened to the girls who leave? Rose, Madeline, Victoria—you remember Victoria— they're all doing wonderfully—"

Isabella laughs bitterly, folding the sheets over her arm.

"What?" Charlotte says. "Do you disagree? What proof do you have that they're being treated badly? That they're

being beaten, or whatever you think? None, that's what."
Isabella ignores her, crossing the room and dumping the
sheets by the door. Charlotte continues to talk to her back.
"You just *want* it to be true. You're a rotten woman, Isabella.
That attitude will get you nowhere."

"Charlotte's right," Mary calls. "It'll get you nowhere,
little crow." Her eyes flick to me. "What do you think?"

"Me?" I say.

"Who else?"

"I think Agnes's broken arm looked bad," I reply, because
that is the only thing I am qualified to speak about. It was
a bad break, like breaks almost always are, and it will take a
few days at least to rule out a concussion and brain bleeds. "I
think it will be extremely painful to set, and there's always
the chance of complications."

Charlotte scoffs. Apparently, I've misunderstood again.
"Listen to yourself," she says. "That's the sickness talking."

*Just like Ellen*, the rabbit says.

I don't understand, so I do not reply.

9

The next day, I am woken by the same sharp bell, the same fluttering of blankets, Mrs. Forrester's feet shuffling across the wooden floor. I have to beg my body to cooperate. It wants to give out from under me, but I force myself upright. Wipe my eyes. Stumble out of bed.

"Up we go, dear," Mrs. Forrester says, taking my elbow to steady me. "Come with me. The Honorable Edward Luckenbill will be here to take breakfast with you."

She says it like it doesn't make me want to scream. The rabbit wheezes, and it sounds something like laughter.

✦

Again, I am taken to the dressing room—the locked room with the mirror, with the odd bump under the rug—and stripped to my chemise. Mrs. Forrester ties me up in an exquisite gown, rose-and-cream-colored silks traced with gold. She smothers me in pearls as perfect as a wedding dress and a corset that accentuates every curve of my body. It's *awful*. Usually, clothing is not so bad. I can convince myself to ignore the textures, the stitching and seams. But yesterday has left me raw.

"Stand still," Mrs. Forrester mutters, turning me around to face the mirror. "Stop fidgeting."

With my pale hair and violet eyes, I am a collection of precious gems sewn up in a cadaver. *Almost a bride.* Then, *almost a mother*, because what is the point of a Speaker marriage if not children and bloodlines? The rabbit digs up everything I know about pregnancy: the biological mechanisms, the diagrams, the notes. For the first time, it becomes a real threat. Something that is possible, not just a bad dream.

Until now, I almost thought I'd be able to avoid it if I really tried.

I know enough about pregnancy to be terrified of it, which is the only sensible reaction to discovering how it works. Seeing a pregnant woman in person, or even illustrations of a fetus in the womb, curled up on itself like a little sleeping lizard, makes me ill. I've studied how to remove a uterus from the body with a scalpel and a few clamps to close off the arteries, and I've dreamed of it so often I swear I know what the muscles feel like; the heat of the innards, the slick of blood between my fingers.

But now, I stand in front of this mirror as Mrs. Forrester pins up my hair, and I imagine it. Really, truly imagine it. I put a hand to my stomach as if skimming the stitchwork of the dress, when in fact I am tracing the curve of a swollen belly that does not exist.

What is it like, to become sick as a fetus rearranges my organs to make room for its body? To feel that hot flush of nauseating panic when it moves for the first time, struggling against the confines of my skin?

From a medical perspective, I would make it. I might even have it easy. Father always told us we come from sturdy stock—I have wide hips to allow for an infant's skull, and Mother said both George and I slipped out with barely a half a day's labor. A million things can go wrong in childbirth, but my body means I would likely survive most of them. I wouldn't *want* to. I'd become like those women who go mad when faced with the power of their own bodies—when it's harnessed to create something new against their will. But I could do it.

Agnes, though, is so much smaller. She's not done growing. She's not ready. If her baby is any size at all, it will get stuck in her hips, and they'll have to split her open to get it out, or they'll crush the infant's head so it fits through the birth canal.

"And we can't forget," Mrs. Forrester says.

She takes my hand and slips a silver Speaker ring onto my little finger.

My reflection is not my own. It is more a sculpture, an artist's creation, than something that actually exists. It is something my parents would have commissioned to replace me.

✦

I am taken to the parlor, the room reserved for visits between girls and their suitors. Mrs. Forrester tells me the parlor is beautiful, with a wonderful view and luxurious furnishings, as if this is meant to make me feel better. I comfort myself by rehearsing what little I know of courtship: of chaperones and the importance of purity, the intricate rules governing contact and conversation. We'll sit across from each other and talk, and Mrs. Forrester will keep an eye on us, and it will all be some strange game I do not understand and I will be exhausted and confused all the while.

"The Honorable Edward Luckenbill," Mrs. Forrester announces as she opens the door. "Gloria Bell has arrived."

The parlor could be a sitting room in Buckingham Palace. A fire, crackling pleasantly, has been stoked in the hearth; flowers spring forth from vases like blooming trees; the towering ceiling is adorned with bright frescoes of meadows and blue skies, held up by bookshelves as tall as a man and then some. A gilded tea set is laid out on the table with milk and sugar, paired with a delicate breakfast that makes my stomach turn. Sun streams through the floor-to-ceiling windows. There are no clouds. It is too bright. I struggle not to shield my face, not to squint against the light.

And there, at the window, is Edward Luckenbill.

I can hardly stand to look at him. It's easier to look at his reflection in the glass than his actual self. He is dressed in more muted tones than at the gala but has managed to hide a spot of color in the sapphire pinned to his collar, the ocean blue handkerchief placed daintily in his breast pocket. The humanity of it startles me.

"Fine," he says. "Bring her in."

Mrs. Forrester nudges me forward. I struggle to take a step into the room. My feet sink into the carpet, and the air smells of fresh-cut flowers and sweets and smoke. It will be okay. Mrs. Forrester will be my chaperone. I am in no danger.

But the door shuts behind me.

It locks.

What?

That's—no. No, it doesn't work like that. Women are not left alone with men and that's final. I stare at the knob, hands shaking. Something pops in the back of my throat like a stitch ripping. Whatever's holding my mask together is failing.

"She's not coming back until time's up," Edward says. He's more composed than he had been at the gala, looking ill while I coughed on the floor, bloody and sobbing. I must be less intimidating now that I've been trapped here. "Didn't you know? The Speakers do it differently. As long as there's a Speaker in this room, they'll excuse just about anything."

I turn, clutching my skirts so tight my fingers ache. The Luckenbill boy hasn't turned to face me. This is preferable to the way he stared at the gala.

*They'll excuse just about anything.*

"But you can relax," he says. "I won't touch you. I'm not a monster."

I don't believe him. I'd memorized entire books on this once; the idea of courtship and suitors was marginally less terrifying if I hid behind the convoluted guidelines. But those are gone now, because the Royal Speaker Society has no respect for the Church or propriety and the Luckenbills can do whatever they damn well please. I can't do this, not here, not now—

"Right." The boy finally turns, leaning against the windowsill. A single curl falls in front of his green eyes. On the other side of the glass, snowflakes start to swirl around him, like the Veil warping the air. I thought it'd be too early for snow. "We have something to clear up. What's your name?"

I answer on instinct. "Gloria."

Edward sniffs. His attention shifts to the curtains, to the ceiling.

He says, "Is that the name you prefer?"

The world snaps into clear focus, the way it does when I start to push a scalpel into skin. A survival mechanism. The body forcing itself alert for the sake of its own safety no matter how much it hurts.

"I don't know what you're talking about," I say.

"At the gala." Edward wanders towards me, fiddling with his cravat. Why is he coming closer? I back away until I hit the door. "David, was it?"

"I stole that name. It wasn't mine."

"You had me convinced you were a boy, you know. You did a damn good job. But this?" He makes a face. "This, not so much."

*"Stop."*

To my surprise, he does. He stops talking. Stops moving. Just blinks.

"I'm sorry." My words tremble. They taste bitter and thick like the spit that comes up before vomit, the saliva that coats the teeth and tongue to protect them from the coming stomach acid. "I don't—I don't know what you want me to say. What anyone wants me to say. I don't know what's going on, or why I'm here, or why you'd want me. I'm sorry."

In the quiet, I can hear the workings of my insides. My heart pumping blood, my ears ringing, the contraction of the muscles in my throat when I swallow.

Something like sadness wells up in Edward's eyes.

Or . . . no. Something more like fear. As if he's seen something he wasn't meant to. And his eyes are so big and beautiful. I hate that's what I'm thinking of. Green, with long dark lashes like Isabella's.

"Oh," he says. "I've missed something. I should start over. I'll start over."

He steels himself the way a soldier steels for an amputation.

"My name is Daphne."

*Daphne?*

In that moment, it's as if I've peeled the skin away from the chest of a patient, revealing a beating heart. A boy could not say that name as if terrified the syllables will break in the mouth. A boy-born-boy could not recognize what I am.

Of course her name is Daphne.

I stand up straight, taking a step from the door; and then another, and another.

She's like me.

For the first time in my life, there is someone like *me*. Who is real, who is alive, who is so close I could touch them. In the span of seconds, standing there in a suit with her cheeks flushing the color of roses and her eyes brimming with tears, the Honorable Daphne Luckenbill becomes the most wonderful girl I have ever seen.

The mask shatters into a thousand pieces. Halfway to her, I stumble, drop to my knees, and begin to cry.

She's like me, she's like me, and I'm safe. After Mrs. Forrester and my naked body in the mirror, after Headmaster, after Mary and Ellen and Agnes, for a moment, I'm safe—and everything falls out. A hernia of awful things breaks the skin. My sobbing dissolves into coughing, a muffled scream into my hands, until I rip off the Speaker ring and throw it across the room. My shoes too, and the pearl necklace. My shoes hit the bookshelves, the necklace hits the wall. It's all so heavy, I need it off me, I need it off me *now*.

Why do I have to find her here? It's a cruel joke. It's not fair.

I fall onto one of my hips. Skirts sprawled and ruined. Gasping for air, pawing at my face until it's numb.

"I'm—" I hiccup, trying to speak, but nothing else comes out. I shake my head, flap my hands, try to dislodge the words stuck by tears. "I didn't—I didn't mean—"

Slowly, carefully, Daphne sits in front of me and holds out a napkin from the table. The Speaker ring on her hand has been turned so the emblem faces her palm.

"Here," she says.

I take the napkin and press it to my face. Breathe in. Breathe out. Like George said.

"Easy," she continues. "It's all right."

My name comes and I throw it to her like a lifeline. I desperately want her to grab it. "Silas." Finally, finally I get to say my name again. "My name is Silas."

She repeats, "Silas."

The stoic expression she's put on is gone. Her chest hitches. She blinks away tears and then, when that fails, roughly scrapes them away with the back of her hand.

"Are you okay?" she asks anyway.

"I'm . . . better."

"You must have had a fucking rotten day." She sniffles a little. "Me too."

We sit on the floor together, crying, until a strand of hair falls into my mouth. I spit it out. It distracts me for just long enough to make me laugh, and Daphne does too. Her eyes shine when she laughs. She's beautiful.

A beautiful thing. Here. I almost don't believe it.

"Bloody hell," Daphne says, "this is embarrassing, isn't it?"

"I'm sorry you had to see that." I have to speak slow. "I'm not usually . . ." *Like this*, I don't finish. I'm not usually loud, or emotional, or pathetic. I was taught better. Don't cry, don't cover your ears, don't beat your fists against your lap like an animal. Mother and Father

didn't spend all that money on tutors for nothing. "I
don't know. I'm sorry."

But Daphne just snorts. "I think you should've aimed for
the window with that shoe; I would've loved to inform my
father he needed to replace it."

She's not making fun of me. She is not mocking my
tears, or telling me to get over myself. Kindness takes me
off guard.

I think it's time to start over, like she said.

"Hello, Daphne," I say.

"Hello, Silas. It's good to make your acquaintance."

There is so much I want to ask her. I want to lay her
down on the couch, smooth my hands over her stomach,
and take her apart to see her insides. To see how much of
our insides are the same. Did she have a brother or sister
to guide her here, or did she figure it out all on her own?
Is she a mirror image of me, or something else entirely?
How much of *this* can be separated from me, how much is
universal, how much is all my own?

"Come," she says. "Off the ground, let's go."

◆

I curl up in a corner of the love seat, knees tucked to my
chest, as Daphne pours the tea. I intended to do so, but
she asked if I had been born in a barn and gently pushed
my hand away. "Though there really should be servants,"
she mutters. "I thought my father paid their salaries. Is
your headmaster pocketing it all?" She hands me my

cup—sugared milk with a splash of Earl Grey, because tea is unbearably bitter—and sits on the couch across from me, sprawled nonchalantly, while I tap a rhythm on the porcelain and watch the ripples.

*Daphne.* I want to repeat it until I memorize the shape my lips make as I say it. *Daphne, Daphne, Daphne.*

"If I may ask," I say finally. "How could you tell?"

"I had a hunch," she says, "and my hunches are always right." Now that she's collected herself, she has a self-satisfied, near-derisive tone to her words; a confidence that is so far beyond me that it's alluring. "It's obvious if you know what to look for. This—" She gestures at me. I can only imagine my hair is a mess, and I still haven't put my shoes back on. That's fine. I don't like shoes. "This is all far more artificial than who I saw at the gala."

I shouldn't be surprised to learn my façade of womanhood is faulty. Daphne could see through it, as could George. But had I seen something similar in her? At the gala, did I notice that her boyhood was a front, something that wasn't really her? It's no surprise to say I didn't. I'm practically incapable of it. I read everything as it is given to me, exactly how it is said, only to discover that the world always operates just below the surface.

The snow continues to fall. It disappears as soon as it touches the grass, as if it never existed in the first place.

I don't believe in luck, or fate, or anything that could be mistaken for them. The world falls into place as the result of a million little things and there is nothing anyone can do to change it.

But I can't think of another word to explain this.

I blurt, "What if you just take me?"

Daphne frowns. "What?"

For the first time, the possibility of escape glitters like fresh bone. "We could make it work, couldn't we? What if you tell them there's no need for any of this? What if you say you'll take me as I am, Veil sickness be damned? You'd get the wife your father wants you to have, and we'd be safe together." I like to think we would. At the very least, we would have one person in our lives who understands. That's more than I ever thought I'd get before. "Right?"

In response, Daphne taps the teacup against her lips. I can almost see her mind working, running through the possibilities. Mine is too. A life laid out in front of us so simply, so plainly, that it could actually be possible. Putting on the airs of a relationship for others. Convincing our parents that I'm barren so we'd never have to force ourselves into being a mother or father. Having some semblance of *safety*.

But—

Daphne studies her reflection in her tea. "That's not how it works. They won't let you out of here until you're cured. The only other option is Bedlam." She considers for a moment. "Or, considering what you did at the gala, a noose."

"But I'm not sick." You can't cure something that isn't wrong. It doesn't work like that.

"Do you believe they give a shit about what you think? They say you are, so you are." Daphne doesn't look up. I'm not sure she can. "And let me make one thing clear—just because I'm not trapped in this school doesn't mean I'm not trapped as well. My father thinks there's something wrong with me too. Deep down, I think he knows." She does not have to say what her father might know. We both understand. The way she laughs into her drink is dry and hard around the edges. "And have you heard about that amendment that's been introduced in Parliament? The one that makes my sheer existence a crime? I'd love to fix this so easily, but I'm just as fucked as you are."

*Bang.*

A cabinet between the bookshelves slams open. Daphne yelps. Tea sloshes across my hand. A bag of speaking tiles—white porcelain squares engraved with letters, light enough for spirits to move—rips open and scatters its contents across the floor. Tiles hit the hardwood. The plush carpet. The back of the settee. It comes with a burst of frigid air, the smell of petals and ozone.

I nearly throw my teacup onto the table and stumble over to the settee to look.

"What—" Daphne gasps. "What is that?"

My heart hammers in my throat. My hands are cold.

There's only one thing it could be.

I say, "Come here."

She gets up from the couch, clutching her cravat.

Most of the tiles, in the positions they've landed, are meaningless. Clumps of letters, vague prefixes and roots. Too organized to be random but too nonsensical to be understood.

But, in the middle, they read:

HELP US

Daphne's throat bobs. There is a spark of recognition in her eyes. The shadow of dread.

The letters jitter, struggling to move again. Tiny pockets of the floor distend and then snap back into place. A shadow flits across the carpet without anything to cast it. A spirit? But there's no haunting here. Nobody is opening the Veil for a ghost to reach through. Without a haunting, without a medium, reaching through to our world is so difficult it burns up the dead like matches; even speaking tiles are a near-insurmountable effort. That's why, before mediums, before the Veil thinned enough for hauntings to show through, burned-up spirits were the only spirits humans ever saw. They were shriveled things rattling plates and scaring dogs, furious but short-lived.

But the words are there.

HELP US HELP US

It's like looking up from your procedure to see that the heart has stopped, or putting your hand to a wound to staunch the blood only to find that it's too late. Daphne watches as the last few tiles slide into place without my touch, mouthing the words.

"Who is *us*?" she asks.

Before the tiles form the words, I know. The empty beds. The hidden chairs.

The tiles slide, clatter, clack. ELLEN WRIGHT FRANCES NICOLL. *Clack clack clack*. STOP THIS HELP US BEFORE THEY TAKE YOU TOO

And, just like that, the tiles stop. The shadows are gone. The world is still. And it's as if none of it had ever happened at all.

is this because i hurt Agnes

i only did it because Mary told me to

i only did it because i thought it'd hurt less to watch her hurt instead

a man in a mask stuffed my mouth with cotton and shut me in a dark room and then i waited and waited and then more men with no faces put me up on a table and covered my nose with a rag that smelled like rotting flowers and i got tired tired tired

i barely noticed when they peeled my eye- open and asked *do you think we can get to the brain through the socket* and another masked man answered *better off going through the skull first* so they took a saw and cut a hole in my skull and i was alive

the whole time

do you understand

i was alive alive alive alive

the men said *we'll find it eventually, we'll cut it out of them eventually* and they said *how is Miss Warwick doing, by the way, what a nasty fall* and then i died and they called it *shock*

i died of shock with a hole in my head

Frances is here now

i don't want to rot down here Frances dont let me please

I tell Ellen there has to be someone who will listen if we scream loud enough.

But can we do it before we burn?

If a dead girl prays to God can he hear her?

IO

"What does that mean?" Daphne asks.

STOP THIS HELP US BEFORE THEY TAKE YOU TOO

I slide off the settee, press my hands against the floor, dig my fingers into the rug. There is no haunting, no weakness in the world for me to tear. No way to get through the Veil.

The spirits are gone.

I don't—

This can't—

*You know what this is*, the rabbit says. The animal feels like a tumor in my chest. Growing larger and larger until it squeezes my lungs, cracks my ribs, crushes my esophagus against my spine.

"Silas?" Daphne whispers. "What the hell does that mean?"

The realization tastes rancid, as if I'd gotten the residue from a ripped-open stomach in my mouth.

Ellen and Frances weren't taken to Bedlam. They weren't taken to that hospital-asylum to rot in cells.

My hands twist together as I force myself to speak, untangling my thoughts as I go. "Girls—students, they just—they go missing. Everyone keeps talking about this girl, Frances, who disappeared before I got here." Daphne's eyes flick to the tiles on the floor. "And then Ellen. She got taken away too. I thought they were being sent to another hospital, but—"

I can't finish, but I don't have to.

They're spirits. That says enough.

And for an awful moment, in that parlor, I don't trust Daphne at all.

Or rather, the rabbit doesn't. It shows its yellow buck-teeth, twitches its black nose suspiciously. *Her father is the president of the Speaker Society!* it squeals. *What right does she have to be surprised about anything they do!*

I tap my palm against my chest to calm myself. The rabbit isn't making sense. Daphne just spoke of her father's suspicions, his disgust of her. He wouldn't tell her anything. Of course he wouldn't.

And if Lord Luckenbill sent *me* here, after everything he said—

He doesn't know what's happening. He wouldn't put this much time and energy into me if he just sent me here to die. When he pulled me out of the gala, he pulled me off the gallows too. He wants me alive.

"Bloody hell," Daphne says. She puts a hand over her mouth. "Fuck. What do we do?"

Even though I know it won't work, I rearrange the tiles. WHERE ARE YOU CAN YOU HEAR US. It keeps me busy while my mind clicks the pieces together. That is how it works; it takes patterns, systems, and unravels them in an instant. It's how I memorized the body so well—it's one big, beautiful structure, everything connected, one thing incapable of functioning without the others. The problem, I've found, is in the translation. My hands flutter as I think. I get up and start to pace.

I am a sick little girl. If I went to Lord Luckenbill, or Mother, or *anyone*, and asked them to look into dead students at this school, not a soul would believe me. If I said a ghost told me, it'd be even worse.

But with proof? With a *body*?

HELP US

"If we find them," I say, "if we can prove—" I shake out my hands one last time and come to a stop in front of Daphne. "We could tell your father. He may be a bad father, but he's a good Speaker. He wouldn't want something like this to tarnish his reputation. He'd shut this place down, and we wouldn't have to spend another moment here."

For the space of a heartbeat, the veins in Daphne's neck stand out. Her jaw twitches. I don't know why she looks like a cornered animal, but she does.

*I told you*, the rabbit says.

Shut up.

"Fuck," Daphne says again. "Okay. Okay. Let me think. Proof? That these girls are—?" She can't say it either. "Okay. I'll write those names down. When I get back to London,

I'll—I'll pull records from local hospitals, asylums, prisons, all the mortuaries I can get in contact with. See if bodies are being funneled through some official avenue, or recorded somewhere." She makes a strangled noise, searches for a piece of paper, grabs a pen. It scratches on the paper with a noise that makes the back of my neck itch. "Put being a viscount's son to some goddamn use, I guess."

She pauses, looks up at me.

"You look like you have an idea," she says warily.

"I might," I admit.

She doesn't say anything to that, and it takes me a moment to realize she's expecting me to elaborate. I don't. She sighs.

"Whatever it is." She points at me with the pen. "Don't get yourself hurt."

I can't promise that, but I nod anyway.

By the time Mrs. Forrester comes to collect me, Daphne has corralled the speaking tiles back into their bag and stands by the window with her blank boy's face. I sit on the couch, eyes downcast, because that is what's expected of me. Mrs. Forrester is none the wiser.

Something terrible is happening here.

✦

I force myself to settle into a routine. I take what my tutors taught me—to scan my surroundings and mold myself to them, prevent myself from standing out at all costs—and bend it for my own purposes. Put the mask up and keep it there. Don't let a soul figure out what is happening underneath.

STOP THIS HELP US

The next day: wake up to the bell. Have breakfast. Go to class, where we have lessons in French, singing, poetry, household management. Out the window, I see the groundskeeper, a hunched man with a scarf around his mouth, sweeping snow from the front porch. Isabella trades me her biscuits during tea when she realizes I don't like the ones I'm given. We do our chores. Go to dinner. Nobody else is thrown over the banister.

HELP US

When something terrible happens—or at least, when you learn about it—it feels like it should affect the entire world. It feels like something should *change*. But it doesn't. It would be one thing if Braxton's was a constant nightmare; if there was always someone sobbing on the floor, broken bones, fear squeezing the heart as tight as a muscle spasm. Instead, Mrs. Forrester sits on the stairs to rest her feet, reading a magazine, and Headmaster reviews his notes in the library.

I can't rush into anything. The most important thing is to learn how Braxton's works. After all, you have to memorize human anatomy before they let you into the operating room.

STOP THIS HELP US BEFORE THEY TAKE YOU TOO

But, that night, when I return to the dormitory, Charlotte is not there.

I hesitate at the edge of my bed, staring at the door. She doesn't come. The girls shuffle, unlace their corsets, braid their hair for sleeping. I fidget.

"Where's—" I start.

"Her suitor came late," Isabella says. "I don't know how long she'll be down there. So we stay up."

Isabella explains that if a girl doesn't get to sleep, none of us do. Even if we don't like her. We'd do the same for Mary, she mutters. We stay up as long as it takes to make sure she gets back in one piece.

I can do that. I'm good at staying awake. I've always gone to bed late, resenting sleep for stealing so much useful time from me. I had better things to do. There were books to read, notes to copy, diagrams to draw. I spent a lot of time in George's room before he went off to university, the two of us hunched over the latest issues of medical journals. Sometimes, when we were much younger, George would lay me down on the floor and press on my stomach, pointing out organs as he went. He'd dig his fingers into my belly and say, "If I wanted to get into the bowel, I'd cut here," and I'd laugh because it tickled.

George would never hurt me. At least, not by action—by inaction, sure, but he would never actually lay a blade against me. So if I told the truth one day, if he came to see me and I explained why I needed him to split me open and take out my womb, would he do it? Would he listen to me?

The rabbit asks, *When has he ever helped you?*

In the dormitory, we light candles instead of gas lamps and force down cups of cold, bitter tea. Louise putters through the room, making beds and dusting and sweeping to keep her hands busy. At the fire, Mary pretends to embroider, picking at thread and fiddling with a needle. And Isabella sits by the door, playing pick-up sticks by herself, pausing between rounds to listen for footsteps in the hall.

After a minute, I come up to Isabella. The only thing to read is *The Angel in the House*, which I can't stand. "Mind if I join?"

She gives me a half smile. "Of course."

She resets the game, gathering up the sticks and letting them drop into a mess on the floor. I peer at the tangled disaster, interconnected and overlapping like broken bones. Good thing I have steady hands—and that I've gleaned the rules by watching her. I've never played before, but she doesn't have to know that. I do not break my attention as Isabella pulls a relatively safe stick from the stack, setting it by her foot. Instead of disrupting the pile, I take one that's rolled away from the tangle. Then both of us pause, listening for the telltale sound of footsteps, the unlatching of a door, anything at all.

Isabella has let her hair down, tied back only by a simple ribbon. Black strands have gotten loose and frame her face.

"Are we locked in?" I ask.

"No," she says, "but do you want to be the one that gets caught wandering around after lights-out?"

I shake my head.

"Exactly." She puts her chin in her hand, mulling over the game in front of her. "So how did the meeting with your suitor go? Mr. Luckenbill, right?"

Her name is Daphne. "It went well."

"Is he decent?"

"Enough." More than *enough*. "I think we'll get on."

Isabella pulls a stick free. They're like little twigs, or bones that are so small they're fragile, like the ones in the ear. "Good." I turn my own twig over in my hands as I search for another; I want to chew on it, but I stop myself. When I try to grab one that caught my eye, the stack shifts, sending some spinning gently or falling over themselves. My turn is over.

We listen.

I say, "Can I ask an odd question?"

"Depends on how odd."

"What happened to Frances?"

Isabella glances to me, then to Mary and Louise. Louise had begun to sweep under the beds but then stopped and is now sitting close to the fire picking a fallen flower petal to pieces. Mary pays no attention. The popping and crackling of the fire drowns out our voices.

"Be careful where you speak of her," Isabella says. "Mary will fly into rage if she hears so much as her name. They were close. Not sisters, but something like it."

I didn't think Mary could be close with anyone.

"And besides, there's not much to tell. There never is." Isabella chooses another stick and sets it aside. "A man proposed to her a few weeks ago—a minor lord from up north, I think, came all the way down to see her—and she drew blood. Cut him right across the face with a pair of scissors. I don't know why she thought she'd get away with it.

Maybe she never expected to. Either way, she disappeared before the day was done." She sniffs. "Just like Ellen."

*She's dead.*

I don't say that.

*Frances is DEAD.*

Why am I so afraid to put it into words? Why does my throat lock up? Why can't I just say it: that Frances is dead, that Ellen is dead, that the girls who leave here without husbands are dead?

Because to mark myself as *knowing* is dangerous.

"And it's not like Agnes?" I ask.

"No. Braxton's never shuts up about girls like Agnes. Our little success stories. Headmaster and Mrs. Forrester will never say Ellen's name again." She takes a shaky breath. "I'm sorry I didn't tell you."

I'm not sure how to respond to that. "It's okay."

"It's not. I just, we didn't know it was going to be a pattern. And I didn't want to scare you. You already seemed . . ." She gestures at me. I'm not sure what she's getting at. "It felt wrong to make it worse. Besides, I've been here longer than anyone else; almost two years now. Girls come and go all the time. You can almost convince yourself you don't see it."

She gets quiet. Another round of pick-up sticks. Another pause to listen.

"So no," Isabella says. "I don't know what happened to Frances. Or Ellen. It's probably that awful hospital, but it's best if you don't think about it."

*Weak*, the rabbit accuses. But I shush it. There's a difference between weakness and survival. There's nothing wrong with wanting to stay out of harm's way, for trying to make it through a world that despises you. I did the same thing for so long. I could never fault Isabella for that.

✦

Eventually, Isabella says, "What did you do?"

We've taken a break from the game. Hunching over the pile for too long has taken a toll on our necks and backs. I'm looking at the ceiling to stretch.

I say, "What do you mean?"

"To get sent here."

Oh. "Tried to get my medium's seal."

Isabella makes a coughing noise. "There's no need to lighten the mood."

"That's what I did, though. I tried to get my seal. Ruined the ceremony. Got caught." The confusion on her face confuses me in turn. "Why? What did you do?"

Isabella busies herself, taking the ribbon out of her hair before slowly putting it back up again. Anything to look away from me.

"Got caught with a boy," she says. "Too many boys. Not that I wanted the half of them, but you know how it goes." I don't. Then she nods to the door, to where Charlotte is, probably. "Outspoken feminist." Then to Mary and Louise: "Prone to violence. Prone to cowardice. Agnes tried to poison herself, Ellen threatened to kill an uncle, Frances made money selling séances in back alleys, Victoria turned down a husband twice her age, Madeline wouldn't stop summoning the ghost of her own stillborn—" She drops her hair. "I could spend the whole night here, listing sick girls and what they did."

My mind does not register the horror of the words. It hardly ever does. I have no emotional reaction to them, no visceral response. All I do is sort through the pattern.

Only three of us are here because we were caught opening the Veil.

Because that's not what Veil sickness really is. The sickness is what comes *after* we open the Veil: being with men, rejecting men, acting out, acting alive. If we are not perfect, obviously our power has corrupted us. It doesn't matter how closely we've followed their laws. It doesn't matter if there's proof or not. We're sick, so we're guilty. That's all the evidence they need.

The only things we have in common are violet eyes, and men who want us enough to bother trying to fix us.

✦

Charlotte comes back some time later. Perhaps an hour, I can't tell for sure. Isabella and I had gone back to playing, but Charlotte opens the door and ruins our game, sending the sticks rolling.

When she sees us all waiting, her face goes flat. Louise immediately hurries to bed. Mary pretends she doesn't notice.

"I told you not to wait," Charlotte says.

Isabella doesn't look up as she begins to gather up the remnants of our game, wrapping the sticks with cloth and twine to keep them together. "We always stay up. You know that."

"And I keep telling you, it's disrespectful." Charlotte closes the door behind her, steps over us, nearly misses my fingers as I try to keep a stick from snapping under her heel. "We'll keep going back and forth about this until one of us relents—and it will *not* be me." She scoffs. "You'd think the rest of you want to be sick for the rest of your lives."

It seems Mary is not putting up with her tonight. "And what makes you think you can talk to us like that?" she spits. "You're one of those damned *women's suffrage* girls."

Charlotte hisses. I scoot across the floor, away from her. "I learned the error of my ways, unlike the rest of you. I'm *healing*. Don't you dare slander me with that again." She takes off her glasses. Points them at all of us in turn. "I don't understand any of you. Don't you want to be happy? Why do you fight it so hard?"

*Charlotte would lick shit off a man's heel if it meant he'd think better of her. At least you would have the decency to gag first.*

11

Another day. Another mask. Keep to the routine, do not flinch, do not tremble. Smile and nod and do as I'm told.

If there is one thing Headmaster and Mrs. Forrester are good at, it is keeping every waking moment of our lives occupied. Classes, meals, chores—we are accounted for at all times, not a single minute left unstructured. It is thankless, draining work. This is what it must be like to be a soldier, hours of business with no escape. I think it's genuinely driving me mad. It builds up like toxins in the body, like fluid in the brain after an accident. The only time I get alone is in the washroom, where I sit on the floor, head in my hands and eyes pressed shut, preparing myself to be surrounded by people all over again.

People exhaust me. They are confusing, and unpredictable, and difficult to understand—and without reprieve, it becomes so much worse.

To counter that, I look at what I *do* understand.

Girls are disappearing from this school. They are dead and begging for help. If, somehow, I find a place where the Veil is thin enough, I can reach in and find them. They can point me toward the proof of their own deaths.

And Headmaster knows.

I don't have evidence of this, but nothing else makes sense. The web of it all falls apart without this one key piece. He is the one that took Ellen away, *he* is the one who digs his fingers into us and decides whether or not we are worthy. And he follows us like flies follow a corpse, studying us, writing notes in his little book, complimenting our pronunciation and posture. His eyes are so watery and pale that if I poked them with a needle, they'd deflate with a stream of saline. He is dangerous.

But anyone can be dangerous. This is a delicate operation, just like any other; I cannot puncture the bowel or the bladder, cannot nick an artery or open a vein.

I am facing a disease I do not know the extent of. I must be vigilant.

*You know what happens to little girls who play with ghosts.*

✦

When it comes time for chores, I am not assigned laundry or dishes. Instead, Mrs. Forrester beckons me to the sitting parlor where I first met Daphne. I hesitate at the door, but she clucks her tongue and motions for me.

"Miss Bell," she says, "come here."

I follow her inside, and this time she does not slam the door closed. Instead, she goes to a vase of flowers. They're the same flowers that were here a few days ago. Who knows how long they've been sitting?

"Come here and look at these," she says. I do. They're drooping and wilted. They don't match the sheer opulence of this room at all. "This is unacceptable. When you are a wife, you will be expected to keep your husband's house as perfect as possible, and this includes sending your maids for fresh flowers. If they can't anticipate your every need, you must know when to mete out punishment, or fire them." I understand just fine how this works. Mother was always nitpicking the work of our help; we could never keep any particular servant for more than a few years. "However, as we have no maid here at Braxton's, I am assigning this duty to you. What do you think you should do?"

The answer is so simple it feels like a trick question. "Fetch some more?"

"Good." Mrs. Forrester gestures out the window toward the glass-and-iron greenhouse. The sun is setting. "You can get them from the greenhouse. The groundskeeper is gathering supplies from town, so it is safe for you to go alone. However." She gives me a sharp look. "Bundle up and come *right* back. No dallying."

It is at once a threat and a show of power. I know I will be punished if I do not do as I'm told—and Mrs. Forrester knows I cannot run, because there is nowhere I will be able to go.

So with a shawl to keep out the cold, I step out the back door of the school and into a half-hearted flurry. The grass is dry and dead, more dirt than anything else. What little greenery persists are stunted ornamental conifers. The greenhouse itself is pressed right up against the wall enclosing the school grounds, tinted purple by all the lavenders and violets and lilacs. It's intricate, the size of a small house, with oxidized metal holding up glass panes. Some of the metal has been bent into the shape of an eye. *Mors vincit omnia*, like always.

Just outside the back door of the school, I pause.

*Run.* It's the rabbit instinct. Flee the predators, burrow into the ground, hide and wait. *Run run run.*

But Mrs. Forrester was right to let me go alone. There's nothing. I hurry across the lawn, breath clouding as I walk.

When I open the greenhouse door, the smell of flowers, of green and dirt and wet warmth, hits me in a wave. There are intricate systems of potted plants, carefully coddled to survive the cold—black drums of water to hold heat, leaves reaching up for the dim sun. I run my fingers along the edges of petals, press them against my lips to feel them, take a lock of hair to chew on it. My shoes click pleasantly on the tile floor, so I slow down a bit to hear it, *click-clack click-clack click-clack*. I let my fingers flex, I let them shake out, I tap my face and chest and neck and palms, squeeze my eyes shut until my face scrunches, breathe in until my chest screams for me to breathe out.

It's good to be away from the school. I'd stay here all night if I could. I'd rather sleep under the leaves and petals than in that damn dormitory, huddled under strange blankets and staring at a dark, taunting ceiling.

But I can't.

Of course, Mrs. Forrester did not explain *how* to fetch the flowers. I sway back and forth a bit, staring at the selection in front of me. Will I get in trouble if I pick the same thing; what rules don't I know about? Is there a certain *way* to pick them? Are some flowers ready but not others? This always happens. Someone tells me to do a task they believe to be perfectly obvious, and I'm stuck struggling because not a single part of it is obvious to me. I put my thumb in my mouth to chew on it. Shit. I'm wasting time.

Just as I reach for a gathering of lavenders—attempting to perfectly replicate the previous batch is the safest bet, I've decided—there is a noise from the other side of the greenhouse.

A clack, a clatter, like an animal dragging itself through the supplies.

I freeze.

"Is someone there?" I call.

Then a large, looming shape shuffles toward me between the leaves.

It's the groundskeeper. The one Mrs. Forrester said was in the nearby village.

He watches me from between shelves of pots and dirt: tall, unnaturally so, all sun-weathered skin and long features. His eyes are dull violet and droopy. A bandage has been wound tightly around his hand, part of a half-seal peeking out from the gauze.

He's not just a groundskeeper. He's an indentured medium. Who holds his contract? Some firm in London? Or Headmaster himself?

"Good morning," I say with a shaky smile. I should leave. I *need* to leave. According to the Speakers, I can be left alone with Lord Luckenbill and Daphne, but I absolutely cannot be left alone with someone like this. The safest thing to do would be to run back to the school and tell Mrs. Forrester immediately, profess my innocence, and make sure the groundskeeper is punished for lying about heading to town.

But his bandaged hand—it doesn't look quite right. This close, I can see the edges of inflammation.

Like a bone setting, an idea clicks. If anyone knows about the secrets of a place—and, in turn, has no semblance of loyalty to it, because why would they?—it's the servants. It's an indentured medium who, I pray, resents the man holding his contract.

And if I help him, he might be able to help me in turn.

The groundskeeper has not responded, so I press forward. I need to make this quick. "I'm here to get some lavender for the school," I say. "I don't want to interfere, if you have a particular way of cutting them. Could you, please?"

The groundskeeper regards me curiously for a moment, then slinks deeper between the flowers before returning with a bundle of blooms, all bright and beautiful, overflowing his arms. They're the same color as his eyes. He holds them out to me, and I make a show of pausing at his hand. His eyes flick to the bandages.

"Does that hurt?" I ask, even though I know the answer. There's no way it doesn't. "My brother is a doctor. Let me take a look."

There is a beat of silence. Of uncertainty. We watch each other like a pair of prey animals unable to recognize the other, waiting for the other to snap. But neither of us do, and the groundskeeper puts the lavenders down gently, like one would set a baby down to sleep, to hold out his hand.

I take it. This alone is clearly indecent. How dare I touch a man the Speakers do not approve of. Just from feel, the injury is swollen, and the heat radiating through the bandages screams that it's infected. His face contorts in pain. I can't imagine what it feels like to work all day with a wound like this. It must be an abscess, and a brutal one at that.

"Has anyone else looked at this?" I ask. He shakes his head. He hasn't said a word. Worry prickles at the back of my throat, but I press forward—there are ways to communicate without words. "That's awful. The pus needs to be drained and the wound needs to be washed. It'd relieve some of the pressure, at least, and keep the infection from spreading." Then: "I could do it, if you wanted."

Truth is, I've always been a little jealous of those who do not, or cannot, speak. I struggle so much with my words, with finding the right things to say, that I imagine it would be almost like a blessing to never have to deal with it again. I could do good work as a surgeon without words.

"In exchange, you have to answer a question. And you can't tell anyone." The groundskeeper blinks. "A trade. I'll do your hand first, so you know I'm honest."

His eyes flick between my hand, his, the wound, the flowers.

Slowly, hesitantly, he nods.

"Right. Do you keep needles here? Anything sharp?"

I am presented with a work knife. It is old but well-kept, keen enough that I barely feel the pain when I draw blood on my finger to test it. So I pull clean water and wash the blade, then his hands, and then my own. Washing before a procedure is a relatively new practice, but George instilled the importance of it when I was little. It used to be that doctors went right from autopsies to childbirths without so much as a scrub. These days, new mothers don't die nearly as much.

"Have you had this sort of thing done before?" I ask as I unwrap the bandages. I've seen far worse than some pus and inflammation, but that doesn't mean I don't pity him. So I keep talking, because as difficult as words can be, I find talking with a patient—or at them—helps take their mind off what's happening. "It can be scary, but I promise I know what I'm doing. Hold your hand steady, please? Actually, put it on that shelf. There you go." I take a rag from the workbench and place it under his hand to catch the mess. "You don't have to watch if you don't want."

He does not turn away. I turn the knife over in my hand, grip it like a scalpel—close to the point—and hunker over his hand to inspect the infected knot by his knuckles, figure out the point of the abscess, where it will drain the best.

"Breathe in," I tell him, and I push the tip of the knife into the skin. Blood and pus come to the surface immediately, yellow-red. His face twists in pain. "Almost done." Just a little deeper, and *there*. I set the knife aside. "It's okay, it's over; that's the worst part." Then I fold the cloth over his hand, cover the abscess, and gently press down. More pus comes out. There is more than I thought, but thankfully I don't see any green or black. That wouldn't be infection, but rot, and there wouldn't be much I could do about that. "There we go. All done."

I wipe up the mess, wash his hand again, and gently wrap the bandages tight.

"Keep it clean," I tell him, "don't bother the wound, and it should heal. Okay?"

The groundskeeper picks up his hand, inspects the bandages, looks at the covered wound from every angle. There's a wide-eyed interest in his expression that doesn't quite match his age, and it reminds me of the face Mary put on to mock me in Mrs. Forrester's classroom that first day.

Then he turns to me, gaze expectant.

Right. The question.

I carefully peel away implication, accusation, context. I cannot imply too much. I cannot be suspicious. "Do you know what happened to one of the girls who left a few days ago?" *It's awful to just say she left, isn't it? When you know what really happened?* "Not the little one, who went with the doctor, but the tall one, with dark brown hair. Did you ever see her leave the school?"

And the groundskeeper grabs me.

He wrenches me away from the shelves, deep into the suffocating clouds of flowers and leaves. Shit, shit, *shit*. The rabbit screeches. I try to pull away, to slip from his grasp, but he fumbles for my sleeve and drags me closer to him, a hand clamped over his own mouth, making a hissing sound. He's so much bigger than me, he's so *strong*.

"*What—*"

"Shhh!"

Wait. He's not hissing. He's shushing.

His eyes flick in a panic over my shoulder, toward the school. He pulls me further in, further, until we're swallowed by the plants, leaves brushing my face and tickling the back of my neck. The air is thick with petals. Sweat collects at the bead of my throat; humidity gathers in the dip of my collarbones.

He lets go.

My heart beats so hard it feels as if it's trying to come up my throat. We're at the center of the greenhouse now, surrounded on all sides so it seems as if the plants go on forever.

Neither of us can catch our breath. I put fingers over my throat to feel my pulse thrumming. The groundskeeper's hands fumble over themselves as if he's trying to reach for something, find something.

He's . . . he's doing the same thing I do. His hands are fluttering. Like mine.

Oh God, he's like me.

Of course. Of course he doesn't speak. Of course he's here. This is what happens to people like me if we don't have the money for tutors, if we refuse to listen, if we don't have wombs that are worth the effort. He's scared. He's cornered. Like me.

The groundskeeper flaps a hand in my direction. I nod desperately. "What?" I say. "What is it? Could—can you write? Could you write it down?"

In a rush, he shakes his head.

"That's fine," I say. "Try to tell me anyway."

He points to the school.

"The school," I repeat, so he knows I understand.

He thinks for a moment, anxiously fidgeting, before he covers his face with both hands. It's a strange movement: one hand across the mouth, with the other above the nose, fingers parted to show his eyes but only barely.

Covering his face.

Like . . .

Like a spirit's face is covered by the caul. Like the spirits reaching out, the speaking tiles.

"Yes," I say. "Yes, yes, exactly. *Exactly.* Is there a haunting here? Can you show me where it is?"

But as soon as I say that, the groundskeeper flinches. He backs away. He steps toward the front of the greenhouse, away from me.

What?

I stumble after him, pushing leaves out of the way as I go. "Sir? Do you know?"

With shaking hands, the groundskeeper picks up the bundle of lavenders and shoves them into my arms. He won't look at me.

"Please," I say. "Just tell me where it is."

With a frustrated, heartbroken whine, he opens the door and shoos me out.

I step outside and turn to face him again, mouth opening to say something, anything, but he closes the door and walks away.

I stand there for a moment, breathing hard, clutching the flowers to my chest. I can't see a thing out here that would have made him panic. It's just the broad, ugly expanse of the school, the walls, the dead grass. Disgust, exhaustion, claustrophobia, but no terror. Not now.

A hand over the mouth, a hand over the eyes.

12

I spend that night thinking of the groundskeeper. What would it be like to be silent? What would it be like to have grown up to be someone like him, instead of someone like me? Whatever I am?

The dormitory is cold, and this late, everyone else is so quiet I almost forget they exist. I roll over in bed, tuck the blankets up to my chin.

There's no point in mulling over impossible hypotheticals. They won't get me anywhere.

But to meet someone with the same hands as mine—

Why does it always have to be *here*?

*A hand over the mouth*, the rabbit says, *a hand over the eyes.*

As rhythmic as the beating of a heart, I press my lips to the bloody handkerchief again, hold it under my pillow, and in the morning, I put it in my pocket like a good luck charm. I don't believe in good luck charms, but I do it anyway.

✦

I have my first of Headmaster's private lessons the next day. "Miss Bell?" he says, poking his head into Mrs. Forrester's room as we're going over canto fourteen of *The Angel in the House*. I'm struggling to keep up with the class. "Why don't we come down to my office?"

Despite the rush of dread, I am darkly curious what the course of treatment will be, if only from an academic perspective. I can't picture the use of medicines or invasive procedures. Besides—it's a *lesson*. Headmaster escorts me from the classroom down to the first floor. He asks how classes are going. I answer, "Fine."

"That's always good to hear," Headmaster says, opening his door for me. "After you."

The war trophies shimmer over his shoulder.

The haunted relics. Right there. In front of me.

I step inside, dipping my head respectfully, and Headmaster takes a pile of cloth from his desk to place it in my arms.

"Here," he says.

It's men's clothes. *My* men's clothes. With the blood cleaned off, the collar starched, the wrinkles ironed out. I thought I'd never see these again. The coat George gave me was lost to bloodstains during the surgery, but it's been replaced by an even nicer one. It's all in better condition than even I'd managed to keep it. When one of the girls was doing laundry, did she have to clean these? Did she know it was for me?

But I don't like the implication. I already feel uneasy.

"Go ahead and change into those," Headmaster says. I turn for the dressing room, but he stops me. "No, here is fine. I'll be outside."

He steps out into the hall and shuts the door.

I've been so desperate to have these clothes back. To have this little part of myself in my hands again. There's even the strip of cloth that keeps my chest flat. After all this, I want nothing more than to slip back into these. No matter how untailored or ill-fitting they are, they're mine, and I missed them. I missed them and everything they mean to me.

But at the same time, I don't want to put this on at all. I don't want to expose my masculinity, bare my manhood in any way that would leave it vulnerable.

*You know what will happen if you don't.*

Disobeying a man like Headmaster is a bad idea.

So I strip, and at least this time I get to do it alone. I put on the clothes. I flatten my hair with pins, put on the hat the best I can without a mirror, even wrap myself up in the scarf. I press the fabric to my mouth and take a deep breath. All I need is just one moment to savor it.

And then, carefully, I go past Headmaster's desk. To his wall of haunted artifacts. None of these belong here, on a shelf in a school. They belong wherever they fell, wherever they were taken from—more broken pieces of statues, a human bone I recognize as a metatarsal, a pale crystal. It doesn't feel right to touch any of them, let alone remove them. These hauntings have been through enough. But I have to, so I find the smallest one. A button, the size of my pinkie nail. It seems the most mundane, the one with the least pain attached to it. I take it and pull the bloody handkerchief from my dress on the floor and wrap it around and around until the shimmer of the haunting is smothered, and jam it deep in my pocket.

Headmaster knocks on the door. "Changed?" he says.

I'm barefoot, so my steps are silent as I fumble back to the chair in front of his desk. "Yes, sir," I say, sitting to put down my shoes like I had been in this spot the whole time.

Please don't let Headmaster notice.

Heat creeps up the back of my neck as he steps in. He glances up and down, regards me, hums. I don't like it, but as long as he's looking at me and not the wall . . .

"Interesting," Headmaster says. "You really do seem more comfortable like this." He goes back to the other side of the desk, pushes his glasses farther up his nose, skims over a page or two of his notes. "That is to be expected. Veil sickness can manifest itself in the strangest ways, and healing will be difficult as long as you cling to this masculinity. Does that make sense?"

No. Because this is not a sickness. This is me. "Yes, sir."

"So it will be in our best interest for you to understand the negatives of masculinity. For you to understand that this is not the role you were meant to take. I'm sure you understand it consciously, but *unconsciously* may be a different story. You need to experience the truth depth of manhood, in your body as well as your mind, so you understand that it is not meant for you."

What does that mean?

*What is he going to do to you?*

Headmaster says, "What is masculinity to you?"

I open my mouth to respond . . .

But I don't know.

I don't actually know what masculinity is. I could sit here and talk about the masculine ideal, the standard men are expected to live up to—competitive, strong, chivalrous. A polite, collected man of good breeding. The problem is, I am none of those things. Any answer I give will be self-incriminating.

*Why are you trying to prove anything to him? Tell him what he wants to hear.*

"Um," I say. "Masculinity is strength. Not just strength of body, but of will. Of being a protector and provider."

Headmaster nods. "*Protector.* Do you see yourself as a protector?"

My immediate response would be that I do. I am a protector of the body, a doctor, a *surgeon*. Or I will be, one day. I know guts and bones. I know how to manipulate the body and change it, how to break flesh to save it.

Headmaster takes my silence as an answer. The wrong answer. "Exactly. Are you a provider?"

I could be, I would be more than happy to be, if only I was allowed to.

"And do you consider yourself strong?"

I've had to be. To make it this far, being a person like this.

"I was a soldier," Headmaster says. "I wasn't a pampered medium in the ranks, either—sure, I did my fair share of spirit-work, but I fought, just like any other man. I did my duty for the crown, and I did it well. And I learned a lot about what it means to be a man in a place like that." I feel ill. "Being a man means being willing to do whatever needs to be done to protect your family, your countrymen, this empire. And it is very, very difficult. It is the sort of thing someone like you is not built to do. That is not an insult, Miss Bell. It is simply a statement of fact."

All at once, I want to take off these clothes and burn them—I would miss them, of course I would, but it's the only way to keep them safe from what Headmaster is saying.

"Do you think you could make it?" Headmaster says. "In war?"

"Does a man have to fight in a war to be a man?" I ask.

Headmaster's face screws up. "If you ask me? Yes. Just like a woman does not fully experience womanhood if she doesn't bear her own children. No man is really a man until he has to defend the crown. War is the greatest creator of real men in the civilized world."

He watches me for a reaction. I'm not sure I have one. He taps on his lip with his pen, glances down at his notes again.

"I do not think you would make it in war," he says.

"I don't think so, either," I reply.

*So you admit it? You're not a man?*

That's not what that means. It just means we are different kinds of men. There's nothing wrong with that.

Headmaster gestures. "And yet, here we are. And yet this persists. This is what I mean by *unconscious*, that Veil sickness is *unconscious*—the body must be convinced as much as the mind. So, to heal, we must convince the body." He stands, straightens up, buttons up his suit jacket. "Put on that coat. We're going for a walk."

✦

Everyone else is in class, so nobody sees Headmaster lead me down the hall, but my head is still on a swivel. My fingers anxiously tap against my leg. Headmaster laughs, puts a hand on my shoulder and squeezes it.

He does not notice the button.

"I can't believe Lord Luckenbill mistook you for a man," he says. "Either it was quite dark at that gala, or he needs a better pair of glasses."

We go out the back door of the school. I look for the groundskeeper but do not see him. It's bitterly cold. It isn't snowing, though it smells like it's trying to, with a crisp wind biting through my coat and ruffling my hair. My lungs hurt when I try to breathe in.

"Have you ever been in a fight before, Miss Bell?" Headmaster asks.

The rabbit watches carefully.

"No," I say.

"Mm." He holds out his hand. "When you throw a punch, make sure that you're not holding your thumb. It's a surefire way to break it, or at least shove it out of its socket. You would know all about how that works, though, considering how much you take after that brother of yours."

He says, "Hit me."

I say, "What?"

And then Headmaster grabs my shoulders and shoves. I can't keep my balance. I fall. Brittle blades of brown grass crack under my hands. Condensation smears my palms and sticks to my legs.

"Sir—" I gasp.

Headmaster stands over me. He puts a foot on my waist, presses down hard enough that the corner of the pelvis aches against his shoe; he reaches under my hat to grab my hair and pull my head off the ground like he's going to rip a chunk out of my scalp.

"Fight back," he says. "You think you're a boy, go ahead, fight back."

He drops me. My skull hits the dirt and my teeth clack together. I try to back away, dig my hands into the grass and claw myself away, but he stops me. He's on top of me.

He's putting his hands around my neck.

He squeezes. Tight. Like it's the easiest thing in the world.

There are two places to squeeze around the neck: the major arteries leading to the brain, and the windpipe. If you squeeze the arteries, the victim can continue to breathe, but it restricts blood flow to the brain. You'll get dizzy, and your vision will start to fade, but it doesn't hurt because the suffocation signal comes from the lungs, not the brain, which is a bit of a design flaw. However, constricting the windpipe itself keeps air from getting to the lungs in the first place. It sends the entire body into a panic.

Headmaster is squeezing both.

I grab his wrists, try to pull them away, buck my hips to get him off me so I can use my legs to kick. But he's heavy. He's too big. My lungs burn. The rabbit screams. *He's going to kill you. He's going to kill you. Say it, say you're not a man; it's the only way he'll let go.* I try to get air into my lungs to speak, to make noise, but I can't. I beat at his shoulders, hit the side of his face.

"Oh, come on," he says. "There's no quarter in war, Miss Bell—go for the eyes, the nose. It's easy enough." He doesn't seem tired at all. I'm barely fazing him. "Do it. I'm telling you to."

I can't. My body won't let me. No matter how much I tell myself to. It's like my first few attempts at cutting open a pig. I couldn't bring myself to do it. It just . . . wasn't something that was done. I didn't have the strength of will.

I can't even protect myself.

There go the edges of my vision. Darkening. The rabbit squeals, thumps its feet, whirls its eyes. Headmaster squeezes tighter, and I can't quite remember what I'm doing. I'm holding on to his jacket. It slips. My head pounds. I think I can feel my heartbeat.

Headmaster just watches.

And then he lets go.

I gasp for air, and it hits my lungs so hard, so wet and cold it stings. I immediately fly into a fit of desperate coughing.

Headmaster's weight leaves my body as he stands, steps away from me. I roll over onto my stomach, face pressed into the freezing grass. My lungs expand and my chest aches. I can breathe. I can breathe. Before the oxygen hits my brain again, I cradle my burning neck. It will bruise. There will be black and purple marks on my neck for days.

He didn't kill me. Of course he didn't. He was never going to. Of course he wouldn't, of course.

"Up," Headmaster says. "Come on. Up you go."

It takes me a minute to get my feet under me, to stand. Headmaster is just looking at me. *Looking* at me. Like he isn't sure what he's seeing. I don't like that. I shy away. My hat has fallen off, and some of my pins have fallen to the grass.

"There," he says, his voice is oddly soft. "See? A woman's body is naturally weaker. Again, I'm not saying it as an insult; I'm saying it as a matter of biology. There's nothing wrong with that. You're just meant for something else, and that's okay."

I know that being a man is not just about violence. It is not just about being able to fight. There are plenty of men who have never fought, have never gone to war, and they're still men. Like my brother, for instance. And then there are men who *have* fought, who were like me. James Barry fought. Which one of them should I be more like? Do I even have a choice?

"Does that make sense?" Headmaster says. "Do you understand why we had to do this?"

I nod, just to get him to stop.

"Good," he says. "Breathe, Miss Bell, breathe. It's okay. There you go." He ducks down to retrieve the hat, then reaches into my hair to take out the last of the pins. I don't like how kind his hands are. I'd rather he was like Mrs. Forrester, who grabbed my head and held it still as she pulled roughly enough to make me wince. "I know it seems barbaric, but the best way to teach the body is to make sure that it *feels*. There's nothing wrong with that. How are you doing?"

"I'm cold," I say, because I can't manage anything else.

Headmaster nods. "Me too," he says. "I know this is stressful. I know it's a lot to take in. But let me tell you that my wife, your teacher—did you know she had Veil sickness once? She still has her struggles, but she is doing her best, and that is admirable. You could learn a lot from her."

I blink away the frost in my eyelashes, which I think are tears.

"Mrs. Forrester was a student?" I ask, voice hoarse.

"Yes, indeed. I trained her up myself." He smiles. "Come. Let's get back inside."

I put my hands in my pockets and feel the haunted button, still there.

After everything.

Thank God.

✦

Once inside, Headmaster hands me a letter. A reward for enduring his lesson. It is unblemished, unopened. "From your dear Edward," he says.

It reads:

> *Hating matrimonial torches like a crime, she had colored her beautiful face with modest redness and clinging with charming arms on her father's neck she said, 'O dearest father, allow me to enjoy perpetual maidenhood! Diana's father allowed this once.' Indeed he complies, but that beauty forbids you to be what you desire, and your beauty resists your vow.*
>
> Ovid's Metamorphoses, *Book I, 483–489.*
>
> *There has to be a better poem out there for us. I'm looking, I promise.*

Daphne's writing is small and smooth. My hand trembles as I press down the edges. I feel like she's trying to tell me something, but I'm not quite sure what.

I don't write back. I don't want to say something I shouldn't. Not like this.

13

The next morning, Mrs. Forrester arrives with the wake-up bell and stares at me. Isabella's eyes flick to my throat with horror.

When I check in the mirror, it's there: a bruise. Sprawling, but not quite dark enough to veer purple-red, not like I thought it would. It's only yellow, green, the sickly colors. I don't get long to look, since I'm with Louise on breakfast duty, but I don't have to inspect it to know it hurts. My head aches where it was knocked against the frozen ground, and my throat feels swollen every time I swallow. Like Headmaster's hands are still there. The poem Daphne sent chews at the back of my neck.

*That beauty forbids you to be what you desire,* the rabbit says.

At least the haunted button is still safe. I've hidden it under my mattress, with Daphne's letter.

Louise and I prepare eggs and sausage to be served with rolls. I can only be around eggs for so long, and if I must make them, I will not be able to eat them. There's just something about the smell, and the texture, that makes them nigh unpalatable after I think about them for more than a minute. They remind me of chyme. Mrs. Forrester watches us closely to prevent any ill talk.

"Your neck . . ." Louise whispers.

"Let's go, ladies," Mrs. Forrester snaps. "Miss Hare, keep your hands to yourself. And Miss Bell, *please* keep the sausages from burning!"

In most situations, I would be chastened—but I have a plan.

I cannot get to the speaking tiles in the parlor, so I make them by tearing letters out of *The Angel in the House* during a lecture on womanly self-sacrifice. I'm nearly caught when Headmaster comes to audit the class and sits beside me. I push the paper bits under the booklet.

"How are you feeling this morning?" Headmaster whispers to me as his wife continues to speak on household management and servant salaries.

"Good," I say.

"Oh, that's wonderful," Headmaster says. "Don't worry if you don't feel any different in regard to your treatment. Sometimes it takes a while; sometimes you don't notice that anything has changed at all." I nod absently. "Nothing worth doing ever happens quickly. I hope those bruises heal soon."

I push my fingers into the darkest part of the injury, right by my carotid artery. "Thank you, sir."

I have been taught all my life to avoid spirit-work, just like every violet-eyed woman in the empire—every violet-eyed *person* who doesn't have that seal on their hand. That's not to say I was ever explicitly told. If there's one thing I know about people, it's that they never say things clearly. Instead, I grew up with the 1841 Speaker Act, the removal of execution from Tower Hill before returning spirit-work crimes to public view, the whispers and hisses of danger. Then, of course, stories run in the newspapers of madwomen drowning their children. Father spoke of unrest in the colonies due to unregulated spirit-work. And when it comes to people like me, our lives are eighty years of promising we are not monsters in waiting. Either you give yourself over to the Speakers or, apparently, you fall ill.

Most violet-eyed women—at least the English ones, with pale skin and posh accents—are more than happy to do what they're told. They will take being beneath powerful men if it means they are placed above everyone else. They will be subservient to Speaker lords, take all the privileges that gives them, and turn on the rest with a smile.

Where do I fall? Someone like me, who is only a woman in the eyes of others?

See, the first time Mother caught me in boy's clothing, she did not tell Father. I was thirteen. She waited until Father had gone to work before she made me tea, sat me down in the parlor, and held my hand.

She told me she knew I had been struggling. That I had made such great progress, but things were still so difficult. She said, with my violet eyes, things might be more difficult for me than they should be, and she was sorry. She would make things easier for me if only she could.

So, she told me, she understood why I would pretend to be a boy. It really does seem like men have it easier. They have more freedom, more chances, more opportunities. But being a woman is a wonderful thing, and there is so much to love about it, and we do important work in the world. We are men's helpers, and we shape the next generation of England with our children. Being a woman is nothing to be ashamed of. You'll come to love it, she said, and there is nothing wrong with us.

"Don't let your father hear that," she laughed. It was strange to hear her talk of him that way—she was able to marry for love, something I would never be able to do, and she'd fallen in love with a man like him? How dare she. "He's a bit old-fashioned."

I didn't know how to explain to her that I didn't want to be a boy because it was *easier* than being a girl. I wasn't *pretending*.

It was just that my girlhood was—and still is—simply, factually, incorrect.

When Headmaster leaves, I scrape the makeshift speaking tiles into my pocket and wait for night to come.

◆

It is hard to sleep. I stay awake in bed, holding the button under my pillow, rolling it between my fingers. The tiles are there too, and I have to be careful not to accidentally brush them away. It takes a while for the dormitory to settle; Charlotte has a difficult time getting comfortable, tossing and turning. The room is so dark that my vision begins to sparkle against the black ceiling, the mind creating little things to focus on due to a lack of visual stimuli.

I wonder if Daphne is lying awake right now too. If she's looking at the same moon.

I hope she is.

When Charlotte finally stops moving, I count to one hundred to assure myself she is actually asleep. One, two, three, four. The fire has gone down to embers, the wind whistling outside. Louise snores lightly. The school creaks and settles. And the rabbit paces restlessly, trapped in the confines of my ribcage, inconsolable. I don't remember how long I've had this thing living in my bones. I just remember being a little child and realizing something was compressing my lungs. It wasn't pneumonia, or consumption, or a tumor. It was just a scared rabbit.

Ninety-eight, ninety-nine . . .

As soon as I reach one hundred, I sit up in bed, loose hair tumbling around my shoulders and one stocking slipped down to my shin. I gather the button and speaking tiles before slipping into the washroom. George and I have quiet feet from years of sneaking around our parents, our memories sharpened by the time it took to learn all the creaking spots on the stairs and floor. It's not that it was *bad* to be noticed. We just . . . didn't want to be. Especially not me.

The washroom is small but impressive for a building that had probably once been a country estate. The indoor plumbing is advanced, especially this far from a large city. It'd be nice to pull some cold water from the tap to splash my face. I'm sure it'd help wake me up, ward off some of this exhaustion. But I don't want to risk the rattling of the pipes. So instead I sit with my back against the tub and spread the paper tiles across the floor.

The haunted button goes right in the middle. It doesn't feel right, to take a haunting. To move it from where it sat. If he were a better person, Headmaster would have left this button where he found it, or at least taken the time to return it to wherever it'd come from.

But if the Speakers can use the dead to guide their hand—if they can ask slain soldiers about enemy plans and demand the truth from executed spies—then so can I.

So why am I afraid?

*Because you know what will happen if you're caught.*

*You know what happens to little girls who play with ghosts.*

I peel the boundary of the haunting. Just a little.

The void is dark and infinite and cold. It is difficult to look at for too long, like eye contact. Chilled air swirls around me like I've opened a window; I smell fresh-cut flowers and thunderstorms. I take the torn edge, pull it, unravel the threads holding the world together. No human should be able to do this. It's nothing like a scalpel going through skin. It's just—wrong.

Behind the tear, something moves. Flitting like a fish under the surface of a lake, or a shadow going by the window.

A spirit.

It is elongated, with the strange proportions that tell me this person has been dead for some time. Its arms are too long, its face blurred, more like a spill of kerosene on cobblestones than a person. I don't know enough about spirits to mark the time of death, but if I had to guess—a decade? More? Despite that, it has the mark of its death: a blasted torso, suspended at the moment it was blown apart, each of the limbs disjointed strangely. Its mouth opens, closes, opens, closes as if it can't remember what to do with it.

This is not Ellen. Or Frances. It can't be.

*But that is what the groundskeeper saw, right? A spirit?*

A hand over the mouth, a hand over the eyes.

I don't know. But this has to mean something, right? Even if it's not who I'm looking for? Maybe I can learn something. Find a clue.

I lean forward, to the void, reaching out for the spirit. My hand burns. This is what the branding iron would have felt like against the back of my palm. That's what the Speakers do; they place the iron through the Veil and hold it there until it is cold enough to mark the skin permanently. I heard, in the early days, it was difficult to keep the metal from sticking to the skin; a botched branding once left a man with no flesh on the back of his hand at all.

The makeshift speaking tiles begin to move. I doubt it for just a second—it could just be a draft, these are paper after all—but when they start to make recognizable patterns, I know it's the spirit peering through.

WHO ARE YOU

I breathe in. Like George taught me.

WHERE AM I

"My name is Bell," I whisper, because I do not want to lie, but I also do not want to tell the truth. But then I pause. Can spirits hear me? I genuinely don't know. I spell my last name with the tiles, just in case: BELL. "You're at a school just outside of London." Then, after a moment, because you can never be sure, I add, "London is in England." LONDON ENGLAND. But I didn't rip out enough Ns. So it actually spells LONDON ENGLAD.

The spirit shimmers. Its mouth, if it had teeth, would click and clack. If it had bones, the joints would pop and snap.

The tiles move again.

WHERE IS CAPTAIN FORRESTER IS H HR

My first reaction is: I swear I made more E's. But my second?

Captain Forrester.

This spirit is talking about Headmaster.

He was a captain once. Right there, on his desk: Captain Ernest Forrester. He must have been somewhere in the colonies, India maybe—there'd been some war going on there, hadn't there? Isn't there always, where the Empire is concerned?

There's only one reason why this spirit would know his name.

Headmaster hurt him.

Headmaster probably killed him.

"Yes," I say, "he runs this school." My heart beats hard in my throat. I try to steady it with a finger to my pulse, but I can't press in. The bruise is too painful. I spell, HEADMASTER. "Why?"

RUN

The scraps of papers flutter. The spirit makes a long, low noise, like the wind howling in a storm or the last rattling breath squeezed out of a dead man's lungs.

HE DID THIS TO US

Spirits have no reason to lie. So they never do.

The tiles in the parlor spelling *STOP THIS HELP US BEFORE THEY TAKE YOU TOO.* This spirit telling us to *RUN.* They know something. They all do. I grab the tiles, start to rearrange them again; FRANCES. ELLEN. "Do you know these names? Do you know these girls? I'm looking for them, something's happened—"

The paper scraps say, NO. My heart sinks.

Then: *click.*

I realize, all at once, that I forgot to lock the door.

Louise stares at me, on the threshold of the washroom, eyes blown wide like she's just stumbled across a murder. The spirit retreats in a fumble of letter scraps. Pieces blow across the wooden floor.

"What—" Louise whispers, pointing to the tear in the Veil. "What is that?"

She knows exactly what it is.

I brace myself on the tub to stand. Louise isn't like Charlotte. She's not going to run to Headmaster and Mrs. Forrester to tell on me. Right?

I say, "It's not what you think."

Louise lets out a long, shaky breath, then reaches for the

little vanity by the sink and plucks a pair of scissors from the sewing kit.

She holds them like a weapon. Pointed right at me.

The blade gleams in the moonlight coming through the little window above the bathtub. Her grip is shaky and unsure, but that doesn't change the fact that scissors are dangerous. Either they are sharp and they will do a lot of damage, or they are dull and they will do a hell of a lot more—and someone who doesn't know what they're doing is a bigger risk than someone who does.

"Close it," she says. Her voice trembles. The scissors shake. "Now."

I raise my hands. My heart thrums in my throat, but I do not let my voice break. A surgeon does not falter. He can't.

I reach down and push the Veil closed. The world sews itself back together. Thankfully, this time it does not hit with the sound of a thunderclap—it is a small enough tear that it only sounds like a pop. It still makes me wince. It still makes Louise look over her shoulder toward the dormitory, her chest rising and falling rapidly. If my ears were any keener, I'm sure I could hear the desperate thrumming of her heartbeat.

"There," I whisper. "There. It's gone."

Louise gasps for air, leaning against the door. She does not drop the scissors.

I have no idea what to say.

"Why would you—" she whispers. "You can't—"

"Louise."

"It's not allowed," she manages. "Why would you do

that? It's not—no." She shakes her head helplessly, pointing the blades at the button on the floor. "Did you *steal* that from Headmaster? Oh God. He'll hurt you if he finds out. He'll hurt all of us."

Of course she's scared. So am I.

I glance to the scissors; her eyes follow. This is just like talking to a worried patient. Right? That's all.

"You're right," I say. "If Headmaster found out, he'd be unhappy."

"He'll hurt us."

I know.

I say, "You don't want to hurt me, do you?"

She shakes her head. Her big eyes fill with tears. "No. No."

"So put the scissors down."

It doesn't work. She only grips them tighter.

*What makes you think she won't do it? Ellen did it, so why couldn't she?*

"I'm not going to put them down until you leave. Go to bed." She wipes her eyes with her free hand. "I'm sorry."

Slowly, with my hands where she can see them, I gather the speaking tiles and dump them into the commode. And then I pick up the button. Hold it up. Show her with fingers spread.

"I'll get rid of it," I say. "I promise." I have no idea how. "Flush that when you're done."

Louise steps aside so I can leave, but she does not point the scissors away from me until the door is closed. She watches me through the crack with one single, whirling eye until the lock slides into place.

✦

The next morning, Louise stares at me across the break-fast table. She grips her fork like she might use it against me. The button itself is wrapped up in that handkerchief again, tucked into the pocket of my uniform, and having it so close makes me too sick to eat. I'm not sure what to do with it. When Headmaster wanders too close, I flinch. I hope he thinks it's just the memory of his hands around my throat. Maybe it is, partially.

While washing the dishes afterwards, I pop open the kitchen door to the back garden—what had once been a servant's entrance—and jam the button into the snow, against the wall, while Mrs. Forrester is busy telling off Isabella for her downcast eyes. The snow covers the haunt-ing's shimmer. It's the only thing I can think of to do that isn't horrifically disrespectful to the spirit attached to it. What other options are there? Burning it? Flushing it?

I pause for a moment, looking out toward the garden, in case the groundskeeper is nearby.

*Stupid*, the rabbit chides. *Too risky*. I know.

"Miss Bell!" Mrs. Forrester snaps. "Don't let in the cold!"

I shut the door. "Sorry. Just checking the weather."

"There's nothing to check. It's bitter out there."

I want to tell Isabella everything.

I want to tell her to run.

I wish that, if I did, we actually could.

14

That evening, I am put on laundry duty with Charlotte. As much as I like laundry, I can't help the disappointment; I prefer to do it alone, as I do most things, and I was hoping I could at least shake the rugs on the steps, or dump the water in the back garden myself.

If I said aloud why I wanted to, Charlotte would accuse me of having a crush. Or worse. But I need to see the groundskeeper again. My first attempt at finding Frances and Ellen didn't work—but more than that, it was the wrong place to start. I've misunderstood what I was told, like usual. There's something I missed. Something he *knows*. And I won't let him run away from me this time.

A hand over the mouth, a hand over the eyes.

The laundry room is a dark closet in the back of the school, badly lit and claustrophobic. There are several large tubs of lye soap, and we take all the dirty clothes to mend them and push them into the vats. Tomorrow, we'll spend most of the day boiling, scrubbing, and wringing the clothes over and over again. Maybe we'll be let out of class to do it. Any chance to get away from Headmaster, I'll take.

*RUN*

"You look tired," Charlotte says as she rolls up her sleeves. "Come on, put a smile on that face. Aren't you excited for the garden party?"

Shit, I'd completely forgotten about the garden party. There's been no sign of preparation, and none of the girls have brought it up, like they're all trying to pretend it isn't happening. If Charlotte is excited, I dread it.

"Frowning causes wrinkles," she says.

I can't help myself. Not because I *want* to correct her, but because I don't like letting incorrect information just hang there. "So does smiling."

"Well." She scoffs as we start filling the tubs. "You know what's meant by smiling. You don't really have to *smile*, show your teeth or anything like that. Just have a pleasant expression." She gestures at herself. "Like this."

But I've learned I am bad at expressions—several times in my life, Mother has admonished me for my dour glare when I thought I looked agreeable—so I don't try.

Charlotte is a conundrum to me. She seems to be absolutely everything Braxton's could want from a girl. She's quiet, and obedient, and believes *everything* Headmaster and Mrs. Forrester say. Do they still consider her Veil-sick? I don't know why they would. She's a better enforcer of womanly virtues than either of them.

Of course, Charlotte decides we must continue talking while we work. "How was your first lesson with Headmaster?" she says. "You haven't said much about it."

I pick up the first uniform dress to push it into the soap. I thought my bruises said enough. They haven't yet begun to fade, and the swelling makes it hard to eat or drink. Charlotte's eyes visibly dart away from them every time she looks at me, as if she is drawn to them but terrified to face what they mean. "There isn't much to speak of," I say.

"I don't believe that." When she passes me another dress, she does it with the most delicate, dainty hand. She's trying so, *so* hard to make everything look feminine and effortless. She even walks with the most choreographed little movements. *You should be more like her. You'd have a better chance of survival if you at least tried.* "I'm interested in Headmaster's tactics. I'm just grateful for him, is all."

I blink at her. "You're grateful?"

"Of course I am," Charlotte says. "Aren't you?"

No. In what version of the world would I be?

"We all should be," Charlotte says. "Mrs. Forrester is. He saved her, did you know that?"

"I did."

For a moment, it seems like Charlotte might swoon. She holds one of the fancier dresses meant for visits with suitors to her chest, spinning around dreamily. This has to be some kind of defense mechanism—she can't actually believe this. "Sometimes, when it's just us," she says, "I call him Captain. Mrs. Forrester is so lucky." She drops the dress from her body, still smiling, and hands it back over to me. "You should think better of him. He's doing a lot for us."

I say, "He tried to strangle me."

"Well, what did you do to deserve it?" The audacity of the question stuns me. "He wouldn't do that for no reason. I know he has unconventional tactics, but—" She shakes her head. I struggle to recover from the mental shock. "He fixed me, but only because I realized I had to be fixed, and we had to convince my body of the same."

Convince the body. Just like how he explained it. "Question."

"Yes?" she chirps.

"When you say *convince the body*, what does that mean?"

Charlotte ponders this for a moment. Her nose wrinkles in confusion before she thinks better of herself, massaging her face to undo the damage that frowning does to the complexion.

"I know there's so much talk about the human soul being corrupt, original sin and all that," she says, "and don't get me wrong, I believe in that. We all have urges we have to work to overcome. But I also like to think our hearts and souls know what's best for us. They *want* what will help us, even if our innate nature isn't quite there yet. It's the body that is stuck in the actions, in the bad pattern. And if we convince the body to do what's right, it can help put us in alignment with what our soul knows it should be. Does that make sense?"

*Headmaster is trying to rewrite you from the ground up. Just like your tutors. Just like everyone has always tried to.*

I hate that the rabbit has a point. Headmaster thinks he can remove my boyhood from me because, to him, it is an affliction of the body. It's part of my Veil sickness. But he's wrong. He can't get rid of it. No matter how hard he pushes me, how many times he wraps his hands around my neck, how many times he tells me what a man really is.

"And you believe this?" I ask.

Charlotte's eyes flash. A darkness shadows her smile. "Of *course* I do."

"I wasn't—" I start, because I wasn't accusing her of anything. I just wanted to know. But she's already gone back to the pile of laundry. I suppose that's my fault, for assuming she would answer honestly.

"Let's make this quick," she says. "I want to get back to my reading."

What is it like, to be like this? To live like this, to believe this. It feels like a fate worse than death. Though maybe this is all an act. Maybe Charlotte is just doing what she needs to do to survive in a place like this. To get out. To make it.

I can't blame her for that.

✦

It's through luck that I find the groundskeeper again. I see him after lights-out, when the fire is down to embers but the grandfather clock on the first floor hasn't rung midnight. I see him through the window by the headboard of my bed, working, sweeping snow. He's bundled up tight, tucked into his scarf and mittens.

It must be easier to work at night. It's colder, yes, but there's nobody to bother you. It's nice to be alone. I'm envious.

I pull my shawl from under the bed and slip out into the hall. It seems strange that the door is left unlocked, but it makes sense, because where would we go? Even if we made it out of the school itself, the wall is brick and the gate is solid iron.

The library is directly under the dormitory, so that is where I look first. And there he is: he wanders down the row of ornamental bushes planted against the school, shaking snow off the branches so they aren't damaged by the weight. I climb on the table in front of the window, careful not to knock over the matching vases of flowers. Knock on the glass twice. *Tap tap.*

The groundskeeper looks up with a start, but when he recognizes me, he smiles. He looks older when he smiles. I unlatch the window and push it open. It's the same kind of suffocating, bitter cold that jammed itself into my lungs when Headmaster brought me out to the back garden. The same cold as the Veil.

*You're alone with a man. Again.*

"You're working late," I say.

He makes an apathetic noise, as if to tell me there's no reason to worry.

For the first time in my life, I've found mirrors for myself. Daphne, and now him. It's bizarre to witness these parts of myself—whatever they are, for if they have names, I don't know them—separated. I'd tied them together in my mind. As if my inability to grasp the intricacies of other people means I failed to also grasp the meaning of my sex at a basic level; as if one thing *caused* the other. Headmaster seems to think they're one and the same. Mother and Father do too. To see them divided disproves that.

And I had to find them both *here?*

I have so many questions, but I can't ruin this. He can't run from me again.

So instead, I gesture to the bandage around the groundskeeper's hand. "How is it healing?"

When he puts his palm in mine, I take off his mitten and unpeel the bandages. His hands are large and rough like gravel.

"Look," I say. "It's doing well." I trace a finger around the puncture site, as close as possible without touching. "I don't see much in the way of pus. That's good. We want as little of that as possible." Then, around what had once been the site of the abscess: "This is far less inflamed, too. Does it still hurt?"

He makes a gesture with his free hand—*a little*, it seems to say.

"That's to be expected," I say. "As long as it's not excruciating."

He takes his hand from me and shakes it out in the same kind of motion I do. I can't keep myself from mimicking him. It feels good, easing the tension in my muscles, letting me breathe a little easier. The groundskeeper's eyes light up. And then it's just the two of us, standing there in the cold—me sitting on the table surrounded by flowers, him with snow stuck to his mittens—laughing quietly into our hands.

It's been a long time since this part of me has felt *joyful*. As my tutors attempted to "fix" me, they belittled and insulted me. They said I would forever be off-putting and unlovable if I didn't train out this part of myself. I had to stop flapping my hands, and rocking on my feet, and repeating the words said to me like some kind of parrot. They told me there was no joy to be had in this. But of *course* there is, because I don't just flap and rock when I am upset. I do them when I'm happy too. When I'm happy, I am so happy my body can't contain it. And the way my mind understands things, like surgery, like the tick and click of a body, like anatomy and all the interweaving pieces of human flesh—I get it, I *get it*, I *understand*. How wonderful is that?

*But it makes you unlovable.*

Right. There it is.

*Nobody cares how happy it makes you if they can't stand to be around you.*

That's not true. The groundskeeper likes me. *He hardly counts.* And Daphne likes me too. She saw my hysterics and agreed to help me anyway. We're friends, aren't we?

*You've met her all of once.*

With a rush of shame, I jam my hands between my thighs to warm them. And maybe to keep them still. The groundskeeper watches me curiously.

I have to ask.

"I. . . um. About the thing you showed me."

I extricate my hands to mimic his motion: a hand over the mouth, a hand over the eyes. In doing so, the misunderstanding becomes clear. Why would he do that when he meant a spirit? Spirits still have mouths. It's the only thing they have left. I drop my hands.

"I tried to look for them, for the girls," I tell him. "I found a haunting, but I didn't find *them*. What did you—"

But before I can finish asking what he meant, the groundskeeper reaches into his pocket and holds out the haunted button.

The one I left outside, buried under the snow in the bushes by the servant's door in the kitchen.

Shit.

"Yes," I say, almost instinctively going to cover it up. He recoils, tucking it to his chest, away from me. "Yes, that's what I used. Please, don't—don't let anyone know you have it." He backs up, and once he's out of my reach, he holds the button to the light of the moon, lets it twinkle between his fingers like a star. His eyes are bright. Anxiety thrums in my chest like the rabbit. Put it away, put it away. "What are you trying to tell me? If it's not a spirit, then what?"

He doesn't answer.

Because his eyes snap from the button to the library door. Right over my shoulder.

The same way a prey animal freezes in the presence of a predator.

"Miss Bell," Mrs. Forrester says. "Groundskeeper."

No. No, no, not her.

*RUN*

Any goodwill I'd built with Mrs. Forrester is dashed against the rocks. I know, logically, this school would not dare to anger Lord Luckenbill. They would not hurt me, risk incurring the wrath of his money and status.

But there are lots of things that can be done to someone while keeping them alive. Surgery looks a lot like torture, and the bruises around my neck have not yet faded.

*Look what you did look what you did.*

"Here I was, going up to check on the girls because I had a bit of a hunch," Mrs. Forrester says, "and guess who was missing? You know, I almost gave you the benefit of the doubt. You've been a polite girl since you arrived, circumstances notwithstanding. And this is where I find you?" She turns to the groundskeeper. "And *you*. What is that? Give it to me. Now."

"He didn't do anything wrong," I whisper.

The groundskeeper shuffles to the window, chastened like a toddler, and Mrs. Forrester snatches the haunted button from the groundskeeper's hand. He flinches. Mrs. Forrester inspects it, rolls it over in her fingers, brings it to her face to sniff.

"I," she says, pointing to him, "will deal with you later. But." Her eyes snap to me. "You. Alone, with a man." Alone with a man that is not a Luckenbill, she means. Alone with a man that is not the *right* man, because they don't care what's done to me as long as it's a proper Speaker that does it. "Do you understand how this looks?"

"I'm sorry." It's the only thing I can say.

"Look at me. Eyes up, Miss Bell, eyes up."

I turn. I do as I'm told. It is like trying to swallow cold vomit, too thick, too heavy, too *much*. The anvil on my sternum returns.

Mrs. Forrester looks so, so disappointed.

"Dear me," she says. "What will we do about this?"

15

I stand outside of Headmaster's office while he and Mrs. Forrester speak inside. None of the lamps are lit. It's dark. I've been told to stay here, so I will. My heel won't stop tapping.

*Tap tap tap tap.*

After a few minutes, Mrs. Forrester steps out of the office. I don't look up, and this time, she allows that.

"I believe we have allowed our lessons on obedience to become lax," she says. "This will be rectified with a presentation tomorrow for all students." Then she shoves a letter into my hand. It's been opened, the paper unfurled. My stomach drops. This one's been opened. "This came for you."

I tuck it to my chest. "Thank you, ma'am."

✦

With a candle, on my bed, I squint at the letter. It begins

without a name, but it's Daphne's handwriting, so there's no question who it's meant for.

> Dearest,
>
> I hope you're doing well, away from me. I'm certainly not, away from you. A shame that our first meeting wasn't warmer, or kinder—but as a show of goodwill, to prove that I only wish the best for your heart, I promised that I would send after some childhood friends of yours. Indeed, I've done so.

I . . . have no idea what she's referring to. I don't have any friends. The sentimental language at the beginning is distracting.

> And because of that, I must admit, I'm hesitant to deliver this disappointing news. So far, I've been unable to locate either of them. No records of marriage or children, or—God forbid—illness or death. Strange, then, that they've just disappeared, but then again, I'm not surprised that someone like you has fallen in with strange friends. My deepest apologies.
>
> I will continue my search; perhaps there are some avenues I've yet to find. Please do take care of yourself, and I cannot wait to know more of you.

She writes as if we hardly know each other. I suppose that's fair, but it makes my stomach twist. And besides, what is she *on* about—

Oh.

Of course. Daphne would be smart enough to disguise this as a letter between lovers; she's writing in disguise. The implications fall into place. There's no trace of Frances or Ellen at all. No death records. Absolutely nothing at all. I let out a shaky breath. Headmaster would be too smart to let the names slip into any sort of record. Braxton's is a very, very good place for people to disappear.

The letter has been signed, simply and plainly, *"Yours."* The paper has been dotted lightly with perfume.

And then, a postscript:

> *Ovid's Metamorphoses, Book I, 510: The places where you hurry are harsh: I pray that you run more gently*

The sweet scent offers little solace as I blow out the candle and plunge the dormitory into darkness again. The smell is covered by smoke. I've done something, and come morning, every girl in this room will be punished for it.

*Harsh* is a good word for it.

✦

Classes are canceled the next day. Instead, after breakfast, we are told to remain in the dining hall. Mrs. Forrester whisks away the dishes as Headmaster calls in the groundskeeper for help rearranging the tables and chairs. I sit up taller as he comes in through the servant's entrance in the kitchen,

but he does not look my way. He cradles his bandaged hand
to his chest.

Did they punish him too?

*Because of you.*

Because of me.

The table is set to the side, the chairs lined up as if we
were the audience at a cheap theater. Like a backdrop for
whatever this will be, the curtains have been drawn to the
back garden, revealing a calm blanket of snow. The world
beyond is smothered, lungs struggling to inflate.

Mrs. Forrester, when she returns, chews on her thumb-
nail, standing at the edge of the room as if trying to get as
far from the kitchen as she can.

"Stop that," Headmaster chides. It's almost the same
tone Father would take with me.

We all sit politely, tucking our skirts and crossing
our legs at the ankles. I end up near the middle; in my
desperation to sit next to Isabella, I find myself with
Louise on the other side. Louise looks at me warily, a
patient eyeing a scalpel. At the end of the row, there is
an extra chair.

"Do any of you know what this is about?" Mary mutters.

Charlotte shakes her head. "And I was looking forward
to class today, too."

On the other side of the kitchen door, something *wails*.

We fall silent. Mrs. Forrester blinks, almost shrinking
against the wall. For the first time, she looks her true age;
only somewhat older than Elsie, as if she could have been
my elder sister in another world.

"What—" Louise begins, trembling.

"It's nothing, girls," Mrs. Forrester says nervously. The rabbit does not scream but its fear makes my chest ache, makes it hard to breathe. I put a hand to my collarbone in an attempt to calm it.

As if to put a stop to this, Headmaster goes to stand at the front of the room. He taps his hands together to get our attention. All of us turn to him, even Mrs. Forrester, who watches him as if she's desperate for his protection.

"Good morning," he says, "good morning. I know we have had a tumultuous few days, marked by all kinds of arrivals and departures, but I do not want the tenets of our teachings to be lost in the bustle. It has come to our attention that a lesson may need to be repeated in a new way." Because of me. Because I broke the rules, I was alone with the wrong kind of man, and it's my fault. "So I am pleased to welcome Dr. Bernthal, one of the head doctors of Bethlem Royal Hospital."

Dr. Bernthal?

A doctor at Bethlem Royal Hospital? At Bedlam?

*Agnes.*

Is that what this is about? All of the students exchange wary glances; even Mary, no matter how hard she tries to conceal it. Was that wail *Agnes*?

Headmaster says, "We all know Dr. Bernthal. In fact, he's brought Mrs. Agnes Bernthal to visit." He waves a hand at the door. The marriage has already been completed, then. Her father or guardian signed off on it, the Church allowed it, the Speakers encouraged it. She is pregnant and she is fourteen and Dr. Bernthal is, what, forty, fifty?

Isabella takes a shuddering breath as if trying not to cry. "Why don't you come wait with the rest of the ladies while your husband prepares?"

Agnes slips out from the kitchen.

She is almost unrecognizable. It's been all of—what, a week?—since she left, and she has already changed so much. Her arm is in a sling. Her hair is done up in a complex style that does not suit her, and her dress is wildly intricate. Part of her face is swollen and bruised from the fall.

There is no swell to her belly. Not yet. Once it gets too recognizable, she'll be hidden away from the world until the baby is born, as is the custom. If she were showing, she would not have been allowed out of the house at all.

*Do you think your parents would have done this to you if they could have?* I don't want to think about this. *If you weren't an imbecile, how young would have been too young?*

Agnes ducks her head and hurries to the group, and we lean out of our chairs to crowd around her. Louise reaches for her and gently cups the bruises. Charlotte already has a million questions: How was the wedding done so quickly? Was it everything she ever dreamed of? Is having a husband really as wonderful as it seems? Mary comments on how the sling clashes with her outfit, and Isabella just murmurs something soft and kisses the top of her head.

"How is your arm?" I ask.

Agnes looks away. "It's healing," she says. "Setting it hurt."

I hold out my hand, asking to inspect it, but she shies away, so I just look from a distance. The whole limb is a disaster. It is wrapped tight and immobilized. Bruising creeps onto her bare wrist and fingers. Hopefully they have a good doctor keeping an eye on her—a doctor that *isn't* her new husband. I don't trust him with her.

When she sits, we adjust to allow for Agnes to sit in the middle of us. Agnes skims the line, as if looking for Ellen, and does not relax until she realizes she is not here. She does not ask about it. I wouldn't either.

Headmaster smiles at her. "Mrs. Bernthal," he says, "you are a wonderful example of what happens when Veil sickness is properly treated. Tell us a little about your new life."

Agnes swallows hard.

"Dr. Bernthal is a very good man," she says. "He is kind, and understanding, and takes care of me." It was easy to forget that Agnes is two years younger than me until this moment. She sounds so small and frail, and I get the sense that her words are rehearsed. "He's looking after me while I'm hurt, and I can't wait until I can start taking care of him instead. We live in a beautiful house in London, and he's taking me to the opera next week."

She looks up and forces a smile. Even I know it is fake. Even I can tell.

*She's been broken.*

"I love him very much," she says. "I'm very grateful."

Headmaster spreads his hands. "How lovely!" he says. "I adore a success story. I urge all of you to take Mrs. Bernthal's words to heart—however, that is not the only reason you have been called here. Today, well . . ."

He takes a deep breath.

"Dr. Bernthal has come with a friend of ours. Another former Braxton's student. Miss Harriet Johnston."

That name means nothing to me. It doesn't seem to mean much to any of the other students either.

But Mrs. Forrester looks up with a start. "Harriet?"

Headmaster frowns at her. "Please refrain from interrupting; it's impolite." Then: "Dr. Bernthal, the floor is yours."

This is my first time seeing Dr. Bernthal—actually, really seeing him, not just catching a glimpse of him out the classroom window. He steps out from the kitchen door with a woman on his arm, and he is all crisp clothes and sharp features. He is a blue-eyed man with a Speaker ring, meticulously clean-shaven, and his every movement, even breathing, is conducted with surgical efficiency. If I cut him open, there wouldn't be organs, but instead some kind of steam engine. The unnatural eeriness of his movements makes Isabella sink further into her seat.

But the woman—

"Thank you for inviting me," Dr. Bernthal says. Headmaster nods. Mrs. Forrester does not move. She stares at the woman, terrified. "I'm grateful for the opportunity to visit."

The woman is dressed plainly, hair cropped at the jaw. From what I've read, in lots of cases, to cut a woman's hair short like that is a sort of uncoupling, a changing, a sign of something horrible. For me, it would be freedom. For those who aren't like me, like Daphne, it is a *taking* of that which belongs to them.

But it is not just her hair.

Her hands are bound with gauze.

Her mouth.

Her eyes.

A hand over the mouth, a hand over the eyes. No. No, no. Is this what the groundskeeper meant? Is this—

*Of course not. Ellen and Frances are dead. This woman is alive on a technicality.*

She walks slowly, relying on Dr. Bernthal for balance. She has the unsteady gait of someone robbed of their sight, but also of someone sedated; laudanum, maybe, or lithium. I swallow hard even though it still hurts to do so, even as the bruising finally has begun to fade. Her face has become featureless, flat, like a spirit's. Like a long-dead thing.

Mrs. Forrester whimpers.

We all know what she is.

One of us. A failure. Alive, but at what cost?

"There's no need to be afraid," Dr. Bernthal says. The woman—Harriet Johnston, that's her name; I want to give her the name that belongs to her—half-flinches at his voice, but her neck lolls under the weight of her head and she ends up with her nose pointing to the floor. "Miss Johnston is perfectly safe to be around. She won't harm you in the least."

What shade of purple are Harriet's eyes?

"I don't bring Miss Johnston here to scare you," Dr. Bernthal assures us. "She is here to help you understand the danger of Veil sickness. You see, we have done everything we can to help her come back from the brink, and yet, this is the state she finds herself in."

Charlotte nods enthusiastically, as if she's been waiting all her life to be told this.

*So this is the choice for people like you*, the rabbit says. *It's this or death.*

Dr. Bernthal takes one careful step and then another. Harriet is so close now. Close enough that I can smell the lye used to wash her clothes and the stale smell of her hair, the same smell as Miss Neuling. The bandages across her mouth throb with her breath. Her hands writhe, looking more like wrapped-up rats stitched to her wrists. There are strange wounds there, right over top of her veins. Not slashes but something else, almost healed but not quite. What—

Toothmarks. If you can't slit your wrists, you try to gnaw your arteries open.

Dr. Bernthal walks her down the line of us. He smiles and I imagine the *click click click* of machinery in his jaw. Harriet makes a low, rasping noise, like a spirit, like something dead, and I know it was her who cried out from the kitchen. She has to be. I hate that my first reaction is to recoil from her, but it's the only thing that keeps me from reaching out to her. It's the way I wanted to reach out to the groundskeeper when I realized he was like me, the same way I reached for Daphne. *Kindred spirits,* the rabbit says.

When Harriet gets to Mrs. Forrester, something in Mrs. Forrester breaks. Tears begin to flow down her face. Her decorum shatters and for the first time since I've arrived, a first name passes her lips. "Harriet—"

Harriet stops. She turns her head, as if trying to pinpoint the voice calling her name.

"I think perhaps you should step out of the room," Headmaster says to his wife, moving as if to escort her away.

But Harriet has begun to reach out. Trapped fingers search for Mrs. Forrester's face—

And Mrs. Forrester, in a fit of madness, yanks down the bandages covering Harriet's face.

Harriet has no tongue.

No teeth.

No eyes.

She's been hollowed. Pieces removed, cut away. I can see the telltale surgical scars, the damage done to her by the doctors. I also see the *lack* of damage that would denote a need for it, something that would prove this was anything but cruelty. They took out her tongue. Glossectomy. It's probably not the whole thing, since the tongue stretches a good way into the throat; just enough to destroy her ability to speak and swallow properly, leaving a strange wet lump awkwardly in the mouth. The teeth, a simple extraction. All of them, of course, one after another, quite possibly after she tried to eviscerate a major artery with them. And the eyes. Enucleation. The muscles around it have scrunched up and left the eyelids limp and caved in. When they flicker, I can see underneath. There is nothing but empty, gaping pink sockets in her face.

Louise screams.

Dr. Bernthal and Headmaster lunge for Harriet all at once, trying to get her away from Mrs. Forrester, but Mrs. Forrester gets to her first, pulling her against her chest. She's repeating, "I'm sorry, I'm sorry, I'm sorry," and Harriet buries her face into Mrs. Forrester's dress. Dr. Bernthal grabs Harriet under the arms and Harriet cries, digs her feet into the floor, tries her hardest to stay close, but she's been brought down to nothing but bones and skin by her time in the hospital. She can't hold on. She slips from Mrs. Forrester's chest and hits the ground.

Harriet Johnston is sedated with an injection into the neck. Dr. Bernthal must have brought one, specifically for cases like this. Harriet goes limp, slowly, slowly, and Dr. Bernthal catches her with all the gentleness in the world. Mrs. Forrester sobs. Dr. Bernthal cradles Harriet on the floor, holding her head up, while Headmaster glares at us all and his thick soldier's chest heaves. Agnes clamps her hands over her mouth.

"I'm sorry," Mrs. Forrester says again, as if it's the only thing she can say, like I did on the floor of the gala while my father slammed me into the tiles and called me an ungrateful bitch.

Headmaster yells at his wife to get out. She does.

16

We—the girls and I, minus Agnes, who we were forced to leave behind—are sent away to the dormitory to "contemplate and reflect amongst ourselves." Isabella stokes the fire against the cold creeping through the windows while Charlotte deposits herself in one of the armchairs, fretting with her nails. Louise picks at the dried flowers on the table, and I just stand there, watching the flames. Mary ignores us.

None of us can look at each other. We're too busy wondering what's happening below us. If Headmaster will punish Mrs. Forrester for her transgression. If Mrs. Forrester regrets the moment of humanity she showed. If Dr. Bernthal is comforting Agnes, or leaving her to worry alone as he wraps Harriet Johnston's eviscerated face back up in its bandages.

Harriet's face . . .

She didn't get better. Mrs. Forrester did.

"So," I say, not quite sure where to begin. *Contemplate and reflect*, the rabbit cackles. It's a bizarre thing to ask of us. "Um."

Mary's eyes snap to me from her spot on her bed. *"What?"*

I falter. "Headmaster said—"

"When people say things like that," Isabella cuts in, "they don't actually expect you to do it." When I look at her blankly, she tries again: "We're not going to be quizzed about it. They just wanted us to go away and be quiet."

"Oh," I say.

Louise whispers, "Her *face*."

Charlotte puts one of her fingernails in her mouth again. It's bizarre to watch her perfectly-poised façade drop. "The doctors had no choice. It's not as if she was mutilated for no reason."

The unsaid *Right?* hangs in the air. *It's not as if she was mutilated for no reason . . . right?* The rabbit shuffles painfully in my chest. *Tap tap tap* goes my heel.

"It's still horrible," Isabella says. "Needed or not, it's sickening."

Louise says, "Why would they show us such a thing?"

"Oh," Mary says, "I know why." She leans against the headboard of her bed and gestures grandly to me. "Ask Miss Bell. I saw her sneaking off with the groundskeeper last night."

Every eye flits to me.

She saw.

I take a step back. My mouth goes dry.

"I was just—" I start, but there's nothing for me to say. Mary gets down from her bed, stockinged feet silent on the wood floor.

"You were just *what*?" she says. "Did you think you'd fuck him?"

"Language!" Charlotte admonishes.

I flinch, resisting the urge to cover my ears. "No. No, it wasn't like that."

Mary's face cracks into an awful smile. "You've been spending so much time with Isabella . . ." Behind her, Isabella fumes, cheeks burned red with anger. Mary pretends to think better of herself, clears her throat sarcastically. "So sorry. Of course, language. Let me try again: did you think you'd have an *affair* with him? I suppose it makes sense; he's just as odd as you. I'd love to see what kind of children two feeble-mindeds make. Probably floppy little things that can't so much as breathe on their own. The Luckenbill boy will be so, so disappointed to learn about this, won't he?"

The other girls do nothing. They've learned their lesson—they don't get in between Mary and her prey.

I haven't learned, though.

*Don't say it.* The rabbit squeals. *Don't. It's too dangerous.*

I say, "I was asking if he knew what happened to Ellen."

"Ellen's gone," Mary says.

"I know. Just like Frances."

Mary stops moving. Her eye twitches.

"When I was with Mr. Luckenbill," I say, even as Daphne's title tastes cruel and bitter in my mouth, "spirits came to us. They spelled their names. Ellen Wright and Frances Nicoll. Right?"

Mary picks up the porcelain vase from the table, dumps the flowers and water across the rug, and throws it at me.

I fling up my hands to protect the soft parts of my face, but it still connects *hard*. Knocks a knuckle into my teeth. I stumble into the side of a bed, where I almost catch myself before I hit the ground. The vase crashes beside me. It splinters into a dozen white pieces. The girls start to yell.

And then Mary is on me. She's grabbing my dress and hair, digging her nails into my bruised neck. Isabella tries to get between us, but Mary knocks her aside.

"You," Mary spits, dragging me up. Her face is so close to mine that her breath is hot on my face. "You don't get to talk about Frances. Don't you *dare*. You don't know a fucking thing about—"

I bite her.

It's what I used to do as a child. I never really meant it. I never wanted to hurt anybody. It's just that I didn't have the words, or nobody listened to the words I had, and I needed to do something, *anything*, to prove how much I was hurting. But I mean it now. My teeth sink into the meat of her cheek, barely an inch from her mouth. Mary shrieks and drops me. I hit the ground, and a shard of broken vase cuts my hand. Blood smears across the hardwood floor.

"You bitch!" Mary screams. There is a bite mark imprinted right at the corner of her mouth. Charlotte hides behind the chair. Isabella has an arm out to protect Louise.

"Frances is dead," I say.

Mary says, "Shut up."

"She's *dead.*"

Mary plasters a hand to her face to check for blood.

"Frances is dead," I say. "So is Ellen. And whatever happened to them, it was terrible."

Mary splutters. She looks around, trying to find support from Isabella, Louise, Charlotte. Her expression, for the first time, is pleading.

No one moves.

Finally, she shows her teeth.

"*You* are the reason we had to see that," Mary says. Her voice is thick, raspy, like she swallowed something she shouldn't have. Pain pulses from my palm with my heartbeat. "I should have told Ellen to throw you over instead."

Nobody helps Mary, but nobody helps me either.

*The places where you hurry are harsh: I pray that you run more gently.*

✦

I clean my wound in the washroom. A small bruise is blooming on my cheek to balance out the sickly yellow-green fading around my neck, and the cut on my hand is deep. Not deep enough to see bone, but deep enough that it hit muscle. I sit on the edge of the tub, inspecting it in the weak light of the winter sun, trying to decide what to do.

I want to see Daphne. Just one meeting and already I am sick without her. I keep her letters under my mattress and sometimes I reach down in the middle of the night to feel the paper between my fingers. I despise poetry, except when it comes from her. Hating matrimonial torches like a crime, indeed.

There's a knock on the door.

"Occupied," I say.

"It's Isabella. Are you decent?"

When I don't answer, she opens the door and peers in. "I just wanted to check on you."

"Could you get me a needle and some thread? Maybe a candle?"

Isabella disappears from the doorway before returning with a candle half the size of my palm, burnt down to nearly nothing. She sets it on the edge of the tub, then passes me the sewing kit on the vanity. Right. The one with the scissors Louise grabbed.

"I get the feeling I won't want to watch," she says.

I don't reply to that either. Still, Isabella sits beside me, her nightgown spread out angelically.

"Did they hurt the groundskeeper?" I manage.

"I couldn't tell you," Isabella says. "I'm sorry."

I thread the needle with the smallest black string I can find—again, I should be using silk, but if this is all we have, then that's fine—and heat the metal in the flame of the candle. George taught me this trick; he said it helps reduce the rate of infections, if you don't have access to any other antiseptic. It's not perfect, but it's better than nothing.

Stitching a wound closed is easy enough. I opt for a running stitch instead of an interrupted stitch, like I always do. If I have to take the time to cut away every stitch as I go, I'll chicken out and refuse to go all the way.

*That's why you'll need George's help for the hysterectomy.*

I won't have to give myself one, though. Not now. Daphne wouldn't do that to me.

Though, Daphne being a woman changes things when it comes to parenthood. Daphne would not turn me into a mother, because if I had a child with her, I would be the father, and *she* would be the mother. Would I choose to bear a child if I was allowed to keep my manhood through it? If pregnancy did not mean shedding my masculinity? I don't actually know how much of my fear and revulsion is linked to the world's inherent gendering of everything reproductive. Or would my changing body still be too much for me to handle?

I don't know. The topic is too big, too much, for me to swallow right now.

So I stitch the wound closed, chewing on a washcloth as I go, Isabella keeping one hand on my knee and looking at the floor so she does not have to witness.

"Where did you learn to do this?" Isabella asks.

I spit out the cloth as I tie the knot. My face is sticky with sweat and my fingers are shaking, but it's done. "My brother taught me."

Isabella takes my hand to inspect the work. A queasy expression passes over her face, but she is intrigued nonetheless. I let her look as long as she pleases.

"A stronger girl than I am," she says, letting go.

"I wouldn't say that."

"I would."

It's strange to be sitting up here on the side of the tub, where for once I am taller than her. I have the vantage point to the curve of her nose, her dark lashes, the muscles of her neck and shoulders. If I feel an urge to cut her open, it's only because no surgeon can ever resist a perfect specimen. I tuck my uninjured hand between my thighs. I don't want to take her apart in the way most men would want to disassemble a woman. Not for any sort of power or hunger. I want to be close, and I don't know *how* to be close unless I'm elbow-deep in innards.

I have to keep reminding myself that I'm a boy. It's almost easy to forget that here. To slip back into the oblivion of just accepting I am what everyone thinks I am.

*If you have to keep reminding yourself, are you really?*

Maybe that's why I want Daphne. Or, at least, part of why I want to be with her. With her, I do not have to remind myself. When she looks at me, she sees a boy. I've never gotten that from anyone before. Not even George. When George looks at me, what does he see? A girl that can never be a boy, not *truly*, but would crumble if she was not allowed to at least pretend?

I'm too deep in thought to notice that something is wrong until Isabella makes a deep, wet noise, and then she's hunched over, vomiting.

"*Oh.*" I grab the washcloth and wet it to clean her face. The remains of breakfast have become a sandy sludge, some of it hanging crudely from her lower lip. I wipe it away. She coughs, splutters, as tears gather in the corners of her eyes. "Here," I murmur, "here."

"Sorry," she says. "I don't feel very good."

I clean up the mess while she leans against the wall, staring up at the ceiling with her knees tucked up close. Then I sit next to her. She leans her head against my shoulder, dark hair tickling my cheek.

Neither of us speak for a while. And then:

"Are they really dead?" she asks.

I run the pad of my thumb across the stitches again, and then again. It makes the wound spark with pain, but I don't mind. Physical sensations are far less confusing than things like emotion. "I know they are."

"Christ." Isabella sniffles, takes a deep breath, blows it out shakily. "I believe you, you know. I want you to know that. I do. And I wish I could help you." She hesitates. "But I'm so scared, and I can't risk it, and I'm sorry. I'm sorry we're such cowards, Gloria, but we can't."

There's nothing I can say that will make it any better.

"You're not a coward for wanting to live," I say, and nestle my cheek against the top of her head. She cries.

17

While rereading Daphne's letters that night—tracing the shape of each word, since her handwriting is much nicer than mine—I get an idea.

The next morning, before the shriek of the wake-up bell, I write one of my own, the page taken from a blank sheet in the front of a book. The dedication is on one side, and this is on the other:

*My dearest brother,*

*I write to you because I miss you. I regret that our last meeting was not the most pleasant. How has your life been since I left? I know work is busy, and your wife needs you now more than ever—but if you were ever to do me the favor of visiting, I would be very happy to see you again. If nothing else, you'd find it amusing how much my French has improved*

*without anything else to distract me. I look forward to*
*hearing from you.*
   *Your loving sister,*
   *Gloria*

Students don't usually write letters. Before breakfast, when
we are let out of our rooms for the first time since yesterday's
disaster, I meekly ask Headmaster to send it. He regards the
folded paper, then tells me I have two choices: I let him read
it, or I take it from him and burn it. I let him read it.

"We don't allow family visits," he says, looking over
the paper at me once he's done. He studies the cut on my
hand, the new bruise on my face. "However, Dr. Bell is an
acquaintance of mine. I suppose we can make an exception."

I don't like the way he says it. "Thank you, Headmaster."

The truth is, I do not want to see George again. I'm not
sure I can stomach it. But I know he works in the London
hospitals these days. I know, sometimes, he comes out to
the villages in the countryside, out here—and Headmaster's
offhanded remark means there's a chance he's come to the
school itself. Maybe he'll have heard something about what
happened to Ellen and Frances. Maybe if he sees the state
I'm in, he'll finally, finally, agree to help.

*Are you sure?*

Of course I'm not.

Just before breakfast is served, though, Headmaster gets
our attention.

"Ladies!" he says. "It's time to start preparing for the winter
garden party." Right. This. I was wondering when it would

come to bite us. "It will be held this Sunday in the greenhouse, and we'll spend the next few days preparing for it. All of you will have a chance to meet eligible bachelors, and work on your hosting and entertaining skills. This will be a wonderful chance to showcase your improvement and demonstrate that you are ready for the intricacies of polite company. So please, be on your best behavior, and prepare yourselves accordingly!"

Charlotte's eyes sparkle, but Mary's darken with something almost like fear as she leans slowly against the back of her chair.

This could be a problem—or it could be exactly the opportunity I need.

✦

After a breakfast eaten ravenously, as none of us have eaten in nearly a full day, Mrs. Forrester sends most of the students up to her classroom for more talk of *The Angel in the House*. There is no discussion of Harriet Johnston at all. There's no reason for it. We've learned our lesson, haven't we? If Mrs. Forrester notices my injuries, or heard us screaming and shouting in the dormitory yesterday, she says nothing. If we notice Mrs. Forrester's limp has grown slightly more pronounced, we do not point it out.

Mrs. Forrester herself, however, whisks me away to the dressing room. "Your suitor is here," she says. "Let's not keep him waiting."

*Daphne.* I want to see Daphne so badly it hurts. It's not a *happy* kind of want, though, and not a good kind of hurt.

It's the hurt of trying to hold your organs in place, desperately waiting for the surgeon to put them back.

When I arrive, dressed in blue florals and silver, Daphne is waiting by the window in the parlor, like she was last time. She's backlit by the winter sun with the edges of her overgrown hair shining gold. As soon as the door closes, Daphne's attempt at a pleasant face collapses. As quick and sharp as a damaged lung.

"Oh," she says. "Your hand." Then: "Your face—"

All of the strength I've put into remaining upright over these past few days, into keeping away the hysterics, into pretending I am not so overwhelmed I want to scream; it disappears at once. I stumble up to her, unsteady on my feet, and pause for just a moment—"May I touch you?" I ask, and she replies, "Of course"—before I collapse against her chest. She is soft and just about my size. My face fits neatly into the bend of her neck. Her next breath comes out as a pained sigh, and if I crawled into her skin, I would fit perfectly.

I say, "Can you squeeze? As tight as you can?"

Daphne wraps her arms around my shoulders and crushes me into her chest. She's not as strong as I'm used to; less like George, who would make my ribs creak, but instead more like Mother, back when she still hugged me. It makes me feel more solid. It makes my skin feel more like mine. It's why I used to pile as many blankets on top of me as I could or pull at my skin until it went taut. I need the pressure, the weight, so I can sew myself back into my own body.

I could stay here forever if she let me. Daphne sways back and forth a moment, skims her hand down my back.

I squeeze her in turn. The little breath she lets out says she needs it just as much as I do.

"Better?" she asks.

"I think."

She pulls back, only a bit, and brushes a strand of hair from my face. It's just to get a better look at the bruises, but the gesture is so calming that I drop my cheek into her palm. She smells of tea and expensive perfume.

Am I in love with her already? Perhaps. Or maybe I'm just confusing love with comfort, and I'm okay with that. Is there any difference between love and a safe harbor from a storm? Should there be? There are a lot of different kinds of love, and though I may not be able to tell them apart from each other, I appreciate all of them the same.

"Can you stand on your own?" Daphne asks. "You're leaning quite heavily."

I'm not quite sure I can. So she walks me to the couch, a hand on my arm to keep me steady.

"I hope my letters made sense," she says. "You got them, didn't you? Your headmaster didn't confiscate them?"

"I got them, though it took me until the second one to figure out what you were doing," I admit. "I've never really been good with poetry. Or subtext. Or anything like that." I settle between the cushions, and she sits next to me. This close, in this light, I can see that there are flecks of brown in her green eyes, and pale freckles on her nose; bits of pigment scattered like droplets. "But I got there. So if they're not recorded at any hospitals, or prisons, or morgues . . ."

"It's not just a lack of records," Daphne says. "I bribed a

bloody lot of cleaners and orderlies too. If one of the girls' bodies had been taken there, recorded or not, I would have known. And there's nothing."

"Which means they're still in the building."

Daphne says, "Or buried out back."

The image chills me. "The groundskeeper would have told me if he'd seen something like that."

Daphne doesn't know about the groundskeeper, so I tell her—our meetings, his silence, the hand over the mouth and the hand over the eyes. She immediately rules out spirits, due to the lack of a mouth, which embarrasses me. I also tell her about Harriet. Daphne looks vaguely ill.

"I hate that I'm not surprised," she says.

The conversation makes us restless. We lay out the speaking tiles and stare at them as if they'll explode to life again, but after a long silence, I jam them back into the bag and shove the drawer shut. I tell her about the button I stole from Headmaster. She explains that Lord Luckenbill caught her talking to a morgue attendant and has been looking at her askance ever since.

"So," Daphne says, "what the hell do we do next?"

"I wrote my brother, asking him to come visit. He works in the surrounding area sometimes, so he may have a clue." My hands flutter. "And then there's the winter garden party coming up. I know we can't do much here, but maybe when the school is busy . . ."

"The *garden party.*" Daphne claps, leaning forward conspiratorially. "Yes, I'll be there. You think you could get away with anything?"

"No," I say, "but I think we could."

She smiles. Her eyes shine like something vicious, and I have never been more attracted to anything in my sixteen years of being alive. "We could."

✦

With a pin in the garden party and my stomach twisted in knots, Daphne finds a book of poetry on the shelves and insists on skimming through, reading her favorite passages to me. She speaks Latin like it's her mother tongue, then reads the translation the way one would savor a particularly soft piece of skin. The snow outside has not yet melted, and the reflection of the sun through the window makes the room feel bright and airy.

I think literature consumes her the same way surgery has swallowed me. She sees the world through the lens of it: she is to stories like I am to meat. I raise the point to her.

"I suppose," she says, sticking out her lower lip as she considers it. "I mean, everyone is made up of stories, when you think about it. You only really come to understand yourself by comparing other people's stories to yours; you find where things are the same, and where they're not." She skims through the book, delicate fingers resting on the edge of the pages. "It's difficult when the story isn't one the world wants to hear, though. I thought every boy would flip a coin and become a woman if they could. I didn't know it was just me. You know?"

Do I know?

I don't really . . . *interact* with people. I've never particularly wanted to. All I wanted were anesthetized bodies and pig specimens and textbooks. I never told my stories, and I never listened to anyone else's either.

But certain people sure tried to tell me what my story should be.

I stare at my hands, tapping my knuckles to my palm. "That makes sense, but it's different for me. Because there's something else in the way. If this . . ." I gesture between us, and she understands what I mean. Our rejection of our birth sex, our attempts to be something else. "If *this* is a joint—please follow my metaphor—then for me there are two muscles controlling the joint, not just one. And I can't tell where one ends and the other begins." I trace an example at my wrist, which isn't exactly right because there are six muscles there, but for simplicity's sake I don't mention that. "Other girls never made sense to me. I never wanted to be one, not really. But was that because I'm not one, or because I'm . . . ?"

An imbecile. Something to be corrected. In possession of a mind that takes everything as it's said and feels it all so strongly it's like drowning.

"Unwell?" I finish.

Daphne winces.

"How am I supposed to separate the two?" My words seize for a moment, so I pull a lock of hair to my mouth and grind it between my teeth. "Maybe I'm just a sick girl, and if someone fixes that, all the rest of it will go away. Maybe these are all just symptoms of one small, nasty thing."

Daphne tries to regain her composure. I try too.

"Do you want that to be true?" she asks.

My response is instant. "No. I like being this. All of it. Even if it makes things hard." And that's true. Knowing these things about myself has given me an insight, an understanding of the way I move through the world that a great many people lack. I would never give that away.

But suddenly, something bubbles up.

"It doesn't matter if I like it, though. Nobody cares if I like myself this way. They still tried to fix me. They treated me like an animal." The words come, faster and faster, before I can stop them. "Training through brute memorization and repetition. No reasoning. No teaching. And I'm not some beast of burden, or a baby that can't think for itself! They could have explained what they wanted, spelled out *why* things need to be a certain way. But they didn't! They just punished me for doing it wrong. How is that fair? How am I a bad person for not knowing things? I was a kid. I didn't know what I was doing wrong. I didn't understand."

I'm crying.

"And now they're doing it all over again. Why am I always sick? Why is it always me? When do I just get to be okay?"

My breathing hitches. My hands are numb, and I press them into my eyes until spots dance in my vision. I should have taken them out years ago. I would have been locked away and taken apart like Harriet Johnston, but at least I never would have come *here*.

Fingers gently wrap around my wrists and pull them away.

Daphne says, "Silas. Silas."

For the first time, her face is too painful to look at, the same way it hurts to look at anyone else. But she doesn't make me look. She doesn't snap at me to make eye contact, call me rude, berate me until I do what she says. She just lets me stare over her shoulder.

"They didn't explain it to you because there's not a good reason," she says. "It's just how the story is to them, and they don't know how to read any deeper." She pulls me closer. "Or maybe they're just pretending. I think the entire world depends on people pretending they don't know they're doing terrible things."

I take those words and hold them like one would hold a fallen tooth to inspect the roots, the ridges, all the little pieces that had been hidden until it came away from the gums.

Before she can say anything else, before I can think too deeply on it and start to cry again, I reach for the book of poetry and push it clumsily into her hands. "Read to me? Please?"

Daphne gives me a long, pitying look that makes me want to rip out my own heart, but does as I ask. *"Id vitium nulli per saecula longa notatum—"* Like she's turned the names of bones and muscles into verse— *"quid non sentit amor?"* She translates: *This defect was noticed by no one through the long generations—but what does love not sense?*

✦

By the time I am able to speak again without making a pathetic fool of myself, Mrs. Forrester has not yet come to gather me. I'm sitting on the floor, watching Daphne look for another book as she bemoans the lack of epic poems; she wants to show me *The Aeneid*, to cheer me up, she says. She pouts as she inspects the collection and asks me if the library has better choices.

Instead of answering, I say, "If we get out of here—"

Daphne corrects me. "*When* we get out of here."

"When we get out of here." Yes, God willing, when. "Would you want to marry me? It seems like the best course of action. The easiest, for us and for others."

"I thought that was a given," Daphne says. "That we would."

"Really?"

"Only if you want."

"Yes. Of course I do. I was just wondering what we'd do about—"

I hesitate. The words taste like gravel on the back of my tongue before I've even spoken them. Is this a dangerous topic to bring up? I know how it makes me feel, how strange and unmoored; I can't imagine how *she* would feel about it.

I finish, "About children."

Daphne regards me for a moment, then leans against the bookshelf. I can't read her face. That scares me.

"Do *you* want children?" she asks.

I'm not sure I have an answer. I try to imagine what that version of life would look like; getting married, my stomach swelling, the mechanics of birth, but then beyond that. A newborn, a toddler, a young child. One version where the child calls me *Mum*, another where the child calls me *Dad*.

I say, "I don't know. I realized I couldn't tell the difference between not wanting children and not wanting to be seen as a mother, so I'm still unsure."

Daphne says, "Oh hell." She pinches the bridge of her nose. "I hadn't thought of it that way at all."

"What?"

"I just . . ." I can see the muscles in her neck stand out, and she turns as if, for once, eye contact is as hard for her as it is for me. "I hadn't thought about being something other than a father."

I say, "For what it's worth, I think you'd be a wonderful mother."

When it's Daphne's turn to cry, I stand and reach out for her, lead her to the couch, and give her a napkin to wipe her face. She takes the napkin, then my hand. She holds them both tight until she can convince herself to let go.

In the face of this, Daphne tells me about her mother. Lady Emily Luckenbill was tall and beautiful and violet-eyed. She was a reader and writer. Her two most treasured possessions were an original edition of *Frankenstein* and Daphne herself. She laughed loudly, and could eat a whole chicken in one sitting, and had one child before she got sick, and sicker, and sicker, and it took five years for consumption to kill her. It's terrible, she says, to watch someone so strong wither away to nothing. Death never goes after those who deserve it. It only ever takes from those who aren't ready.

Daphne got her love of reading from her. She got her hard mouth and big eyes and know-it-all attitude too. Lord

Luckenbill did not deserve Emily, not for a moment in his life.

But at the heart of it, Daphne is torn—she wants her mother to be a spirit, in hopes that one day Lady Luckenbill could meet her daughter; but she also wants her mother to rest in peace.

"And she would love to meet you too," she says. "She'd think you are a wonderful young man."

18

George arrives the next day.

We are preparing for the garden party when the carriage clatters up to the front door. I only see it because I'm next to the window, the gate swinging open then closed again in my peripheral vision. Mrs. Forrester is at the front of the classroom, reminding us of our manners: to never have private conversations at a gathering, to always remain with an escort, to never express affection for one another (it is a mark of low breeding). I know the handbook she is teaching from. Mother gifted it to me once. I tried to memorize it, but it made no sense to me.

I see George step down from the carriage, thanking the driver as he goes, and I stand up from my seat in a rush.

"Miss Bell," Mrs. Forrester snaps.

"I—" I collect myself, embarrassed. "I'm sorry. That's my brother."

"Your brother?" Mrs. Forrester limps to the window, peers out, watches George come to the front door. Her face screws up, as if she's been told to let me go but doesn't want to. Clearly I need the help of this lesson more than anyone else. "Fine. Go."

I find George and Headmaster on the first floor as George cleans off his shoes and tucks his hat under his arm. I pause halfway down the stairs. Look at him. So grown, without me, leaving me to suffer Mother and Father and Braxton's alone.

But he came. That has to count for something.

George sees me over Headmaster's shoulder. He almost drops the coat he's taking off, just about kicks over the doctor's bag at his feet. Oh. My throat. I put a hand to it, softly, where the bruising has almost faded but not entirely, leaving sick-colored splotches that are only visible in the right light. This must be the right light. The stitches in my hand ache.

"Lord," he says. "Look at you."

Headmaster turns and smiles. It's not a very convincing smile. It twitches at the corners. I remember the spirit spelling out his name on the washroom floor, Harriet's broken face, the groundskeeper unable to tell me what he knows. "Good morning, Miss Bell."

I come up to George, take his hand. "You got my letter."

"Of course I did," he says. "Thought I might make a day of it, as your headmaster asked for my assistance while I'm here." He turns to Headmaster. Assistance? "Do you mind if I take a moment with my sister before I talk with your wife?"

"I don't mind at all," Headmaster says. Headmaster's presence taints George's safety, the way a punctured bowel causes a body to go septic. "I think you may enjoy our library; Miss Bell, stoke the fire for our guest."

So that is where we end up. George comments on a lack of servants and sits heavily upon a chair and gestures for me to do the same, even though he knows I hate to sit. Instead, I stoke the fire as I was told, then wander aimlessly through the books left on the tables and pick at the threads on the backs of the chairs.

The rabbit is uncomfortable. Clearly afraid. I imagine its beady black eyes staring at nothing as it shivers. *He won't believe you. He stopped believing you as soon as everyone else noticed how sick you are. He abandoned you.*

I shut the rabbit up. It'll be okay. I know he comes up to the villages. He does it all the time since he's come back to London, going wherever the Speakers and his hospital send him. Maybe he's heard something, or knows something, or knows someone who does. If he does, he'll tell me. He has to.

"George—" I begin.

"You look like hell," he interrupts. "Let me see your hand."

Yes, I do look like hell. I come over, let him take my wrist and turn it over. The worse condition he sees me in, the more I can beg him to take pity. *Let him see what's happened to you here. What they've done to you.* He inspects the ugly run of thread across the heel of my palm, then the discoloration of my face, my throat.

"They're healing well," he says sadly. "You've always healed well."

My legs suddenly feel weak. "You're not going to ask what happened?"

"I don't need to. Headmaster said you'd gotten into a few fights. I know this new environment is challenging, but I really hoped you'd settle in better."

The rabbit stares. The words sit uncomfortably, but I can't articulate why. When I fall silent, unable to speak, George sighs.

"Mother told me you'd been sent here the day after the gala. She visited Elsie and me to talk about it, like she suddenly wanted confirmation she'd done the right thing. As if she could have done anything about it if it wasn't—it's up to Father, not her—but—"

I don't care about Mother. "So you knew about Braxton's."

"I knew *of* it."

"You've come out here before."

"To the countryside," he corrects. He seems miffed at my interruptions, as if the rules of a polite conversation actually matter here. "For a house call, once or twice, when the doctor in the village has to take leave."

"So you haven't come to the school before?"

"No. That's the village doctor's job, not mine."

"Because—"

He cuts me off. Again. "Look. This has been an upsetting time for you." *Quite the understatement.* I pick at the loose threads on the armchair in front of me to give my hands something to do, so I don't start ripping things the way I did on the floor of the parlor. "I can't imagine how difficult it is to be taken away from family, away from the city, surrounded by people you don't know. But I do think Mother and Father did the right thing."

"They *didn't*."

"Tone."

Tone doesn't *matter right now*. I'm done playing with this back-and-forth. If I don't say it now, I never will.

"George, listen to me." He blinks in confusion, startled. Good. "Something terrible is happening here, and I can't tell anyone but you." I've told Daphne, but I can't incriminate her. I've tried to tell Mary and she— "Just listen to me. Hear me out. Please."

George says, "Okay. Okay." Like he's talking to a confused patient who has become distressed coming out of anesthesia. I want to cry. "I'm here now. I'm listening."

This is it.

"There are spirits here," I say. "The spirits of dead students."

"And how do you know that?"

"They talked to me."

"Christ. Silas—"

Him using my name is not going to stop me. "No. You said you'd listen, so *listen*. Students are dying here. They're *dead*. And I just need you to tell me if you know a single thing about it." My voice chokes. My hand thumps against the back of the chair because I have to do *something*, and if I flap my hands (*like a child, like an imbecile*) it'll just be one more reason to brush me off. "If you know of any unlabeled bodies at your hospital, any rumors of disappearances, anything, you have to tell me. You have to help me stop this."

George is quiet for a good, long while. Watching me. I dig my nails into the upholstery.

Please.

He says, "I should've known."

"Known what?" I whisper.

He mulls like he's trying to decide how to break some terrible news to me.

"Recently," George says, "at the behest of the Royal Speaker Society, I've begun researching Veil sickness. They needed a surgeon on the team, and I agreed."

This isn't how the conversation was supposed to go. He's not answering me.

"The topic, it felt close to home," he continues, "considering how many violet-eyed people I know and love dearly. And we've learned a lot. We used to believe violet-eyed women were more susceptible to the illness the more they interact with the Veil—but the truth is, we've learned that any contact at all can cause extreme deterioration over a long period of time, even if it only happens once. It can cause irrationality. Delusions. Violence. Like Miss Neuling."

He pauses.

"Like you."

*Like you.*

I know what that means. I shake my head, take a step back. My hands tap against my chest. He can't do this. He can't say this. "George. You know that's not true."

George says, "Look at the evidence. The gala, the fights you've been in, and now this?" His voice chokes for a moment. "If it's anyone's fault, it's my own. I encouraged these behaviors of yours. I gave you those clothes, I taught you—" He reaches for my hand, my stitched-up hand, but I won't let him get close. Oh God, he regrets helping me be a boy. He regrets showing me his notes, he regrets *everything*. "I refuse to deny you care. I am your brother, and I care about you. You and Elsie both."

Both the rabbit and I pause. We take that word, *Elsie*, like we aren't sure what to do with it. It burns, but we can't let go.

I say, "Elsie?"

George looks sad. Distraught, even. Like he's on the verge of tears too.

I say, "No. George, no. You can't really think—"

"The miscarriage," he says.

The miscarriage. Elsie's miscarriage, the baby she lost, that both of them lost. He can't really blame her for that. Can he? Tragedies like this happen all the time. It's not Veil sickness, it's just a failure of the human body. There's no morals attached to it, no grander meaning. It doesn't mean a damn thing, it's not a sign of something bigger, it's just a *tragedy*.

"No," I say. Another step back. Away from him. "That wasn't her fault."

"It's a *sickness*," he says. "She is sick, and so are you, and, considering the symptoms . . ."

George gets up from the chair, walks over to me, put his hands on my shoulders. I flinch.

He says, "It is important for a caregiver to be skeptical of what a sick girl says."

*Girl.*

*Sick girl. Sick girl girl girl. You're a sick girl playing dress-up, you're a sick girl lying to yourself, you're making things up and you need to be fixed and you're sick sick sick sick sick*—

I point to my throat. "Headmaster did this. Look. Look at the bruises." I'm crying now. Like I always do. Like the manipulative little bitch Mother and Father always said I was. "You have to believe me. Please."

And the look he gives me—

He thinks I'm mad. He thinks I'm fucking mad.

George leads me toward the door. When I try to resist, he grabs me by the arm. It hurts. It's the first time he's ever hurt me.

"Come," he says. "Headmaster asked me to treat Mrs. Forrester while I visited, and we agreed that it would be a good idea for you to come along."

◆

The first time I opened an animal on my own, it was a fetal pig that had been discarded by the abattoir. It wasn't developed enough to be roasted as a suckling. Not even enough to survive outside the womb. It was destined for fertilizer or cheap meat markets for the poor; the bones had not yet hardened, and the meat was gelatinous and unpalatable. Pigs are the closest to humans you can get without actually dissecting a person, George explained. It was hard enough to get bodies for the medical schools as it was without resorting to body snatchers. If I wanted to learn, I'd have to make do with what I could get.

*He regrets ever having helped you.*

I gathered the pale little creature in linen and took it to a forgotten corner of London where I wouldn't be disturbed, where the air smelled of rubbish and horse manure, and the summer days lasted long enough that there was still enough light to see by. The piglet was soft, with its closed eyes and little hooves. Its mouth hung open and its tongue stuck out. The umbilical cord looked like a worm peeking out from the stomach.

*Your own brother thinks you're mad.*

I'd cut it apart with shoddy bladework, my hands shaking and vomit catching in the back of my throat. The skin was thicker than I thought it would be, made of so many layers, like puff pastry, the grey-pink organs jammed so carelessly into the abdominal cavity that it shocked me. They reminded me of drawings of coral I'd seen in books of fairy tales. There was a lot of liquid. Things stuck to each other with sinew and tissues I couldn't yet name. The hair on its body was soft and sparse.

I think of that now as George lays out his doctor's bag on the floor of Headmaster and Mrs. Forrester's bedroom. I've never seen this room before; it's small but beautifully decorated, nothing like Headmaster's spare study. The gas lamp is dim, so he tells me to draw the blinds and let some light into the room. I wipe my eyes and try to steady my breathing.

Even if I was mad, there's no excuse to treat someone like this. Madness isn't a reason to stop caring about someone, is it?

Mrs. Forrester sits at a vanity, with George at her feet, a basin of water and disinfectant on the floor. The disinfectant makes my mind calm. Or at least, calmer. A procedure. I can do that. I would rather do this than anything else.

"Come," George says, "down here. Sit."

I do, folding my skirts politely under me. George offers me half a smile as he begins to wash his hands in the basin.

"How are your feet feeling?" George asks Mrs. Forrester. When he's done washing, I scrub my nails, just to give myself something to do. "Any infections you're worried about?"

"No," she says. "You cleared Miss Bell's presence with the headmaster, right?"

George snorts. "It was his idea. He has unique treatment plans, I'll give him that."

Then he takes off one of Mrs. Forrester's shoes.

Her foot is a mess of mangled meat and torn bandages. The smell and gore of it shocks me. A tiny piece of something loosens from the sole and hits the wood floor with a delicate *clink*.

Broken glass.

There are shards of glass in her shoes. Little pieces, dozens of slivers, the bandages torn to shreds and stuck to the wounds. George unwraps the soiled gauze and sets it aside. I lean in, inspecting the carnage. It's awful. I can't believe none of it is infected. It's as if a dog has been chewing on her foot for days. *No wonder she limps.* Honestly, it's a miracle that she can walk at all.

Mrs. Forrester doesn't seem particularly comfortable being used as an example. She won't look at us. George takes off the other shoe—it's the same mess—and peels out a bit of lining from each of the shoes and places them in a bag for disposal.

He hands me the shoes and a new set of liners from a box on the vanity. "Change these out for me, please."

He acts as if this isn't a surprise at all.

"You see," George says to me as he lifts Mrs. Forrester's foot onto his knee, "Mrs. Forrester here was afflicted with an extreme case of Veil sickness. Isn't that right? She even attacked her first suitor when she was a young woman." *Just like Frances*, the rabbit says. *Why does this bitch get to survive that?* I ignore the rabbit and do what I'm told, though I wonder what the man did to deserve it. "Years ago, we might have locked Mrs. Forrester up for the rest of her life."

*Or killed her.*

After I finish putting new liners in her shoes, George beckons me closer and has me hold Mrs. Forrester's leg as he sets about pulling the glass from her wounds. Some of the pieces are far longer than I expected.

"Instead, she became the first student at Braxton's, and she got better. It was a long road, and a difficult one." George gives her a look as he works. She glances away, embarrassed, and all I can think of is when she collapsed into Harriet's arms. Or Harriet into hers. What did Headmaster do after that? What punishment did she deserve? "This treatment does not look kind, and yes, it is painful, but Headmaster discovered it's what her body and mind require in order to keep her and others safe."

He's been putting glass in her fucking shoes. He mangles

her. He makes sure she is in pain with every single step, all to make sure she is a perfect wife.

"Can I try?" I ask, half-reaching for the forceps, desperate for something to do.

George barely hesitates. "What do you think my answer is going to be?"

He keeps working.

The glass in her shoes is a brutal treatment, but it is an effective one. It keeps her grounded. The pain reminds her of the truth. Without it, her mind would degrade all over again, and she would be left no better than where she started.

George says, "So, you see now, don't you? That women with Veil sickness can still be productive, good members of society? They don't have to be locked away. Not all of them." He shakes his head. "But you have to want to get better. I hope that can be you one day. Lord Luckenbill will make a good father-in-law."

He finishes removing the glass without looking at me. He washes the pieces with strong, stinking antiseptic.

Mrs. Forrester puts the glass back in her shoes herself.

19

The rest of the day goes by in a blur. Mrs. Forrester avoids me during supper and chores. The rabbit berates me for my naivete: *He was never going to help. You knew that. You and that girl are alone alone ALONE.*

No. Not if we find proof.

By now, the word *proof* has begun to grate on me. It's upsetting to acknowledge that the proof we're looking for is, technically, evidence of a body—but it's the truth, isn't it? Daphne and I looking for dead girls.

*Even if you find something, you can't trust your head. Nobody can. It's perfect, isn't it? They've put you in a position where they can discount every single thing you say. They never have to listen to you again.*

I just have to make it to the garden party. The whole school will be distracted, and Daphne will be by my side, and . . .

It's not perfect. Of course it's not. We don't know what we're doing, or even where to begin. But I pray that we will be able to at least *start* to crack open the ribs of this building and pull out whatever rotten shit has been packed down inside of it. After all, there are only so many places to hide a haunting, or a corpse. This school is only so big.

That night, we have to stay up for Isabella. She has a suitor, and he's come late. Charlotte puts up a fuss about it, saying that she doesn't know why Isabella dislikes Dr. Jessett so much, or why we all seem so scared. He's been away in Scotland for so all those weeks; it should be wonderful to see him again! Mary tells her to shut the fuck up. I chew on the edge of the bloody handkerchief until my jaw aches.

Isabella comes back silent, an arm around her stomach like she's sick. Louisa offers her cold, watery tea.

✦

With the day of the party pressing in on us like a tumor compressing the brain, our days are filled with mindless preparation: freshening up our manners, reminding us of pleasant conversation topics, quizzing us on the minutia of hospitality. None of it makes any sense to me. So it's almost a relief when Mrs. Forrester ushers us to the piano in the parlor to take stock of our musical abilities. My parents were too busy cycling through new tutors to bother finding me an instructor; for once, I won't have to do much of anything.

Except Headmaster catches my arm just inside the door. Shit.

"I'll be pulling Miss Bell for another private lesson," he says. Mrs. Forrester waves us off. Isabella gives me a sad look over her shoulder. Most of her looks seem sad now.

So there I am again, in the chair in front of Headmaster's desk as he flips through his pages of notes, staring at the shimmering hauntings hung on the wall behind him. The broken shards of statues. The metatarsal. A bracelet that looks like it was made by a child.

The tiniest one, the little button, has been put back in its proper place.

I don't want to move my leg, so I tap the side of my chair with my nail. *Tap tap tap.*

"Before we begin," Headmaster says, not looking up from his notes, "why a running stitch? The military doctor I served with insisted on interrupted stitches; said running stitches were for clothes, and interrupted stitches were for men."

"It's a personal preference," I reply.

"Ah. And is that cotton thread? Really, if you require silk thread, please ask. I don't mean to encourage this sort of behavior, but I don't want you doing more damage to yourself in the meantime. Now. Stand, please, would you?"

I do what I'm told. The rabbit snuffles, looks around, keeps its ears back. I put a hand on my pulse to feel it kicking. The bruise on my neck is almost entirely gone now; it doesn't ache anymore.

Headmaster stands too. He leans against the desk with papers in hand.

"What we witnessed with Miss Johnston was," he begins, "unfortunate. But be that as it may, it was still an important lesson. She was prone to indulging in spirit-work, and oh, you can see how far that got her. That poor woman." He clicks his tongue. "It's awful, how far she's fallen. Even with London's best doctors, and the most supportive family, there was still nothing we could do. She simply did not want to be helped."

He flips a page in his notes.

"We talked previously about how this sort of unlearning can take time. There is no shame in failing this early in the process. It is not a moral judgement, simply weakness, and everyone is weak at first. In fact, I had only planned for the two of us to have a discussion. Talk about your life, what's led up to where you are today.

"However."

Headmaster sucks on his teeth.

"Considering what has happened over the past few days," he says, "I think we may need to take a more aggressive approach."

*He's going to do something. He's going to do something to you.*

"I don't know what you're referring to," I say, even though I do.

Headmaster walks to his wall of haunted relics and picks up the little button. He rolls it absently between his fingers. He watches me for a reaction. I do not give him one.

"Do you recognize this?" he says.

*Yes. Yes yes yes.*

"Yes, sir."

"That's what I thought," he says. "I noticed it went missing a few days ago. Funnily enough, it turned up in the hands of the groundskeeper. He had it with him when the two of you were . . ." He tries to come up with a word. "Associating."

"Oh." That's all I can say. *Oh.* Anything more and I'll collapse.

"When I thought about it, I realized it went missing right after our first lesson. Right after I left you alone here." He doesn't meet my eyes. It's the one mercy he's giving me right now. My body hardly feels like mine, like it's overheating, like the skin is too close to my bones. "Really, Miss Bell. Out of everything I've learned about you, I genuinely thought you were more intelligent than this. You *steal* this from me, and actually believe I wouldn't notice? What did you do with it?"

I shake my head. "I wasn't trying to do anything."

"Don't lie to me."

"I wasn't."

Headmaster takes a deep breath. "Right," he says. "Right. Of course. Well. Maybe you just didn't get the chance."

I did. I absolutely got the chance, and the soul behind the haunting was afraid. Headmaster killed him. *HE DID THIS.* Did Headmaster kill all the people on the wall behind him?

"Here's your chance," he says.

He sets the button on his desk and plucks at the edge of the Veil. A small rip forms. It feels like a draft has been opened into the room, wisps of cold air, the smell of a summer thunderstorm in the distance.

"There. Whatever you were going to do. Go ahead."

Violet and silver spark from the edges, frayed threads of the world.

This is a trick.

"No," I say. "I'm okay."

"Don't be coy. Go ahead. I've even started it for you."

"I'm fine."

He opens the tear a little further. I can see a spirit, just beyond the Veil—the one that told me to run. I can't see much of it. It doesn't move, as if it doesn't want to draw attention. "Do it. Now."

I do not.

Headmaster circles the desk once. Twice. I look at a particular part of the wall, the wallpaper where the floral print looks like a face. Focus on the shape, the pattern; do not look Headmaster in the eye.

"You," Headmaster says, "confuse me."

Do not look. Do not speak. Breathe in, breathe out.

"I thought you, of all the girls at this school, would be the one who best understood the danger of Veil sickness. You have a silly little medical mind. You've read all those journals, haven't you? You understand the dangers of leaving a wound open. So, here I was, under the impression that you would be the most open to treatment. You are at once exceedingly logical and horrifically illogical. Can you explain that to me, Miss Bell? Can you help me understand?"

I cannot. Because I do not know the way my mind works either. It is a mind that experiences the world too much. It is a mind that at once experiences everything in its smallest details, but without sensing the deeper meaning the rest of the world seems to inherently understand. It is a mind that sees the patterns and clicking, ticking systems all around us, but crumbles as soon as something falls out of place. It is a mind that operates, it seems, in a mirror version of the world, where the same actions and reactions are experienced so differently it's like we are not even the same species.

But that's not true, is it? We are the same species. We're all human. It's not that people cannot understand me; it's simply that most of them don't want to.

"Fine." Headmaster grabs a letter opener, then my hand. He wrenches my palm upward. *Don't move don't move don't move.* "If you're going to be silent like an animal, I'll treat you like one. If you don't open the Veil, I'll cut your stitches and open that wound right back up."

The rabbit pictures it for me. The sharp edge of the letter opener jamming underneath the loops of the stitches and wrenching them out of the skin. Because I used a running stitch, pulling on one will make them all tighten, ripping through the flesh in a chain reaction. I should have used an interrupted stitch. I should have just bitten down and done it.

"It'd be easy enough," Headmaster says. "That's only just now begun to scab, hasn't it?" His hand is covered in calluses. I don't think I remember how to breathe. "It wouldn't take much."

*Would he do it?*

"Go ahead. Open the Veil. That's all it'd take to make me stop."

I do not.

He puts the letter opener against my palm.

I do not.

A little pressure against the wound. Pain spikes. I jerk. He holds tight. "You're just going to let me do this. Interesting. Do you take pleasure in it? Would you have let the groundskeeper do this?"

He does not know that my tutors taught me to be silent. They forced me into shoes that made me cry, they played high notes that made me cover my ears, they dragged me out into bright light and berated me when I dared to squint—and they did it over and over again until I *stopped*. I learned to work through discomfort, through pain, and smile all the while.

The scab snaps. Blood wells to the surface, a little red drop. The stitches strain but hold.

It's so easy to say nothing. For a moment, I wish I could do this forever, like the groundskeeper. Just sew my mouth up or reach down my throat to destroy my vocal cords for good. Daphne would understand. We could write back and forth to each other, or she could talk and I could listen. I think I'd like that. A good surgeon does not need to talk; his hands do the talking for him.

Headmaster says, "Jesus Christ," lets go of me, drops the letter opener, and shoves all the papers off his desk with a roar.

Pages flutter. Pens scatter. Ink spills. Books thud onto the floor. I do not move, do not move, squeeze my eyes shut, pretend I don't hear him, pretend it's not happening.

Don't breathe.

*He's going to hurt you.*

*"I know you opened the Veil!"* he howls. His feet hit the ground, *thump thump thump*. I know where he is by the sound of his shoes, by the ragged breathing between his teeth. "You insolent, disrespectful *bitch*. You come here so that we can *help* you, and you disrespect us every step of the way. What do we have to do to get through to you? Do we have to put glass in your shoes too?"

Something breaks on the floor.

*He's going to HURT YOU.*

"So when I tell you to do something, you do it. When I tell you to open the Veil, you bloody well *do it*. Am I *clear*?"

Don't move.

A long, long silence.

He says, "If you are a good girl, and do as I say, and open the Veil," with his voice low, ragged, worn, "I'll stop."

And he's kissing me.

He—

He's—

if we still had the fingers to take out their eyes

we would feast on them like witches

I've never been kissed before.

Sure, men would kiss the top of my head, or my knuckles, or even my cheeks, where they would often miss on purpose and press their lips to my temple, my ear. I learned to deal with it, because I was a little girl and men can do whatever they want to little girls.

But not like this.

Not with teeth like a bone saw and tongue like loose intestines, beard scraping my skin raw. Not with a hand holding my head still.

All the softness of an amputation without the reason.

I do not stop him.

I was taught not to stop him.

I don't know how long he stays there.

Like that.

Touching me.

I don't remember him sending me away. I don't remember stepping out of the office, or shutting the door behind me, or looking for Isabella. By the time my mind is coherent enough to remember anything at all, I am curled up in her bed, her stomach pressed to my back, her fingers running through my hair. She's whispering.

"I know," she says. "I know."

She says, "It never gets any easier."

Two days until the winter garden party.

Isabella takes care of me. She ushers me from class to class, reminds me to eat, does my chores with me. Even Charlotte, even Mary, know not to come too close.

Have they been through this too? Do they understand?

During breakfast the day of the party, Headmaster comes up to address us with a hand on my shoulder. Be on your best behavior, he reminds us.

He squeezes tight. The rabbit translates: *You'll be a good girl, won't you?*

20

"Gloria?"

I blink unsteadily, vision blurring before it clears. The strings of Isabella's corset are in my hands. She's standing in front of me, facing one of the mirrors set up in the dining hall but looking through the reflective surface at me. Her long, dark hair has been piled into an intricate bun. A few artfully chosen strands rest against the pale nape of her neck.

Oh. We're here.

I look around, trying to get my bearings. Everyone is in the dining hall except Headmaster, because it would be improper if he was, considering the various states of undress we're in. Mirrors have been set up on every wall, shawls and gloves and hats strewn about. Each of us fiddles with our dresses, or our hair, or whatever thing we've nervously fixated on. Mrs. Forrester walks her circuit around us, looking for errors to correct, but she doesn't have to do much with Charlotte bemoaning every little stitch out of place. And, for the first time, there are servants: maids fussing in and out of the kitchen, hired help out in the back garden and greenhouse. My head spins. Why are there so many people? There are never this many people. Isabella sees my confusion and sighs; I catch my reflection in the mirror and I realize I'm almost hiding from these new people like a mouse.

It doesn't help that my memory of coming down here is hazy. It wasn't until Isabella said my name that I became aware of what I was supposed to be doing. Right. Helping her with the corset. Charlotte snapped about it being too loose, so we're doing it again. Through the window to the garden, the groundskeeper sweeps away bits of snow from the path he'd shoveled from the backdoor to the green-house, shrinking back from a servant that comes too close with a chair. I can almost discern the altered shape of the greenhouse interior, all the plants pushed to the edges to make room for tables.

"Are you all right?" Isabella asks me.

"Yes." The answer is automatic, because I don't know the truth. Am I all right? It doesn't feel like it. I gather myself and pull the last string on her corset. "There."

I peer over Isabella's shoulder, into the mirror, to see what outfit I've been tied up in. A structured white dress, buttoned to the throat, bustle cascading to the floor with a silver scarf. With the hat threaded with violets, I look like a Speaker wife already. We all do. Across the room, Louise fiddles with her buttons and inspects gloves she hasn't put on yet. Mary paces restlessly. The air hums with anxious energy.

I get to see Daphne again.

Her name feels like a scalpel held tight in the hand, or the comforting smell of antiseptic. We will search for the rotten core of this place, the haunting, the bodies, wherever they are—and if we find it, we will squeeze. While Braxton's is consumed by the party, we will cut it open.

The rabbit does not like the flicker of hope I feel in my chest. It grabs whatever it can find and throws it at me: *You really thought your first kiss would get to be her? Pathetic. You know that men take what they want.*

I do not cry. I don't know if I've allowed myself to cry about it yet.

"We'll finally get to meet the Luckenbill boy," Mary says as I tug at my collar to give myself space to breathe. I hadn't noticed her come up to us. Isabella sighs. "I, for one, am intrigued."

"Don't start," Charlotte warns over her shoulder. "He is Miss Bell's, and that's that. It's not as if you have a chance with him."

Mary hums, fiddling with the string around her neck, the one that disappears into her dress. That ring again. "It's just morbid curiosity, Miss Hudson," she tells Charlotte. It's odd for us all to be using our surnames, but this is a proper event and Mrs. Forrester is breathing down our necks. "To be honest, if he wants Miss Bell, I'm not sure I'd want him."

Mrs. Forrester comes up behind her and tugs on her ear. Mary yelps. "Quiet."

It's strange to see Mrs. Forrester walking around when I've seen what's inside her shoes. Now, if I pay a little too much attention, I can almost hear the glass crunching when she walks. Infection will get her eventually—it can't not. She tells Louise to put on her scarf, and then leaves us to check on Headmaster.

"I saw your brother," Louise says to me as she picks a scarf from the pile. "He's a handsome man."

"He's married," I say.

"Oh."

"What about you, little crow?" Mary asks Isabella. "Is Dr. Jessett visiting you today?"

"Mm," Isabella says.

"Not that it matters. You'd let all of them have their way if you could."

The suitors arrive around noon. Speakers, of course, each and every one of them. Charlotte peers out of the room to introduce them to us as they arrive, whispering dreamily. There's Dr. Church, a doctor from Liverpool; Mr. Macalister, a young bachelor with a massive inheritance; Mr. Kidd, the nephew of the Queen's medium. When the name *Dr. Jessett* comes up, I glance to Isabella. There's more men, of course, but I can't focus when Isabella looks like she wants to crawl into the floor.

Isn't Dr. Jessett the man who came to see her a few days ago?

Dr. Church dips his head toward Charlotte, who he sees peeking out of the door. She curtsies in turn, then flees back into the dining hall with a giggle. The men greet each other down the hallway, laugh, joke with Headmaster. I can hear their voices, a garbled mess of low murmurs.

And then: Daphne and Lord Luckenbill. *Those* voices I would recognize anywhere. I peer through the crack in the doorway, then open it further, a bit immodestly.

Daphne is stunning. Her clothes, like all men's clothes on her, are strange and drab, with the heavy coat slung around her shoulders. But her cheeks and nose are reddened from the cold and her green eyes are bright. A dark curl falls over her forehead. And, yes, there it is—she's placed a flower from the entryway vase in her breast pocket.

She smiles when she sees me. I duck my head demurely, because I cannot bring myself to smile back, not now. Lord Luckenbill raises a hand in greeting.

"That's Mr. Luckenbill?" Mary says from behind me, eyeing Daphne. I jump and duck back into the dining hall. "Looks like he'd rather bugger men than you."

*If you told Daphne what Headmaster did, she'd be disgusted.*

I feel the sudden urge to beat the side of my head. No. No, she wouldn't be. She would be disgusted with *him*, not with me. No.

*So don't say a word. Be a good girl, won't you?*

Mrs. Forrester rings her bell. We hurry to put on our gloves. "All right, girls, in line, in line."

Each of us receive our escort. When Daphne comes in, I struggle to stay on my feet. She comes up, smiles a bit lopsidedly, and allows me to put my arm through hers. She's so warm, even as the cold radiates off her clothes, and it

240 Andrew Joseph White

takes everything I have not to lean against her and beg her to keep me upright.

"Ready?" she whispers.

No. How am I supposed to do anything when I ache all over? When my stomach hurts from fear and anxiety? "I have to be."

Dr. Church takes Charlotte's hand, the age difference making my skin crawl. Louise keeps her eyes down at the floor, avoiding Mr. Macalister's hungry gaze. Mr. Kidd takes special interest in Mary, but a Mr. Humphrey (I don't know anything about him) takes her arm instead. And Dr. Jessett approaches Isabella. Isabella tries to smile. She looks just as sick as she did when she came back to the dormitory.

Daphne ducks her mouth to my ear. I shudder. *Don't tell her, don't tell her, she'd be disgusted.* "Who is who?"

"Mary there was the one who got my hand," I whisper. "And that one is Isabella. She's my friend."

"You have friends?"

When I laugh, it comes out pitiful and shaky. I know she doesn't mean it as an insult—it's a genuine question—but it still feels odd. I want to say I'm not sure, I'm not sure how to tell. I've never had friends before. But I don't.

◆

The greenhouse of Braxton's has, indeed, been transformed.

All the shelves of plants have been moved to the edges, a beautiful border surrounding tables with lace tablecloths, fine china, polished silver. Mrs. Forrester has set up an endless row of cakes and teas, most of which are aggressively unappetizing. Snow blows in with our feet as we enter. Place cards have been set up for each of us, which Louise painstakingly wrote yesterday, as she has the best handwriting. We are surrounded on all sides by bright greenery and the smell of pollen and servants. There are too many people. I feel a bit ill.

Headmaster greets each of the men as they sit, and Daphne too. Headmaster's smile is plastered on. It's not real. It's never been.

He watches me all the way to our table.

"Hope nobody is allergic," Daphne grouses as she pulls out my chair and settles down across from me. "What is all of this, anyway? Lavender?" She wrinkles her nose. "At least they finally hired some damn help."

Everyone finds their seats. All of the other escorts leave their girls with a gentlemanly bow to go sit at their own set of tables on the far edge of the room—that is, except for Dr. Jessett. He has a place card at the table beside us, where he sits with Isabella. Their cards are set up like Daphne's and mine. The rabbit notices. Shit. Is Isabella engaged? Or betrothed? No; she would have told me if she was. I try to catch her eye, but she doesn't look up.

Lord Luckenbill is up at the front, speaking with Headmaster. Something must strike Lord Luckenbill as funny. He laughs.

If we told Lord Luckenbill right now, would he believe us?

*Of course he wouldn't.*

"Good afternoon," Headmaster says, tapping his fork against a glass of wine. The servants stand at the side of the

room, as still as possible, so as not to be in the way. I skim
the line for the groundskeeper but don't find him. Of course
I don't. If this is too many people for me, I can't imagine
what it's like for him. "I am pleased to announce that today's
guest speaker is Viscount Luckenbill; the president of the
Royal Speaker Society and benefactor of the Braxton estate.
Thank you, thank you, for agreeing to address us this afternoon. Why don't we all give him a warm welcome?"

We clap politely. Daphne meets my eyes across the table
and pulls a quick face. Despite myself, I smile.

"Thank you for the introduction," Lord Luckenbill says.
"Now, I must say I've rarely given such a speech in mixed
company—forgive me if some of the things I say come across
a little much for delicate ears, ladies, but I do mean well . . ."

And he speaks of Veil sickness. He speaks of Miss
Neuling, and Bethlem Royal Hospital, and the uptick of
women struggling under the weight of their power. He
speaks of how this sickness spreads through the body,
through the mind, until we become not just a danger to
ourselves and others, but to London as a whole. And then,
he talks of how anger is a poison of the mind, how we
should avoid it at all costs, how we must be vigilant to be
sure we are nothing like those sad, sad women who have
given over to moral impurity and sickness.

He says that a woman's best defense against this sickness is the warmth and love and guidance of a husband—I
glance to Daphne, hoping my gaze conveys *What the fuck is
he on about?*—so, Lord Luckenbill says, how lovely is it that
we are all here today?

He toasts to our frail constitutions, weak minds, and easily tempted spirits, though not in those words.

And then the garden party begins in earnest.

It's been so long since I've been allowed at an actual party that I realize, quickly, I have no idea what happens at them. The servants pour tea and pass out little snacks. I fret with my sleeve. Whatever Daphne and I need to do, it can't happen in the middle of the greenhouse, surrounded by so many people.

"How do we get back to—?" I whisper.

"I've got it," Daphne says.

She gets up to bother her father's table: the table with Headmaster and Mrs. Forrester. Across the room, Charlotte politely asks if she may be allowed to play a song on the piano, which Mrs. Forrester agrees to. As the notes rise, I cannot hear what Daphne asks. Headmaster's face cracks into a smile that, for once, is not fake. It looks unwell. He leans across the table, clasps Daphne's hand, shakes it vigorously. I don't like that he's touching her. He shouldn't touch her.

*Don't tell her.*

She comes back and quietly slips back into her seat. I frown at her.

Daphne reaches into her pocket to reveal a key tucked into her jacket pocket. "Parlor room key," she says. "Said I wanted a moment alone with you and he handed it right over. I know they let the Speakers do whatever they please, but—" She makes a sick noise that's obscured by the piano. How did they get that damn thing out here? "He's disgusting," she says.

He is.

We wait until more people begin to stand, until there's a bit of mingling, before Daphne offers an arm to help me to my feet. We're doing this, then. When Daphne pulls me through the door to the outside, the only person who sees us go is Charlotte, who watches, horrified.

"Charlotte will call me a slut afterward," I say as the greenhouse door shuts. At the edge of the lawn, the groundskeeper continues to shovel snow—there he is. I raise a hand in greeting, but he doesn't see me. I want to ask if his hand is okay. If Headmaster hurt him because of me. But we don't have time.

"Do you care?" Daphne says. "If she does?"

"No."

*Don't tell her.*

Daphne holds the back door open for me and I slip inside, immediately taking off my hat and gloves because I can't stand the way they feel. Without the students, Braxton's Finishing School and Sanitorium carries the same silence as when I first arrived: stillness like an anesthetized patient. The ceilings feel higher, the hallways wider. Even the air itself presses down on my shoulders.

"Proof," I say, even though I hate that word. A haunting—a haunting that isn't the artifacts, the stolen ruins, but the girls, the girls, the girls.

Or a body. Either one.

"Proof," Daphne repeats, and she takes my hand and pulls me deeper into the empty school.

*Don't tell her.*

"Where first?" Daphne asks.

We have the key to the parlor, but if something was there, we would have found it already. I lead her towards Headmaster's office. The rabbit is nervous. *Ellen went into his office and never came back. You never saw her again.* The office is at the end of a long hall with no windows and one light. The sun has a hard time reaching down here, the same way light can't go far past the back of the tongue. I squeeze Daphne's hand tighter. At the very least, we'll be able to find something here. Right?

But the door to the office is locked. Figures. Daphne tries the parlor key on the off chance that it's a master key. It's not. She squints, crouches down, peers through the keyhole.

"Can you pick locks?" she asks.

What kind of question is that? "No."

"Do you have any hairpins? A hatpin?"

"I doubt that would actually work—"

Down the hall. Around the corner.

The creaking of hinges.

Feet thumping on carpet.

Low, muffled voices.

"What?" Daphne says. "It can't be *that* difficult, can it?"

I yank her away from the door and put a finger to my lips.

Her eyes blow wide. She stops moving.

". . . probably rotted by now," someone says. The voice is familiar, and my stomach falls to my shoes. *Rotting*, the rabbit says, *rotting rotting rotting.* I press a hand to my pulse just to feel the thrum. Just to remind myself that it's there. "It's going to smell like the devil down there."

"Well, unless you want it to *keep* rotting, then be my guest."

The muscles in Daphne's throat tighten: the platysma, all the other delicate pieces.

Who *is* that? Why do I know that *voice*?

. . . Why do I know both of them?

I take a step closer. And another. Daphne hisses, grabbing for me, but I'm already out of her reach. She follows with a strangled noise. Closer, closer, until the end of the hall, and then—

Two men. In masks. Haphazard masks, leather and linen wrapped around the head like burial shrouds, showing only the eyes. I realize, at that very moment, that I've been misinterpreting the groundskeeper's motion: it was never a hand over the eyes. It was one hand over the mouth, the other with fingers *split* to show the eyes.

This was what the groundskeeper was trying to tell me. Oh God. This is it.

The two of them, dressed in fine doctor's suits, one fumbling with a set of keys, grumble at each other impatiently in the hall.

Daphne grabs my shoulders and brings me back against her chest. I can feel her heartbeat. "Speakers," she says. "They have rings." It's too far away for me to see clearly, but I see the glint of metal and the smooth backs of their hands. They're not mediums.

The Speaker with the keys finally finds the one he's

looking for and shuffles down the hall to the dressing room, which he unlocks.

Wait. The dressing room?

All of a sudden, the other man turns away from him.

"*Hey,*" says the Speaker with the keys. His voice, his voice, his voice. "Where are you going?"

The other one hesitates. "I'm not abandoning you." He takes a folded document from his coat pocket, his voice oddly flat. "I'm dropping off your letter at the office."

The office? Headmaster's office.

He's coming toward us.

I duck back behind the corner. There are approximately five seconds before he sees us. We can't leave this hallway, all the doors are locked, we can't be caught like this—

And in those five seconds, I look at Daphne. She stares back, green eyes wide. Her nostrils flare with panic.

*Don't tell her.*

Headmaster took my first kiss from me. He took it like it was nothing. I wasn't ready, I was waiting, and he plucked it from me before I had the chance to claim it for myself. And he didn't do it out of carelessness or ignorance, but because he knew it'd hurt me. He wanted to hurt me. He wanted to punish me for my disobedience.

I thought—the rabbit thought—that I'd never get that chance again.

*Don't tell her.*

But it doesn't work like that.

*Don't tell her.*

He doesn't have to be my first. He doesn't count. Not if I don't want it to.

And I don't want it to.

*Don't tell her what he did to you, it's disgusting, it makes you disgusting, he tainted you the same way he taints everything he touches.*

I say, "Kiss me."

It would hide our faces. It would give us plausible deniability—a young man and a young woman in a back hallway. But it would also be a kiss to do it right this time. That I asked for. That I agree to.

Daphne hesitates.

I say, "Please."

She does.

Before this moment, the idea of kissing never really appealed to me. Observing it from afar, it seemed strange. I've always been prone to pulling things apart clinically: What is a kiss but a touching of lips to show affection? Or devotion, or a show of power? I see the social benefits of it as a marker, yes, but only in the way one knocks on a door or shakes hands. It's done because it's what's expected. I know what it looks like. I know, in a sterile manner, how it is generally done.

But when I kiss Daphne—she is soft and her breath is warm. Her eyes flutter shut, and she reaches for me as if she's terrified I'll disappear while she can't see. I don't know how I ever spent so many days apart from her. The idea of stepping away is suddenly unfathomable, as if we are the only steady things we've ever had. Maybe that's true. Maybe we've only known each other for a few days, but the world has seen fit to put us together, and what beautiful luck it is, then, that there's such a sweet thing in such a terrible place.

Beside us, I hear the Speaker stop.

I hear a sharp intake of breath.

I hear him walk away.

Daphne breaks from me. Her lips are pink. Her eyes half closed. We wait there, our faces close to each other, nose against nose, and listen in silence until the dressing room door shuts.

Daphne whispers, "Is there—"

I say, "There's something in the dressing room."

There is a long moment where I know what we are both thinking. We are both thinking that we run. That we take one of the carriages outside, leave this place behind, demand that the driver ride and ride until we are so far away.

But we would be hunted like dogs. Because that's what the Speakers do. They will never let go of us.

*There's something in the dressing room.* Something rotting. Something that needs to be kept hidden by Speakers in burial shroud masks. Whatever it is, I'm terrified of it.

And we need to find it.

Nobody else is going to.

✦

We go back to the garden party in silence. My hands tremble. Daphne returns the key to Headmaster, who smiles that same awful smile.

"I wish I could stay with you," she whispers across the table, her voice almost drowned out by the laughter and talking. I wish she could too. She has found herself in part of my chest, and I know that it will begin to ache as soon as she's gone. Her hand squeezes mine. "Please don't do anything dangerous alone."

I am about to whisper an apology—that I can't promise that—when there's a cheer from the other side of the room. Daphne leans forward, as if to protect me.

By the piano, Isabella's suitor has taken her by the hand.

"The time has come, hasn't it?" Dr. Jessett says. Isabella retreats, but not in any real, visible way; I see it in the vague distance of her eyes. She's not really here. Mrs. Forrester takes down her little reading glasses to watch them. "Won't you join me?"

Isabella has no choice but to say, "Yes," which she does, and some of the suitors cheer, and every girl claps the way she knows she should. Only Charlotte looks genuinely happy.

Isabella is leaving us.

It is like watching an animal being led to the slaughter, and there's something in her eyes that says she's going to do something about it.

✦

When I catch her during clean-up—after Daphne has left, after the servants have been sent away, after we are alone— Isabella says, "I'm okay, dear," and presses her lips to my forehead. "He's a fine enough man. Better than some."

21

I kissed Daphne.

And there's something in the dressing room.

*Probably rotted by now.*

Sometimes, while I was looking for slaughterhouse rejects to study, I came upon animals that had been left to fester in the London sun. It was always the smell that hit me first. Sick, heavy, a miasma that lodged in the throat. And then, when I found the carcass, I always thought for a moment that it might still be alive. It moved. Writhed. Eventually, like clockwork, I would realize it wasn't moving, but instead it was the *worms*, the maggots, crawling through the body and devouring it. The meat had gone black and somewhat green in the sun. Parts of it had liquified and reflected the sun.

Something like that couldn't be in the dressing room. I would have noticed. Anyone would have noticed.

Right?

*But why else would the room be locked?*

Why, indeed, would a dressing room be locked from the outside?

I have trouble sleeping that night. I open my eyes every few minutes, watching the girls to make sure they're still breathing. The rabbit wants to convince me something will happen to them if I don't keep looking at them.

We just need to get into the dressing room. That's it. That's all.

The only thing stopping us is a key.

I toss and turn, heart beating fast, the thrum of a rabbit. Which is why, in the middle of the night, I hear something in the washroom.

It's distant, but my body's physiological response to it is immediate. It's a sinking in my chest, the way I imagine it feels when a mother hears her baby cry. A leaden weight in the stomach. Painful and impossible to swallow. The sound of someone in agony and desperately trying to hide it.

Nobody else moves.

I sit up, clutching the quilt to my chest. The girls all look asleep to me; nobody twitching, seemingly dead to the world. Slowly, I slide out of bed, wincing when my stockinged feet touch the cold floor. The noise comes again, quieter this time, quiet enough that maybe I'm imagining it. There's a dim light coming from behind the washroom door.

Isabella's bed is empty. I go over to it anyway, as if it's a trick of the shadows that the sheets are flat, that the curve of her body is gone. It's not. She's not there.

The sound comes again.

I walk over to the washroom door and tap my fingers on the wood. "Isabella?" I whisper.

"*Shit*," comes the voice inside—broken, terrified.

"Are you all right?"

Nothing. Another pained gasp.

I grab the knob. "I'm coming in."

"Wait—"

I open the door and stop.

Bile rises in my throat. My head turns light and my knees threaten to buckle.

Then the reality of the scene before me snaps into place, and I am calm and composed, the way a surgeon should be. The nausea in my stomach, the beating of my heart, are all replaced with a long, deep breath. With stillness.

Assess the situation. Find the best course of action. Save the patient.

Isabella has situated herself in the porcelain bathtub, long white nightdress unbuttoned to her belly and folded down over her legs; her chest is bare and blood smears her hands, her stomach, her thighs. With her dress pulled down, I can see the bare flesh of her stomach and the slightest, vaguest bump of pregnancy. My guess is three months, maybe four. Not far enough along that it couldn't be hidden with certain corsets and sucking in the belly.

The damage is as follows: she's cut herself open along the stomach. Parallel to her body, off to the side, as if she couldn't bear slicing through the navel. The wound is deep enough that it's gone black, the same way it was in my fantasies of hysterectomy. No doubt she's hit important things. The cut is jagged, and messy, and in the completely wrong direction—a Cesarean should be opened lengthwise, just above the pubic bone, not stretched out tall. She's used a kitchen knife from the party. The only illumination comes from a few candles on the windowsill, guttering a bit since they've burned so low.

"Gloria," Isabella splutters. Her face, usually bright with pink in her cheeks, is sallow and sickly. "Close the door."

I do. My movements feel incredibly slow. She's losing so, so much blood. She doesn't have much time. "What is this?"

She looks down at the gaping wound. "I need to get it out." Her words are a keen, barely audible between her teeth. "It's *his*. It's his."

*Of course it is*, the rabbit says.

"*You know what to do*," George might have said, if he were here. My mind is a traitor. I don't want to think about him. "*You've read my notes enough. Put it into practice.*"

Traitor or not, he's correct. I can do this.

"I understand," I say. I gently peel the knife from her limp fingers. The blade is sharp enough to work, but I really wish I had something better. "Will this stop him from marrying you?"

"It'll show him I'm fucking mad." The blood loss is making her delirious. "I'll show him and everyone that I'm better off—" *In Bedlam. In prison.* Something. Anything. Her voice turns to a whisper. "You don't go to Heaven if you kill yourself, Gloria."

I know. "You're not going to die," I tell her.

She closes her eyes. Her breathing is quick and shallow. "Get it out of me," she says.

I turn to her just-so-slightly swollen belly, the blood pooling around her. "Okay."

I gather all the spare linen I can find in the bathroom; she's bleeding so much that I'll need to soak it up repeatedly, and even then, I'll only have a few seconds to work at a time. Like her, I unbutton my gown to the waist to keep blood from weighing down the sleeves. My mind doesn't have enough spare room to bother worrying about modesty. I climb into the large tub with her, straddling her long legs and the red mess of her clothes. The knife is too steady in my hand.

"Do you want me to talk to you?" I whisper.

"Yes," Isabella says. "Talk to me, talk to me. I don't care about what."

I nod and fold a small hand towel to wad it between her teeth. "All right. All right. Here."

And as I press my hand to her belly, stretching out the skin and dabbing away blood so I can see the damage already done, I begin to speak.

"My name is actually Silas." Without clamps, I have to spread the gap apart with my fingers to see inside. Her innards are warm and slippery. Isabella's foot jams help-lessly into the side of the tub as she whimpers. "I'm a boy. Well, not in the way you think. If you took off my dress, I'd look just like you. But the thing inside you that tells you that you're a woman, deep in your chest—I don't have that. I never have."

A person's insides are nothing like the clean, mono-chrome drawings in medical notes. Everything is the same shade of red, cut through with pink and bits of flaxen fat. Just like the medium. Just like the pig. She's made the cut in a strange place, which makes it harder to work with. And she hadn't gone all the way through the muscle like she needed to. She could have just found some way to abort the fetus—expel it, starve herself, poison herself.

But she was correct about one thing: this is the way a madwoman does it. No man will ever look at her again.

This is how a Veil-sick woman does it.

"I thought there was something wrong with me for the longest time," I murmur. "I thought I was alone. But there was a doctor who died a few decades back. James Barry, his name was. He did procedures just like this one. And when he died, they discovered he was a woman." I push the knife into the muscle and split it carefully. More blood, always more blood to wipe away. Isabella's head slams against the hard edge of the tub. "But of course, he wasn't. He was a man like me. And he got a chance to *be* a man. Will I ever get that? I genuinely don't know anymore."

I reach into the muscle, and she *screams*.

It's muffled by the rag, but it's so hoarse and desperate that it strains the walls. The air reeks of sweat and meat.

Someone knocks on the door.

"No," Isabella pleads around the rag, "no no no."

There's no time; I can't afford to stop. I push my hand deeper, and it's like reaching into a fire. "My brother knows," I say. My voice hitches. The door opens and someone steps inside and clamps a hand to her mouth. I can't see who it is. "He's the first person I told, and—he used to use my real name. He used to let me wear his clothes. But now I don't know if he actually *sees* me as a man, or if he's just humoring his silly little sibling. He doesn't listen anymore, and I don't know what I did wrong."

Isabella begins to pull away from me. I turn, blinking at the girls who are beginning to crowd into the washroom.

None of them move.

I point to the closest person. Charlotte. "You, hold her by the shoulders. Keep her as still as you can." Mary. "You, grab one of these rags. I need you to soak up the blood for me so I can see." Louise. "And you, bring me more candles."

Louise scatters. Mary grabs a rag and wrings it out. Charlotte doesn't move.

"What happened?" Charlotte asks.

"She opened herself up," I snap. She doesn't get to waste my patient's time, not like this. "I'm just finishing it. Isabella, look at me. Are you still with me?"

Isabella opens her swollen, red eyes just a crack. She's sobbing. I need to be quick, quick, quick.

She nods.

"Okay. I'm almost there. It's almost done."

I pick up the knife again. Louise brings in candles, lights them wherever she can. The blade cuts through the membrane of the small, hard uterus easily, and it pops like a cyst, fluid soaking my hands.

I keep talking. I have to, or I'll lose my focus. "My parents hate me for it. I'm nothing but a disappointment to them. You know, I always thought I'd get to be a surgeon one day. I'd do what Barry did. I'd get George to vouch for me, convince a medical school I'm a man, and join the ranks. I'd be a doctor who helps people like me. I'd be a doctor who understands." And then my hand is in the little organ, searching for— I don't know. I don't know what it will feel like. My fingers press into every corner. "I always thought I'd be able to get out somehow. That I could live as a man, and everything would be okay. Now, I don't know anymore."

I find it. It's smaller than the palm of my hand, burning hot, tethered to Isabella's insides with a wet little cord.

"I'm not sure where I'm going with this." I pinch it between two of my fingers. It's delicate. Something twists unnaturally. "But my name is Silas. I'm a boy. And I hope the man who did this to you dies a long, horrible death, so that he can feel as much pain as you're feeling right now."

I pull the fetus out.

It's a pink, curled creature that fits right into my palm, beady black eyes staring at nothing, frail arms tucked to its mouth. By taking it out, I've broken part of it. The body is twisted strangely. Even its face is still lumpy, like clay. And its head is bulbous and misshapen—the skull hasn't fully hardened yet, pulsing rapidly like a double-time heartbeat.

The fetus does not move. It does not cry. It does not react to the darkness, or the cold, or the pain.

Should it?

I sever the cord and wrap it up in the rag to hand to Louise. She stares at it, wavering, as if she'll be sick.

"Dispose of it," I say. "Mary, I need the sewing kit."

The bundle is taken away, and the sewing kit I used to stitch my hand is given to me. Isabella stares at the ceiling, sheet white and shivering, as I stitch her up one piece at a time; first the womb, then the muscle, then the burning skin of her belly.

"There," I whisper to her. "It's done."

"It's done?" she whimpers.

"It's done." I place a hand on her leg, squeeze. To show her I'm here. She's cold. She shouldn't be this cold. "I promise."

The dormitory door opens. Someone shrieks.

Shit, *shit*. I drop the knife down the back of the tub and start desperately pulling Isabella's gown up to cover her. The movement makes her sob. "I know, I know. I'm sorry."

But it's too late. Mrs. Forrester and Headmaster burst into the washroom, still in their sleeping clothes.

"What in the devil—" Headmaster says before his eyes land on me. Me, with my bare chest, hair tied roughly from my face, blood smeared my hands and gown.

I don't even think to cover myself. The only thing I can do is hunch over Isabella, her hand clasped in mine.

"What did you *do*?" Headmaster snarls.

"I did it," Isabella sobs. "I did it. Don't touch her."

"It was a Cesarean," I say. "Call Dr. Bernthal, or the village doctor, or my brother, please."

"There's no time for that," he says. "Mrs. Forrester, some assistance, if you please?"

And it's as if I'm not there at all. Mrs. Forrester drags me out of the tub, away from Isabella, who wails and reaches for me. She wrestles my dress up over my chest— *How dare you*, she hisses, shoving me against the wall when I struggle. Headmaster lifts Isabella from the tub and he does not hesitate, no matter how much she screams.

Then she's gone.

You know what they did.

22

After Isabella is taken, there is nothing for us to say. Headmaster locks the dormitory door so we cannot leave.

Charlotte, Louise, Mary, me.

I wash my hands, and the tub; I change my nightgown and leave it to soak in an attempt at saving it. I wear Isabella's spare, even though I have one of my own. The washroom smells of copper and amniotic fluid, the vague smell of afterbirth. Louise cleans the spots of blood on the floor. I don't ask her what she did with the fetus. Charlotte extinguishes the candles one by one, licking her fingers to pinch the wicks, while Mary strips Isabella's bed and folds the quilt.

When I step out of the bathroom, Mary has put Isabella's quilt at the foot of my bed. I open my mouth to say something about it, but she shakes her head, so I don't. The only thing I can think of to do is unfold it again, wrap it around my shoulders, and sit on the edge of the mattress.

Again, we do not change beds.

We are so spread out now. So distant from each other.

✦

"Silas?" Louise says in the middle of the night. The sudden appearance of my name, like a spirit, startles me. None of us are asleep. I don't know how any of us could sleep now. Louise in the bed beside me, rolled over onto her side to watch me. "Did you say your name was Silas?"

"I did." There's no use denying it.

"You want to be a boy?" Charlotte says. Her tone is inscrutable.

For a moment, I almost say yes. But the wording isn't quite right. There's a difference. I remember the feeling in my stomach whenever my family passed advertisements for performances at the West End Theatre, showing women dressed as men. I remember Father's newspapers—the sensationalist ones he bought for fun on the weekends—languishing over bizarre stories of "female husbands" and cross-dressing. I remember desperately wishing to be something other than what I was.

I don't want to be a boy.

I already am.

*And the world will do anything to stop you.*

"I think it just takes some boys longer than others to figure it out," I say.

✦

In the morning, nobody comes to wake us. Instead, we rise slowly, by ourselves, with the sun. It shines, weak and watery and pale, through the large windows. I am awake first, sitting up in bed with my arms tucked around my knees. Mary follows soon after. She takes down her braids and doesn't bother putting them back up again.

Eventually, I hobble over to the hearth to pile in wood and start the fire. It takes a few tries for the flame to catch. It's warm here, and my eyes close for a moment, still weighed down by sleep. But instead, I get up and go back to my bed, where Daphne's letters are hidden under the mattress, then take them back and sit in front of the fire. I'm not going to burn them or anything of the sort. I just want to hold them is all.

*"There has to be a better poem out there for us."* I press one of the letters to my lips, the same way I did with the bloody handkerchief. The paper doesn't smell like her anymore. *"I pray that you run more gently."* I kept the envelopes too. It's strange to see the wrong name on them, above the address. I turn the envelopes over so I don't have to look at it.

Behind me, Mary sits in one of the chairs. I try not to make eye contact.

"Silas," she says. "That's your name, right?"

"It is," I say.

She nods at the chair beside her. "Sit."

I hesitate.

"*Sit.*"

I sit.

And there we are, in opposite chairs, a book of poetry on the table between us filled with pressed flowers. Maybe Daphne would like this. Maybe I should give a copy of *The Angel in the House* to her to see how she rewrites it, to discover what beautiful thing she could turn it into against the author's wishes. I think her voice could do something like that.

I realize, belatedly, that I should have written Daphne back. Even if it was just to say that the letters arrived. The rabbit mimics my tutors: *Such a thoughtless little girl.* I try not to let it worm its way into my head. The bits of social life that are so obvious to everyone else hardly ever occur to me. Thank-you notes, tone of voice, the simple concept of reciprocity; the back-and-forth that makes up human connection just . . . doesn't happen.

Daphne understands. She knows it's hard for me.

It's just that, if something happens to me, I would've liked for her to have my handwriting.

"Isabella started it?" Mary says.

"She'd just about cut into the muscle when I found her," I say.

"And you just kept going?"

"She was going to do it anyway. Might as well have someone with steadier hands give it a go."

Mary laughs bitterly. Her smile is cold and cruel. "Someone like you, then."

"You wanted her to ask you?" I don't look at her, just hold

the letters, focus on the feel of pages between my fingers. I know I get defensive of my work; no need to provoke her any more than that. "You'd sooner perforate the bowel than do any good. Or pop the bladder and infect the whole mess. She'd even made the incision in the wrong place. I had to make do. If you think you're capable of that, be my guest."

Mary says, "That's the most I've heard you speak."

"It's the most I've had to say."

"Mm."

She leans her head back, exposing her throat. She has no bruises, not like Isabella did. Certainly not like I did. Does that mean Headmaster and the suitors were rougher with Isabella, or does it mean that Mary simply hides it better? Men all hurt us in their own unique ways. None of us carry the same bruises, the same aches.

It makes me wonder what Headmaster has been doing to the other girls. I've never found out. We don't talk about what people do to us. We all have our own pain, so it makes sense that we wouldn't want to burden the others. Sharing pain is meant to make it easier, but all of us are at our limits.

And . . . I don't know much about any of them. I don't know childhood friends. I don't know pets, or favorite colors, or holidays they've been on. I don't know the names they have picked out for their firstborn children, or their favorite Christmas carols or hymns at church; I don't know their least favorite seasons or the foods that make them wrinkle their nose. I don't know first kisses, whether their parents loved them, if they have brothers or sisters, what countries they've dreamed of visiting, if they thought they'd ever escape and be alive.

"Frances was taken a month ago," Mary says.

I stop moving, as if startling her out of this train of thought would cause her to flee like a wild animal.

She says, "It took some time to realize she *had* been taken. She went to meet a suitor and never came back. At first I thought she was just taking her time, that maybe they'd gone for an evening stroll of the gardens—it wasn't so cold then—or, perhaps, he was having his way, like men do."

She makes a disgusted noise.

"Why would you want to be one of them?" she says. "How could you live with yourself?"

I've asked myself that so many times. How *could* I ever want to be a part of the section of humanity responsible for so much of my suffering? In what ways *haven't* men hurt me? But then again—in what ways haven't women? In what ways hasn't everyone?

I say, "I don't believe in original sin." Mary looks at me askance, frowning. "What they've done isn't my burden to bear. It's theirs."

"You actually believe that?"

"I do."

Mary says, "Lord, you're so naive."

I know. Mother and Father loved to remind me that my innocence was no longer cute. I was too old to act like this. Even George started chiding me for it eventually. *"Nothing is as black and white as you think it is."*

Mary continues. "But Frances would agree, if she were here. She was a better person than me. I thought God was good, and nothing would happen to her, because *she* was good too. So when she didn't come back, I convinced myself that nothing was wrong, because it couldn't be.

"And then she didn't come back, and her seat at the table was gone, and her book was gone, and when I said her name to Mrs. Forrester, the bitch hit me for it. I just wanted to know where she was. I was just scared for her."

A pause.

"After that, Isabella started staying up when a girl didn't come back. I hated her for it. Why was she trying to protect Agnes? Or Ellen? And not *her*?"

When she pauses again to collect herself, I offer silence. Her teeth grind together.

"I loved her," Mary says. "I would have done anything for her."

If my tutors were in the room with us, they would tell me there's a certain way to comfort somebody—to offer a reassuring hand, to say I'm sorry. But that's always felt hollow to me. It's performative, a script repeated over and over until it loses all meaning. I've never wanted to give anyone something like that, not really. Maybe that's why my tutors called me callous and unfeeling.

I'm not. I never was. I just express things differently is all.

Behind us, Louise wakes. I hear the shuffling of the blankets, the quiet noise of a stretch, feet hitting the floor. She comes up to the fire. The light makes her look young. Lord, I don't even know how old any of them are. Agnes was fourteen, but the rest of us? Louise might be my age. Maybe. I don't know how to ask.

"Nobody yet?" she says.

I shake my head. So Louise sits on the floor, watches the flames, and we do too.

Charlotte continues to sleep. Outside, the wind blows. It's no longer snowing, but drifts swirl off the roof, shake off the limbs of naked trees. The sky is bright and has that sharp, crisp edge. If I opened up a window and stuck my head out, it would be cold enough to hurt my lungs. I cradle the letters to my chest as if they might flutter away.

"So they're dead," Mary eventually says. Louise tucks her knees up to her chin. "All of them. Frances, Ellen, Isabella . . ."

"They always have been," I say. Mary drops her face into her hands. Louise picks at the hem of her skirt, glancing between us. "Their spirits—"

Mary lets out a strangled scream, grabs a teacup from the table, and flings it into the hearth. It shatters with a terrible crash. Pieces scatter among the wood and ashes. Louise jumps. Charlotte sits up with a gasp.

"Fuck them all," Mary says, jamming herself farther into her chair. She looks like a wolf curled up on itself, baring its teeth, hackles raised. Behind us, Charlotte fumbles with her blanket and crawls out of bed. "Fuck every last one of them. I hope they burn in hell."

And I say, voice so low that only Mary can hear: "They will. Because I think I know where they're hiding the bodies."

Mary's eyes slide to me.

"Where?" she asks.

After all these days. Finally. Finally.

"The dressing room. All I need are the keys."

Mary breathes in.

She breathes out.

"Okay," she says. "I can get those for you. As soon as I cross paths with Headmaster or Mrs. Forrester, you'll have them. But you better be right, Silas Bell, or I swear to God, you'll wish you were in her place."

◆

Eventually, Charlotte makes her way to the fire. She doesn't sit, but instead stands, glasses perched on her button nose, leaning against the bricks next to the hearth in silence. Louise offers her a tight smile. Mary offers nothing.

If she heard anything, she doesn't let it show on her face.

"You're not planning to do anything stupid," she says, "are you?"

Even I understand what she means. The way she defends Headmaster makes me ill. Men won't give her special treatment just because she'd smile and thank them if they struck her. She'd probably love them even more for it, thinking that they were doing God's work by correcting her.

"What do you care?" Mary says. "Go ahead, let a husband wring you out like a dirty washcloth. It's what you want, isn't it?"

"Not every man is so *cruel*." Charlotte's voice is small. As if she's not trying to convince us, but herself. "You think they're all monsters." She points at me. "See? You even have your suitor's letters. Hypocrite."

We don't bother responding to her. My fingers dent the papers in my hand. She doesn't get to talk about Daphne like that. She doesn't get to talk about Daphne at all.

Slowly, to fill the silence, Louise starts to tell stories. About Frances—how Frances stood up to the teachers, how she constantly had a handprint mark on her cheek, how she'd steal cigarettes from suitors and smoke them out the window. About Ellen—how she was a struggle to get along with but she still made sure to be kind to the groundskeeper, how they all skirted around her but still remembered to pass along shortbread biscuits, because nobody denied anyone their pleasures in a place like this. About Isabella—how she'd been here so long that she'd memorized the names of every girl she'd ever seen pass through, how she'd fallen asleep holding Agnes on Agnes's first night in the school, how she would've crossed out *Gloria* and written *Silas* in the ledger in the back of her mind if she'd lived long enough to do so.

While she speaks, Louise leans her head against my leg, burying her face in my skirts. I put a hand on the top of her head, lean over, and press my forehead to her hair. Mary watches the fire. Charlotte watches nothing.

23

Mary said I'll have the keys as soon as she crosses paths with a teacher, but for the longest time, we wonder if anyone will actually come for us. *The lot of you*, the rabbit says, *princesses trapped in a tower, forgotten until you waste away.* I know that's not how it works, but I hate when the rabbit says something I might agree with. Eventually, I put Daphne's letters safely under my mattress again, which seems to make Louise panic.

"They've never left us for this long," Louise says.

"It must be for a reason," Charlotte assures her.

I get up to check the door, as if I'm not the third person to do so, and it's still locked, because of course it is. We're running low on wood for the fire, and without food, we're becoming cranky and irritable. I don't mind being hungry—the gnawing ache makes me more aware of my body, so much that I've sometimes forgone food just to remind myself what it feels like—but that doesn't mean it's pleasant. Louise tries to nap it away. I wash my bloody nightgown until my fingers wrinkle. The stains are dark brown and stubborn.

It isn't until late, late in the afternoon, after we've missed breakfast and luncheon and tea, that we hear footsteps coming up the stairs to the third floor. I drop the sodden nightgown and peek out into the main room. Mary's head has turned from the fire, snapping her gaze to the door.

"Finally," Charlotte says.

Mary gets up, fingers curled. I can't stop comparing her to a wolf, hackles raised, slinking toward an injured fawn.

People are talking on the other side of the door. No, not talking. Arguing. I breathe slow, trying to make out the words. Louise comes up beside me. Her hands are wringing.

Mrs. Forrester: "I can't believe you made Dr. Bernthal come out all this way—"

Dr. Bernthal: "It was no issue, I promise."

Why is the doctor here? There's no reason for him to come out here.

Unless it's for one of us.

The rabbit says, *You.*

Mrs. Forrester: "Lord Luckenbill will have a conniption—"

Headmaster: "Are you implying I can't do my job?"

*Click.*

The door unlocks. It opens.

There's Mrs. Forrester, storming away the best she can with her painful, mangled feet. *That is what Headmaster did to her. That is what her husband did to her. She does it willingly, she believes him, just like Charlotte.* And then there's Dr. Bernthal and Headmaster. In the doorway. With the keys. The medium's seal on Headmaster's hand stares menacingly. I keep waiting for it to blink but it never does.

Dr. Bernthal dips his head respectfully, keeping his eyes down; we're immodest in our nightgowns, intensely improper for any strange man to witness. He's carrying a doctor's bag, one of those big heavy ones that George has. I can imagine everything inside. I have the contents memorized. The scalpel, the forceps, the chloroform and laudanum.

Headmaster says, "Good afternoon, girls. I hope you all have had time to rest since last night."

The way he says it disgusts me. *Last night.* As if we don't know Isabella is dead. As if we don't know how this school works.

As if any of us got any rest at all, knowing we would not be able to save her.

"Supper is prepared downstairs," Headmaster says. "I know it has been a while since you've last eaten, so we decided to relieve you of cooking. Mrs. Forrester has spent the past hour preparing your favorites. Miss Hudson, Miss Hare, Miss Carter. Please head downstairs. You may remain in your gowns, if you like; there are no suitors here to see you."

But not me.

Of course not me.

Mary says, "What about Gloria?"

Dr. Bernthal says, "Miss Bell will stay behind to talk with us for a moment."

*Scalpel, forceps, chloroform, laudanum.* Harriet, Harriet, Harriett.

I'm fucked.

Charlotte glances between us all. Her eyes are hard and set. She takes a step forward, then glances back again.

"Well?" she says to the others. "Aren't you coming?"

Because of course Charlotte would leave. Why wouldn't she? After everything she's been through, after all the time she's spent here—she'll always pick them over us.

She holds out a hand. "Louise? Come."

Louise makes a weak little noise.

"*Miss Hare,*" Charlotte says. "You're being rude."

"Okay," Louise says. "Okay. Can I just—" She hurries over to her bed, beside mine, and crouches down in the space between them. "I'm sorry. I needed a ribbon. For my hair." She sheepishly holds it up, one hand nervously in her pocket. "Yes. Okay. I'm coming. I'm coming."

Mary practically hisses. I know I said I can't blame any of them for trying to survive, but God, watching this, how am I supposed to do anything else? Even the rabbit twitches its ears in disappointment.

"As I thought," Charlotte says, taking Louise's arm. "I won't waste my breath trying to convince you, Mary."

"Good," Mary says. "Don't."

Charlotte pulls Louise to the door, their white nightgowns fluttering behind them. Dr. Bernthal respectfully steps aside to let them pass. Louise looks over her shoulder at us, her face drawn in pain, before she disappears around the corner.

There's a long pause. Headmaster sighs.

"Miss Carter," he says. "We don't have to do this."

"Don't we?" Mary says.

Headmaster steps into the room. So does Dr. Bernthal. The door shuts.

"May I ask what this is about?" I ask in the calmest voice I can manage. The sweet voice my tutors made sure to teach me. The mask is in place, my diction perfect, my expression nothing but openness and femininity. It is the voice of someone who has never been touched by Veil sickness at all.

"Dr. Bernthal and I merely want to have a private discussion about what happened with Miss Rossi last night." Headmaster tilts his head, as if he understands, as if he has any sympathy for me at all. *Headmaster screaming in your face. Throwing his papers and pens and ink to the floor. Pressing the letter opener to your hand, putting his mouth to yours, pushing you to the grass, wrapping his hands around your neck.* "And what the best steps from here may be."

"Best steps," Mary says. I hold out a hand—don't go further, don't say anything, please. Mary pushes against it like a dog on a lead. "Like what you did to Harriet."

Dr. Bernthal pulls a face. "No. Not at all."

*Do you believe him?*

No.

The possibilities, then, are slim: because Lord Luckenbill wants me for Daphne, he wouldn't risk losing me. He pulled so many strings for me. He wouldn't throw me away now. *But*, the rabbit says, *there are lots of things you can do to someone while keeping them alive.* And that much is true. Because you can take out someone's tongue. Or their eyes.

The rabbit paints a picture; Dr. Bernthal cutting me to pieces as a punishment for both me and for Daphne. A private wedding, Daphne holding my broken hands, pressing her finger against my teeth to make my mouth open so she can see the severed stump of the tongue. Lord Luckenbill saying it is the best thing for both of us. Daphne can learn to be a real man with the help of a wife who cannot fight back. This is what I deserve for disrespecting the Luckenbills after everything they've done to help me, after every chance they've given me. At least my womb still works, yes? At least I can still bear children. I don't need to be whole to do that. Men have plenty of practice doing terrible things like this. *What makes you any better than your ancestors, boy?* he'd say over Daphne's shoulder. *Real men take.*

Because that's how it always goes.

And what reason would Dr. Bernthal have to tell me the truth, anyway? Why would he tell me what he was really going to do, if it would only make me fight harder? It's easier when there's the benefit of the doubt, when we have been told all our lives to give grace, to be polite, to refrain from defending ourselves in case we were wrong and cause offense. Besides, doctors have a long, storied history of lying to their patients.

*The doctor's bag.*

*Bedlam.*

*Harriet.*

Headmaster reaches for Mary's arm. "I can escort you down, if Miss Bell promises to be good while I'm gone."

Mary lunges.

A wolf, a *wolf*. She snaps forward, a trap with sharp teeth and claws. She takes Headmaster to the ground, the crash of body hitting body muffled as if heard through water. Dr. Bernthal stumbles back, knocks into a bed, catches a foot in the rug. Headmaster grabs for her face, her neck, wrenches her to the side. His keys clatter to the wooden floor. The metal glints in the winter sun coming through the windows.

I grab the keys.

Mary howls, "*Go.*"

I run.

Out of the dormitory. Down the stairs. Hit the landing awkwardly, nearly twist an ankle, keep going, keep going. On the cold, silent second floor. Down the stairs again. Hit the first floor.

Run. Like the rabbit, rabbit heart thudding, like I've never been able to run before. Mrs. Forrester is in the door to the dining hall, where she says, "Hey, *hey*," but I'm already past her. "*Headmaster!*" Down the hall. Grab one of the keys. They're not labeled. Footsteps thud down the stairs behind me, Mrs. Forrester's voice, the clatter of plates. Stumble to a stop in front of the dressing room door. Try one key. Doesn't work. Fumble for a second key. Doesn't work.

"*You little cunt!*" Headmaster roars.

Third key.

It works.

The door unlocks. I yank it open, slam it shut, fumble the

lock into place just as a body hits it with a *thud*. And then more. A fist beating on the other side. I grab a chair and jam it under the knob. Kick it for good measure. Headmaster is screaming. Mrs. Forrester's voice is there too, and Dr. Bernthal. I can't breathe.

The dressing room. It has to be the dressing room.

I stumble through the mess of boxes, mirrors, shelves. I tear off sheets to find dusty old clothes boxes. Nothing that would have a *person*. No smell of rot. Nothing.

"*Get your bloody keys!*" Headmaster snaps. At someone. I don't know who.

I don't have much time. This room makes my heart rate spike, makes my mouth dry. In the mirror, the massive mirror that Mrs. Forrester forced me in front of while she stripped me naked, I barely recognize myself. I am feral, hunched over. I am haggard and gaunt. There is a hungry spark to my eyes too, something strange, unrecognizable.

There has to be something. There *has* to be.

More footsteps outside. A jingle of a new set of keys. Fuck, *fuck*. The rabbit thuds over and over; *find it find it find it*. Maybe there was something I missed, something I overlooked? I start for the mirror. Maybe there, behind it, like some kind of fantasy story from a book. But I trip over something. A lump in the rug. My toe snags it and sends me sprawling. I catch myself, turn with a snarl—I fucking *tripped*—and it's the same place where that stool caught when Isabella dragged it over for me to sit—

The same place—

I pull up the rug. A key fumbles in the lock just meters away.

It is a nightmare, then, to see it. As if this were some awful thing, and not real life, a metaphor for itself, not itself.

Because there is a trapdoor in the floor of the dressing room, and when I pull up the rug, I can see it shimmering with a haunting. It is almost suffocating, impossible to look at for too long, so warped and sick that I worry it will shatter if I reach for it. A padlock lays heavily on the floor. That's it. That's what I've been tripping over.

The door unlocks. Someone attempts to open it, but the chair holds fast. I think, I think I hear Mary scream. The thud of bodies, the roar of voices, piercing and droning and high and low, all around me, until there is nothing else, until the cry of the rabbit and the beating of my heart drown out everything. I try two keys. The second one works. I plunge my hand into the haunting and haul the trapdoor open and reveal a set of narrow stairs leading into a deep, dark hole.

I go down the stairs, reach up, and slam the trapdoor closed above me.

✦

This is not Veil sickness. This is not my *illness*, my difference, the incongruencies of how my mind works. This is not my boyhood, the flaws in my thinking, the tutors' annoyance and notes and adjustments. This is not whatever George thinks is wrong with me, what Lord Luckenbill thinks is wrong with me, what Dr. Bernthal and Headmaster and the world think is wrong with me.

This is Hell.

24

I have—against the wishes of the majority of the medical establishment—been in several operating theaters over the past few years. That's not to say there haven't been "females" in medicine before. There have been a few, yes; that much is true. But for most of England, our existence is a rarity. I've even heard that the men of the school even vote for whether women should be allowed admission. So it was obvious I would attend operations in the clothes George had left for me, pretending to be some baby-faced student or another, hiding at the top of the steep tiers of observers. The air always smelled of alcohol and sweat and thick, coppery blood.

From so far away, in the back of the room, it was difficult to make out the details. Still, I could see the blood on the surgeons' aprons, the glint of the scalpels, the body laid open. Maybe once, I thought that being the attending nurse

in her little bonnet was the best I was ever going to get—
bringing supplies, cleaning up the mess. I wanted more. I
wanted to be the one with my hand in the chest cavity, on
the scalpel, on the pulse of the patient while it beats slow
and steady.

I wanted nothing to do with spirits. I wanted the soul
while it was still attached to the body, when it still thrummed
with life. I wanted to feel the body move, burning hot under
my fingers. I wanted to dedicate the rest of my life to the
only thing that has ever made sense. I wanted to be at
the heart of the operating theater. On the floor, with the
patient. Leaning over them. Whispering that it would be
okay as the anesthesia took them under.

I am at the heart of an operating theater now.

It is a vicious mockery of what I remember. There are no
tiers surrounding the table, only an empty floor. There are
no bright lights or rays of sunlight, only weak gas lamps I
struggle to ignite with a pack of matches left on a nearby
shelf. It all warps under the weight of the Veil. The floor
under my feet does not seem solid. The ceiling does not
feel like the ceiling, does not seem like it should lead to the
dressing room above. The air pulses with the dead like it's
filling up my lungs. I can't breathe without someone else's
soul working its way into my oxygen supply. It's so cold.

But I do not open the Veil. I do not reach for the spirits
and tell them I'm here, I'm finally here, I've found them—

Because at the heart of it is Isabella.

Taken apart. Broken to pieces. Made into ruins, crum-
bled to bloody pieces, left out to decompose.

What they have done to her is, of course, surgical. I pick my way to her, bare feet tiptoeing against the freezing floor, reaching for the table as if I'll fall without it. Above us, there is thumping, the sound of feet, but it's miles away. Isabella smells of death. Insides, copper, petals, ozone.

What have they done to her?

*What will they do to you?*

Whoever did this stopped in the middle, rushed away for some reason or another. They used a sheet to cover her to her neck, as if her modesty still mattered once they'd cut her open. This is a dissection. Head shaved, skull opened, brain exposed. Eyes removed. One missing, the other picked to pieces on the table next to her jaw. The skin peeled away from the socket, flaps held in place by pins. Slivers of skin cut out and removed. So sallow the blood had clearly been drained. I reach under the sheet, take her cold hand, pull it out—or, at least, I try. Her hands are lashed to the table. Her ankles, her legs, her chest. Her wrists are bruised.

She was alive when they opened her up.

Not dissection, then. Vivisection.

I reach farther. Toward her stomach. Just to feel it.

They ripped it back open. They took out my stitches. The stitches I put in her so carefully, each turn of the needle a plea for her to be okay. They undid them—they undid everything, every prayer that held her together.

*Nothing you did could have saved her.*

*She was gone as soon as she decided.*

The same as I was. The moment I realized I was going to cut my womb out of me—

There's thumping upstairs. The beat of footsteps. Are they really above me? Are they in the room, the hall? I can't imagine that they haven't gotten into the dressing room.

I reach out to the haunting, and rip open the Veil.

someone is here someone someone someone we are not
alone anymore we are not alone the veil is open i can *breathe*

It splits with the feel of a scalpel going through flesh. The tear, the resistance before it opens wide, the insides glimmering, beckoning, begging. And, behind it, the flicker—the movement—the dead.

The spirits stop. Their blank, gape-mouthed faces turn to me.

Three of them.

Frances. Ellen. Isabella.

It shakes me to my core, I think, that there are only three. Why three? It's such a small number. This is a tragedy that has only begun. It has not taken root, or forced society to become desensitized to its own horror. There's a difference between horrible things that have gone on forever, because you can almost convince yourself of the inevitability of an age-old cruelty, or almost its necessity. But not a new one. With a new one, the change is too great, the wound too new, and you cannot convince yourself that it is simply the way of the world.

No. No, that's not correct. This *is* a cruelty that has happened forever. It's happened to so many different kinds of people, taking so many different forms of human sin. Maybe that's why the Veil opened. Because God knew there was no other way for us to come face-to-face with what we've wrought.

And the Speakers refuse to listen.

This is not Veil sickness. This is the ones who did not make it reaching out screaming.

◊

We come pouring out with teeth bared ravenous for warmth hungry desperate *desperate* to return to the world. Our mouths can no longer make words our throats cannot make sound but still we reach out.

The living are so warm.

Have you seen what has been done to us? Do you understand? Do you feel it the way we felt it? Please say you do please

The worst part about a spirit to me—what makes my heart hurt the most—is that their body takes the form of the worst thing ever done to them. Or the worst thing they ever did. Either one, whatever left the biggest scar on their soul.

It's not always what killed them. It hardly ever is.

Ellen's head is blurry. It can't hold up its own weight and it melts, hunched like a weeping willow, dissipating like fog at the ends. By the end of her life, her mind was so muddled, her life so confusing, that she was not herself. Even her mouth is stretched beyond recognition, climbing up toward her ear on one side, if that is even her ear at all.

Frances is twisted, stretched, broken to pieces. Her parts don't fit together the way they should. Ellen's mind was not her own and Frances' body was not her own. Whatever rule she broke that caused Headmaster to bring her down here, it was a dehumanizing, brutal violation of the body. I can guess. I don't want to guess. I don't want to think about it at all, how terrifying her last hours were, how quickly they disposed of her like rotten meat.

And Isabella—

Isabella—

She watches me without eyes, mouth hanging open. There is no gash on her belly. She is whole through strength of will, through anger, an amalgam of rage and love and desperation. I know it is her because she does not move. She does not writhe, she does not rail against the world or the air or the Veil. She is still, and she is watching me. Like she knew I'd come.

Silas, what did you have to do to get here?
Silas, what did you do?
You're alive, you're alive, you need to *run*.

Above me, the trapdoor opens.

Dull evening light, the last of the day, pours into the operating theater. The hinges squeal. Someone made it into the room. Shit, shit. I turn, reaching toward Isabella's body on the table—the rabbit says, *There has to be a scalpel*, but there isn't, and I wouldn't be able to use it even if there was—

At the top of the stairs, there is Headmaster. He's holding Mary by the hair. She has been beaten. Her face is swollen, blood dripping from her mouth, hands mangled. In turn, Headmaster's face is a vibrant wound. She must have fought him. She must have fought him so hard, and I wonder if Headmaster knows he is lucky to be alive when Mary would have torn out his throat with her teeth if she could.

Headmaster throws her down the stairs.

She tries to take him down with her, but he's too strong. She falls. Howling. Hits the stairs, tumbles down, crashes to the floor. Her shoulder takes the brunt of the fall. She makes a sound so guttural I hardly believe it's human.

"Don't do anything stupid, girls," Headmaster says, turning a padlock over in his hand and slamming the trapdoor shut.

25

Mary sits up, gulping down cold wet air and clutching her arm in the endless dark of the room. Her torn hands leave bloody prints on the fabric of the dress.

The first thing I think: she's alive, thank God, her head didn't take the brunt of the fall, she's upright and breathing and alive.

The second: we're trapped. *You're trapped you're trapped you're trapped.* The rabbit chews on my ribs like it's trying to gnaw its way out of my body. It's that one kind of torture, the kind with the rat placed against the soft stomach until it eats its way to freedom. I press hard on my chest to stop it and feel only my heartbeat. *Headmaster trapped you down here like he trapped all the others; you're going to die down here; you're going to die you're going to die.*

To keep from beating the sides of my head, or collapsing into a useless, sobbing wreck—neither of which are going to help us—I focus on the one thing I know I can fix. Mary's arm. I can't make out the extent of the damage; her hands are cut but not to the muscle, not like mine were, so that will probably only take bandages. But the arm.

"Mary?" I whisper.

She doesn't acknowledge me. She's not trying to triage her wounds, or screaming at Headmaster, or even stumbling over to Isabella's corpse.

She's too busy staring into the dark.

"Frances," she says. She reaches out with her undamaged arm, fingers splayed like a small child desperate for warmth even though she's reaching toward the cold. The dark wounds splay as she stretches the skin. In the dim light of the gas lamps, tears spill over her sharp cheekbones. "Franny. Is that you?"

Frances turns. Sweet Frances, dead Frances, Frances who fought back and was killed for it, Frances whose spirit is a beast with too many limbs with too many joints that don't come together the way they should.

She sees Mary, as much as a spirit can see.

She *wails*. So loud and broken that the temperature of the air plunges and my breath clouds. She rushes to Mary's side. She tries to hold her, but her hands are too ethereal.

I shouldn't be here for this. It feels wrong.

"I'm sorry," Mary says. Her voice is thick and wet. "I'm sorry. I should have come looking for you, I should have known, I—"

Frances moans.

"No. Don't. I should have come for you." Mary sniffles. "What did he do to you?"

Instead of this, I try to imagine the two of them together, when Frances had still been alive. Mary never told me what Frances looked like, so I invent her. Hair chopped short in a fit of rebelliousness, narrow and lithe with eyes like midnight, the fox to Mary's wolf. I imagine her leaning over Mary's favorite chair in the library, the two of them tracking Headmaster across the room in unison. I imagine pacts to kill future husbands, sharpening their teeth on nail files, Frances tangling her fingers in the necklace hidden under Mary's dress. There will be blanks in their lives I'll never know how to fill. I don't know if they're like me—where I could fall in love with anyone, man or woman or anything else, if the world would let me—or if they would rather die before they touch a man. I don't know if they ever had the optimism to plan for a life together, or if they were just trying to find the future that would hurt the least. But I do know they intended to survive. I know it wasn't supposed to end like this for them.

Something is hissing, and I realize it's Frances. She's trying to get my attention. Mary blinks at me, eyes watery and wide with confusion. I don't have to ask what's wrong.

I try to speak again. "Mary. Your arm." I can tell by the way it's held, by the way the cloth of her sleeve is resting on it, that it's dislocated. Dislocations are better than breaks. It's easier to fix than most things. But that doesn't mean it's not excruciating in the meantime, or that it won't take weeks for the aching and swelling to come down. Mary is going to feel this for a long time.

She snaps at me, "It's fine."

"It's not."

Mary tries to move it, but the pain is instant—her breathing picks up, and she bites her tongue to keep from wailing. She tries again. That's fair. When it comes to an injury, the body will aways try to deny it.

But there's no denying it anymore. She turns to Frances first, then to me again.

"It's okay, right?" she says. The hard, dangerous edge that I'm used to in her voice is gone. She sounds like a child.

"Lay down," I say. "I can fix it."

"Will it hurt?"

I do not want to be the kind of doctor who lies to a patient. "Yes."

The best course of action would be to have her lie on the operating table and pull her arm back into place that way, but I don't want to move Isabella's body. I certainly don't want to take Mary over there either; I don't think it's clicked for her. I don't think it's really clicked for me either, that the slab of meat on the table across the room is someone I crawled into bed with just a few days ago. She kissed my head, held my hand, then begged me to save her. No—no, I can't think about that. The longer I put off the crushing weight of loss, the better I can do my work.

So I guide Mary onto her back, where she stares up at the spirits looming above her. They gather to watch. Frances leans down, her ghostly form pressing close. First, I rip the hem of my dress, and then wrap up her hands to protect the wounds from the dirt and dust on the floor. Then I take the wrist of the dislocated arm and squeeze it like I'm reassuring her. She runs warm, *hot*, like a furnace, like she's so burnt up with rage it radiates from her skin. She could power the world with how angry she is.

"On the count of three," I say. "One—"

I move her arm away from her body, at a precise forty-five-degree angle, and plant a foot against her side. I've never done this before. And I certainly don't specialize in field medicine. I'm made for carefully calculated cuts and keeping a steel stomach in the face of blood and guts, not this.

I say, "Two—"

And pull until the bone snaps back into the cup of the shoulder joint.

Mary stifles a shriek. She tears away from me and rolls onto her side, clutching the arm to her chest. Frances flutters about anxiously.

"Three," I say. I guide her back to me, press my hands against her cheeks until she stops hyperventilating. "There you go. It's okay. It's over."

Then, on the floor, holding her arm, she starts to laugh. A terrible giggle comes to her lips. Her eyes spark with a sick light.

"Oh my God," she says, "we're going to die."

The rabbit agrees.

I don't respond to that, because that would mean responding to the rabbit, and I can't do that right now. Instead, I help her sit, leaning her against the flimsy stairs, and wipe away a tear with my thumb. Mary is still laughing. The spirits flit about, unsure. When I don't know what to do, I rub the stitches in the meat of my palm. I don't know how much longer it'll be until I can take these out. Maybe they should have already been removed; I can't remember. It's hard for me to remember things down here. What bones are in the joint that I just fixed? The names escape me.

I should not have to keep fixing the damage done to us. It would be so easy to not hurt us, and the Speakers can't even do that. It's *more* work to hurt us. It's *more* work to be cruel. And yet they continue.

Why is it always like this? Over and over, repetition like poetry.

I want Daphne. If anyone could make sense of it, it's her.

The spirits gather at the trapdoor, staring at it, pushing against it. It doesn't work. Whatever surrounds us—holding the spirits in this place, concealing this haunting until you are practically inside of it, Headmaster's handiwork no doubt—it is strong. Even Mary, once she's collected herself, tries to climb the stairs and press against the door. We take the key ring and try to push open the door just a crack, just a little bit, so that we can reach the lock, but it doesn't work. When Mary's foot slips, I demand we stop. She trudges down, growls, and stares at the floor so she doesn't have to look in Isabella's direction.

We search the room. We take up the matches and debate setting fire to the wooden door, but I don't trust we'd make it out before the smoke suffocates us. We pull chairs from the dark back corners, overturn trays and carts to look for something. Anything. But there is nothing here except us, the stairs, the table, the ghosts, and the body.

*If you're trapped down here, will you have to eat your friend?* the rabbit supplies, over-eager to look at the most terrible possible outcome. But my brain draws a heavy iron gate against the thought. It offers only the descriptions of dehydration and starvation I found in George's notes: the shriveling of the flesh; the body's realization that hunger and thirst no longer serve a purpose, and therefore stopping the urge for food and water; the fact that there is a point where, once crossed, a person cannot be saved, even if they have not yet died.

When it is clear there is no way out, we go to Isabella.

Isabella's spirit stays where she is as we come closer. She's at the back of the room, standing tall, impassive. The only movement is the vague ripple of the Veil, like the few seconds after a pebble has been thrown into a pond.

"Does she know who I am?" I whisper.

Mary says, "Of course she does," as if it's the most obvious thing in the world.

We do not take the sheet off her body. I keep holding one of the frayed edges, running it between my fingers. I already reached under the sheet to feel what they'd done to her, but I want to see it too. I want to *know* instead of letting my imagination run wild with terrible things. But she deserves her privacy, so I don't.

Mary pauses at the edge of the operating table, sees the pins holding Isabella's face open, and turns away.

"Christ," she says.

"Do you want me to fix it?" I ask.

"Please."

So I go to Isabella's head and pull out the pins. The last time we touched, I was hands-deep in her guts, and the time before that, I was curled up in her bed with my head on her chest, a loose wave of her hair brushing my nose. A snip of her dry, dead hair sits on the floor by my foot. Her skin is cold and clammy; mine too. The flesh under my fingernails is starting to go blue. The pins slide out, and the flaps of skin come loose, and I gently put them back in their places.

There.

I back away, and when Mary finally finds the courage to approach, she puts her head to Isabella's chest as if listening for a heartbeat that will never come.

◆

"How did you pick the name Silas?" Mary asks me.

We've huddled together for warmth, to rest, to collect ourselves, our feet tucked together, heads on shoulders. We can't think properly if we're out of our minds. Around us, the spirits crawl like animals, hiss, crackle. It's hard to remind myself they are no longer the people they'd once been; this is the heart, the soul, not the body, not the chains. As much as I hesitate to call a body a chain.

*You're going to die*, the rabbit says. I put the side of my thumb into my mouth and bite it.

"I thought it was pretty," I say around my hand, which is true.

Mary snorts. "That's not very masculine."

"I'm not very masculine," I admit.

"So you thought it was pretty? That's it?"

This is a more complex question than I thought. I take my hand out of my mouth. "Well. I was going through the names of contributors to a medical journal my brother gifted me. It seemed like the best place to get a doctor's name." I tried a lot of different names before I told anyone. They were all too long, too stuffy, or conjured a picture of the wrong kind of man: always taller, always stronger, always bearded or deep-voiced. I was never going to be that, so I needed to name myself accordingly. "That one just stood out to me is all."

"Dr. Silas Bell," Mary says.

"Has a nice ring to it, doesn't it?"

"It does." Even though I'm going to change my last name if I survive this.

*If.*

Mary looks up to the ceiling, as if she could hear the footsteps again, feel them, even see them if she tried hard enough. "All right, Doctor. Tell me this. What are they going to do to us down here?"

I don't know. All I can do is picture all the terrible things we've seen: Harriet cut to pieces. Isabella's body taken apart. The shattering of corpses, of live flesh, as if it is nothing more than rock meant to be carved, as if meat cannot feel pain.

"I wish I knew," I say.

"I don't. I'm not sure why I asked. You're rocking, by the way."

I hadn't noticed I was until she pointed it out. Just a little bit, side to side, because it helps keep me calm. "I do that sometimes." And because she started this conversation, because now I recognize it as a good idea, I ask a question too: "Why did you tell Ellen to throw Agnes over the banister?"

Ellen's spirit pauses above us somewhere, the cold settling on the back of my neck.

Mary scoffs at first, pulling away just a little bit, but eventually she decides to speak. "Less competition. If I couldn't have Frances, I wanted the best chance at a man who wouldn't fucking kill me." She won't look at me. "I didn't think she'd actually do it. I just . . . wanted her to get caught trying."

I can't help my reaction. "Jesus."

"Don't look at me like that. I'm not a monster for trying to ensure the best chance of survival."

As much as it's at odds with my own moral compass, I have to agree. We don't consider animals monsters for surviving. Why should we expect different of a person?

"Then why are you helping me?" I ask.

"You're my best chance of survival."

What a thing to say, in this dark cellar with a corpse on the operating table, behind a locked door, the ghosts of dead girls watching us from the other side of the room.

I say, "And look how that turned out."

✦

"If they hurt either one of us," Mary says, "it will be me."

"No," I say.

"You have the Luckenbills. You have someone who wants you." I hate that she's right. I have a future, no matter how bleak, no matter how ill it makes me in the pit of my stomach—I will always have Daphne, I will always have *something*. A terrible noise comes up in the back of her throat, and I realize it's another laugh. This time, I hardly recognize it. "My father threw me in here to be rid of me, you know. He knew his family would be better off without me." She looks to me, then away. "I got a lot from him."

"No."

"Don't lie. It's not becoming." She says it in a mimicry of Charlotte's voice, and it almost makes me laugh, but the levity of the moment is already gone. "Besides. I did that to Headmaster's face. I broke a mirror and tried to slit his throat."

She holds out her bandaged hands. The wounds make sense now. The scuffs across her knuckles, the cuts across the palm where she held the shards of glass tight.

"He'll want me to suffer for that," she says. "I know he will."

I want to comfort her, but I don't know how.

✦

When Mary asks about Daphne to fill the awful, ugly space in our heads, I tell her everything. I tell her that the two of us are the same, mirror images of each other, our experiences so fundamentally opposite that they become identical again. I tell her of the letters Daphne sent, the poetry, and about the bribes, and the search, and our first kiss, and the way our eyes met while I was on the museum floor with blood on my hands, and how she held me when I cried, and how Daphne is the first person I met who did not look at me and immediately see something broken.

Mary doesn't say anything for a while.

Then: "If I was a better person, I'd call that beautiful."

It is.

26

It's easy to lose track of time down here. You can only count so many heartbeats; you can only guess so accurately in a void. Even the spirits have gone still, huddled together like Mary and I, a strange form together on the other side of the room. It's heartbreaking that they keep their distance from us. They have to. We wouldn't be able to stay warm any other way.

"It's fucked," Mary says, "that we have the keys and we still can't get out."

I hold up the ring with a humorless smile. Mary groans. The rabbit berates us for just sitting there, says that we deserve our fate if we're just going to let it happen. But we need to rest, don't we? We need time to calm down, to think. We won't help ourselves if we tire ourselves out doing useless things over and over again.

Mary dozes off against my shoulder once or twice, and I let her have that because I can't bring myself to close my eyes. My stomach is gnawing at itself. The last time I ate was supper after the garden party. I'm so thirsty that my eyes feel dry and my lips stick together.

We do not know how much time passes before we hear footsteps on the floor above us, the clatter of the lock, the creak of the trapdoor as it opens.

Mary wakes with a snarl as dim light cuts a line across her bruised face. Her bandaged hands shield her eyes. Bruises climb up the side of her cheek, dried blood on the corner of her lip, right next to where I bit her days ago. That fight was a lifetime ago. Now, down here together, I feel an animal instinct to grab her and lunge for the sun, because if we don't both escape here then what is the point, I'm not leaving without her, I'm not—

But that instinct is strangled the moment we realize who is peering down at us.

Headmaster. Flanked by two men in masks. Keys jingle, metal clacking against metal like chains, taunting. Mrs. Forrester stands to the back, wringing her hands. She doesn't get to be worried. Not now. Not after everything she's done, after everything she's excused. It doesn't work like that. How dare she.

She doesn't have a mask, but Headmaster does. It's a burial shroud, just like the others, leather and linen, stained and awful. It's the face of a monster from a fairy tale, or one of Daphne's epic poems. The gall he has, to not even bother to cover himself now. He wants us to see everything—his eyes, the bandage over his cheek, the smile on his face. He wants us to know it's been him all along.

*Cover the mouth, cover the eyes.* Just like the groundskeeper tried to tell me. These are the men Daphne and I saw in the hallway. The men disappearing into the dressing room, men who talked about our friends' corpses rotting beneath our feet, men whose voices I knew.

Frances, Isabella, and Ellen shriek. They *scream*, unraveling from each other like organs. The temperature plunges and frost gathers in the corners of the room, creeping against the stairs and walls. But Headmaster holds out a hand and they stop. They can't get close. A medium who had once been in the service of the Queen's army—of course he can do this. He can tear and change the Veil like it's nothing. Mary puts an arm across my chest. I hold her hand because it's the only thing I can think of to do.

I've frozen like a rabbit.

"Right," Headmaster says, and settles the mask over his face. He turns to his wife. "Lock the door behind us, will you?"

Mrs. Forrester slams the door as quick as she can, as if desperate to look away from what these men will do to us. It sounds just like the snap of the Veil closing. The operating theater is plunged into near-darkness once again, and it is just us. Trapped. With beasts.

I sort through as much information as I can because information is what keeps you alive in a situation like this. Headmaster knew about this all along, but that much is obvious. Frances did not survive being taken down to this room, and neither did Ellen, and neither did Isabella. I'm holding keys to a door I cannot get to. The suit and doctor's bag of one of the masked men is horribly familiar, and I realize it's the same suit and bag that Dr. Bernthal brought up to the dormitory. His eyes are the same pale, icy blue. Agnes's husband plucked her from this school for himself and has left the rest of us here to rot.

But the third man—

The rabbit is berserk. It is slamming against my ribcage, clawing up my throat, making me so sick with fear I can't focus. The third man hesitates halfway down the stairs, still a little hunched under the trapdoor. Nothing about him stands out. Shouldn't there be some actual *reason* my brain is screaming, looking at him? Why the rabbit is howling *him him him?*

The third man slowly makes it to the bottom of the stairs and goes to turn up the gas lamps. He does not turn his back on us, like we are dogs he cannot back away from. There is an awful humanity in his eyes. I hate that. I hate that someone so awful could be human, but George would tell me that only humans are capable of evil. An animal does not have the higher thinking needed to be malicious, or cruel. It's as simple as that.

Then Headmaster waves his hand. The Veil rips open, flickers, devours, and then is gone. Isabella, Ellen, and Frances disappear. Just like that. They're there one moment, white crystals of ice sparkling across the wall and floor, and then they're not. Mary makes the smallest, most pathetic sound. "No," she whispers. "No, no, no, Frances—"

A childish part of me thinks that there should have been more to their disappearance than that. More than just a simple snap. But the world does not care about sentimental significance. It will not slow the passage of time just because you care. They are there, and then they are not. I want to hold Mary's hand tighter, but it's wounded and I'd only cause her more pain.

"Damn mess you've made of the place," Headmaster says. "Look at this. Ghosts everywhere." He clucks his tongue. "That's Veil sickness if I've ever seen it."

Mary lurches forward. There's spittle on her lower lip. "Fuck you."

Dr. Bernthal sets the doctor's bag beside Isabella's broken head, pulls out a scalpel, and points it lazily in our direction. "Easy now."

There are a lot of things he could do with that.

*You're fucked. You're fucked you're fucked.* Bile rises in the back of my throat. I try to talk the rabbit down, but it doesn't work. *You're going to die alone down here and you'll never see the sun again and it's going to hurt, it's going to hurt it's going to hurt hurt hurt.*

There has to be something we can do. Even if it's just give in, capitulate, make things easier while we look for a way out.

I'm not sure Mary is capable of that.

"Hand over the keys," Headmaster says. I'm not sure who he's talking to, but when he gives me a pointed look, I realize I've been holding them like claws between my fingers. Anything is a potential weapon down here. "Now."

Mary tries to stop me, but I slide the ring across the floor. I just need to make it easy for myself. That's it. That's all. I'm not giving up, I'm just ensuring the best chance of survival, like she said.

Headmaster reaches down to grab them off the floor, inspects them to make sure they're all there, and stuffs them in his pocket.

"Thank you, dear," he says.

I hate the way he says it.

"You fancy yourself a doctor," Mary whispers against my cheek. "If you took that scalpel, could you do anything with it?"

Could I? If I grabbed it, could I turn the blade against someone fighting back? I imagine the miniscule weight of the blade in my hand, the delicate edge, the map of arteries and veins under the skin that would be the best place to strike. I stretch out my hand, feel the stitches, try to imagine *doing* it.

I say, "No."

Because I am not a wolf. I am a rabbit. Why would I be anything else? My tutors taught me to bow my head and follow the rules. They taught me to do what was expected of me and nothing else, to be perfect, to be a good girl, for so long that they may as well have overwritten my mind. I cannot fight. I can only freeze. I can only do as I'm told.

*It's going to HURT.*

The men—Headmaster, Dr. Bernthal, the silent one— unbuckle Isabella's body from the table and put her in the corner like she's a pile of laundry set aside to be folded later. The autopsy table is a child's painting of red and brown. If Isabella's spirit were still here, she'd chase her body, desperate to have it back. But she's not.

The silent one pauses, looking at us, wavering on his feet, a too-tall tree in the wind.

"Which one first?" Dr. Bernthal asks.

Headmaster grits his teeth. I can almost hear the grinding enamel under the mask. "Luckenbill will be furious if he loses Bell, and Carter's a fighter . . ."

I press myself farther against the wall. Yes, that's exactly correct; Lord Luckenbill will be so upset if he loses me. They can't do anything to me without risking his anger. That's right.

But if it's not me, then it will be Mary.

"Well," Dr. Bernthal says, "if Bishop cut our subject budget, we have to make do with what we have on hand." *Budget?* I try to follow their words, but I don't know enough about the inner workings of the Speakers to understand. Dr. Bernthal continues. "Tell Luckenbill something happened. Maybe she did it to herself. Cut herself open like that one girl."

Headmaster ignores him and begins to pace. His attention turns to me, and his eyes behind the mask are wild. This is the Headmaster who screamed at me and put the letter opener to my injured hand. This is the Headmaster who gave the key to Daphne with a sick, disgusting smile, the Headmaster who makes his wife put glass in her shoes. All of this has been boiling under the surface for so long. He doesn't care what he does as long as it hurts me.

"Why *is* Lord Luckenbill so enamored with you?" Headmaster says. "He could have engaged his son to any woman in the country, and he chose *you*. A half-imbecile with Veil sickness who won't listen to a damn thing anyone says. A pretty face doesn't make up for the rest of it." I know it doesn't. I know everyone thinks I'm mad. He doesn't have to say it, I *know*. "What is it, then? He doesn't even have a penchant for blonds!"

"She's not going to reply," Dr. Bernthal says, impatient. The silent Speaker remains silent.

Headmaster snarls in frustration, then says, "Luckenbill can find a new one. I'm sick of her." He flicks a hand at me. "Fine."

They come for us.

Mary gnashes her teeth and tries to rip open the Veil in a desperate attempt to get them to stop—but they're too strong. Headmaster slams the Veil closed once more and wrenches her injured arm behind her back, making her shriek and plead for him to stop like I've never heard her beg before. Dr. Bernthal grabs me by the hair at the back of my neck, hauls me off the ground, snaps for the other doctor to help him.

"No no no," Mary sobs, "let me go, please, it hurts, it hurts."

Dr. Bernthal and the silent doctor drag me onto the operating table. The rabbit kicks in. I try to bite Dr. Bernthal's hand. I jerk my head to get him to let go of my hair, but a chunk of it rips out. Pain sparks across my scalp. The silent one grabs my naked ankles, lifts them onto the table, and pins them there.

He breathes in.

He breathes out.

I breathe in. Breathe out.

I fall still, watching him. His shoulders rise and fall. His eyes meet mine. Hazel. Dark, shaded from the holes in the awful mask. Breathe in. Breathe out. I mimic him like it's the easiest thing in the world. Stop fighting. In. Out. Dr. Bernthal grabs the leather straps hanging from the sides of the table. In. Out.

His eyes.

"Chloroform?" Headmaster says, tying Mary's ankles together with a strip of cloth. Her hands have been wrenched behind her back and tears streak her face. "Might stop the squirming."

"Still debating," Dr. Bernthal says. "Can't be sure if that's affecting the results. Should we try without it?"

The silent one stares at me. Breathe. Breathe.

I'd know those eyes anywhere.

They're the same eyes that used to meet mine across the dining room table, both of us trying not to wince as Father said awful things about the stories in the weekly paper. The same eyes that sparkled when I said I wanted to be just like him, and the same eyes that watered when he said his wife's name and admitted that she was sick, that he wanted to fix her no matter what it took.

I whisper, "George?"

He jerks away as if I've burned him.

It is. It's him. It's him.

George grabs one of the straps and brings it down over my chest.

"George." I say it again, louder. He has to listen. He's my brother, he's my brother, he can't do this. "*George.*"

*Maybe he thinks this is worth it. Your life for Elsie's.*

"Ignore her," Headmaster growls. "Ignore her, Bell, ignore her."

George knew about Frances, and Ellen, and Isabella. He knew what happened in this school and he did not help me. He called me sick, he said I was imagining things, he said I was ill and couldn't be trusted. And now he's here, doing this, for what? For his career? For Braxton's? For the Speakers? For a girl he only met two years ago?

He had his hands in *all of it*.

It was George all along.

My brother.

My anger is not white-hot rage. It is not the rabbit screaming. It is a rip of pain through my stomach and the taste of blood in the back of my mouth. If we make it out of here, I'll tell Daphne, and we'll tell Lord Luckenbill, and he'll have to do something. He's the president of the Royal Speaker Society. His family donated the land this school is built on. I'll make George regret turning on me, and he'll spend the rest of his life atoning for what he's done to me, to us, to all of us.

*If,* the rabbit says. *If you make it.*

Vivisections are illegal in England, but this obviously hasn't stopped anyone in this room. Functionally, they're just like a dissection, except the subject is alive when the procedure begins. Nobody uses a vivisection as their first option. This is something they've come down to. Whatever these men are looking for, they've failed to find it with a normal dissection. They need the heart to keep beating. The brain to keep functioning. Because maybe they'll find something *now*.

The rabbit is right. I don't know if I can survive a cruel man's desperation.

"George." I whisper this time. Beside me, Dr. Bernthal begins to set out his surgical supplies. I grab the edge of George's coat as it passes, straining against the leather. "If Lord Luckenbill finds out about this, he'll ruin Mother and Father for life."

George says, "Shh."

*Thump.*

The sound of feet. The clanking of metal.

The opening of the trapdoor.

Mrs. Forrester stumbles down the first few steps, holding on to the edge of the door. Her face is red, burned from the cold, and her eyes are wild. Mary struggles to sit up.

I hear distant, distant yelling.

*"If you don't tell me where she is right this instant—"*

Daphne.

Daphne. Oh God. I stare at the ceiling and begin to cry. It's her. She's here.

"Get her up," Mrs. Forrester says, stamping her heel on the stairs. "Get her up, *now*."

Headmaster says, "What the bloody hell is going on?"

"Edward Luckenbill is here." Mrs. Forrester is so panicked she looks as if she might scream. "He wants to see her. *Now*. He's threatening to get his father to pull every single ounce of funding and you *know* how he's been lately—"

She's *here*. I don't believe in miracles, but this is the closest thing to one I have ever seen.

Daphne's voice again. *"This is unacceptable!"*

Dr. Bernthal growls. "Shit."

"Get her up," Mrs. Forrester says again. "Get her up!"

Headmaster immediately yanks on the straps, drags me off the operating table, holds me up roughly by the arm that, for a moment, I think might dislocate as well. I can't keep up. Mary starts to yell too. Her voice is hoarse from crying. I want to put a cup of warm tea to her lips, tilt it back, let it soothe her throat. She deserves that. Once this is done, I will stitch her together and patch her wounds and make sure nobody ever touches her again.

Dr. Bernthal notices me watching her. He glances between us, then grabs the scalpel again, smiles, and brings it over to Mary's side.

Mary tries to jerk away—"No," she gasps, the only thing she can say now—but he grabs her jaw to tilt her head back. The pale white expanse of her throat looks sickly in the dull light. George, holding me upright, digs his fingers into the soft meat of my arm. It's pitiful that he won't even speak. He can't open his mouth to acknowledge me, like he can hide behind his silence. What a coward.

"You squeal," Dr. Bernthal says to me, "and I'll make sure her death is as slow and painful as possible." It's fascinating what Dr. Bernthal becomes down here. Gone is the automaton. The mask has changed him, granted him the anonymity to be someone else. Why is it that when they hide their faces, men become monsters instead of angels? "I'll make sure it hurts."

The scalpel pierces the soft part of Mary's jaw. A single ruby droplet comes to the surface. It trails down her neck.

"You won't tell, will you?" Headmaster says to me.

I am going to tell Daphne everything, and all of them are going to regret all they've done to us. I hope Mary can see that in my face; I am not abandoning her. I couldn't. Not now.

"I won't," I say.

"Good." Headmaster hands me off to Mrs. Forrester, his pale purple eyes wild. I know that look. It's the look of a man who may have done something that will ruin him for life. "Clean her up. Make her presentable, and get any pens out of that damn parlor. Miss Bell, don't say a fucking word." He nods toward his wife. "She'll be listening."

27

She'll be listening.

Even in this beautiful evening gown—is it evening? There's no sun behind the thick curtains of the dressing room; how much time did that dark room swallow?— my reflection in the mirror is a ghoul. I'm so hungry I'm unsteady on my feet and my head feels light. Mrs. Forrester had to run out into the hall to deal with Daphne again, even though we were in the middle of putting up my hair; Daphne is throwing such a fit that I can hear her from here. A few pins sit discarded by my side.

*"I just want to see her, and apparently that is too much to ask!"* I close my eyes and try to picture Daphne in the hall. She's here. I can't believe she's here. For the first time, yelling does not scare me, because I know she would never hurt me. She is doing this for my sake. Is this what it's like for someone to stand up for you? *"Am I being unreasonable?"*

"Of course not," Mrs. Forrester replies. Her voice sounds like it's coming from a million miles away. "Please, if you make your way to the parlor, I'll bring her in just a moment, there's just a few more things to attend to—"

Beneath me, Mary. Headmaster. Dr. Bernthal. George. If Headmaster goes back on his promise and hurts Mary anyway, will I know if she screams? Nobody heard Frances. Or Ellen. Or Isabella. If they had time to scream at all. My hands flutter, then dig into the overwhelming blue fabric of my dress. Despite that there's nothing in my stomach, I have the strong urge to vomit. My head pounds.

How do I tell Daphne without putting Mary in danger? I can't say it aloud, using the tiles would draw too much attention, and Headmaster said to take any pens out of the parlor. *Pens.* They're covering everything. The rabbit repeats it: *she'll be listening she'll be listening she'll be listening.* Mrs. Forrester will be listening. My lips will be sewn shut.

I think I might lose my mind.

Mrs. Forrester comes back, her keys jingling. "Christ," she says. "Your hair looks awful." As if that is the only thing in the world that matters.

✦

Daphne is waiting in the parlor, by the window, and after everything the normalcy of it nearly brings me to tears. That's where she always waits for me. Hands behind her back, chin up, the brightest thing against a black window. She's here, she's here, and it takes everything I have not to run to her, to bury my face in her chest, to *hold* her. After this, I swear to God, I am never going to leave her again. There has to be something more than marriage that can tie us together after everything is said and done—something deeper, on the level of flesh. The morbid parts of my mind suggest a swapping of blood, or taking a piece of meat like communion, and while I could never speak those thoughts out loud, I would not say no if Daphne were to suggest it as a sort of terrible poetry.

Is that ghoulish of me? Or just lovesick?

I should have written her.

"I'm so sorry for the wait," Mrs. Forrester says, a hand on the small of my back to push me inside.

"It's fine," Daphne snaps. "Leave us."

Mrs. Forrester flinches, but I do not feel bad for her. The door shuts. It locks. Good.

Daphne immediately pushes away from the window, crossing the parlor to grab me. She's shaking. I missed her so much. Her hands take my bruised wrists, cradle my face to wipe away a tear. She's going to cry too. Is it so obvious what's been done? Even in a fancy dress and my hair pinned up, do I still look broken? I spent so long staring into the mirror waiting for Mrs. Forrester that I stopped being able to make sense of my reflection. The whole of my appearance splintered into a hundred little things I couldn't put back together.

"What happened?" Daphne says. *Shit.* "Why did you—"

No. Don't speak. I put a finger to my lips. The way I did outside Headmaster's office door. The words die in her throat.

I point to the door. Then my ear. Mrs. Forrester is listening. If she hears anything out of line, they'll hurt Mary. They can't hurt Mary—not because of a situation I put her in, because of something I did. I won't let them.

"What are you talking about?" I say brightly. "I've had a wonderful day."

It takes Daphne significantly less time to catch on to ruses than I do, but that's to be expected. "Oh. I must have been mistaken." She's a better actress than I. Her voice does not match the terror-struck look on her face. "Fancy a snack?"

Food? *Food.* I hadn't even noticed the trays on the table behind her: snack cakes, bite-sized meat pies, tea and finger sandwiches. I'm starving. In fact, I'm hungry enough that I'm forgetting how the mechanism of hunger works in the first place. It's a muscle contraction, isn't it? I barely restrain my voice. "I would, thank you."

Daphne takes me to the table, unwilling to let me go. I don't even check the ingredients of the small tart I grab before I shove it in my mouth. It tastes awful—I hate baked fruit with an almost violent passion, as the texture is repulsive—but I swallow it anyway. Then the tea. I usually hate tea, but for once it's palatable. I need anything my body can get.

Mary is probably hungry too. That alone suddenly makes all the food and drink in my mouth taste thick and bitter.

"What happened?" Daphne whispers, glancing urgently toward the door as I force myself to swallow. "What did they do? Are you okay?"

I ignore her questions entirely, wiping crumbs from my mouth. I can't answer safely. "Why are you here?" Then, louder, because Mrs. Forrester will get suspicious if she doesn't hear anything at all: "Oh, these are delightful, aren't they?"

Daphne blinks at me, mouth open, before running a hand over her face. "I don't . . ." She trails off. She watches me as I grab another piece of food and cram it into my mouth with what must be a somewhat distasteful expression on my face. I always say I'd rather starve than eat something I can't palate, but I've bullied myself into eating terrible things more than once.

Then she says, "Come here." She puts a hand on my waist and my traitorous heart skips a beat. I hate how much I've wanted her to do this. I shouldn't want anything at all right now, not when Mary is trapped. I wipe my mouth anxiously, then press my hands against my stomach to keep them still. "In case she's watching, love, come here."

I'm about to say that Mrs. Forrester is only listening; she didn't say she would *watch*, but—there's a keyhole. Shit. It's always so easy for me to forget that people lie. Why wouldn't she watch? Why wouldn't she do anything she could to catch me?

"Okay," I say. "I'm here."

Daphne draws me in close to her, close enough that I can smell the hints of her perfume, what must be her mother's, light and floral—and drops us both onto the couch. I fall against her in a rush of skirts.

*Onto* her.

I'm in her lap now. She's holding me in place, her hands that should be gentle instead stiff with anxiety, her eyes trained on the door. Her lips brush against my cheek. If I turned just a little bit to the side, we'd kiss. Instead, our chests are pressed together, and my hands are on her shoulders, and we are both as still as prey animals that have heard a predator.

I can't let them hurt Mary. I can't, I can't, I can't.

"Why are you here?" I whisper.

Daphne gives me an odd look as she runs a hand down the back of my dress. This is a show. We're putting on a show. We need to make it look like nothing's wrong.

"What are you talking about?" Daphne says. "I got the letters."

My head spins a little, or maybe that's anxiety making my vision swim.

"I never—" I start. "I never wrote you back. I never wrote you anything. I'm so sorry. I should have—if anything happened to me, or to you—I'm so thoughtless—"

"Silas." My name, said so quietly that it stops me in my tracks. Daphne takes one hand off me to reach into the pocket of her waistcoat. She uses my body as a shield, between us and the keyhole of the door. "You didn't send these back?"

She has the letters. A transcription of Ovid, hating matrimony like a crime; the apology for not having found Frances or Ellen, disguised as a search for a childhood friend. I take them from her, carefully holding them near my belly, and nearly rip them open to check. I memorized the way she wrote the words, the loop of the letters, the way they sat on the page. Something has to be different.

But they're not. It's exactly the same. These are the letters she sent *me*.

"No," I whisper. "I didn't send these."

I mentally scramble through all the possibilities. Headmaster and Mrs. Forrester should have no idea where I hid these, and as far as they're aware, Daphne is nothing more than the son of a viscount who wants a violet-eyed wife and doesn't care how. They'd have no reason to use these as a trap. That only leaves one of the girls. But Mary was trapped with me, Charlotte wouldn't care enough to save me, and Louise is a coward.

"I don't . . ." I say.

Daphne stuffs the letters back into her pocket. My attention comes back to her. "I came as soon as they arrived," she says. "Left in the middle of tea, grabbed a horse, didn't even bother to tell my father where I was going." She catches her voice getting loud and grits her teeth, muffling her mouth against my shoulder like she's kissing the crook of my neck. "I didn't know what you were trying to tell me, but I knew something was wrong."

She was correct. Something is awfully, terribly wrong.

And I can't say what it is.

"Look at you," Daphne says. "What did they do?"

I have a moment of incandescent rage that is swallowed up by sadness: of course, this is the first time I get to touch her like this. When it is a disguise. When it's a lie. No, no, this isn't how this is supposed to go. When you're in the lap of a beautiful girl, this isn't what you're supposed to talk about. Your throat isn't supposed to ache, you aren't supposed to feel sick, you aren't supposed to hold your breath and listen for the sound of screaming under the floor. In a better universe, Mrs. Forrester wouldn't be listening or looking through the keyhole. I would have my friends with me. We would be smiling, and laughing, and I would reach down and kiss her and everything would be okay.

But that is not reality. And the moment I open my mouth to tell the truth, the world will become so much more dangerous than it already is. They'll hurt Mary. They'll cut her open. They'll kill her to spite me, to keep me silent, to punish me—it will be *my fault*—

I take a deep breath. Close my eyes.

We deserve to be together on our own. Without death hanging over us like a scalpel. But we're not, and this is what we face now, so we have to make do with what we have.

I would not want to be in this situation with anyone but Daphne.

Because Mrs. Forrester is listening, because she may be watching, I lean in close to Daphne and kiss her.

For the first time, when I tell myself how my future will go, it is not the instructions for a hysterectomy. It is not hot blood, yellow fat, the soft edges of internal organs slipping between my fingers. There are no implements jutting out of a wound and no stitches. There is nothing to cut, or clamp, or sew shut. I don't even have to take out my eyes.

Instead, my future is calm. Once this is done, once this is over, it will be just us. There will be no Braxton's and no

Headmaster. Daphne and I can be married. We can start our lives over, away from this, the way we deserve to. Mary will be okay. Isabella and Ellen and Frances can rest in peace. It may not be perfect—who knows how much of ourselves we will have to hide, how much of our lives we will have to give up—but it will be over, it will be over, it will be over.

One day, things will be better. But first, they have to get worse.

So I have to say it.

Against her lips, I whisper, "Headmaster trapped Mary in the basement of the dressing room."

Daphne jumps with shock, but I grab the back of her head to keep her still. Don't let Mrs. Forrester notice. Daphne's hands tighten around my waist as if she's terrified to let go of me.

I say, "She's in the basement with Isabella's body, and the ghosts of all the dead girls. Headmaster has been controlling the haunting so they can't leave the room. But they're all down there. Headmaster, and a doctor from Bedlam, and—" My brother. I stumble. Even now, it's too much to swallow. "They've been killing us. And if I tell you any of this, if I tell anyone, they're going to kill Mary too."

Daphne stares. Her eyes are so beautiful. They're the only eyes I can bring myself to look at. Her lips are parted and it would almost be sweet if it wasn't an expression borne of pure terror.

"So what do we do?" she says.

That's the question, isn't it? I hold her face. She tucks her cheek against my palm the same way I did to her, her eyes fluttering closed for just a moment, despite the fact that I can hear her heartbeat thrumming, panicked, at her jaw.

A letter to Headmaster, left by the monsters in burial shroud masks.

A girl in the basement.

Spirits behind the Veil.

And movement outside the window.

My mind—the wonderful, inexplicable thing it is—puts everything into place. *Click, click, click.*

All of it should be enough. Not just to end this school, but to make sure that everybody involved gets what they deserve. I will not let the rabbit eat me alive from the inside out, and I will not let those tutors puppet me around with invisible strings for the rest of my life. I will not be beholden to the voices in my head telling me to be a good girl, to be quiet, to do as I'm told. No matter how scared I am.

Some things are more important than just surviving.

I get up from Daphne's lap. She leans forward, tries to hold me, so I lead her off the couch, my hands squeezing hers tight. Like lovers holding each other close, like my heart is not beating so hard in my throat I can almost taste it.

"Darling," I murmur to Daphne, and it is the most natural thing in the world. My voice is so soft, so sweet, that her cheeks flush pink. "Would you be a doll and distract Mrs. Forrester for me? And maybe get those damn keys?"

There is a moment of horrible silence as she stares at me, and I worry that I've misread everything we've done, every conspiratorial look that Daphne has ever given me—but all at once, Daphne smiles that same vicious smile I saw when we planned for the garden party. An amalgamation of anger, excitement, fear. Something terrifying and exhilarating all at once.

She mouths, "*Keys*," with an animal grin. I love her, I love her, I love her.

And she does as I ask. Without hesitation.

So I turn to the window, where the groundskeeper shovels snow from the path all over again, stuck in an endless repetition of tasks that Braxton's traps us in. Daphne, I think, would call it Sisyphean. I wouldn't be able to blame him if he didn't want anything to do to with me. The last time we spoke, I got him hurt.

But if this goes right, Braxton's will never hurt him again.

I force the window open. The groundskeeper turns with a start, nearly dropping the shovel.

"Hey," I say as gently as I can, sliding out so that I'm sitting on the windowsill. My feet dangle over a blanket of snow, and the wind catches my skirts. The rabbit wants me to run—but I wouldn't in a million years. I'm not leaving Mary behind. I'm not leaving anyone else behind. "Do you mind breaking something for me?"

28

From the parlor, behind me, Daphne's voice as I slip off the windowsill and into the snow: "Excuse me—oh, hello, Mrs. Forrester. That's your name, right? I had a, ah, quick question; do you have something for monthlies? Like, the blood?" Brilliant girl. I swear I hear Mrs. Forrester squeal with horror. "I'm so sorry, but we *really*—"

I turn to the groundskeeper. The sunset has bled from a soft gold to the same color as gangrene, and his worn face is lit by the pale half-moon hanging above the garden. He holds the shovel to his chest. There's still bandages peeking out from underneath one of his mittens.

I don't know what to say to him. Headmaster hurt him because of me, because found the button I threw away, because I begged him for help. I wish I knew more about him, the same way I wish I knew more about the girls. His name, his hometown, his favorite flower. What color he would use to describe his eyes when he looks in the mirror. You would be able to tell a lot about someone by what color they pick, I think. I'd call mine *amethyst*. I'd call his *orchid*.

*Leave him.* The rabbit is back. Its sharp voice startles me—I never hear the rabbit when I'm with Daphne, do I? As soon as she leaves, it's there again, trying to chew me to pieces. *You only make it worse. Why would he ever want to help you?*

I can't listen to it.

I hold out a hand. The groundskeeper flinches and it's like I'm on the floor of the gala again, like I'm smeared in blood.

"I'm—" Snow crunches under my shoes. A freezing wind blows, and it sends up swirls of loose snow, waves the branches of leafless bushes, pulls at the groundskeeper's scarf. "I'm sorry. If Headmaster hurt you, it's my fault." I swallow hard. "He doesn't treat you right."

The groundskeeper whines in the back of his throat.

I say, "Nobody treats people like us right."

I've heard the way people talk about us when they think we aren't listening—or when they know we are, and they don't care what we overhear. They call us broken, weak, feeble-minded imbeciles. And if that's what *I've* experienced, what has the groundskeeper lived through? He was never taught to hide this part of himself, not like I was. Or maybe he was, and he couldn't. Maybe he lived through what I did, but worse, berated for his silence and downcast eyes. They only tried to fix me because I would make a good wife one day. If I didn't have that, would Mother and

Father have thrown me aside entirely? What has this man been through?

We don't deserve that. None of us do.

I lean in.

"Headmaster's office window," I say. "I need it gone."

The groundskeeper turns on his heel, hefts the shovel over his shoulder, and starts walking. Breath billows from his mouth in a long, steaming growl. Does Headmaster hold his contract? Does the groundskeeper hate him for it, the same way I hate him? He must. It radiates from him so violently I can almost taste it. He was the one who showed me: the hand over the mouth, the hand over the eyes. He knows what Headmaster does. He wants him gone too.

We come around the long east wing of the building, snow crunching under our feet. The windows leave distorted rectangles of light stretched across the ground, warped like we're looking at them through the Veil. And the window to Headmaster's office is right there, a little high due to the tilt of the ground underneath the building. Inside, I can see his desk, his chair, his shelf of awful trophies.

No Headmaster.

I back away and duck my head. Translation: all yours.

*No going back.*

The groundskeeper swings the shovel off his shoulder and smashes it into the window. The glass spiderwebs. The wooden muntins holding the panes in place crack. Again. The glass breaks. Pieces scatter across the floor, the same kinds of pieces resting in Mrs. Forrester's shoes, leaving shards like an open mouth of fangs. The groundskeeper doesn't hesitate—he jams the shovel through the hole and scrapes the edges of the window, knocking out the teeth like he's done this a hundred times. The noise of it makes me wince. If anyone at all heard that, I won't have much time.

Then the groundskeeper takes off his mittens and hands them to me. I stare at them blankly. Mittens?

After a second, he grabs my wrist and begins to put them on. Oh. So I don't cut my hands climbing through.

Once they're on, he holds out a hand to boost me up.

But instead I take the hand and squeeze it.

"Hey," I say. "Thank you."

The groundskeeper stares, confused. That's fair. I am too. I don't really know what to say, but I need to say something. Because he's like me. He's bad at this too, and he flaps his hands too, and things don't make sense to him either, and we are both just doing the best we can in a world like this. That has to count for something.

After Braxton's, I don't want to leave him.

I say, "I'm glad I met you."

*Hurry hurry hurry run run run.*

The groundskeeper begins to cry. He scrubs his bandaged hand against his eyes, shakes his head, then holds out for me again. When I reach for him, he hugs me—so tight my ribs creak, that I lose all of my breath— and then he lets go and lifts me through the window into Headmaster's office.

I grab the broken edges with my gloved hands and pull myself through. A small shard of glass catches my belly and tears my dress. That's fine. I don't care. I fall through on the other side, barely catching myself before I hit the ground. The stitched wound on my hand screams. I hiss, cradling it to my chest as I struggle back onto my feet.

I'm in. I turn to thank the groundskeeper again, for what might be the last time, but he's gone. His footprints lead out of sight.

I almost laugh, because I'm bad at goodbyes too. I take off the mittens and clutch them to my chest. I'll keep these, then, so I can remember him.

Now.

If I were Headmaster, where would I hide incriminating evidence?

I go for the desk and begin ripping out drawers, shuffling through notebooks and stacks of paper. Christ, there's so much here. Files on students the thickness of a finger, names I know—Charlotte, Mary, Agnes, Harriet—and names I don't. I almost don't recognize my file when I find it, but there's my old name, *Gloria Bell*, written in Headmaster's precise, unerring script.

There's no need to look inside. All it would do is hurt me. I don't want to know how I'm spoken of behind closed doors.

But—I do. I *do* want to see what Headmaster thinks of me. I want to see it written out, I want to make it real. I want to see whatever he thinks is so broken about me that warrants everything he's done. What, exactly, is so wrong with me *this* was only option?

Even though I do not have the time, I open the file.

*High-functioning imbecile. Veil sickness exacerbating cognitive and social delays, despite above-average intelligence; several years behind peers in understanding nuances and cues. Seems to experience distress and confusion regarding sex characteristics. High potential for success if these are compensated for or eliminated.*

This is me, then. Boiled down to my deficits, as if those are the only things about me anyone will ever be able to see. There is nothing here about my steady hands, or my sense of justice, or my honesty, or my kindness, or anything else. It is simply everything that is wrong.

The voice reading along in my head sounded a lot like the rabbit.

The rabbit follows me everywhere, even here.

I fling the file across the room to get it away from me and open another drawer. If I keep thinking about Headmaster's words, I'll be stuck here forever. I came for the letter and that's all. I don't even need the *exact* letter. That doesn't matter. I just need *something*. Anything that will back up my stories of the spirits and dead girls and the Veil-sick wives nobody will ever listen to. A cold wind comes in through the window. Breathe in. Breathe out. Concentrate. It's okay. Daphne is out there. I have time. Breathe.

Underneath a book of Veil sickness case studies, I find it. George's handwriting. Headmaster's name, Captain Ernest Forrester, in his doctor's scrawl.

My hands shake as I unfold the paper. There is no salutation, only George's words.

> *Do not presume to twist my words. Yes, I am a Speaker; however, I am and will always be a surgeon first, so I am obligated by my profession to inform you that our current path will lead us toward nothing but ruin. I cannot in good conscience perform <u>vivisections</u> on our <u>children</u> in pursuit of wishful thinking.*

A knock on the door.

Shit.

I've ransacked the room. Headmaster's files are a mess, papers flung across the desk and onto the floor. Glass glitters on the hardwood, the window an open maw of broken pieces, and I'm red-handed. But it could be Daphne. Okay. Okay. I fold up the letter, jam it into my pocket, and rush to the door to look through the crack between the door and the frame. The rabbit tells me that if it's Mrs. Forrester, we'll be able to jam the chair against the door like I did in the dressing room, but then I'll only have so much time. If it's Charlotte, maybe I can pretend I'm not in here. And it's—

It's Louise. *Louise.* No matter what I think of her, I don't want her to be here when all of this comes to a head. I need to grab her, tell her to run as soon as she has a chance. I unlock the door from the inside and crack it open.

The words are already on my lips: Mary is in the basement, I know what's happened to the girls, you need to *go.*

But I open the door wider, and Louise whispers, "I'm sorry," because Charlotte is there too.

*That bitch.*

The girl that would ruin all of us as long as it made Headmaster happy.

Before I can get a syllable out of my mouth, Charlotte drags Louise into the room and slams the door shut behind them. She stands between us and the way out. The hauntings on that shelf thrum with energy, as if they can feel the anxiety rising. I glance towards the window. I could get out that way, maybe.

"No," Charlotte says. She points a single, accusatory finger at me, then the window. She used Louise—she knew I wouldn't have opened the door if it had just been her. Louise shrinks from her. "Don't you dare."

I hold up my hands, no matter how much I want to flap them or shake them out. I spread my fingers. Show I mean no harm. *She's going to hurt you*, the rabbit says, and I hate that it's right. Out of everyone, it was always going to be her. *Mary is going to die because of her. Shut her up shut her up.*

"You—" Charlotte tries to talk, but something chokes her.

The expression on her face is disgust. Pure disgust.

"You," she begins again, "are supposed to be gone."

"You're right," I say. "I am." Charlotte's nostrils flare. Louise takes a step back, and her shoe hits a piece of broken glass. "Do you know what's happening down there? In the basement, under the dressing room?"

"We don't have a basement," Charlotte says.

I'm running out of time. Daphne can't distract Mrs. Forrester for much longer. I have to come clean. If I tell the truth, maybe they'll join me. Maybe the horror of it will shake some sense into Charlotte and we can do this together.

One more try.

"There is a basement," I say slowly. "Headmaster— he's been killing girls. He killed Frances, and Ellen, and Isabella."

Louise clamps a hand over her mouth like she's going to be sick. Charlotte, though, starts to shake her head: "No," she says, "no, you're lying, you're lying."

But I continue. "He tried to kill me, and he's going to kill Mary if we don't do something *right now*. We have to help her. Please."

Louise says nothing. She's silent, as still as a statue. This I expected. I can deal with a coward. She's not the one I'm worried about.

Please let Charlotte see sense.

"Headmaster isn't going to love you just because you're a good girl," I tell her. "And anyone who does will never give a shit about you."

Charlotte meets my eyes, and the weight of her loathing makes me ill.

"Both of you," she says. "You and Miss Carter. You're both sick. You're both—you're both sick, and disgusting, and ungrateful. Absolutely ungrateful." She makes a wretched, pathetic noise that only makes me despise her more. My own anger terrifies me. It makes the rabbit *squeal*.

It burns my throat, my face, the tips of my fingers, and the depth of it makes me ill. "Both of you should be ashamed. You're a disgrace to this school, and if you end up with a man that beats you and fucks you like you're so afraid of, then maybe you deserve it."

She breathes in deep.

It strikes me, at this very moment, that Charlotte has always been the most dangerous girl in Braxton's. And not just because she's a snitch. But because she *believes*. She believes the lies, or at least she believes that regurgitating the lies will save her. She'll fuck over anybody if she thinks it would make her look better in the eyes of the people who want to hurt her.

We cannot afford to pity her. We can only fear her.

Charlotte screams, "*Mrs. Forrester!*"

Louise tackles her.

They hit the chair in front of Headmaster's desk, the same one I sat in while he asked if I abused myself, and fall to the ground in a tangle of limbs and skirts. "No," Louise is sobbing, "no no no." Charlotte screeches. She digs her nails into Louise's face and leaves long red gashes over her cheek. Louise leans forward to puts an arm across Charlotte's throat, jams her fingers into her mouth, does not hesitate when Charlotte bites down. I take a step back and my heel catches broken glass. My shoulder hits the shelf. Stolen trophies rattle. "Shut up," Louise cries, "shut up shut *up!*"

And outside:

Footsteps.

*They'll fucking hang you.*

If I go out the window, then Louise is alone.

If I stay, they'll kill Mary.

*They'll hurt you, they'll put a rope around your neck, they'll cut you open while you're alive just like they did to Isabella—*

The door flings open.

Mrs. Forrester lurches through. Her eyes are pale, rotting bruises jammed onto her face. Charlotte screams for her, reaching out a hand as Louise looks up with a strangled gasp. Daphne's not there. Shit. Where is Daphne? *Where is Daphne?*

*THEY'LL HURT YOU THEY'LL HURT YOU THEY'LL HURT YOU. YOU'RE TRAPPED AND THEY'LL FUCKING KILL YOU.*

"You *wretch*," Mrs. Forrester howls at me.

But I'm not trapped. Not like I thought.

I opened the Veil. I spoke to the dead. And I know what Headmaster did, because the dead always tell the truth.

I reach for every relic, every war trophy, every stolen chip of someone's life, on the shelf. Every little piece of cruelty he took off the bodies of those he killed, that he robbed from their final resting places. The bone, the button, the stone. I cradle them all, gently, the way they deserve to be held. I find the edge of the world. I pull.

And the rage—

The pain—

It tears apart everything, and it is beautiful.

29

Do you know how angry the dead can be?

The air is so cold that the skin under my finger-nails turns blue: the vessels constrict, leeching away the blood that gives pale skin its pinkish tint. Tears gather in my eyes from the sting. Snow flurries in through the broken window.

Whatever I've done, I've broken the Veil. I've destroyed everything Headmaster has put in place to keep Braxton's quiet. There are more spirits than I've ever seen, a flood of them, shattered and whole and everything in between. There's the spirit I met on the washroom floor. Isabella. Ellen. Frances. So many others I've never met and I'll never know. The world is torn apart in my hands. The other side of the Veil is dark and empty and nothing.

Frost swallows the walls and the floor and creeps up the hem of my skirt. The desk, the walls, the floor, they all shimmer and shake and freeze. It is so deep, so instant, that the wooden boards by the window begin to crack.

If I don't get out, all the water in my body will freeze, and I will absolutely die.

*Run.*

Ice crystals pop across Mrs. Forrester's face and hands. She looks down, stares at them, and begins to laugh.

Charlotte throws Louise off her and scrambles to her feet. Louise hits the ground, sobbing, trying to wipe blood from her eyes. The mess of fluids has frozen to the soft hairs on her cheek and jaw. It sparkles like dew on an early spring morning.

"Mrs. Forrester," Charlotte squeals, rushing to her side, grabbing her hands to warm them. "Mrs. Forrester, it's okay, it's okay—" But Mrs. Forrester is just *laughing*, high and hysterical, watching as frost swallows her fingers. Isabella looms behind her, slash-mouth open, and if I didn't know any better, I'd swear she was smiling.

We have to go.

I grab Louise's arm and drag her off the ground. She tries to pull away from me. "Come on, *come on*."

"I—" Louise whimpers.

Another voice: "*Silas!*"

Oh my God. Daphne. It's her. In the hall, past the open door. Part of her cheek is raw. I want to scream—who hurt her, who would dare hurt her?—but the world alters around us again, ice creeping forward, the cracks digging deeper into the foundations of this school. The hard edges of the world don't line up anymore. Everything shimmers in the corner of my eye. The spirits are devouring everything.

The rabbit, again, like a mantra, or a heartbeat: *They'll hurt you.*

Daphne holds up Mrs. Forrester's keys, silhouetted by snow and air so cold that it's gone hazy. How is it snowing inside? It doesn't work like that.

"Oh," Louise whispers at my side, barely audible above Mrs. Forrester's coughing laughter and Charlotte's pleas for her to be okay, to just get up, to get somewhere warm. "The letters made it."

Louise sent the letters?

She was next to me, every night, when I took them from my mattress to read them. She saw me cradling them in front of the fire, running my hands over the pages. And she ducked between our beds to grab that ribbon—the ribbon that's in her hair now—the perfect excuse to grab something, anything, that might save us.

Louise sent the letters. Charlotte's face is marred with three massive gashes tearing open her cheek, and Louise has the blood under her fingernails.

She saved me.

Daphne says, "*We need to fucking go!*"

We do. Every second that we spend up here is another one in which Mary could be bleeding out on the operating table, another second that I can't put pressure on the wound and hold the artery closed. Do I remember how to use a tourniquet? I take Louise's hand and start for the door.

But she doesn't follow. She's rooted to the spot like her feet have frozen to the floor. I glance down in a panic to make sure that hasn't actually happened.

Why isn't she coming?

*Leave her.*

"Louise?" I say.

She shakes her head. Her red hair, the color of a burning sunset or a sweet summer fruit, has fallen from its pins in a ragged mess. Charlotte must have hit her, because a bruise is starting to form just under her eye. "I can't," she says, so quietly that I almost can't hear her over Charlotte and Mrs. Forrester. "I'm—" Her eyelashes are dotted with ice crystals. "I'm scared. Please just go. I'm sorry."

Mrs. Forrester has given up, slumping over, still giggling. Charlotte shrieks at her. I think I hear Isabella laughing.

I let go of Louise's hand—one finger and then the next, slowly, until the cold is too much to bear. And then I leave her and run to Daphne, who catches me by the shoulders, lets out a strangled sob, and pulls me down the hall.

Braxton's Finishing School and Sanitorium shatters with the cold of the dead.

✦

The walls and floor crack and crumble. Plaster rains down from the ceiling, and when I look up from the bottom of the stairs up, up, the white sheen has climbed up the railings, the banister, the windows. It hurts to look at for too long. The air smells of petals, the sharp shock of winter snowstorms. Ellen crawls across the ceiling and disappears into the dark.

Daphne unlocks the dressing room, but the door sticks until she rams her weight into it once, twice. The room is *white*. The curtains are frozen solid. Icicles jut down from the shelves and hanging skirts. I can feel my joints screaming as I throw the rug aside, the wool crackling as I yank it away from the floor.

The padlock is frozen in place. The key strains but the mechanism doesn't budge. My hands so cold it hurts to move them. Then a spirit reaches across the floor—the same spirit from the washroom floor, the one spelling words with me from scraps taken out of my poetry book, the one who told me to run—and shatters the ice. The pins give way. The lock springs open.

*They've already killed her. They've already opened up her head and her face and you're going to find her taken apart, ripped to pieces, broken broken broken.*

Daphne and I haul the trapdoor open. "Mary!" I scream into the dark. "*Mary!*"

The world beneath our feet is absolutely, utterly still.

A thick sheen of snow covers the floor, revealing hoarfrost at the deepest corners, climbing up the sides of the operating table in a hungry, swallowing arc. And two ice sculptures stand with their hands up, mouths open, faces shrouded like a caul. Like spirits.

They're not sculptures; they're people.

Dr. Bernthal on one side. Headmaster on the other.

And then Mary.

Mary is strapped down to the table, but the ice has not touched her. Frances looms above her, disjointed limbs bending in too many places, melting and reforming in constant motion. Watching over her. So loyal that she will not leave Mary's side even after death. Keeping her from the cold, trying to comfort Mary as she cries, even though they cannot touch, not really.

Daphne and I are beside her as quickly as we can be. I nearly twist my ankle at the bottom of the stairs. Frances growls at us as we get close, but I hold out my hand as Daphne begins undoing the straps. Daphne shivers. Frost has begun to collect in her dark hair.

"It's okay," I say. "We're here." I try not to think about Headmaster and Dr. Bernthal frozen in this room, their organs grinding to a halt as all the water in their bodies turns to jagged ice crystals, how quickly or slowly they died. I try not to think about how there are only two people in this room. Stop, stop thinking. "We're going to take care of her, I swear."

Daphne gets Mary up. Part of Mary's head has been shaved, leaving a bald spot right at her temple. A circular wound is torn into the scalp. It's deep and bleeding a hell of a lot. I search through my mental catalog of surgical implements until I come to the right one: a trephine. Meant for trepanation. They were going to drill into her skull while she was alive. That's what they did to Isabella. They had already started. They'd—

Mary sobs. She leans against Daphne, wraps her arms around her like a child looking for her mother. Frances jerks forward, crawling over the operating table.

"We're leaving," Daphne whispers to Mary, leading her to the stairs. "We're leaving, we're leaving, it's over."

They start up the stairs.

I don't.

Around us, Braxton's groans as the foundations and beams and walls start to give out. Breathing hurts. I can't feel my toes, and my fingers tingle: the precursors to frostbite. The operating theater in the basement of this goddamn school is cold, and silent, and dark.

There are only two men here. Both of them deserved what they got. I hope it hurt. The trephine froze in Headmaster's hand. He died in this school, in the guts of it the way so many girls did before him. And then Dr. Bernthal, the man who took a child for his own, who hurt her and broke her.

George, though, is gone.

He's not here.

I'm supposed to feel something about that, I think. I'm supposed to be angry that he dared survive when so many others did not. Maybe a dark part of me is supposed to be relieved, because no matter what he did, he's still my brother. Or it doesn't even have to be that specific. I should feel a rock in my stomach, my insides tying themselves up in knots like a twisted bowel constricting itself on accident.

But there's just nothing.

"Silas!" Daphne pleads from the top of the stairs. "Let's go!"

Right.

I climb the stairs, back to the shattering school, and Daphne leads us down the hall, out the front door, into the white world of snow and moonlight and fresh air. Somehow it's warmer here. I look back towards the school as we walk. I'm not sure what I'm looking for. Mrs. Forrester?

Charlotte? Something, anything, that would betray them. But there's nothing. It is silent. It is all dead.

Ahead of me, Mary stumbles and nearly falls out of Daphne's arms. When Daphne tries to help her, Mary pushes her away—"I'm fine," she gasps, "I'm fine"—so Daphne pauses in the middle of the cobbled road leading up to the school, breathing hard.

She is lovely in the moonlight. Standing tall, breath clouding. Frost and snow clings to her clothes. And she's looking at me like I'm something at all worth looking at.

Maybe I'll get used that one day. But not now.

"I tied my horse by the gate," she says. "She can't handle all three of us. Do you think we could walk to the nearest village?"

"I'd have to keep an eye on you for frostbite," I say.

Daphne almost laughs. "Frostbite."

And there, in the distance:

The squeal of the gate opening. The dark, far-away silhouette of the groundskeeper. And Louise. Maybe. I can't tell if it's her, no matter how hard I squint, because there's not much time for me to look. As soon as the gate is open, she's gone. She disappears into the darkness. I breathe in, breathe out, and try to make sense of what I see as the gate opens wider.

It's . . . a carriage. A carriage with matching chestnut geldings. It rattles in on its massive wheels, closer and closer, and comes to a stop right in front of us, the horses snorting and steaming. Mary, shaking with sobs, reaches behind her to find me. I take her hand and squeeze.

Daphne says, "Father?"

Lord Luckenbill steps out of the carriage.

"Oh dear," he says, taking off his hat. "It's much too cold for you to be out here alone."

Past him, the groundskeeper stands by the impenetrable wall. Behind us, Isabella stands in the front door of Braxton's just as the foundations give. The entranceway collapses. Windows shatter. Glass rains down, pieces reflecting Ellen's weeping-willow face.

It's over.

It's done.

The rabbit says, *Right?*

30

I remember . . .

I remember hesitating in the snow, staring at the carriage, because I'm so tired and cold and unwell that I can't remember if I should be relieved. I remember Daphne helping me and then Mary up into the coach, and me leaning against Daphne's side as we leave the crumbling ruins of Braxton's behind. "What a shame," Lord Luckenbill says, peering out the window. I remember Mary holding her necklace as she falls asleep against my shoulder, the ring at the end shimmering, a haunting. It wasn't like that before. As she dozes, I reach for it.

It's Frances. She's here, with us.

It's such a simple gesture—yes, that is how it's supposed to be, that is exactly how the world is supposed to work— and it nearly brings me to tears.

Daphne wraps an arm around me to pull me close. Lord

Luckenbill looks between us all, the three of us crammed into one side of the carriage, him alone on the other side. I don't know where we're going and I don't care. I don't ask. We're going away, we're leaving this all behind, and that's the only thing I need.

I remember trying to get the letter from my pocket, reaching for Lord Luckenbill to tell him everything. But he takes my hand and holds it. He says, "The world can wait. You need to rest."

"Father," Daphne says, like she might cry.

"Rest," Lord Luckenbill says. It is the kindest word he's ever said to her in my presence.

So I do. We all do.

✦

I wake up in a room I have never seen before, and this does not scare me.

It's early morning, the snow reflecting the sun, the walls of this luxurious bedroom covered in scientific diagrams of flowers and bookshelves and paintings of gardens. I am swaddled with blankets in a four-poster bed. The world is silent, and still, and calm. My heart does not beat with fear. I am alone, and the air is pleasantly chilly, and my chemise—I'm not in a nightgown, I must have simply undressed and fallen into bed—is warm from my body heat.

I sit up in bed, wrapping a quilt around my shoulders. If I listen carefully, I can hear the distant patter of servant's footsteps; it's early if they're still about. On the other side of the room, my dress has been laid out to dry. It was wet with melting ice. There's even a large mirror right from the bed, and for once, when I inspect my own reflection, I look bright. Healthy. Tired and worn, but alive.

I'm . . .

Okay.

I'm not in Braxton's. Mrs. Forrester is not ringing her bell to wake us. Headmaster is not here to drag me outside or put his hands around my throat. No more locked doors, no more dead things. Just me in this soft room. I imagine Daphne is asleep too, and Mary must be just down the hall, in her own bed, sleeping deeply like she deserves.

We made it. We're safe. Braxton's is gone, and Lord Luckenbill came for us. I have proof. I have people who will listen to me. All of the anxiety, all of the fear, it leaves my body in a rush.

Except for the rabbit.

*You're alone.*

I thump the top of my left breast with my fist. No, I'm not. Daphne is here, and Mary, and Lord Luckenbill. Everything is fine now. Or, it's not entirely fine. Daphne and I still have to figure out what we want to do with the rest of our lives. I'm worried about what will happen to Mary after all this. Will we be blamed for the destruction of Braxton's? There are things nagging at the back of my skull, but nobody is actively trying to *murder* me, so it doesn't matter. Right now, it's over.

Don't I deserve a chance to rest? Even just for a little bit?

*Rabbits never get a chance to rest. Something always wants to hurt us.*

*No matter how close we are.*

That is a terrible reminder: the letter in my pocket. I slide out of bed, onto the cold floor, and go to my dress. The letter is still there, thank God. It's a little wrinkled, and the ink is smeared, but it's readable.

I don't want to read it, though. I try to unfold it but can't. My fingers won't let me open it, my eyes won't stay on the words, my mind blanks out what script I accidentally manage to glimpse.

It's not fair that George wrote this. It should have been some stranger, some man I'd never met and feel nothing for. After everything, it's not right that I should have to lose my brother too. And I don't even have Headmaster or Dr. Bernthal to blame for taking him from me—this is something he chose all on his own. He took his heart, weighed it against the world, and decided to do the wrong thing.

If I read this letter, then he is gone forever.

There's a knock on the door.

My heartbeat explodes as I tuck the letter protectively to my chest, and I have to calm myself down. It's not like the knock on the door of Headmaster's office. It's okay. I'm okay.

"Who is it?" I say. Then, in case it's a servant: "I'm sorry, I'm not quite dressed."

"Oh, my apologies, dear." It's Lord Luckenbill. His voice is shockingly soft. It's unnerving to realize where Daphne gets it from. But I'm not afraid of him, certainly not as much as I once was. He's a product of the Speakers, yes, but not a monster. Nothing like Headmaster. "I was just wondering if you were awake. I have a housecoat, if you'd like."

I go to the door and stick my hand out for the house-coat. Lord Luckenbill laughs as he hands it over. In just a chemise, I'm practically naked.

I shut the door. "Thank you," I say, putting it on. The letter goes in the pocket. "Is anyone else awake?"

"You mean Edward?" Lord Luckenbill says. I haven't heard that name in so long that it surprises me. "Or your friend? They're both still sleeping. Which is understandable—it was a difficult night."

That's one way to put it. I tie the housecoat closed, then pause there with it wrapped around me. I catch sight of myself in the mirror again. My long blond hair is loose, and my cheeks are pink. The housecoat itself a bit big, but other than that, it fits well; strange, how immaculately this has been tailored to someone who is not me. I do not have the kind of body that is easy to pass off as male, and it is impossible to hide my chest and hips. *You make such a pretty girl.* I scrub my eyes and look away. Maybe I'll never be able to convince the world of my true self, but at least I can have that with Daphne.

Speaking of the world.

"Can . . . ," I say to the door. "Can we talk, my lord?"

"Only if I'm allowed to come in." A pause. Usually that would be indecent, but then again, Speakers are allowed to do whatever they like—and if he was the one who wanted Daphne and I engaged, there's no reason to worry. "And only if you stop calling me that. It's a bit stuffy, isn't it?"

The banality of it shocks me enough that I laugh. He's right. I'm never sure when or how to address someone above

my station; titles never made much sense to me anyway. "Of
course."

I open the door to the bedroom, and Lord Luckenbill
comes in. He's dressed plainly, in a morning suit and
comfortable shoes. He's not as intimidating as he once was.
In fact, his face sports an almost apologetic smile that makes
the wrinkles at the corners of his eyes stand out. He's not an
intimidating viscount. He's just a father. Not a perfect one,
of course, but certainly a kinder one than my own.

There must be a look on my face, because Lord Luckenbill
says, "Oh, poor thing. It's okay. It's over."

I say, "What?" but it's too late. I hadn't realized how
badly I'd needed to hear someone say that until he did, and
my mask crumbles. Before I can stop myself, I'm crying all
over again, weeping into my hands, because I have spent
the past weeks tired, and scared, and cornered, and overwhelmed, and it all comes falling out of me in a single
moment.

"I'm—" I hiccup, shaking my hands to get this under
control. Then, when I realize I'm doing it, I grab the housecoat and squeeze the fabric until it hurts. "I'm sorry."

Lord Luckenbill reaches out, holds my arms, rubs them
up and down. It's a strangely familiar gesture, not the sort
of thing someone like him would do, but what else do you
do when someone cries in front of you? "There we go," he
says. I sniffle, scrubbing my face. "Breathe, dear. Easy.
What happened to the school wasn't your fault."

The simplicity of that statement nearly shocks me out of
my sobs. It *was* my fault, though. I am the one who opened

the Veil and let out the spirits that tore the building to splinters. And I'm not upset that it happened, not at all; it *should* have happened, it *needed* to happen. But to the Speakers, this should be just as terrible as what I did at the gala. They don't need another excuse to see me as a madwoman. So why—?

"The Veil is dangerous," Lord Luckenbill says. "This's why we've put so much work into helping you. It's heartbreaking what's happened. It must have been terrifying." I wipe my eyes. "But you're alive, and that's what matters. I had been upset with Edward for leaving without warning, but I'm very glad he was there to protect you and your friend."

Her name is Daphne. She got her letters, the letters Louise sent back, and she knew. She had a hunch, and her hunches are always right.

"Of course," I whisper.

"If it makes you feel any better," he says, standing and crossing the room to the hearth, "this sort of bizarre event has been recorded elsewhere."

I follow him as he stacks the logs, starts the fire, stokes the flame. "Really?"

"Mm." He takes an iron poker and pushes kindling into the fire to help it catch. "Mostly in the colonies. Calcutta, for example, had a similar event recently. The home of one of our generals simply froze. Trapped him and his family inside. A horrible thing. I've heard the same happened in America recently, though I can't remember the details—old buildings on some plantation swallowed whole by ice." He shakes his head. "Lord knows why."

I can guess. Dead men have no reason to lie, so they never do.

They have no reason to not fight back, so they will.

*Mors vincit omnia*, right?

"That's . . ." I don't want to say *good*. It's terrible that the world has come to this. But if the dead are so angry they are able to turn their rage on the living, no matter how many times a medium tries to seal them away, then I say let them break whatever parts of the world they want. "A lot to take in."

"I know, I know." Lord Luckenbill straightens up, wipes his hands on his pants. There's that smile again. "So I just want you to know that what happened there is not your fault."

This time, I am not confused. He's right. It's not my fault. It's Braxton's.

"How are you?" Lord Luckenbill says, offering me a handkerchief to wipe my face. I do. "What did you want to discuss, dear?"

Oh. Right. I take the letter out of my pocket and hand it to him.

*He won't believe you.*

"What's this?" Lord Luckenbill says.

"A letter from my brother," I say. The fire crackles. I can see all of myself in the mirror on the wall behind Lord Luckenbill, my face splotchy with tears. I am not composed, but I look more sure of myself than I ever have. "To Headmaster."

Lord Luckenbill holds up a hand to quiet me.

In shock, I comply. I should press forward, like I did with George, but I don't want to upset him, not now. I rock on my feet as he unfolds the paper—and then, carefully, I lean over to read it.

> *Captain Ernest Forrester,*
>
> *Do not presume to twist my words. Yes, I am a Speaker; however, I am and will always be a surgeon first, so I am obligated by my profession to inform you that our current path will lead us toward nothing but ruin. I cannot in good conscience perform <u>vivisections</u> on our <u>children</u> in pursuit of wishful thinking. I do not care about budgets, or Parliament, or orders from on high. I swore an oath and I will stand by it.*
>
> *To that end, I say: There is no evidence that violet eyes are anatomically different from any other. The brains are no different, the bodies no different. There is <u>no difference</u>. There never has been and there never will be. I too believe that there must be some way to control such a dangerous power, but basic biological mechanisms simply are not the way. My wife deserves better than this.*
>
> *Find the goddamn budget for our previous subjects, or I am done.*
>
> *Best,*
>
> *George Bell*

There it is. It's written out plain. Headmaster was killing us. He was taking us apart to look at our insides. To—to learn what gives us the ability to do spirit-work, so that it could be taken from us.

Taken from us?

Of course. People like Headmaster would never be content with just teaching us not to use our powers. He wanted to make it *impossible*. And why wouldn't he? If he learned how to do it, he could turn around and give the discovery to the Speakers—what if they wanted to bring this to the colonies, to take away spirit-work from the people they deem unfit to have it? Only the worthy could ever be mediums, and pesky outliers would have it cut out of them, and the empire would be just as the Speakers want it. A petty part of me wonders what Charlotte would have done; would she have willingly submitted to the procedure? What would all of the Speaker wives do to make their husbands happy? Would they campaign for their own destruction all because they wanted to take from those deemed undeserving?

What a terrible, selfish thing to play God. Monsters, all of them.

And George was a part of it. The only thing he ever balked at was cutting open people like me and Elsie. If he couldn't look at them and see us, he never would have flinched at all.

"Oh," Lord Luckenbill says. "You found this?"

"In Headmaster's office." My voice is stronger now. "They were hurting us. They were hurting so many people. I know, I know you wouldn't allow that to happen, but—"

Lord Luckenbill folds the paper back up. I stumble over my words. He's not looking at me. He's usually the kind of person who insists on looking me in the eyes, even if I don't want him to.

"Did Captain Forrester touch you?" he says. "Did he—" A flash of rage flickers in Lord Luckenbill's eyes. "Did he put his hands on you? Did he try?"

Oh God, finally. Somebody is listening. Somebody is *listening*. I remember every time he put his hands on me no matter how badly I want to forget. Phantom fingers wrap around my throat and lips touch mine. I almost start crying again. "Yes. He did."

Lord Luckenbill says, "He was never supposed to touch you."

To touch me.

*Me.*

I say, "What?"

"I told him to keep his hands off you," Lord Luckenbill says. "I told him you were off-limits."

No. Wait. No, no. "You knew?"

"Of course not. Not what they were doing to you."

"But you knew about the basement?"

He does not reply.

The rabbit screams *NO NO NO NO NO*.

He knew too. Everybody in my life knew, and nobody did a fucking thing to stop it. He signed off on Frances, on Ellen, on Isabella, on everyone that came before us. Student or not. Like me or not. Everything that Headmaster ever did, every person that has ever been hurt, Lord Luckenbill knew.

Every time, except for me.

What makes me so special? Why did it have to be *me*? Why couldn't it have been Isabella that survived? Or anyone else? This isn't right. This can't be how it goes.

"I never wanted you to be hurt," Lord Luckenbill says. When I take a step back, he takes a step forward, hand outstretched as if to show he means no harm. "I needed to keep you safe. Because—you hear so much about these women, women with Veil sickness. And perhaps the late headmaster and I have different views of the world, because I—I think a woman can be made well again if simply given a chance. Like Mrs. Forrester was, like Emily was." Emily. Daphne's mother. Lord Luckenbill's voice changes as he speaks, and suddenly he is sniveling. Pathetic. His softness becomes disgusting, the underbelly of a pig just before I cut it open. "The two of you look so much alike, did you know that? You and Emily? Not in the face, but in the soul. In the eyes. You have the same color eyes that she did. I would never hurt you. I never would."

*HE KNEW AND HE DID NOTHING.*

One more step back. Stop following me. Stop. He needs to stop talking about my eyes right *now*, the way those men did as I was growing up, the way those men did as they played with my hair. I was ten years old. I was nine. I was eight. I was a *child*.

*ALL OF THE SPEAKERS KNEW THEY ALWAYS KNEW.*

"Wait," Lord Luckenbill says. "Here. I'll prove it to you." He reaches into his pocket to reveal a little velvet box. He opens it—and it's a ring.

Small enough to fit my finger. Elegant diamonds set into gold, a line of them, and a small piece of parchment tucked into the velvet explains that they were mined directly from the most beautiful vein in South Africa.

"Your parents helped pick this out," Lord Luckenbill says.

What is he talking about? Too much is happening at once, and I can't make sense of it. If this is for Daphne—or to be from her, I suppose—I don't understand why Lord Luckenbill is giving it to me now. We're engaged, not yet betrothed, promised but not yet bound. This isn't how it works. Right?

"I wanted to wait," Lord Luckenbill says. "But I've discussed it with your parents. And. Well. I've heard the way he speaks of you, seen the way he interacts with you. Edward is a good boy, but he needs time to mature, to come more into his manhood. He's a bit of a ponce, isn't he? A bit soft around the edges? Haven't you noticed?"

Lord Luckenbill's voice is changing. Becoming something else.

"If you were my wife," Lord Luckenbill says, "you wouldn't need to be fixed at all."

The rabbit presses on my lungs. I can't get a breath in.

"I'm not—" I have to drag the words out because they don't want to come. I want to scream, I want to sew my mouth shut, I want to tear out my throat like a madwoman to keep him from ever looking at me again. *He wants you. He wants you and you're telling him no? You know what men do, you know what they do.* "I promised Edward. You said it was going to be Edward. We're engaged."

*But not betrothed. Not bound.*

*Speakers can do whatever they want.*

"Gloria," Lord Luckenbill says. "This is the best possible option for you, is it not? A marriage to a high-born, wealthy man and not his weak, ineffectual son?" He tilts his head. "Be honest. I understand you are a proud, intelligent woman. Other Speakers, well, they'll only see the tutors you needed. They'll only see the Veil sickness. I won't do that to you."

Breathe in. Breathe out.

*Just do what he says.* The rabbit is pleading. Begging. *Just do it. Just agree. He'll stop if you agree.*

In another world, maybe I would have said yes to this. I would have looked in the mirror, steeled myself, and taken the best chance the world had given me. People like me are not supposed to have anything. We are meant to be shut away, ignored, locked up. And Lord Luckenbill is here, offering me a chance for something else. Anything else.

*He'll hurt you if you don't.*

I know.

"I know it seems a bit . . . distasteful from your point of view," Lord Luckenbill says. "But it's the best thing for you, and generations of women before you have done the best thing for themselves. Is it really so hard to do the same? Is it so hard to accept a life of idleness and wealth, if you choose?"

He's right. If I swallow it all and agree, I would never want for anything ever again. If I turn away from the Speakers' wrongdoings and pretend I never noticed them, my life would be perfect. I would have money, and nice clothes, and a warm bed, and more power than I would ever know what to do with. It is what so, so many people have done. It is how the world works.

*Just do it. Just say yes just save yourself just do it please.*

I throw the tear-stained handkerchief to the ground. "I'd rather fuck a rotten corpse than you."

Lord Luckenbill lunges for me.

He grabs me like he's hungry. Like he's starving, like he needs to take a piece out of me before I bleed out in his mouth. The force of him slams us both into the mirror hard enough that I bite my tongue. He's holding me by the wrists, but the whole weight of his body has me pinned. He's so much bigger. My ribs press into my lungs like they're going to break.

"We met when you were little," he says. "When you and Edward were still so little. Don't you remember?" I wrench my head away from him because I can feel his breath in the back of my throat. I don't remember. I begged God to help me forget the men that ran their hands through my hair and pulled at the ribbons on my dresses for fun, and I don't remember it at all, I don't. "I would have taken you then, if your father had let me."

*Be good.* It's the same thing the rabbit said on the carriage ride down. *Be good just like you did for Headmaster. Just be good it'll be over faster he won't hurt you as much if you just do what he says just do it do it.*

"I won't hurt you," he says. "I promise." He presses his face to my cheek. I jerk away, hit the mirror harder. "I'm a good man. I can wait until the wedding."

He lets go of one of my wrists to rip the housecoat, grab a handful of my chemise, and *tear*.

The sound is like skin ripping. A wound opening, a scab peeling away, a saw going through bone.

He says, "But you just look so much like *her.*"

*Let him.*

But Mary with her bloody hands and bruised face. Frances with a pair of scissors. Miss Neuling with the metal.

Hurting them is the only way they learn.

*No don't no no no you know what they'll do.*

Hurting him would be no different than cutting open a piglet. A patient. Pulling a tooth. Amputating a limb. A hysterectomy, a removal, an excision of a rotting piece of flesh.

*HE'LL HURT YOU.*

He already is.

I grab the rabbit by the throat. The creature between my ribs screams, thrashes, makes that awful high-pitched noise that all rabbits make when set upon by foxes or hounds. It begs me not to hurt Lord Luckenbill even as I squeeze its throat, collapse its esophagus, constrict the arteries to keep blood from reaching the brain. The bones grind. The rabbit's eyes whirl. *DON'T HURT HIM HE'LL HURT YOU DON'T HURT HIM HE'LL HURT YOU.*

The neck snaps.

And I bash my hand into the mirror.

It does not explode into a storm of little pieces, the way I thought it would. It spiderwebs with a horrific crack. Lord Luckenbill looks up with a start, like he's been shocked out of a trance. "What are you—"

I jam my hand into the broken mess. Splinters dig under my fingernails and rip open my palm. Lord Luckenbill starts to back up, dragging me by the arm—*What are you doing, what are you doing*—but I force a shard from the frame and rip it away and plunge it into Lord Luckenbill's throat.

Like Miss Neuling's knife into the medium. Like Mary cutting Headmaster's cheek. Like Isabella and her split belly.

The glass tears through flesh and tendons. It's so much duller than a scalpel and does so, so much more damage. Muscles pop and give and shift under the skin. The edges slice open my palm, tear apart the stitches, rip my fingers to shreds.

Lord Luckenbill's eyes bulge. His mouth flops open. He makes a sound like a choking cow.

He trips on the edge of the rug and falls.

He pulls me down with him. On top of him. The glass severs an artery, and the pressure sprays blood across my face in the rhythm of a heartbeat. Again. Again. He's still trying to grab me, coughing and choking, but now he's rasping, wheezing, sick, wet.

I pull out the glass. It leaves a large, dark wound. I can see all the little things inside. Broken arteries. Severed skin. Sallow fat.

I shove it in again, but I pick the spot carefully, with a surgeon's precision. The esophagus this time. At the base of the throat. Tough and leathery. He writhes and squirms, but he's losing blood fast. Strength goes with it like it always does. Find another vein. Sever that too. Dig until I can count all the inside bits of his throat that should never see the air.

He's still watching me.

No. He's done watching. I reach into his eye sockets and pull out the eyes—muddy, dull, something he never deserved. *Pop.* Like the cork in a bottle of wine. The orbs are tough yet pliable in my hand. I sever the optic nerves with my teeth. It tastes tough, and meaty, and salty, and it's just as satisfying as if I had done it to myself.

I sit up.

I breathe.

Blood drips off my hands. My chin. My white chemise is soaked all down the front, clinging to my chest, and I spit to get the salty taste of insides out of my mouth. Loose hair clings to my face.

I breathe.

I drop the shard of the mirror. Part of it broke off in his neck. The man underneath me is nothing more than a cut-open pig, a medical cadaver, his empty eye sockets staring up at the ceiling. I hope, as his spirit slips away into the Veil, that Emily Luckenbill finds him. I hope she finds him and tears him apart. I hope he suffers for everything he's done, for hurting Daphne, for hurting me, for hurting all of us.

Breathe.

Sometimes, when a surgeon does the right thing, it looks a hell of a lot like this.

I look up, and there's Mary and Daphne. In the doorway. Watching.

31

Daphne pulls me against her—whispering, *"Silas, oh God, oh God, Silas"*—and I do nothing. Outside the window, the sun rises and shines bright and beautiful.

Lord Luckenbill breathes for a few seconds more, then stops.

32

I didn't hit any major veins or arteries in my hand. Sitting on the washroom floor, that's what I focus on: that my bloody, torn-up hands are not damaged beyond repair. If I flatten my palm, the wounds open in a collection of little mouths. The broken stitches lay sprawled. I can see inside the meat. The pain is a distant throb, as if hidden by cotton. All of my head is fuzzy and dull.

Mary sits on the edge of the tub as Daphne dabs away the blood and pulls out each broken stitch. She is gentle, but her hands tremble as she works.

"You okay?" Mary says.

I don't respond. Words are beyond me.

"Silas?" Daphne whispers. "Are you okay?"

I try to open my mouth to speak—to say what, I'm not sure—but instead I heave. Nothing comes out except hot spit. Mary holds my hair back from my face. In turn,

Daphne wets a rag and presses it to my lips, and I pull it into my mouth to suck on the water.

"Here." Mary grabs the rag from my mouth and wrings it out. "You're a mess."

"Of course he is," Daphne says. Her voice cracks with tears.

"And so are you." Mary gives her a stern look. "Let me handle this."

So Daphne holds me against her while Mary cleans my face. I let them. Daphne's heart drums in her throat, so hard I can almost hear it; there is blood on her sleeves where she's wrapped her arms around me.

"Silas," Mary says, "look at me." It's bizarre to hear Mary's voice so kind. I almost don't recognize it. "He's dead. You killed him. You did it."

All I can do is whimper. Daphne holds my face.

"And I'm sorry you had to," Daphne says. "I'm so sorry."

Mary's eyes have locked on my torn chemise. Her jaw twitches. Daphne must have already seen. She understands. They both do.

"I hope he rots in hell," Mary says.

"He will," Daphne says. And then she's crying too. "Fuck him," she's saying. Mary sits on the floor beside us, wraps her arms around us both, rests her head on the place where our shoulders meet. "Fuck him, fuck him, fuck him."

✦

Mary fetches clothes for us, because I can't get off the floor and Daphne refuses to leave me alone.

"Come on," Mary says when she returns, holding a mess of skirts and blouses and trousers. Some of them are Daphne's old clothes; some had once belonged to Lady Luckenbill. Daphne opens her mouth, but Mary interrupts her. "I told the help to take a day off. At the viscount's expense."

"Shit," Daphne says. "Did they ask—"

"I made it clear there'd be much bigger problems than a nice day off if word ever got out," Mary says. "Considering the going rate for gossip around here, that should buy us about a day or two."

We help each other, the way we should. Mary takes a dress dotted with little blue flowers, the kind that offsets her hair and dark eyes beautifully; she holds the ring on her necklace to her lips, looking at herself in the mirror curiously, as if it's been years since she wore anything but the dark Braxton's uniform. Daphne helps tie the corset. Mary holds the haunted ring tight.

Afterwards, Mary says, "I think I'll leave you two to this."

She goes out to the hall, and then it's just Daphne and I.

I help her out of her sleeping clothes. Her skin is smooth, and her back, the dip of her shoulder blades and spine, is all lean muscle. This isn't my first time seeing a girl undressed, but my hands are still unsteady. The crook of her jaw, her collarbones, are just as perfect as a medical diagram. I am so tired that I want to put my cheek against her chest and close my eyes and never open them again.

But there's something else, too. Across her back, from the trapezius muscles to the latissimus dorsi.

Tattoos.

Stars, and birds, and ribbons, and laurel trees, twisting around each other in a beautiful sort of clutter. It's all done in rough black ink, riddled with imperfections that only make it look more human. I press my fingertips to her bare skin, run them around the edges because I cannot bring myself to speak. Daphne shudders and looks up at the ceiling.

At the center of the birds and leaves, there are words. Latin.

> *fer, pater, opem! si flumina numen habetis,*
> *qua nimium placui, mutando perde figuram!*

I trace the words, and Daphne speaks. She translates.

"Father," she says, "bring help. O rivers, if you have divinity, destroy my shape by changing it." She glances over her shoulder at me; her cheeks are pink. "That's not the exact translation, but it's clunky if you phrase it literally. It's from Ovid's *Metamorphoses*. Daphne and Apollo."

Destroy my shape by changing it.

This is the poem she took her name from.

I lean forward to kiss her shoulder, then lean my forehead against it, and we stay like that before I give her Lady Luckenbill's old underclothes. She's taken up an old riding habit, severe and all black. It suits her. I show her how to settle the blouse so it rests properly, how to make sure everything sits comfortably. I work in silence. If I open my mouth, I don't know what will come out, if anything. I keep hurting my hand as I adjust her sleeves. Daphne sighs sadly.

Next to her—her in this dress, me in my torn and bloody

nightgown—it's so obvious what I've been lacking all my life. It's so obvious what I really am. How could anyone have mistaken me for a girl when I stand beside one now, and see how clear the divide is? It is willful ignorance on the part of the entire world. I have never been anything but this. Neither of us have ever been anything but this.

"Now you," she says.

Then, for me: trousers, a vest, a heavy overcoat for the cold. They're hers, so they're a bit old-fashioned, with more color than a modern winter would allow for. It fits me with a few rolled hems. It's just so different from the ratty, awkward clothes I wore to the gala. It makes me laugh and it's a hollow, terrible sound.

But it's not right. Not yet.

I take a pair of scissors from the vanity.

"Silas," Daphne says. "What are you—"

I grab a hunk of my hair in my injured hand and saw it off with the scissors before I can stop myself. It comes out ugly and uneven, right at the shoulder.

Daphne comes up behind me. Her hands skim my arm before she pulls the scissors from my hands, uncurling my fingers.

"Here," she says. "Let me do it. Please."

I let her.

She cuts my hair short, but not too short. I don't want to look like a gentleman. I don't want to look like anything a Speaker could want. I want to be messy, overgrown, wild; hair a bit too long, buttons undone, bandages and bruises. I lean against her, and she smiles the best she can, even though the smile doesn't really reach her eyes. She hums as she works. I can feel it in her chest. I want to take her apart and crawl inside.

She says, "I won't miss him. Nobody will."

When Daphne is done, my hair is only hardly shorter than her own. My head is not weighed down with braids or pins. Without the long blond locks, my face is plain, unframed. I don't recognize it; it's a stranger's.

I do not look like my parents' perfect violet-eyed daughter. Good.

✦

We find Mary in the hall. She's whispering to her ring. The Veil has been torn, and Frances' ghost is there in the hall. Mary is crying. I wrap an arm around her shoulders, and Daphne kisses her forehead.

"We'll leave when you're ready," Daphne says.

✦

The sun rises as we step out of Luckenbill Manor, faint light sparkling off the swirls of frost. The three of us pause on the steps. The world continues, as it always does.

Without the rabbit, my chest is hollow. A cage with nothing inside. There are scars on my ribs, signs of a struggle, and an ache every time I breathe. But there is nothing within.

I almost miss it. The knowledge that something was

there with me, hyperaware of danger, keeping me safe. But it wasn't keeping me safe, was it? It was only ever torturing me, reminding me of what my tutors said, making sure that I remained frozen and afraid like a prey animal. Just like a rabbit.

Mary is silent, staring aimlessly. Daphne huffs into her palms, huddling into the scarf around her throat.

I should, I think, be more upset than I am. I am in pain, and hollow, and feel vaguely ill in the pit of my stomach, but that is all. I blink. I breathe. I am still in one piece. I am still here.

"Fuck," Mary says.

"So," Daphne whispers. There's a snowflake stuck to her eyelash. "What do we do now?"

I say, "I was about to ask you."

Mary keeps fiddling with the letter I took from Headmaster's office. George's letter. She turns it over in her hands. "What about your brother?"

It takes me a long time to reply to that. He wasn't in the basement. He's still alive, out there, somewhere. With Elsie. With Mother and Father. I could take this letter and make him face everything he's done. I could throw it at him, and he'd beg me for mercy, or for forgiveness. Or he could burn it and call me mad. He could bring the Speakers down on our heads. He could ruin our lives. And for the first time, I don't know what he'd do. I don't know my brother at all.

I never want to see him again.

We all look at each other, breath clouding in front of our faces, as the sun finds its place high in the sky.

It isn't until Daphne reaches out to hold me that I scream.

When the dead men come, we are waiting. We have been waiting so long.

They must have convinced themselves they would never
rot in the same dirt we do.

# One Year Later

Mary invites Daphne and I to spend Christmas in Manchester. "To celebrate the newlyweds," the letter explains, "and as an apology for being unable to make it to the ceremony." But neither of us particularly believes it, and I don't think Mary does either. We didn't invite a soul to the wedding anyway. Our witness was a local clerk, and we'd had to buy forged documents to get around the minimum marriageable age; legally, we are both in our early twenties now.

The real reason for the invitation, which none of us has to say, is the first anniversary of Braxton's collapse.

In front of the window overlooking a cluttered Liverpool street—we maintain a cramped flat under the surname Barry—Daphne flutters the letter at me to get my attention. She says, "Well? Do you want to go?"

I stare over her shoulder, out the window. Across the

street, someone is gathering their laundry from a clothes-line before the snow comes. A mess of carriages clatter down the street, the horses huffing and puffing. Has it been a year already? The scar on my hand has faded to nothing; Daphne's hair is grown out to her shoulders. I've spent the months studying for entrance exams and legitimizing the money we've stolen from Lord Luckenbill's accounts—she's straightened up the mess her father's murder left behind. There are speaking tiles scattered around our flat, messages from Ellen and Isabella. We had a pregnancy scare last month, but otherwise, our lives have been quiet. For a year.

But when I wake up from a bad dream or smell fresh-cut flowers, it doesn't feel like a year at all. I feel like a scared little girl again.

"Silas." Daphne comes over and puts the letter on top of the used textbook I've been memorizing, forcing it into my line of sight. My notes lay scattered across the table. *Tap tap tap* goes my heel. I haven't told her that I'm consid-ering traveling to mainland Europe for medical school, or maybe America if I can't brush up on my French in time; I'll go anywhere that doesn't have the Speaker system, just so we'd be safer. I also haven't told her I'm too nervous to go outside most days. That I can't hold a conversation with anyone anymore, even if I want to, which I don't.

Granted, I also haven't told her I haven't left the flat in weeks, but she knows that already.

"Silas. Do you?"

I almost tell her no. But it's Mary. She'd burn down half of England without someone to keep an eye on her.

England would deserve it, sure, but I'd really rather have a plan in place for the aftermath before turning her loose with kerosene and a book of matches.

I breathe deep, close my eyes. "We should. Go, I mean."

Daphne reaches down to kiss me. I think she can hear the panicked flutter of my heartbeat. It's not a rabbit heart anymore—it's just me in here, and sometimes that's worse. I reach up to check her pulse in turn. I have to. Just to make sure her heart is beating too.

"Good," she says. "I'll write her back."

✦

We arrive in Manchester late on Christmas Eve, the day the almanac predicts a blizzard will roll in. We've agreed to meet at a coffeehouse in the heart of the city. It's a little place, hidden by winding streets and nestled underneath a line of dark, empty shops, and by the time we arrive we are numb down to our toes. Nobody glances up at our arrival. A young man languidly washes teacups behind the counter; the gas lamps have been turned down low, candles flickering on every available surface. There aren't too many people out right now. Most are probably home with their families, staying away from the cold. That leaves only a few stragglers at the counter or reading newspapers by the fire.

Between the days it took to reach the city, the blue skin under my fingernails, and the anxiety of new places, I'm almost starting to regret coming up. I fiddle with the stickpin holding the cravat in place under my scarf.

But—

"If it isn't the happy couple."

Mary comes up to us, clasps my hands and then Daphne's. A year hasn't changed her much. She still has the same sharp-toothed smile, the same shimmering ring. Of course. Frances, the charm worn around Mary's neck. It's a gentle haunting, the air twinkling around the metal, the same way a gem sparkles when it's held up to the light.

I can't help but smile.

"How is married life treating you?" she asks us.

"If you're expecting some grand wisdom about love," Daphne drawls, "you're sorely mistaken." Daphne talks for me sometimes—she doesn't expect me to chime in, so neither does anyone else. She is a blessing in every way I could ask for. "It's merely asking the other person what they want for supper every day for the rest of your life."

"And you're not even twenty," Mary says. "What a bore."

The girls laugh.

Now that I live as a man, which is more than I ever could have asked for a year ago, I've found myself on the outside of things like this. Women exclude me; they no longer see me as one of them, no longer a natural member of the group. It aches a bit. There will always be sacrifices with things like this, and I have to come to terms with it.

But, for once, I understand why the two of them are laughing. How funny it is to joke about the bores of marriage when once you thought you'd never live to experience it as your true self. How funny it is to describe something as tedious as supper when some days you wake up crying because you are so grateful for it. How many times have I woken up next to Daphne, rolled over and pressed my face into her neck like she might be taken from me? Even Mary considers the ring on the chain around her neck to be her wedding ring. The last time she wrote to us, she referred to Frances as her wife. We sent back a parcel of dried petals for Frances to blow around the speaking tiles as she pleased.

Are we too young? Perhaps. Did we rush into this? Almost certainly. But, nevertheless, here we are.

Daphne's eyes sparkle when she smiles.

How lucky we are.

"Well," Mary says, starting toward the back of the coffeehouse and gesturing for us to follow her. "I didn't drag you all the way here from Liverpool just to chatter at you. I think an hour of pleasant conversation might give Silas a fever. Come, I have some friends I want you to meet."

I blink. "You didn't say anyone else was going to be here."

"You know he doesn't do well with strangers," Daphne says, stepping sharply after her.

Mary flicks a hand at us both. "See what I mean? Silas, you'll recognize her. And no, it's not Louise. I sent for her too, but she just wrote back *how did you get my address, never speak to me again*, a mess like that. You know how she is." She scoffs. "Anyway. Agnes and Adam are here to say hello."

Little widow Agnes Bernthal sits in the back booth of the coffeehouse, with her baby.

I grab Daphne's arm to steady myself.

Agnes offers a gentle smile. God, she's still so young, and somehow even smaller than I remember. There is a scar on her wrist from when Ellen threw her over the banister. She must be fifteen now, or sixteen, barely. And the *baby*; she has a *baby*. My first instinct is to press my hands to her, make sure the doctor took care of her, that she didn't tear, that they didn't sew her up an extra stitch to make her tighter. But I don't. All I can do is chew on the inside of my cheek. The baby is only a few months at most. Did Mary say his name was Adam?

And, a year ago, I killed his father.

I don't know what to say, but that doesn't matter. Agnes starts talking for me.

"You look so *different*." Agnes blinks owlishly at me. "When Mary said you were a boy, I didn't think—you actually look like a *boy*."

"Yes," I say slowly. "I mean. I am. What's going on?"

"Not that we're upset," Daphne translates for me. "We're just confused is all. It's been a long few days getting here."

Mary gestures for us all to sit, putting us down in the booth. "Look, over there." She gestures toward the carving over the hearth; I hadn't paid much attention to it, but that's just because I'm used to eye symbols being everywhere. "Did you notice that?"

But now that I look—

It's not the eye symbol. Not the one that was carved above the door of Braxton's, on all the Speaker's propaganda. Instead, it is a side view; the orb of the eye, the globe, flattened a bit right where the pupil would go, with the iris, the bubble of the cornea. But that's not the most prominent thing.

That would be the crude approximation of a needle sticking out of it.

The message is clear: *Fuck the Speakers.*

Agnes says, "Mary told me about the letter from your brother."

I shuffle awkwardly. I've been trying to forget about that letter for a year. I ran from London to Liverpool to get away from that letter, to get away from the chance of seeing George on the streets, to keep from losing my mind.

"What about it?" I whisper.

Mary takes Adam from Agnes's lap, bouncing the baby on her knee as he makes a strange gurling noise. He has a bright face, nothing at all like his father's, even though his eyes are the same shade of icy blue.

"I was just wondering," Agnes says. "Did you want to kill him?"

Just like Lord Luckenbill gasping for bloody air on the dressing room floor.

Like Headmaster and Dr. Bernthal and Mrs. Forrester, frozen.

Agnes, Mary, Daphne, me, all of us—we already know what we can do. What we've done, what we've picked out from under our nails, what we've buried. What we're going to cut open and sew shut.

Daphne and I glance at each other.

*Mors vincit omnia.*

# Note on Historical Accuracy and the Representation of Medical Experimentation

*The Spirit Bares Its Teeth* is as much a historical novel as it is a horror or fantasy. Even as I took liberties with the setting—sometimes a lot of liberties—it was important to me that I remained at least somewhat grounded in the real world. Thankfully, I had the help of a queer historian, Sebastian Crane, to strike that balance. Any anachronisms in regards to social attitudes, etiquette, or social understandings are included on purpose. Probably. (As the historian noted: Victorian chaperoning rules are narratively inconvenient.)

However, it would be negligent to leave my readers with the impression that what you've read in *The Spirit Bares Its Teeth* is the full picture of historical attitudes towards experimentation and medical harm. If I'm going to be honest, it's not even close. While terrible things were done to all kinds of people deemed "unfit" by Victorian society, when it comes to medical experimentation, so much of that pain and hurt was inflicted on racial minorities in particular, and it would be incorrect not to acknowledge that. For my older readers, there are several books on the topic. As a starter, I recommend the following two: *Medical Apartheid: The Dark History of Medical Experimentation on Black Americans from Colonial Times to the Present* by Harriet A. Washington, and *Medical Bondage: Race, Gender, and the Origins of American Gynecology* by Deidre Cooper Owens.

That is real history; this fantasy novel is not.

# ACKNOWLEDGMENTS

I don't think it's an overstatement to say that writing *The Spirit Bares Its Teeth* was one of the hardest things I've ever done. Seriously, my master's thesis was easier than this. While working on this book, I released my debut novel, completed my graduate degree, moved way too many times, lost family members, started a full-time job, and more—all while struggling with burnout and a severe case of second-book syndrome. I've joked that we're lucky to see this book in print at all.

But it made it! Despite everything, this strange, heartbreaking book made it. And I have a lot of people to thank for that.

Obviously, we're starting with Ashley Hearn at Peachtree Teen. I could sit here and repeat all the wonderful things I said about you in the last book, but I'll also add on to that and say *thank you* for giving me the opportunity to write my first openly autistic protagonist. You always create a space for your authors to feel safe and heard. And another massive thank you to the entire Peachtree Teen team because, just, oh my god y'all. Between this and *Hell Followed with Us,* you've knocked it out of the park every time.

Jennifer, thank you for looking after my YA books like your own, even if you didn't sell them. Evangeline Gallagher and Melia Parsloe, every author should get the chance to work with a cover team who *gets it* like you do. Eli, Alina, and the little savior—thank you for shaking me when I needed it, and also being soft when I needed that too; I couldn't ask for a better chosen family.

Mom, Dad, Mamaw, it's been a rough year, but we have each other, and I love you. (Papaw, I miss you.) Barbara and Gordon, thank you for letting me sleep in your guest room for several months, and for helping us with the house, and the million things you've done to keep us on our feet. And then all of my friends; thanks for being there, even when I don't have the mental fortitude to respond to your DMs. Sorry about that.

Then, there's Alice. The day after we moved into the house, the two of us sat at the dining room table with plates of broccoli cheese chicken, surrounded by unpacked books and mismatched furniture, and I don't remember if I said it out loud when I realized I never thought I'd get this far, but we did it, and we're here now, and we can breathe.

# ABOUT THE
# AUTHOR

*Andrew Joseph White* is a queer, trans, *New York Times* bestselling author from Virginia, where he grew up falling in love with monsters and wishing he could be one too. He earned his MFA in creative writing from George Mason University in 2022. Andrew writes about trans kids with claws and fangs, and what happens when they bite back. Find him at *AndrewJosephWhite.com* or on Twitter **@AJWhiteAuthor.**